Kiana
+
Roderick

The Golden Princess and the Moon

Anna Maria Mendell

The Golden Princess and the Moon

A Retelling of the Fairy Tale
"Sleeping Beauty"

♛ ♛ ♛

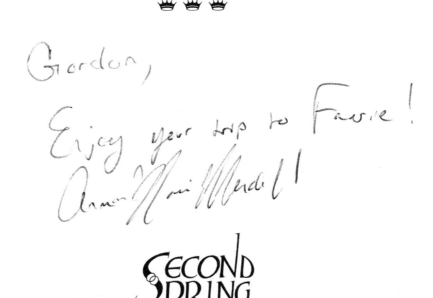

Gordon,

Enjoy your trip to Faerie!

Anna Maria Mendell

SECOND SPRING

First published
by Second Spring, 2016
www.secondspring.co.uk
an imprint of Angelico Press
© Anna Maria Mendell 2016

For information, address:
Angelico Press
4709 Briar Knoll Dr.
Kettering, OH 45429
angelicopress.com

978-1-62138-193-8 Pb
978-1-62138-194-5 Cloth
978-1-62138-195-2 eBook

Cover Art & Design by Gwyneth Thompson-Briggs
Back Cover design: Michael Schrauzer

Contents

To my parents:
without your love and support
you would not be reading this now.

♛ ♛ ♛

Acknowledgments

I WOULD like to thank Our Lord and His Blessed Mother for watching over me and blessing my work. This story belongs to them. I would like to offer my sincerest thanks to all those at Angelico Press and Second Spring who helped make my book possible, especially my publisher, John Riess—his vision brought this book out into the world—and to copyeditor Mark Sebanc, whose careful edits and suggestions gave my work the polish it needed! I would also like to thank James Wetmore for his typography, which greatly enhanced the text. My deepest love and gratitude go to my first and dearest editor, Lucy Wells, who read every single chapter as it came out, and whose continual advice and support spurred me on to complete my work. I would also like to specially thank Nathan Pinkoski, Laura Bement, Mark Forrester, and the incomparable Rodkey siblings, Erik and Krista—traces of their creative insights glimmer in my story. I would also like to acknowledge my indebtedness to the grandfather of all fantasy writers, George Mac-Donald, most particularly as it relates to his story, *The Wise Woman*. My book is, in a way, a dialogue with all the haunting impressions that story has left on me ever since I was a child. I also would like to acknowledge the inspiration I drew from Michael Ward's book *Planet Narnia*, his insights into C.S. Lewis's works having helped shaped my faerie world. I would like to thank all those others who encouraged me through the labor of a first novel: Sarah Hinkle, Rebekah Lamb, Beatrice Ellis, Gemma Myers, Tessa Cialini, and Sophie Lippiatt. Last but not least, I would like to thank my parents. They took me in, jobless and homeless; they gave me the time and the space to write and never once told me that I should be doing something else. Without them, my dream would never have become a reality.

A NOTE ON THE WORD *Faerie*: The word "faerie" is both the adjectival and plural form of the singular "faery." When it is capitalized, it then describes the "realm" of the faeries.

♛ ♛ ♛

Chapter One

Ninny Nanny

A SHARP THORN of sorrow pierced the young prince's heart. He had stolen deep into the forest to cry alone under the elm tree, where no one could hear him. But he was not as alone as he had thought, for a shrill cackle of laughter broke in on his sobs.

He craned his neck to peer through the thick gloom of the wood, where he glimpsed an old woman peeking at him from behind a tree trunk. Her eyes glittered from the shadows and fixed him with their keen gaze. Then, as she hobbled toward him with another cackle, the boy rose, warily watching her approach —there were stories of a witch that lived in the forest who drove men mad and was mad herself. The old woman certainly seemed mad, for she muttered as she hobbled.

> *Under the dark side of the moon*
> *The old man went fishing for trout.*
> *But he only found shoes,*
> *And he only found spoons,*
> *For there were no fishes about.*

She cackled again and circled around the elm, reciting this time:

> *Old Ninny Nanny's bones did moan*
> *Rattle tattle bags.*
> *Old Ninny Nanny's bones did groan*
> *Skittle skattle skunk.*
> *Speak to Ninny Nanny's bones.*

1

Then she popped out from the other side of the tree and, fishing a little handkerchief from her voluminous coat of tatters and rags, held it out to the boy. He stared at the old woman. She was stretched and gaunt and stooped; her silver, wiry hair stuck out in knots like whiskers; wrinkles crisscrossed her face; her eyes were bright and sharp. Her handkerchief was white and clean, but the boy did not take it.

The old woman cracked into a smile and tucked her handkerchief back into her tattered coat.

"Why have ye been crying?" she asked.

"I wasn't crying."

Salt tears turn sweet when they water your feet.
Tears that are dammed poison the land.
They slay your enemies and worse,
Yourself!

"Tell me why ye have been crying."

The boy's lips trembled but his voice remained steady. "My mother's dead, and my father married again yesterday. He says that it is weak to cry." Two lone tears trailed down his face. "My father is the king, and I cannot shame him."

The old woman whisked out her handkerchief again, and this time he took it.

"Princeling, what be your name?"

"Erik."

"Come to my cottage, Erik. Ye can wash your face an' eat some hot soup, eh?"

"I don't know if I should, aren't you a…"

"…Witch?" she finished for him. "Some would call me that, but everyone gets everything backwards. I promise ye that no harm will come to ye through me. Ye can even cry in my cottage an' I won't tell."

He took her outstretched hand, and his feet crunched the dry leaves as she led him on a winding path through the forest until they came to a small, thatched cottage with a picket fence. In the yard were hens and geese, a bleating black and white goat, and a well in the far corner.

The old woman opened the creaking gate and led the prince into the cottage, sitting him down on a wooden chair at the table. Then she hobbled over to the hearth to kindle the fire and get the pot boiling. Erik heaved the occasional sigh, but mostly he watched the old woman's goings on with interest. Soon she placed before him a bowl of soup, and the warmth of the rising steam soothed him. The old woman sat beside him and did not say a word, which relieved the prince because he did not yet feel like talking. After he finished, he leaned back against his chair and gazed into the old woman's rough but friendly face.

"Are you one of the good wood folk my mother told me about?"

"What makes ye ask that?" the old woman chuckled.

"You are kind to strangers in the wood. No one else that I know is kind to strangers. I wager you can speak to animals too."

There was once a young maid who bathed in the river an' lost a silver trinket from round her neck in its shiny waters. I spied the silver, thought it was a trout, an' fished the gleaming thing from the river. I found the maid weeping over the loss of her favorite bauble an' returned it to her. An' here 'tis now!

With a swift jerk, the old woman yanked a silver pendant from under the prince's tunic before he could even blink in surprise. The pendant was shaped like a half moon, its straight edge notched in places. On its face was the delicate carving of a bird in flight clutching a fish in its outstretched talons.

"You knew my mother!" the prince exclaimed.

The old woman nodded.

"Did you know who I was all along?"

The old woman grinned.

"What else do you know?"

"Now that would be telling."

3

"What is your name, then?" asked the prince.

"Ninny Nanny."

"That is a children's rhyme. What is your real name?"

The old woman was silent.

The prince saw that she was not going to answer him.

"My mother used to tell me stories about Ninny Nanny and her old bones. Didn't you marry the old man of the moon, so you could live on the moon too?"

Ninny Nanny grunted. "Backwards... Why does everyone always get the stories backwards?"

"My father doesn't like the old stories. He says that the time of magic is now past. If there is any magic left, it is wild and dangerous."

"And what do you believe, princeling?"

"I don't know... but I miss my mother's stories. Ninny Nanny, can you tell me more about her?"

The old woman took the prince's chin in her hand, and he could feel the rough calluses on her fingers.

"Your hair is dark as the raven's wing, an' your eyes are the clear grey of the sky after the rains. Ye take after the western peoples like your mother."

The prince nodded. "She used to tell me about her people from the west and how their ancient lands were once the Golden Kingdom from the old stories, and that their king traveled throughout his realm and spoke to animals like one of the good wood folk. Then the Golden Kingdom was lost and became a part of Lothene, and the king now wanders throughout the kingdom searching for his golden crown."

"A gentle woman was your mother an' she loved the old stories. I told her a few myself before she married your father. She had traveled far from home an' was lonely. Mind ye don't forget the stories she told ye."

"Of course not! They are all I have left of her. That and this." Erik held up his silver pendant.

"Did ye know that silver belongs to the moon?"

"Does it?" Erik asked. "What does that mean?"

The old woman fell silent, and Erik heard the crackling of the fire in the hearth. A drowsiness swept over him, and his eyes grew heavy.

"Would ye like to take a nap on the heather?" the old woman asked. "I'll make sure an' waken ye before it gets dark."

He nodded sleepily, and Ninny Nanny led him to a mattress that smelt of straw and heather in the corner of the room.

Erik fell asleep.

A warm light surrounded Erik and, as he blinked back sleep, the light turned into the clear light of day.

He was standing in a silver field of tall feathery grass that rustled in the breeze and was spangled with little white flowers that looked like stars. Gazing to his right, the prince saw that the field went far into the distance and turned into a dark wood and then finally grew into blue-grey mountains that faded on the horizon; to his left was a riverbank sheltered by soft, purple trees.

Erik accepted his presence in this otherworldly landscape with the calm acceptance of a dream. The purple trees shading the river bank and the wind in the leaves seemed to rustle secrets that drew him through the field to the shaded bank, where he peered into the river water.

The prince gasped in surprise.

The river was so clear he could see right through it and count every pebble. But what truly took his breath away was that, drifting on the bottom of the river bed, a fair maid lay sleeping.

Erik knelt down by the bank and stared long and deep into her lovely face. She was the most beautiful creature he had ever seen. Her floating hair formed a soft golden aureole about her face, and her expression was gentle and peaceful, if a little sad. If only she would open her eyes, he thought.

Slowly the prince stretched out his hand and touched the surface of the water. Ripples radiated from that point, and the water shimmered and blurred as the whole world about him dissolved.

"No!" he gasped.

Then he found himself lost in the dark.

He must have woken up. Night must have fallen, and the fire gone out in Ninny Nanny's cottage.

He called out. There was no answer. All he could hear was the thump of his heart growing faster and faster. He was alone, trapped in a mad woman's cottage in the absolute darkness. Erik fought down panic. If he found his way outside, the moon and the stars would shed enough light for him to make his way home.

Erik fumbled about the room until his fingers finally found the door and clutched the latch. He pushed the door open.

No cold, night air rushed to greet him. Instead, he stumbled into a large room lit by candlelight and firelight, with large candelabras hanging from the ceiling. Rich, red curtains were draped over the windows, and the walls were painted with garlands of stars, their colors shining subdued in the flickering shadows.

The prince saw that he was not alone. A stately lady, wearing a crown, sat embroidering by candlelight. He supposed she was the queen of a wealthy kingdom; her gem-encrusted dress was richer by far than any dress he had ever seen his mother or step-mother wear. He spotted the king standing before a table on which lay a box painted with stars of all different colors. Beside him was a girl about the prince's own age. Her perfect milk-white face looked almost unreal, as if she were a doll, and her eyes were latched on the box with such greedy intensity that Erik grimaced, though he could not help being struck by how pretty she was, how golden her hair and blue her eyes.

Nobody noticed him. I must still be dreaming, he thought. Strange, to feel so awake and yet know he was dreaming.

The princess snatched the lid off the box, and, for an instant, her face was transformed by wonder. But then her expression vanished, replaced by a dark look glimmering with rage. She reached into the box and held aloft a glass globe that sparkled in the flickering light.

A wild howl burst from her lips.

The princess hurled the globe across the room, and it splintered in a heartrending crash against the wall. Shocked, Erik watched as she flung herself to the ground, punctuating the air with cries and shrieks.

A flood of disgust washed over him. What a brat, he thought. Her parents were just as bad. There they were, trying to calm her down when they should just give her a sound spanking. His father would have had him beaten with a stick if he had behaved like that, and rightfully so.

He turned his back on the scene. A door stood before him, and he pulled it open, hoping to step into another dream, maybe even return to the field with the beautiful sleeping maid—she was so peaceful and serene, so different from the princess shrieking behind him.

He stepped through and found himself opening his eyes. Ninny Nanny's thatched roof loomed above him, and he smelled straw and heather. The prince swiftly sat up, and there was Ninny Nanny herself, sitting in her chair, knitting by the fire.

She chuckled. "Ye slept soundly, princeling. I didn't know if I should waken ye."

Erik rubbed his eyes and rose to stand next to her by the fire. The searing heat blasted his face. He sprang away from the fire and wondered how the old woman could stand it.

He gave Ninny Nanny a curious sidewise glance. Who was this old woman with her bizarre words and riddles, who might or might not be mad, and who lived all alone in a cottage deep in the wood?

"I had the most strange dream," he said. "It was so real." He described his dream of the selfish princess, but did not mention the sleeping maiden in the waters. It was as if his vision of her would be spoiled with words.

"What did you think of the young princess, princeling?"

"I don't like her. She's spoiled and cries too much."

The old woman raised her eyebrows.

The prince straightened. "But she had no reason to cry. She's a brat and a baby."

"Ah, but we have to allow that little ones grow. An' sometimes people's goodness is hidden very deep inside. Sit ye down beside me at the fire and let me tell ye a story. It's about a princess who wished for the moon."

Chapter Two

The Princess and the Moon

THE PRINCESS FLUNG the moon across the room, and it shattered against the wall into millions of slivers of glistening glass. She trembled violently and let out such howls and shrieks that the flustered king immediately ran to her side and the queen dropped her embroidery. Together, the distressed parents managed to soothe the screeching child enough to sit her on a chair and hush her piercing screams.

"I told you I wanted the moon. Why did you give me that silly glass ball?" the princess gasped from her heaving chest.

King Aurleon IV stroked his beard, which was as golden as a lion's mane, and, as he stroked it, he patted his daughter on the head.

"It is not a simple task to bring the moon," he said. "The moon is hard to come by. Besides, that was not just an ordinary glass ball—it was a globe hand-blown in the east. I went through much trouble to find one with just the right silvery complexion. Why it cost me half of my kingdom. I'll have to raise the taxes!"

The princess glared at him. "You promised you would bring me the moon. Kings do not break their promises."

He sighed. "Dear heart, how about I give you a little dog?"

The princess shook her head.

"I know." The queen wrapped her arms around the child and lowered her face down to the princess' ear to whisper, "How about I give you my pretty pearl ring? I know how much you like it."

Tears welled up in the princess' eyes, and she started crying again.

"Shh! Shh! Enough! I shall bring you the moon, but please, no more tears." The king wrung his hands.

The princess sniffed and her sobs subsided. "You promise?" she whined, her tear-stained face upturned.

"There, there." The king stroked her hair. "Don't look so sad, kings always keep their promises."

The princess snuggled into his warm chest, burrowing her face among the smooth folds of his robes. She turned her head aside and gazed at the moon through the window and smiled triumphantly.

"Now, now." The king gently pushed his clinging daughter away. "Why not go and amuse yourself? In a week's time, I will bring you the moon."

The princess smiled and skipped out into the long hall.

The queen looked at the king doubtfully, her fine eyebrows raised. "And how, pray, will you bring her the moon?" she asked. "She has become unbearable. I do not understand why you indulge her so."

The king smiled ruefully. "I had hoped that you might devise something convincing to show our daughter?"

The queen shook her head and then knit her brow. "Perhaps," she murmured after a moment, "perhaps a necklace. She likes those kinds of pretty things. A little round, shiny, silver bauble about the size of the moon from a distance—she might think it was the real thing."

"Yes." The king sighed in relief. "And we will keep her from looking out the window and make her go to bed early for the next few nights. Then she'll forget about the whole thing like she does everything else. My queen, you should be the one on the throne ruling the kingdom!"

He kissed her, and the queen smiled wryly. "Truthfully, I would be pleased to simply rule our daughter. But that, I fear, is as difficult as ruling the kingdom."

The king strode out of the room, roaring for a silversmith.

MEANWHILE, instead of going out to the garden to play, the princess sat alone in her room. A large room cluttered with toys, ribbons, and priceless jewels, its walls were covered with intricate tapestries depicting forests and gardens full of playing monkeys and colorful birds. Over the princess' door hung the woven crest of the kingdom of Aurlia, the Golden Kingdom, with its heraldic beasts on a field of the royal sapphire. A golden gryphon stood emblazoned in the center of the crest, with two birds flanked on either side: a heron on the right and a kingfisher on the left. Seven stars were woven above in the brightest silver thread.

At the moment, she sat with her brow furrowed in concentration, deeply engrossed in following the trail of a dragonfly hovering over the woodwork of her canopied bed. It settled tentatively on a projecting wooden leaf, and the princess sprang forward to trap it. There was a crunch. She peered under her fingers and recoiled with a cry.

The crushed dragonfly dropped to the ground, and she prodded it with a daintily slippered toe.

The princess' nursemaid burst into the room. "Rosa, we must prepare for dinner! I napped and over-slept, and now we are going to be late. Make haste and let me help you out of your dress."

The princess, cross over the dragonfly and despising baths, plopped on her bed and crossed her arms.

"Now, Rosa dearest, please don't make this a trial. You know the king and queen wish you always on time for dinner."

Rosa narrowed her eyes and waved her hand. "I am the princess and you must listen to *me*, and, if you don't, I'll have you hanged, chopped up, and scattered about in tiny pieces for making me angry. Just like father did to the thief in prison the other day."

The nursemaid stepped back in horror. "Princess, what a cruel thing to say! Have I not cared for you since you were a baby? I think you owe your poor Alice a larger debt of gratitude than that. Besides," said the nursemaid, scooping the girl under her arms and dragging her kicking and screaming to the tub in the adjacent room, "no one else could endure this thankless task of looking after you, and look after you I will."

Alice pulled off the princess' dress, under-shift, and slippers, pinioning her arms and feet so Rosa couldn't run off. She then dumped the squirming girl into the tub and held Rosa down while she poured bucketfuls of tepid water over her. Sputtering, the princess quieted down and let her nursemaid lather soap into her hair. Rinsing the princess off, Alice helped her out of the bath and dried her.

Feeling unusually submissive after the warm glow of the bath, Rosa allowed her nursemaid to dress her in a more formal gown, a deep blue trimmed in silver, with a yellow girdle tied about her waist. Then setting her before the mirror, Alice began her favorite task of brushing the princess' golden waves.

The princess looked smugly at her reflection in the mirror. She was beautiful and she knew it. But then a somber look settled on her face and she furrowed her brows like she was puzzling something out.

"Alice, do I always get my way because I am beautiful, or because I am a princess?" she asked.

Alice paused in surprise and saw the princess' serious blue eyes looking into hers in the mirror's reflection.

"Well…" Alice answered slowly, "you are your father's only child, and I suppose that many would wish to please you, hoping that you might speak words in their favor to the king."

The princess gazed at her reflection again. Abruptly she made a hideous grimace. "So if I looked like this, I would still have what I wanted?"

"Now stop that!" Alice chided sharply. "Beauty certainly helps in getting your own way. I am sure that, when you reach womanhood, which is sooner rather than later, if one could but believe it, you will have your choice of princes far and wide. So don't go spoiling your looks."

The princess scowled and narrowed her eyes. In a sudden fury, she swept her arm across her dresser, violently knocking over an empty vase, so that it shattered on the floor with a loud crash.

"If I can have whatever I want, then I want you to pick up this mess. I feel quite prepared for dinner." With that, the princess flounced out of the room, leaving Alice down on her hands and knees to gather all the broken pieces of the vase.

THE hours between sunrise and sunset of each lingering day seemed long for Rosa, while she waited for the moon. Finally the seven day cycle passed, and she once again entered the king's chambers to hold him to his promise.

"Father, did you bring me the moon?"

"Of course, my little rose, how could you ever doubt me?"

On the king's outstretched fingers there dangled a delicate silver chain on which hung a tiny, silver ball. The princess stopped short and stared at the shining globe with suspicion.

"I thought the moon was larger than that."

"Do not be foolish, my dear," the king said. "Have you not ever closed one eye and looked out at the moon with the other, and covered the moon completely with the thumb of your hand? See, the moon's circumference is the size of my thumb. Would I ever lie to my little Rose?"

The king gently laid the silver moon on the princess' outstretched palm. She brushed her fingers over the shiny, polished surface with wonder. Turning to the queen, she held out the necklace. "Mother, will you help me put this on?" she asked.

"Of course, little one, turn around," the queen replied.

When her mother had finished clasping the necklace, the princess threw herself at her father crying. "Oh, father, thank you! I am so happy."

"Do not just thank me. Thank your mother. It was her idea to put the moon on a necklace," the king said, extricating himself.

The queen bent down, and the princess encircled her neck with her arms, raining down many kisses on her face.

"There now, that is enough," the queen said in annoyance. "Go be seated."

"Only if you kiss me back," the princess pleaded.

The queen kissed the princess coldly on the forehead and then gave her a little push towards the seat next to the table at the other side of the room.

Princess Rosamund twisted the moon about her little finger, while the queen took up her embroidery, stitching golden gryphons on a field of blue. The king poured himself a glass of dark red wine from a crystal decanter.

A silence and stillness filled the room.

The silence grew so silent and the stillness so still, that it was almost a tangible thing. Rosa became aware that she and her parents were not alone. A shadowy figure, robed in a cloak of dusk that covered its face and flowed down to the ground in heavy liquid folds, was observing them from the corner of the room nearest the door.

The moment Rosa realized that she was being watched was also the same terrifying moment she realized she could not move. Cold fear gripped her heart and she could feel it thumping heavily in her chest. Her throat felt dry, but she could not swallow.

The shadowy figure glided across the room, its robes a smooth swish against the marble floors. When it made its way to the foot of the table before the princess, it lifted up its hood to reveal its face.

Rosa found herself staring into the deep, limpid eyes of a beautiful lady. She had an ageless look, so that the princess could not tell if she was young or very old and wise. Her features were regal, her skin ivory, her hair thick and dark as the night, though mostly hidden beneath her hood.

Rosa found the spell was broken and that she could move again.

The king abruptly rose and bowed. "My lady, you should have informed us of your coming. We would have had a room prepared. Be patient but for a moment, and I will order the servants to bring you refreshments."

The robed lady raised her hand in silence and continued looking at the princess.

The king spoke impatiently, "Stand up, Rosa, and present yourself properly. This great lady is your godmother."

The princess rose nervously and curtsied. "I am Princess Rosamond, only daughter and sole heir of His Majesty King Aurleon IV of Aurlia and Her Highness Queen Eleanor…" But instead of continuing the memorized address, the princess once again gazed into her godmother's eyes.

They shone like twin stars of twilight.

It was staring into her godmother's eyes, eyes deep and old as the first dawn that also shone like the new day, that made the princess pause and say, "…but you may call me Rosa."

The ageless lady smiled at the girl, and her smile made her look young.

Encouraged by the smile, the excited princess fingered her necklace and then showed it to the lady. "Look! This is the moon. My father the king gave it to me. I do not think any other princess in the whole world has worn the moon about her neck."

The lady's smile vanished, replaced with a stern look that made her ageless again. She gazed at the princess and then at the king and queen, who lowered their eyes. Then she strode to the large window and swept back the damask curtains.

15

"There," she pointed, her voice ringing as clear as a tiny sil-ver bell, "is the moon."

The princess' eyes widened, and she ran to the window and gazed up at the moon. The moon shone mockingly, and the stars twinkled in laughter. She spun around, ran to the center of the room, and stamped her foot. "You lied to me, you lied! You said it was the moon. I want the moon!" The last she said with a howl and then flung herself on the ground, filling the room with her shrieking. Her parents were aghast at the spectacle, while the robed lady watched the scene in silence.

After a spell, the lady knelt by the screaming princess and touched her shoulder. The princess quieted down at the gentle pres-sure and looked up at her godmother with a red, tear-streaked face.

"You are being very ugly right now, Rosa," the lady said qui-etly.

"I do not care! I never asked to be beautiful."

The lady's silence seemed to engulf all sound. Finally she asked, "Why do you behave this way?"

Ready to make a quick reply, Rosa was stopped by the keen fire of her godmother's penetrating gaze. After a moment, she whispered, "I do not know," and threw herself into her god-mother's arms.

The princess' godmother held the sobbing girl tightly to her breast. The king and queen stepped forward, crying in a chorus, "We do not know what to make of her."

"She does not usually act in this way."

"We will make sure to punish her properly."

"What a poor, poor, young girl," the lady said.

"What do you mean?" cried the indignant king. "We are the ones who have to endure her constant tempers. She is always in a fury."

"We give her everything she asks for," the queen chimed in nervously. "I have never come across a more indulged and yet ungrateful child."

"Furthermore, you could have bestowed upon the princess gifts better befitting the demands of her duties," the king accused, growing heated. "You could have made her an obedient and submissive child or have given her a sweet disposition. What use is beauty when it but covers this… this fright?" The king pointed to his daughter.

The lady's arms tightened soothingly about the girl. "You have no one to blame but yourselves. You gave what was not needed and withheld that which would have made her grow. Together you have both helped squander the gifts we bestowed upon her as a baby, and, coming back thirteen years later, I find her a baby still. You have left her ill prepared for the future awaiting her."

At this the two parents fell silent, and the queen looked at her husband with pleading eyes. "But what should we do now?" the queen asked, turning back to the princess' godmother.

"You have done enough."

The lady swept the princess up into her arms, and Rosa fell instantly asleep. "I am taking her with me. When I deem it good for her, I will bring her back."

"Oh, Aurleon," the queen cried, clutching the king's arm. "You will not let her do it?"

"I am not certain I have a choice," the king said. "And perhaps it is as she says. Maybe the princess should be taken out of our hands. The faerie have better knowledge of the future in store for her than we do."

The queen composed her features and loosened her grip on her husband's arm.

"Very well." She turned her back on her daughter and walked out of the room.

The king watched the robed lady carry away his sleeping child down the hall and out of the castle.

Chapter Three

Ninny Nanny's Bones

THE PRINCESS WOKE drowsy and befuddled, trying to recollect the events from the night before. She blinked sleep away from her eyes and, sitting up in her bed, realized she was in the strangest house she had ever seen.

In the center of the room was a little stone well. Planted around the well, flowers bloomed of all kinds, giving off a sweet, fresh scent—a scent that reminded her of springtime.

The wall to the left of the well had a large, open window before which was a table set with seven glass goblets all in a row. Each goblet was a different color, blue and gold, red and silver, green and the clearest crystal, and one the color of quicksilver. The sunlight streamed through them and cast their vivid, dancing hues on the whitewashed wall near the fireplace. On the mantelpiece perched two golden statues of two birds, and Rosa recognized them as the birds woven in the tapestry over the door in her room. These two statues were carved so perfectly that she would have thought they were alive if they had not been made of gold.

Rosa climbed out of bed and made her way to the strange well. She peered down into it, but could not make out its bottom.

Then she caught something moving out of the corner of her eye, turned, and saw what she thought to be the most wondrous thing of all: in the corner of the room hung eight shining globes suspended in the air. Seven of the globes were each a different color, matching the goblets on the table, and they spun around an eighth globe, which remained still, though it swirled with all the colors of the seven globes together. They whirred about furiously, but did not make a sound, and Rosa was just about to touch one of the globes when she heard a voice behind her.

"That is a model of Time's turning wheel. But you must not touch it, for you will stop the spinning."

Rosa whirled around to face her godmother in her cloak of shadows.

The lady smiled. "Come and sit down and I will give you breakfast."

The princess nodded, shy before this mysterious woman, and sat down on one of the two wooden chairs by the table. Her godmother plucked a bowl from the wooden cupboard beside the fireplace, and filled it with something bubbling from the pot over the fire.

While she was eating, the princess overcame enough of her shyness for her to ask, "Why do you have a well in the middle of the cottage?"

"Why not? The water is fresh, and I use it for drinking, cleaning, and watering my flowers."

"Oh. And why are the two birds on the mantelpiece the same as the two birds in my room?"

"They are the two guardian birds of Aurlia. Have you not heard the story of *The Heron and the Kingfisher?*"

Intrigued, the princess shook her head.

"Would you like to hear the story, then?" the lady asked.

At Rosa's nod, the lady began:

Long ago, when the kingdom was new, the Golden King wandered throughout his land. He came upon a heron and a kingfisher squabbling by the reedy margin of the water. The king, faerie-gifted with the animal tongue, demanded to know the cause of their discord, and the two birds told him they were quarreling over the best way to catch fish. The kingfisher main-

tained that it was best to swoop down suddenly from a branch on high, while the heron said it was best to wait motionless by the darkness of water and reed. The king said he would settle their dispute and that the winner in turn would grant him a gift. The kingfisher promised the gift of peace, and the heron promised the gift of prosperity.

So the Golden King set up a contest to see who could catch the most fish. The first day he had them hunt as they were wont, and, by the day's end, both birds presented to him seven fish each. On the second day, the Golden King had them hunt again, but this time they switched places, the heron hunted from the high tree branch, and the kingfisher from the reeds in the water. At the end of the day, neither of them had caught a single fish. For the heron could not swoop down from the tree branch fast enough, nor could the kingfisher stand amongst the reeds still enough. The Golden King declared them both winners and losers, and demanded that they both pay him their gifts. The birds were content with his judgment, for they saw it was just and their quarrel foolish and that they were given gifts according to their needs, and the Golden King ruled in peace and prosperity for all his days.

When her godmother had finished, Rosa asked, "Who is the Golden King?"

The lady's gaze was filled with pity as she spoke. "The Golden King is one of the founding kings of Aurlia and he was gifted with the animal tongue because he was faerie-born. It is also the title given to the one who sits on the Aurlian throne, so that the monarch is called the Golden King or Queen. Did no one ever tell you this?"

Rosa squirmed uncomfortably on her seat, and the lady looked sad.

"I will tell you more stories of the Golden King, but some of them must wait until you are ready to hear them. But enough questions. I'll leave you to freshen up. You will find a new dress at your bedside. You may come out and join me when you are done."

With that, Rosa's godmother stepped outside and closed the door behind her.

Left alone, the first thing Rosa did was to go over to the shining globes which her godmother had told her not to touch. She watched in fascination as the globes spun about, then she reached out to pluck the nearest sphere that shone the clearest crystal. The instant her fingers closed around the orb, every suspended globe lost its color and thumped to the ground.

She opened her fingers and saw that she held nothing but a lump of dusty, burnt out coal in her hand.

Rosa started at the sound of the door latch and darted to her bed in fright, swiftly hiding the lump of coal under her pillow. She turned just as her godmother entered the cottage.

The lady looked from the coals on the floor to the princess' guilty face. "Rosa, did you touch one of the globes?"

"No, they fell on their own."

The lady gazed back down at the black, coal lumps. "Rosa," she said, "one of the globes is missing, do you know where it is?"

Rosa pursed her lips and refused to meet her godmother's gaze. She shook her head.

The lady's voice grew stern. "When you have known me better, child, you will know that I do not allow untruth in my home. Tell me where the globe is."

"I will not!" Rosa burst. "You are a mean and horrible woman and I hate you!"

The princess started crying. Rosa had never felt guilty before and she did not like it. That nagging guilt transformed her sobs into piercing shrieks. But the lady did nothing and continued to gaze sternly at the princess.

The princess felt the challenge in her godmother's silence, and fury hit her like a crashing wave.

She darted to the table and with a single sweep, sent every single glass goblet hurling down on the ground with an enormous crash.

"You are an evil woman and I hate you," she shrieked. "My father would punish you dreadfully if he knew that you had kidnapped me to turn me into your servant. I do not wish to stay here and want to go home. I command you to take me back to the castle."

The lady strode to the door and opened it. "Rosa, you are free to go. I will not force you to stay here."

Rosa glared into her godmother's serene eyes resting in her terrible, unsmiling face. Seething with anger and resentment, she stormed out the door barefoot, fists clenched. She did not look behind her or notice her godmother watching her until she disappeared in the thick gloom of the shadowy woods.

👑 👑 👑

"YE MUST BE getting back to the castle or ye will be missed," Ninny Nanny said.

"Must I? But what happens to the princess?"

"I thought ye didn't care much for the spoiled princess, princeling."

Erik stiffened. "Not really, but it's dangerous for a silly girl like her to be alone in the woods. She doesn't even have a knife to protect herself from the wild beasts!"

The old woman chuckled. "Ye must go home, princeling. For if ye are missed, then ye will be watched carefully an' not be able to visit me again."

Erik tried to disguise the interest in his voice. "And then you can tell me more about the princess?"

The old woman's face cracked into a grin. "That I will, princeling."

She took him by the hand and led him out of the cottage and through the forest until they reached the edge of the woods in view of the castle. "Now run along. But before ye go, take this bag of dried sticks. If ye want to find my cottage shake the bags and say:

Old Ninny Nanny's bones rattle, tattle,
To Ninny Nanny's cottage skittle, skattle.

"Then cast my sticks an' they will fall in a straight line. Do that as many times as ye need, an' if ye follow faithfully the way of the sticks, then ye will come to my cottage."

Erik grasped the bag and then impulsively threw his arms around the old woman. She gave a loud "oomph" and the prince started back as if he had been caught doing something he shouldn't have. The old woman chuckled, patting him on the head, and he turned and ran back to the castle.

"That one don't smile much, does he?" The old woman muttered to herself.

MIDLOTH Castle was hewn into the side of a mountain, fortified by thick walls circumscribing whatever part of the castle was not naturally defended by sheer rock. Erik heard a falcon's cry and spotted the bird of prey wheeling over the castle ramparts. Buzzing traffic to and from the castle passed through the heavily guarded main gate, but the prince instead went to the left side of the castle walls and ducked around the overhanging boulder shielding the postern gate from view. The postern gate was left open during peacetime, and he knew the guard's rounds well enough to slip in and out of the gate unobserved.

Erik stole into the castle and almost made it to his room before he was stopped by Kenelm, the captain of the king's guards, who also happened to be his own personal sword trainer.

"The king sent me to find you. You are to go to the feasting hall."

The prince's shoulders slumped. He did not want to go to the feasting hall and see his father with his new stepmother. But Kenelm was a grim man of few words and a sword arm strong enough to bear the weight of the command in the mountain castle. He was not someone Erik wished to cross.

"I didn't know I was wanted during today's celebration," Erik mumbled.

"You are to toast the new queen's good health."

The prince nodded reluctantly and followed Kenelm into the feasting hall.

The rafters in the large hall's highly vaulted wooden ceiling were obscured in the dim, evening shadows. The only light came from capped torches that cast their light on the floor below and the large fire whose raging flames radiated warmth into the cold night and cast shadows on the grey stone walls.

Erik saw that the king and queen sat at the head of the long feasting table, while everyone else stood, ready for the toast. The king and queen were swathed in furs, the king in a black bearskin and the queen in white ermine; her fair hair rippled through the ermine like water trickling through snow and her fingers sparkled with rings. Someone shoved a goblet into the prince's hands, and he saw his father's gaze turned on him.

The prince bowed first to his father and then to the queen.

The king seemed satisfied and raised his glass, thundering, "To the queen's good health!"

"To the queen's health! Hail to King Mark and Queen Sigrid of Lothene!" boomed the resounding replies followed by cheers. Everyone drained their cups, and the prince backed up against the door and then snuck out of the hall.

THE prince lay in bed, thinking over the events of the day. Meeting Ninny Nanny had brought back to life a world he had thought buried with the dead queen. He remembered his mother's soft, grey eyes and gentle expression. She had been the only one he ever laughed around, and that was because, whenever she gave him one of her rare smiles, those smiles were meant only for him. They would curl up on the fur rug before the fireplace, and she would tell him stories while running her fingers through his dark hair. She told him about her people in the west and of the golden kingdom from long ago and how its court was full of laughter, song, and dancing. She told him tales of the Golden King with his golden crown, who traveled throughout the kingdom and watched time pass by.

One day King Mark found the queen telling the prince her stories, and Erik was sent from the room. When he returned, his father had gone and his mother had tears in her eyes. From that day on, she stopped telling the prince stories of the golden kingdom.

But he hungered after stories; so he wandered throughout the castle's dark and secret places until he came across two old women whispering before the fire.

At first they fell silent when they saw the prince, but he sat by their feet at the hearth, and they saw by the look in his eye that he would not tell. So they began again to talk in hushed voices, and their tales were very different from his mother's stories.

They whispered of a wandering king searching for his stolen crown, but this king was different from the Golden King he remembered. If the wandering king thought you had taken his crown, he would hunt you down, and, when he touched you, your body would wither and your remains scatter like dust in the wind.

The old women also spoke in ominous voices of the Shadowood, a dark wood in the west where the ancient faerie race was banished—they were vengeful spirits who preyed on those foolish enough to wander past the margin of their wood. Not least of all, the old women would murmur between their stories of witches caught and burned at the stake, and these witches were women from the west.

Erik remembered how he had asked his mother why her stories were so different from the old women's stories by the fire, and she said it was because the people of the west had long memories, and those from the north were new to the land and did not understand it, and therefore were afraid. Then Erik understood why his father did not like his mother's stories, and why his mother was sad, for she loved her people and their long memories.

Then the queen had died. Not many in the castle mourned her, for she had not been one of them, and the king found a new bride.

Erik brooded over all this and wondered how Ninny Nanny was connected to his mother. He knew that he could never tell anyone about the old woman, for, if he did, she would surely be burned as a witch. Somehow the prince knew deep in his heart that Ninny Nanny was no witch, that she was his friend.

The next morning the prince grabbed the pouch of dried sticks that Ninny Nanny had given him and snuck out of the castle. Kenelm would thrash him for missing his morning sword practice, but he didn't care. When Erik reached the edge of the forest that skirted the edge of the town, he said the rhyme that the old woman had taught him and cast the sticks on the ground. He raised his eyebrows as he saw that the sticks all rattled and fell pointing in the same direction.

After gathering the sticks up again, he set off into the woods. Whenever he thought he was swerving off the path, Erik cast the sticks again and followed where they pointed. Sometimes they even sent him off on an entirely new direction, full of twists and turns, but eventually he caught sight of Ninny Nanny's cottage with its picket fence, thatched roof, and smoke rising from the chimney. Erik opened the gate and knocked on the cottage door.

"Come in, princeling," called the voice from within.

♛ ♛ ♛

THE PRINCESS had not traveled far from her godmother's house before she regretted not wearing any shoes. When she had first stalked outside into the forest, fuming rebellion, she was so lost in a hornet's nest of anger that she was oblivious to anything beyond her injured feelings.

Finally the sharp pain from crushing sharp branches and small rocks with her feet broke through her cloud of anger, and with a sob Rosa crumpled against the trunk of a large tree. She sat there crying, waiting, and hoping that her father and mother might have regretted their decision to send her away and be looking for her even now. But in her heart she knew that they were not looking for her, but were instead relieved that she was gone.

This realization woke a deep pain within Rosa that eclipsed the pain in her feet. She set her jaw, pushed herself up against the rough bark of the tree, and stubbornly set forth again. This time she was not searching for the castle, but was instead aimlessly wandering, trying to find her way out of the woods. Rosa walked for hours, her feet numb, her body exhausted. Dazed with hunger and thirst, she thought that the trees about her all looked the same.

Darkness descended on the forest, casting its shadowy veil lightly pricked with stars. Rosa broke through a thick line of thick trees into a clearing of tall grass scattered with wildflowers bowing their heads in the on-setting dusk. She watched in horror as the glowing sun sunk below the tree line and the sky grew dim and then black. The trees surrounding the clearing became menacing, reaching out clawed, grasping branches gnarled like witches' fingers. The rising moon was a ghost, yellow and worn.

She wrapped her arms tightly about herself, while she stared up at the ghoulish moon in terrified fascination. Its flat, yellow disc grew larger and larger, and the wild thought leapt through her mind that the moon wanted to roll around the floor of the sky like one of her clay marbles until it tipped out of the sky and crushed her flat.

A sharp howl, eerie, mournful, and long, pierced the cold night air and sent a stab of shivering fear through Rosa's heart. What a fool I am, she thought. Now I'm all alone out here in the dark with the wild beasts. A groan escaped her shivering little body, and she sobbed, "Godmother, please help me!"

Branches snapped, and a low growl emerged from the darkness behind her.

She spun around and glimpsed a flash of silver before an onrushing force sprang and toppled her over, its heavy mass pressing her to the ground. Rosa felt a panting breath hot against her skin. A pair of golden-yellow eyes loomed above her, blocking out the moon and paralyzing her with fear so that she could not utter a sound. The yellow eyes blinked shut, and the night fell into absolute darkness. Her senses reeled in terror, and the last thing she remembered was hearing a sharp, unintelligible command before she herself was lost in the inky blackness of the dark night.

Chapter Four

The Silver Wolf

THE SCENT OF FRESHNESS and springtime surrounded Rosa. Her head rested on something as soft as a pillow, and she realized that she was back in her godmother's house, being cradled in godmother's arms.

Rosa heaved a great sob and flung her arms around her godmother, tightly clinging to her while her godmother hushed her with soft, murmuring words until Rosa's tears died down.

"You saved me from the wild beasts!" Rosa gasped.

"Hush, hush, you have nothing to fear. No beast can harm you as long as you are under my protection."

Rosa's godmother gently laid Rosa down on the bed and then went to the wooden cupboard to pull out a large copper basin, which she filled with water from the well and brought to Rosa's bedside. Rosa gazed into the basin, and its clear water reflected her dirty tear stained face, with shallow scratches flaming red across her cheeks and forehead.

Her godmother soaked a soft cloth in the water and carefully washed Rosa's hot face, dabbing her cuts until Rosa no longer felt a sting. Next she knelt down, gently lifted Rosa's feet into the basin, and tenderly wiped her bleeding toes until the water's coolness soothed the burning in the princess' feet.

Tears again sprang from Rosa's eyes, but they were tears she had never shed before. Gratitude and love sent their wet trails down her face, and, when her godmother finished, Rosa wrapped her arms around her and fell asleep.

Rosa woke the next morning, tucked in bed and in a new nightgown, to the cheerful sight of her godmother tending the bubbling pot over the hearth. She had cast off her dusk cloak and was clothed in a gown as green as the new leaf, while around her waist hung a simple belt of copper links that bounced off the light like the sparkle of fire.

"Godmother, you look so pretty!" Rosa exclaimed.

Her godmother gave Rosa a glowing smile that made her appear as young as a maiden before she returned to stirring the pot.

Then Rosa remembered the events from the day before and felt under her pillow. Her fingers closed around the lump of coal she had hidden there, and, as she pulled it out, it left an ashy trail behind on the bed cloths. She shamefully held it up to her godmother.

Without a word, the lady took the coal and blew on it. There must have been a glow deep inside it that she fanned back to life with her breath, because it shone again the brightest crystal. The lady went to the corner of the room and placed it in the air where it hung suspended before her. Then she breathed on each of the fallen globes, and, when the last one hung suspended in the air, they all again wheeled and spun in their endless circle.

Rosa breathed a sigh of relief. Then she spotted a broom and leapt out of bed to sweep up all the broken shards of colored glass scattered across the floor. When she finished, her godmother drew up the bucket from the well, and Rosa poured all the tinkling glass shards into the bucket, and then her godmother lowered them down deep into the well. When the lady drew the bucket back up, Rosa saw to her amazement that each goblet was made whole.

"This is my well," her godmother explained, "and it makes whole again what was broken. Whatever is bathed in it turns into what it was before it was hurt or damaged."

Rosa stared at her godmother in wonder and asked, "Is it magic?"

"That depends on what you mean by magic. Some think of magic as tricks and illusion, willing things to be otherwise than what they are. That is not magic but deception. Magic is true to the harmony and nature of things, nurturing things to grow into what they really are, or purifying them into what was originally intended. So yes, in answer to your question, my well is magic."

"So I shattered goblets that were always meant to be goblets and never anything besides?" The princess widened her eyes. "No wonder it was so wrong of me to break them."

The lady burst into a peal of laughter. "How single-minded you are, my princess. When faced with a magic well that can restore all things, you are still thinking of my goblets. But you are right. Magic is as wondrous in the smallest of things as in the mightiest."

"So what happens if I drink the well water?"

"That depends. Sometimes it takes a long time for the magic of the water to bear fruit. Other times it takes effect right away. Whatever happens, it is different for each person, and it only changes you as far as you are willing to be changed."

The princess gazed at her faerie godmother. Rosa had heard that her godparents were all faerie, but, until now, she had not understood what that meant.

"Are you the one that made me beautiful?" she asked.

Her godmother nodded. "I gave you beauty, and others gave you different gifts besides."

Rosa pondered all that she had heard. The lady laughed again and tucked one of Rosa's golden curls behind her ear. "You are thinking so seriously, Rosa. Things will come to you in their proper season. But come; I have a gift for you."

She rose and pulled out from the cupboard a simple dress, soft and blue, along with a dove grey cloak. "It will be much easier for you walk through the forest in these clothes than in that elegant dress you were wearing before. And I am afraid your old dress is torn." Then she laid out a pair of calfskin shoes on the bed. "These will protect your feet."

Rosa blinked at her gifts. "I'm not sure if I want to go out in the forest anymore. I want to stay with you and be safe."

"Rosa, did I not promise you no wild beast will ever harm you while you are under my protection. Now get dressed and come outside. I wish to show you my garden."

When Rosa was ready, her godmother showed her the garden and explained what each growing thing was, when it could be picked, and how it should be tended and watered. With her godmother's promise to look over her, Rosa grew brave and ventured every day deeper into the forest, dancing from rock to rock and gathering the white hawthorn flowers that grew in profusion throughout the wood.

One day, when she was napping in the cool shade, Rosa woke to a robin chirping high up in the branches of a tree. She espied the robin's nest and was overpowered by the sudden desire to peek into it.

She shimmied up the trunk, and perched herself on the lowest branch in triumph. Climbing a tree was much easier than she had thought! Her heart bounded faster and faster as she climbed higher and higher up. She was almost at the top when a branch bent with a terrifying crack under her weight. For a breathless instant she was falling, but she flung out her arms, grabbed at the outreaching branches, and wrapped her limbs against the trunk. She remained motionless for a while, trying to still her breathing while her heart throbbed painfully against her chest.

All thoughts of the robin's nest were forgotten. Rosa just wanted to make her way down as quickly and safely as possible. But then she discovered, much to her dismay, that climbing down was much trickier than climbing up. Rosa's foot floated in indeterminate space below her, her body trembling like a leaf in the air, while she blindly felt for footholds.

She slid down to sit on the high bough with a loud groan. It was only midday, and she knew her godmother would not look for her for hours! The thought of being trapped in the tree until it grew dark was unbearable and sent tears of frustration spilling down her cheeks.

"Child, why are you crying?" A commanding voice from below broke through her sobs.

Rosa quickly dried her eyes and peered down through the branches. Below her stood a tall woman slender and straight as a spear-shaft. She wore a cloak that blended with all the colors of the forest, and her hair blazed the brightest red that Rosa had ever seen. At her side was a wolf, his coat silver and his eyes a yellow gold.

At the sight of the wolf, Rosa's breath stuck in her throat.

The woman repeated her question with an impatient edge to her voice.

"I am stuck," Rosa replied in a wavering tone.

The woman with flaming hair sternly gazed up at Rosa. "You should be able to climb down from the tree, for the branches are close enough together. It is your fear which stops you. Come down from the tree, child. You will not fall. "

Rosa nervously looked down from her height, the fear of falling, along with the presence of the wolf, made her hesitate.

"If I fall, will you catch me?" she finally asked.

"I have just told you that you will not fall."

"Do you promise that the wolf will not eat me, if I come down?"

At this the woman smiled. "My wolf harms no one under my protection. You are quite safe."

The woman's words reminded her of her godmother's promise, but still Rosa hesitated.

"Princess, does fear grip your heart so strongly that you doubt my word? Climb down from the tree."

Rosa felt herself grow flushed with shame, and she stood up

on the branch to try again. She lowered herself further and further down, her leg dangling precariously from the tree-limb, until, with a sinking heart, she realized she could not pull herself back up. Then she found a firm foothold and dropped down from the tree's lowest branch.

Rosa stood before the woman, unable to tear her gaze from the piercing yellow eyes of the silver wolf who stood up to the woman's breast.

"You are not still afraid?" the woman asked sharply.

"I think this wolf once tried to eat me."

"Nonsense. If my wolf had wanted to eat you, then he would have. You may touch him. He will not harm you."

Rosa wasn't so sure, but a fierce desire awakened inside her to prove that she wasn't afraid, so she reached out to brush the fur on the back of the wolf's neck. The wolf's hot breath panted against her face, but he did not twitch or otherwise give a sign that he noticed her except by peering back at her with his golden-yellow eyes.

"What is his name?" Rosa asked.

"You may simply call him Silver Wolf, for you would not be able to say his true name."

The princess fixed a curious gaze at the woman with the flaming hair. She recognized the serene, ageless look on the woman's face and realized that she stood before a faery.

"May I ask what I should call you?"

"I am the Lady of the Hawthorn Wood, which is this wood in which you stand, and that is what you may call me."

"Oh, I thought my godmother was the lady of this wood."

"You are both mistaken and correct. Mistaken, because the one whom you think of is not mistress of these parts, though she often comes to visit me. Her true home is an island, full of cypress trees, perfumed cedars, and warm breezes, though, when she abides here, she stays in her own house. But you are correct as well, because I am also your godmother."

"Oh," said Rosa, "godmother mentioned that I had others."

"Indeed? You have seven. You should call your other god-mother the Green Lady. Her greenness is different than mine. She is the greenness of new life, though she is by far the eldest among us. I am all the colors of the Hawthorn Wood. I am stone, earth, water, the ore that can be found under the earth, the ruby that can be mined from the caverns nearby, and the red hawthorn berry."

She leaned over and took the princess' hand. "My wolf here will be your companion for as long as you stay in my forest. You should obey him, for he knows the laws of this place and he will look after you and protect you. I will visit you again when my wolf says you are ready."

Rosa responded with a deep curtsey, and the red haired lady disappeared in the trees and the undergrowth.

The princess stared at the wolf in awe. He exuded a regal air of power, and she could feel the wildness deep within him. She no longer believed that the wolf would harm her, but she was mystified over what to do with him. Perhaps speaking to the beast was the most fitting.

"I am going back to my godmother's house. You are wel-come to come with me if you like."

The wolf gave no sign that he had heard her, but, as she walked back home, he followed her with dignified, firm padded steps. When she reached her godmother's, the wolf would not cross the threshold, but remained outside.

Rosa's godmother was within, and the princess excitedly related her adventure.

The Green Lady spoke, "I was wondering when the Mistress of the Hawthorn Wood would show herself to you. She has bestowed upon you a great favor in giving you such a companion."

Rosa nodded, but then said, "Yes, but I am not sure what to do with him. He does not seem to want to be friends."

"I wouldn't try to *do* anything with him. He is a companion for you, and so you should accept him. You will soon discover what kind of friendship may be had after you spend some time together. He may not be sure of you either and is waiting to discover what sort of young girl he is being asked to watch over."

Rosa went to the window to look out at the wolf, but did not see him. "He is gone!" she cried.

"He will come and go as he pleases, I suspect," the Green Lady said, "You will see him again soon."

The princess went over to her godmother. "The Lady of the Hawthorn Wood said I should call you the Green Lady."

"You may if you wish."

"Oh," said the princess, "I was hoping I could still call you 'godmother.'"

Rosa's godmother broke into a warm smile.

"I would like that as well," she said.

WHEN Rosa left her godmother's house the next day, the Silver Wolf was waiting for her at the edge of the glade. As the days went by, the grave mood surrounding the wolf lessened, and she took to chatting with him about her godmother and the life she used to have at the castle, but she could not tell if he understood her as he watched her with his yellow eyes. She also shared her lunch with him, a little bit of bread and cheese and ripe berries gathered from the bush, but she had the impression that he did not particularly enjoy their meals and ate only to be polite.

Sometimes the Silver Wolf would bound off ahead of her, disappearing into the woods, then she would later find him observing her from a distance. But he would not leave her for long.

Other times the wolf guided her through the forest, intruding upon her path, pressing her in a different direction with his heavy weight. There was a time when she willfully ignored his lead, clenching her jaw with stubborn determination, and so disturbed a bee hive. She fled and escaped with only a few stings.

Sitting on a tree stump, she cradled her smarting arm, but the wolf offered her no sympathy and gave a snort that seemed to say, "Serves you right."

The weeks passed by for the princess and her wolf, and Rosa gradually became aware that whenever they walked for a long period in a north-easterly direction away from her godmother's house, the wolf would inevitably push her away from her course. Sometimes she would pretend that she did not notice him, and he would growl and snap his fangs until she was forced to follow.

Curiosity overwhelmed Rosa. What didn't the wolf want her to see?

The next time Rosa left the cottage, she spent the whole morning digging holes in the garden. Rosa snuck a sideways glance at the wolf: his eyelids were half-closed, his tongue lolled out. If ever a wolf looked bored, it was the Silver Wolf.

Rosa smiled to herself and stretched herself under a tree, pretending to take a nap. When she opened her eyes, the Silver Wolf was gone. Rosa immediately rose and dashed off in the forbidden direction.

The sound of crashing branches behind her told Rosa that the wolf was not far behind, and that he was rapidly gaining. She broke into a full sprint, her heart thumping wildly in her chest. A thundering sound reverberated ahead and her flight was forced to a sudden halt at the edge of a wide, rushing river.

The Silver Wolf burst through the trees, snarling and bristling, crouching and snapping. Rosa gave a cry and retreated back into the wood. But the damage had been done. She had seen the other side of the river bank, with its silver glades and trees shrouded in purple shade, and the vision of it was seared into her mind.

Chapter Five

The Faerie Ring

WHEN SHE LAY ABED that night, Rosa could not sleep. Her heart yearned to cross the river, walk in the shade of those mysterious trees, and lie amid the silver grass.

The next morning, the Silver Wolf watched her with a displeased eye. At first she felt guilty for tricking him, but he was such a cold companion that her remorse quickly dissolved. Whispers of the forbidden wood haunted her, and the only thing that kept her from attempting a second escape was the knowledge that her godmother would not approve.

That evening during dinner, Rosa wanted to tell the Green Lady about what she had seen, but she could not. She was torn between her desire to please her godmother and to lie down in the shade of the dark and silver wood. She could not choose, and the moment passed.

"Tell me another story of the Golden King. You promised to tell me next about how he fought the Golden Gryphon on my tapestry," she said instead.

Rosa and the Green Lady curled up before the fire and the lady began,

Long ago, when the kingdom was new, the Golden King wandered throughout his land and he came upon a Golden Gryphon trapped in a net. Though the cords were thin, the net was a faerie net, and the mighty beast could not free himself. The king asked the gryphon why he was trapped in the net, and the

gryphon answered, though he was surprised to hear a mortal speak in the animal tongue. "A faery trapped me in his net for stealing a single ram from his flock, though its white fur shone like the sun." "If I free you, will you serve me?" asked the king. The gryphon said he would do so, and, when the king freed him from the net, the gryphon looked down upon him. "I will serve you by sparing your life, for you are mortal and not strong enough to bind me." He spread his vast wings and flew into the sky, but the king grabbed him by his lion's tail and thrust him to the ground. Then the two wrestled for three days and three nights, the gryphon with its pinions and sharp beak, the king with his bare hands. On the morning of the fourth day, the gryphon's strength failed and the king pinned him to the ground. "Will you serve me?" the Golden King asked again. This time the Golden Gryphon gave the king one of his golden feathers and his name. And whenever the king held the feather aloft and called out the creature's name, the gryphon would come and was bound to do whatever the king asked of him. And the feather and the gryphon's name were treasures passed down to each heir of the golden throne, and the gryphon saved the kingdom in a great battle one day, but that is a different tale.

By the time the story was finished, Rosa felt dazed, a steady ache thumping behind her eyelids. The Green Lady felt her forehead.

"You are feverish," she said with a worried expression and then drew a cup of clear water from the well. "Drink this. It will dispel the cloud you are under."

Rosa drank the fresh water, and it cooled the heat of her cheeks. The Green Lady then put her to sleep, smoothing her golden hair away from her forehead and kissing her cheek.

"Call me again if the fever returns in the night, and I will give you another draught from my well," she said.

Rosa nodded and quickly fell asleep, but her sleep was restless, full of twists and turns, and she finally awoke with the burning desire to go to the river and gaze at the purple and silver wood.

She rose, put on her shoes, and tiptoed to the door. Lifting the latch, she peered through the dark night and did not see the wolf. She left her cloak hanging on the peg, since it was a warm, summer night, and set off toward the river.

Rosa drifted through the starlit forest until she reached the riverbank. The dark waters flowed smoothly and gently, and across the river lay the silver grass and the trees that whispered secrets unfathomable. The delicate branches cast intricate shadows in the moonlight, and the rustling leaves beckoned Rosa to come into their shade, where they would drape her in their darkness. Her soul strained at the river's edge, drinking in the sight of them.

The moon shone across the river water and cast a path made by moonlight. In the path she saw stepping stones, shining and white, leading across water. Her heart leapt. She could cross the river!

Rosa nudged the first glowing white stone with her foot to make sure she was not dreaming. It felt solid enough. She leapt nimbly from stone to stone, her heart fluttering with joy—the path must have been made just for her so that she could find it at this exact moment in the moonlight.

Later, she wondered if it was because of her exultation, or perhaps a trick played on her by the treacherous stones, but, when she reached half-way across the river, her foot slipped, and with a cry, she tumbled into the dark waters.

While the river had seemed gentle when she had sat on the bank, it was now an angry, tumultuous maelstrom. The river entirely submerged her, its churning waters dragging her down in their merciless current. In her panic she screamed. The waters slammed into her chest and lungs, choking her, paralyzing her. Icy fear gripped her heart.

Suddenly she felt something yanking her upwards, dragging her up onto the river bank.

It was her wolf! He had saved her, even though she had

tricked him. Panting and trembling, she threw her arms around him, sobbing apologies against his wet dark coat.

The wolf let her clutch him and burrow her face into his fur, and he licked her face to dry her tears, so that she laughed and burst into tears again. He took her back to her godmother's house, where the Green Lady stood by the door with the light of the fire behind her.

The next morning, the Green Lady did not bring up Rosa's nighttime escapade, but only laid out the breakfast table in a somber silence. Rosa knew that her godmother was waiting for her to speak, and, all the while, the silence was growing more and more uncomfortable. At last she could stand it no longer and asked directly, "Godmother, did you send the Silver Wolf to rescue me?"

The Green Lady laid down her egg basket on the table with a deep sigh. "Yes. When I saw that you were gone, I realized you had seen something that you were not meant to see, and that you had been called to it. So I asked the Silver Wolf to bring you back."

"If you had not sent him, I would be drowned. I am sorry for sneaking away. I knew I was going somewhere I should not. But the woods..." here she paused. "I could not forget them... Please forgive me."

"My Rosa," the Green Lady reached across the table to grasp her hand, "you do not need to say more. And there is nothing that I can say that your near escape from death does not say for me. There are some things for which you are ill-prepared. You were not meant to glimpse the other side of the river, for it is one of the overlapping margins between the faerie and mortal realms and holds a strong enchantment for mortals. It would have been dangerous to many stronger than you. Only..." and here the Green Lady smiled sadly, "I wish you could have spoken to me about your longing. I would have been able to help you."

Rosa hung her head in shame. The Green Lady lifted the princess' chin and smiled warmly. "No more worries, my princess. All is well, and I believe there is someone outside the door who is eager to see you."

Rosa leapt from her chair to the door. There was her Silver Wolf, waiting for her. She threw her arms around him and buried her face in his fur. He licked her face and then pranced around her like a puppy.

"Go now, and enjoy yourselves," said the Green Lady, handing the princess her lunch. "But I want you back home before dusk."

Rosa and her wolf scampered off. The princess did not feel too adventurous that day, and mainly kept her fingers tangled in the wolf's coat. They chased each other about, and the princess teased him by pulling his tail, something she never would have dared before. They lunched together and she tossed berries into his mouth, which he caught with a snap of his jaw. Finally, they curled up together in the afternoon sun, and she lay her head against his warm, heaving side and fell asleep.

She woke to the wolf licking her face and saw that it was nearly dusk.

"It is time to go back home, isn't it?"

THEY returned to the house together, and the Green Lady was waiting for them at the door. Rosa kissed her wolf goodnight and recounted her day to her godmother. Then, as the evening shadows lengthened, a cloud passed over the princess's eyes, and she heard a ringing in her ears. Her yearning for the purple wood and the silver grass grew with the rising moon.

The Green Lady draped the princess' cloak over her and took her hand.

"Come with me. We are going out," she said.

Surprise and curiosity momentarily dispelled the throbbing in her head. The Green Lady wrapped herself in her own cloak of shadows, and the two entered the wood in the darkening night.

Rosa could not tell for how long they walked, while the stars spangled the heavens above them, and the woods thinned into aspens and young birches tall and straight. They walked on until they reached a cove with a pebbly beach and the sea stretching out before them.

"I did not know we were so near the sea!" Rosa gasped.

"We are not near as you would term it," said the Green Lady. "But no distance is near or far when you travel in the faerie realm. Follow me."

The lady took Rosa down around the bend in the cove, and they came upon a little white ship. The prow was carved like a swan in flight, and the sail gleamed white in the moonlight. She could hear the waters lapping against the hull as they boarded the ship and took off into the horizon.

Time was meaningless as the steady rocking of the ship lulled Rosa to sleep. She woke to her godmother singing a wordless melody so beautiful it hurt to listen. The Green Lady's eyes were closed, and she seemed to be listening to something Rosa could not hear. When the princess' heart was full of the song, she fell asleep again. On they traveled through the night, and, between her waking and sleeping, Rosa thought the night would never end. She did not mind, for the soft breezes carried sweet perfumes that dispelled the dull hammering in her head, and the moon was full and bright.

The light grew on the horizon, and Rosa beheld an island in the distance. The breezes blew across her face and carried the ship toward the island, where they banked on a white, sandy beach. They watched together the most glorious sunrise, and then, hand in hand, the princess and her godmother found a path that led from the beach into the interior of the island.

Rosa's godmother had shed her dark cloak and was garbed in the green of springtime, with flowers in her hair. Cyprus trees, tall pencil-like evergreens, lined their path until they passed into a grove of olive trees that shimmered like silver-green mist in the sunlight. Through the olive grove wove a stream whose source was a fountain springing from a white rock at the heart of the island.

The Green Lady led Rosa to a basin in the rock, where the water was so clear it almost shone like a diamond glowing with a fire in its heart.

"Drink," the Green Lady commanded, "drink from my spring and be renewed."

Rosa obeyed. The water was so cold and pure that the cloud in her head vanished, and the desire to lie down in the shadow of the purple trees and forget all her troubles was replaced by the tranquility of the olive grove.

Rosa caught her reflection in the basin and was startled. She knew that she was beautiful, or, at least, so she had been told, but the glowing reflection she caught sight of was of a different kind of beauty, a beauty that seemed to radiate from the inside and shine through her eyes and face. But the instant she had glimpsed her reflection, the radiant beauty was gone, replaced by the natural order of her features.

"What was that face I just saw now," she asked, a little frightened, "was that my own?"

"Yes, the fountain reflects what is within as well as that which is without. And after drinking from its waters, you were renewed and made beautiful again. This fountain is the mother and source of the well in my house, which is only a lesser reflection of it, as my house in the wood is only a reflection of my home on the island. Only its purity was strong enough to release you from the thrall of faerie enchantment."

The princess fell silent, but the Green Lady spoke, "Speak what is on your mind. I see that you have another question you would ask me."

"Then, please, why did you make me beautiful?"

The lady breathed on the princess.

"Do you ask why you breathe? Even breath is a gift. Therefore, do not ask why you are beautiful, but be glad that you are so, just as you should be glad that you breathe. Beauty reminds us of a time when the world was unbroken, when there was harmony and love in all things. And when a heart is moved by beauty, it strives to return to the time when things were unbroken."

Rosa did not think she fully understood what her godmother had said, but she felt that she had been answered. They left the olive grove and returned to the ship. She saw that time had passed differently there on the coast than it had in the grove, and that it was already sunset. The light pink stained the hazy margin between the sea and sky, and it seemed as if a rich girdle of blues and pinks encircled the world.

They sailed off again towards the horizon, and this time Rosa slept through the whole journey to find herself waking in the morning in her bed at her godmother's house.

IT was not many nights after her visit to the Green Lady's island that Rosa heard a rapping at the windowsill as she lay in bed. She opened the shutters and saw the cloaked figure of the Lady of the Hawthorn Wood outside. Tendrils of her red hair peeped out from under her hood, and the Silver Wolf sat on his haunches beside her. The lady beckoned, and Rosa threw on her cloak and shoes to join them.

The Lady of the Hawthorn Wood led the way, and Rosa followed with her hand against the Silver Wolf's back, for she was a little frightened of this stern lady. They traveled for a long time, and, when the princess looked up at the stars, she saw a red star shining bright above that seemed to journey with them. Then, at a distance, Rosa could hear the faint sounds of singing and laughter. The sound grew until they finally came to a wooded clearing, brightly lit by the tall flames of a bonfire. There were many figures dancing and singing, their pale limbs gleaming in the moonlight and firelight.

The lady led her to the edge of the circle, and the princess sat down to observe the reveling before her. Never had she seen so many graceful creatures dancing or heard such a vibrant chorus of voices, accompanied by a delicate lyre and ringing bells. She watched the dancers form patterns in arcs and waves as they were carried by the spirit of the music. As she watched, she saw that some of the dancers seemed akin to the trees, long and slender, with leaves in their dresses and garlands in their hair, while others seemed to spring from the water with rippling movements and flowing garments. There were creatures that seemed embodiments of air and fire, so did they dart and flash among the dancers.

She watched the unworldly scene before her in amazement, half entranced, but also a little frightened by its strangeness. One of the creatures, whose skin seemed to flame and whose feet barely touched the ground, approached her. He offered her a cup engraved with vines, a challenge spoken in his glowing eyes. She took the cup and sipped the golden liquid, warm and honey sweet. Instantly her fear disappeared, and she felt a tingling down to her toes and a bubbling mirth welling up within her. The spirit of air and fire laughed and darted off to join the dance, and Rosa soon found herself laughing and singing with all the other faerie creatures, though she was content to remain seated and watch the dancers. The Silver Wolf's head lay in her lap, and she stroked it gently. Some of the faerie murmured at this.

The Lady of the Hawthorn Wood cast off her cloak and joined the dancers. One by one they left off their dancing to watch, and soon she was the only one dancing in the center of the glade. The music was soft and gentle at first, and each move the lady made was grace and fire, strength and beauty. Rosa felt a deep longing stirring within her heart and tears sprang in her eyes. But slowly the music grew and grew, and the lady spun and spun and flew about the clearing with such energy that Rosa felt it was a joy to be alive. The song ended, and silence filled the glade as every faerie creature had been captured by the lady's dance. Then someone laughed, the music started again, and the dancing went on as before.

The Lady of the Hawthorn Wood approached the princess and held out her hand. Rosa clasped it and was pulled into the dance. There she forgot everything, who she was and where she was. All that she knew was the music, that she was alive, and that she could dance. She did not notice that one by one the other dancers stopped to watch, until she was the only one left in the clearing. She did not come to herself until the music ceased and she realized all the faerie creatures were watching her, some with tears in their eyes. She covered her face in embarrassment.

"No, do not be ashamed," cried one of the dancers who rushed up to the princess and gently took her hands. Rosa saw that she was tall and slender, with birch leaves in her hair and that she had tears in her eyes.

"Do not be ashamed," she repeated, "you were beautiful. We of Faerie seldom cry, for we are joyful and take delight in living, and nothing ever fades for us. But you have the beauty of the perfect flower that will wither or the glorious sun that will set. Oh, what a sad thing mortal beauty is, for it must end."

The dancing began again, and Rosa remained with the dancers until the Lady of the Hawthorn Wood took her by the hand and led her from the clearing, with the Silver Wolf stalking regally behind them. Dawn stained the sky, and they wandered through the freshness of the dew and the early morning birdsong.

The Lady of the Hawthorn Wood broke the silence, "Tell me, Rosa, when you saw the purple wood and silver grass on the other side of the riverbank, how did it tempt you?"

Rosa flushed that the lady knew of her folly, but she answered after a moment's thought, "I yearned to cross the river and lie in the silver grass and sleep in the dark shadows."

"You yearned for sleep," the lady murmured and then fell silent.

"But I was rescued by your Silver Wolf. Thank you for sending him to watch over me."

"He was careless in his duty!" the lady snapped, and the wolf whimpered, laying his ears flat against his head.

"You should never have seen the riverbank," she continued, "For you see, it was a test for him as well. My wolf is proud and was not content with his charge over a young girl, princess or no. He did not realize how much you meant to him until he almost lost you."

Rosa glanced down at the wolf and once more buried her fingers in his fur. They continued in that manner until they reached her godmother's house, but, before the lady could depart, Rosa said, "Godmother, may I ask you what is the gift you gave me at my christening?"

The lady looked surprised. "Do you not know? Do you think that there are many mortals who can dance so as to make a faery cry?"

Rosa was glad that it was still the morning twilight, for she could feel a flush spreading over her features. The Lady of the Hawthorn Wood looked out into the distance, her eyes seeming to pierce the horizon beyond the tree line.

"But there is something more, I see that now. There will come a time when you must face an ordeal in the formless darkness, and all will abandon you. At that time my courage will come to you and help you to endure." She looked down at the princess, "Farewell, Princess Rosamund. We shall not meet again for a long while, but my gift goes with you."

"Thank you," said Rosa, "and goodbye." She did not know what else to say.

The lady disappeared among the trees, her Silver Wolf following her. Rosa felt a pang at her going. She went inside the house to sleep and woke with the sun at its brightest. The events of the night before seemed but a dream, but the beauty of the memory of the Lady of the Hawthorn Wood's dancing remained with her.

THE summer passed into autumn, the oak trees grew heavy with acorns, and Rosa walked into her godmother's house one afternoon, carrying a hawthorn branch laden with its dark-red berries.

The Green Lady bid Rosa sit down and said, "Rosa, it is time for you to bid farewell to my home and return to the castle, where your mother and father await you."

A wave of varied emotions passed over the princess. She felt joy at the thought of seeing her parents again, anxiety over returning to her old way of life, and a little stab of fear that maybe, just maybe, no one would be glad to see her back.

"Godmother," she said, "this cannot be goodbye forever? I will be able to come back and visit you, will I not?"

"Your time in the forest has ended, and you will not return to my house in the wood. Though that does not mean that we shall not see each other again," the Green Lady said.

Rosa embraced her. "The Silver Wolf, will I see him again?"

"I am sorry, Rosa, you must say goodbye to the wolf. Tomorrow will be your last day with him, and then I fear your time together has passed. The Lady of the Hawthorn Wood has other tasks for him now."

"Oh, no!" Rosa cried, and sobbed in her godmother's arms.

The next day was bittersweet for Rosa. She spent it with the wolf and said goodbye to all her favorite haunts in the forest. When he took her back to her godmother's house, she could not help but weep. "You have been the best of friends, and I will miss you terribly," she said and buried her face in his fur.

He licked her tears away and nudged her into the house and into the Green Lady's arms. He stayed for a while, staring at the closed wooden door, and then silently strode through the growing mist into the woven shade of the forest.

Inside her home, the Green Lady comforted the princess, for she understood Rosa's sadness at leaving.

"I don't know, godmother," Rosa whispered, "but maybe I would rather stay with you here in the wood after all." She anxiously looked up at the Green Lady.

The lady knelt down and smoothed back the princess' golden hair. "My dear, it is time for you to return to your own kind. You cannot be alone in the forest any longer."

"But I have you and the Silver Wolf," the princess cried, "I am not alone!"

"That is not enough," the Green Lady said firmly. "You must learn to make friends among your own kind. And you must further discover your gifts. You have learned all you can from the forest as you are now. I have a gift for you, Rosa, one that I hope will aid you when you are in the castle."

From the folds of her gown she pulled out a small, square mirror the size of her outstretched palm.

"This mirror was bathed in the waters of my fountain and is therefore imbued with its grace. At most times it will merely give a true account of your outward features, but, when the inspiration takes it, it will grant you a glimpse of your inward self. But let me give you a word of warning. You cannot force the mirror to bestow upon you its vision, and it can be dangerous if misused, and, if misused, it will be taken away. It is not meant to be used for vanity's sake. But come…" The lady opened her arms. "I will take you back to the castle now."

"Oh," cried Rosa, "are we going back tonight? How are we getting there?"

"We will return the way we came," the Green Lady replied and encircled the princess in her arms.

Chapter Six

Mnemosyne

PRINCE ERIK WOKE early for his morning sword training with Kenelm. The Captain of the Guard wore the prince to the bone, and, after his lesson, the prince made his way to the cistern in the castle keep to pour water over his burning arms and head. He slumped on a bench to rest his aching limps and fell into a daze, until his thoughts were interrupted by an inhuman shriek that filled the air.

The prince leapt in surprise and dashed toward the sound. Bursting upon the castle courtyard, he found a group of servant boys, as well as the sons of some of the castle guards, gathered together to form a ring. They were jeering and throwing stones at something in the center of the ring, and, by the yowling cries piercing the air, Erik knew they had trapped a wild animal.

The prince grimaced and pushed himself into the crowd. In the center of the ring was a large brown sack flailing violently with what could only be a frenzied animal inside. Another stone hit the bag, and a sharp cry of rage and pain pierced the air.

"Hey! That is enough!" Erik cried.

He stepped out into the center with a show of confidence that he did not feel. One of the older boys held up his arm to stop the others from throwing stones. They all watched to see what the prince would do next.

Erik knelt down by the sack, from which emitted a low, reverberating growl. He pulled his hunting knife from his belt and cut through the cord. The frantic head of a cat thrust out, its grey hair standing on end, its ears flat against its head. It immediately struggled to escape, but, in its frenzy, the cat tangled itself further into the cord. Erik reached forward to disentangle it, but the terrified animal slashed at him with its free paw, and the boys in the circle laughed.

"Ach! You stupid cat. I'm only trying to help," the prince exclaimed.

He took off his tunic, wrapping it around his hand, and, with soothing noises, tried to calm the frightened animal. The cat was beyond soothing, however, so the prince finally held it down with his wrapped hand despite its hissing, spitting, and scratching, until he managed to cut it free.

The cat streaked out like lightning from the courtyard.

Erik turned and saw the other boys glowering at him. A tall broad chested boy called Selwyn gave him a particularly dark glare; he had been the one who had halted the others from throwing stones at the prince, and he acted as a ringleader for the other boys. Erik was sure it had been his idea to trap the cat.

No one spoke. Erik pulled his tunic back on and was about to walk out of the ring when Selwyn blocked his way.

"Want to have a fighting bout?" The boy grinned, but there was no friendliness in his eyes.

Erik's heart sank. He should have known that he could not have saved the cat without a price. He could not refuse the challenge without being forever branded as a coward, and, when he accepted, cries for "Selwyn" echoed about the ring.

Only a few cheered for the prince.

The fight ended quickly. Erik was no match for the older boy, who was taller than he was and much broader. The prince was quick and managed to dodge the first strike, but he could not break Selwyn's defense and only landed one blow before he was knocked flat on his face with a few clean strikes. Erik tried to get back up on his feet, but Selwyn landed another blow when the prince was on his knees. The boys all laughed and dispersed, leaving Erik curled up in a ball gasping for breath.

"What have we here?" said a voice from above.

Erik looked up and saw one of his father's hunters, a man called Cynric, looming above him. The hunter was lean and nimble, with a brown, weather-beaten face and sharp, quick eyes.

Cynric pulled the prince up off the ground. "Hmm, let's have a look at your split lip." He took Erik to the gatehouse, where the castle physician stored supplies. "You're going to have a nasty bruise over your eye as well," he observed while tending to the prince's cut. "Whom did you fight?"

"Selwyn"

The hunter whistled. "That was foolish. Who started it?"

Erik explained about the cat.

"Well, this should teach you to stay out of things that don't concern you."

Erik didn't say anything. He was still glad that he had saved the cat.

"THE door is open, princeling."

Erik pushed open the door to Ninny Nanny's cottage and found the old woman pouring milk from an earthenware pitcher into two large mugs on the table.

"Sit ye down and refresh yourself."

The prince slipped into his seat and sipped the frothy milk the old woman set before him. Ninny Nanny then hobbled to her chair by the fire and sighed in contentment as she stretched her weary bones.

She eyed the prince. "How did ye get that purple flower o'er your left eye?"

The prince explained about the cat and the bruises. "I just couldn't watch them all ganging up on a small creature that couldn't defend itself. The cat didn't have a fair chance, and I am glad that I saved it."

"I'm sure the cat's glad as well. Come inside, Mnemosyne," she called, "did ye hear? The prince is glad he saved ye!"

The prince had left the cottage door ajar, and through it slinked a large, grey cat.

"Why, it's the same cat I saved this morning!" Erik exclaimed.

Ninny Nanny chuckled as Erik knelt beside the cat. Mnemosyne sniffed him and allowed the prince to stroke her this time. She soon had enough, however, and stalked in an aloof manner over to the fireside, where she stretched and settled herself down to groom her fur with a rough, pink tongue. Erik watched the cat in fascination.

"I didn't know that it was your cat," he said

"Mnemosyne is not really my cat. She travels around an' sometimes condescends to sit by the fire an' drink milk. In return she catches mice. But she goes where she pleases, an' there are times when I don't see a whisker or tail of hers for weeks."

Erik tore his eyes away from the cat and pulled his legs up, so that his chin rested on his knees. "Ninny Nanny, tell me another story about the princess," he said.

The old woman grinned, "And I thought that ye didn't like her."

"Oh, she's not too bad. In fact, she can be rather nice. I feel sorry for her, now that she has to leave the Silver Wolf and her godmother behind."

"She gets in trouble again at the castle."

"Does she?" Erik rolled his eyes. "Surprise."

But instead of beginning her story, Ninny Nanny picked up her knitting by the fire. The crackle of the flames and the click of the knitting needles formed a soothing rhythm. Mnemosyne yawned, and the prince felt his eyelids growing heavy.

"Would ye like to take a nap?" the old woman asked. "I'll make sure an' waken ye before it gets dark."

The prince nodded. "I don't know why, but I suddenly feel very sleepy."

Erik almost fell asleep on his feet as Ninny Nanny led him to the heather.

"I bet you can talk to Mnemosyne and she answers back," he mumbled before drifting off to sleep.

THE next thing he knew, Erik was surrounded by darkness, but with a white light behind the darkness like when he shut his eyes against the sunlight. Then the light faded, and it was as if night had fallen and there was nothing but the dark.

The prince looked down, or at least he thought he looked down. He was not sure if there was any up or down anymore. Then he realized that there must be some light, for he slowly made out an even darker shape looming before him in the blackness—a dark tower, tall and isolated, with no beginning discernible in the murky depths of the world of shadows below.

By fixing his gaze on the tower, Erik felt that he was descending until he was level with it. He found that he could see through its walls, which were transparent like a veil with gossamer threads as thin as a spider's web. In the darkness and the stillness he could see a figure climbing up the tower's winding steps. When he first saw the figure, it was blurred like a shadow among shadows, but, as he continued to gaze at the climbing form, it was as if his own eyes began to shed a light and he recognized the ascending figure. She was the sleeping maiden in the river from his dream.

Erik could tell that the beautiful maiden could not see in the darkness, since she held out her arms blindly before her, brushing her hands up against the walls of the tower. Her face was white and her mouth determined as she slowly climbed up the stairs. Then she stopped climbing. Her body grew rigid, her face crumbled as she sank down to her feet to bury her head against her knees. With a pang the prince saw that she was trembling and he reached out his arms to her. He found that he was flying through the air, swiftly traveling towards her, and he passed through the gossamer veil separating them and landed on the tower step above her crouching form.

"Are you frightened?" he asked. "Don't cry."

The maiden did not hear him and continued to lie huddled in the darkness. She looked so alone and helpless that Erik's heart instantly reached out to her. He knelt down and kissed the top of her head, feeling her smooth hair against his lips. The beautiful maid did nothing for a moment, but she stopped shaking. Then she slowly raised her head and looked past the prince, and in her features was a new strength and resolve. She stood and continued her climb up the tower steps. Erik watched until her figure was absorbed by the shadows, and he feared what she would find at the top. But then the darkness swam over him, and the white light shone behind his eyelids.

The prince woke and found that Ninny Nanny was knitting in her usual place by the fire and that Mnemosyne was staring at him with her wide, yellow eyes. The cat blinked, stretched, and then began to purr as she rubbed herself against him. Erik stroked her behind the ears and then made his way back to Ninny Nanny's hearth.

"Ninny Nanny, do you remember when I first dreamed of Princess Rosamund?" he asked.

"That I do, princeling. It was the day ye first came to my cottage."

"I had another dream before that, one that I never told you about. I saw a maiden sleeping in a river, but when I touched the water, she disappeared."

"Did ye, now?"

"She was very beautiful, Ninny Nanny," the prince whispered.

"Was she?"

"I just dreamed about her again, but this time she wasn't sleeping."

"No? What was she doing, then?"

Erik told Ninny Nanny about the beautiful maiden climbing the dark tower and how she had seemed frightened.

"I know she is real," he whispered. "I could not dream her up."

"Your heart speaks truly, princeling."

"What was at the top of the tower?" he asked.

"A curse."

A moment's pause.

"What sort of curse?"

"She falls asleep."

The flames crackled, and a log shifted with a clunk in the fire.

"I will wake her," he said at last.

"Will ye?"

"Yes! Tell me where she is."

"She's in a dark place in a dark tower in a dark wood, the Shadowood. There she sleeps as time passes by."

The prince's eyes grew wide when he heard the name of the cursed wood. He thought of the old women's stories before the castle fire and of the fearsome things, magical things, that lived in the wood.

"How do I find the Shadowood?"

"Ye are too young to go looking for the sleeping maid, princeling, and, if ye found her, ye could not wake her."

"Why not? I dream about her, don't I?"

The old woman chuckled. "Yes, but ye are a young boy still and she is a grown woman. It will be a man, not a boy, that'll waken her."

Erik felt himself flush and stared down at the ground. Finally he asked, "No one else will wake her before I grow up?"

Ninny Nanny raised her eyebrows and then laughed. "Jealous are we? Nothing is certain. But ye dream of her, do ye not? That means something. Ye will know when to look for her when the time ripens."

His face still burning, the prince stood up and said with an earnest gaze, "Promise me, that, when the time comes for me to look for the maiden, you will let me know."

"I promise."

The prince settled down on the ground again and stared gloomily into the fire.

"Would ye like me to tell ye a story of the princess to get your mind off the sleeping maid?" the old woman chuckled.

Erik grunted.

"Do ye not like the princess, now that ye are thinking about your sleeping maid?"

"Oh, it's not that. But she's only a story and she's not really in trouble."

"Is Rosa any more a story than the maiden ye dreamed of? Do ye think it's an accident that ye dreamed of them together?"

Erik furrowed his brow. "Very well, Ninny Nanny, you win. Tell me another story."

♛ ♛ ♛

WHEN ROSA AWOKE, she blinked steadily at the bright stars on a field of blue above her. They were the stars of silver thread woven on the canopy above her bed in the castle. She rubbed her face against the cool softness of her silken cushions and then sat up and saw that she was back in her old room. Her playthings had even been gathered and neatly put away, evidence of Alice's tidying.

Her godmother's mirror glimmered beside her, so she tucked it under her pillow. Her first thought was of her parents. Perhaps she could surprise them in their chambers for breakfast.

She sprang out of bed and ran out of her room into the hall, but her plan was interrupted by Alice, who at that moment turned the corner at the far end of the hall and gave a loud shriek as she caught sight of the princess.

They ran toward each other and Rosa found herself enveloped in her nursemaid's arms. Amid more shrieks and laughter, she realized how much she had missed her nursemaid. Servants gathered at the commotion and Rosa saw with chagrin that word would get down to her parents that she was back before she could surprise them.

"Oh well, never mind." Rosa laughed. "I wish to see my father and mother now."

Alice took a step back and narrowed her eyes, gazing up and down at the princess' clothes. "You cannot see your parents looking like that! They would never forgive me."

Rosa saw that she was still wearing her simple blue dress from the forest. "Don't worry, Alice, they won't mind what I'm wearing."

"I insist, Rosa. You cannot wander about the castle in a peasant's dress, and with such tangled hair! You look absolutely wild. No, it will not do."

"Alice, this dress was a present from my godmother. Surely if she gave it to me, then it is right for me to wear it."

"But at least your hair," was her final, wailing protest.

Rosa sighed with impatience, but went back into her room and gave her hair three quick yanks with a comb and gathered it all into a ribbon. Then she scampered past Alice and ran all the way to her parent's chambers, where she slid to a halt before the door.

The guard let her through and she burst upon her parents at the breakfast table.

"Well, if it is not my beautiful princess." The king rose with outstretched arms.

"Father!" Rosa flew into his embrace.

Then the queen gave Rosa a light kiss on the forehead and then gestured for her to join them at their meal. The queen's glittering eyes searched her daughter's face. "Did you see or learn anything at your godmother's house that made you... worried?"

"Oh, no! I had a wonderful time."

The queen held her daughter's gaze, and then gave her a quick smile and seemed satisfied to ask no further questions.

Rosa, however, could not contain herself, and excited, jumbled words tumbled from her mouth, and it wasn't long before she had recounted all her adventures.

The princess' tales were met by silence from both the king and queen. Their faces looked grave, and Rosa began to feel apprehensive.

"Such tales, Rosa…" the queen said at last, "…I am certain your godmother had more sense than to expose you to such perilous things. A silver wolf and dancing faerie rings indeed!"

"But it is true!" Rosa cried in astonishment. "I am not making it up."

"So much the worse," the king interrupted. "For if true, then you were in danger and, by the sound of it, nearly drowned. Is this what we are to expect from Faerie, then? Such negligent guardianship of our children?"

The queen continued, "I do not understand what your faerie godmother was thinking, forcing you to live in the wood, and in such a dress as well! How you could appear before us in such costume is a sure sign of the bad manners you have learned at her home. You will change as soon as you have finished your meal."

"No, I will not!" Rosa cried. "This dress is from my godmother, and you cannot make me take it off."

The queen arched her eyebrows and gave the king a significant glance. "I see that the princess has exchanged one manner of willfulness for another, and I am not sure if I did not prefer the former."

"No," said Rosa in confusion, "I will change my dress."

"See that you do," the queen replied.

Rosa miserably looked down at her plate.

"Well, let us have no more unpleasantness," the king said.

"You will not believe it, Rosa, but I found you a tutor while you were away."

Rosa was startled out of her reverie by surprise. A few years ago, Queen Eleanor had taken it upon herself to teach Rosa her letters. The princess had learned quickly and, in fact, had pretended that reading was more difficult than it was so as to prolong the time she spent with her mother. But as soon as Rosa had mastered her letters, the queen stopped their lessons, and Rosa had stopped reading. Since then, a quick succession of tutors had found Rosa an impossible student and declared her "unteachable." They had all been banished from the court, and since then she had not touched a book nor picked up a pen.

"Only a few days ago," the king continued, "a learned scholar was passing through our court looking for a place to spend the winter months. He comes from far away, I cannot exactly recollect from where—and had to leave his previous post for some reason or another—I can't rightly remember the details—but, upon hearing that you lacked a tutor, offered his services at once. I explained that you were not at the castle. You have no conception, Rosa, how inconvenient it has been to explain your absence to the court. One cannot say, 'Yes, she was taken away by her faerie godmother.' 'Where?' 'Oh, somewhere or other.' Seems very careless. We said you were visiting a relative, though we never settled on which one. But to continue... I explained that you were not presently with us, but he said he could wait. And look, within a few days you are returned to us. What a fortunate coincidence! Now you can learn something useful after that summer of play in the forest."

Rosa gave a deep sigh.

After breakfast, Rosa returned to her room to change her clothes. She burrowed her face in her dress; it smelt of the forest and of hawthorns. She folded it neatly and placed it at the bottom of her chest, then Alice helped her into one of her elegantly embroidered gowns.

"It's a bit short," Alice commented. "You've grown while you've been away. We will have to let it down."

When her nursemaid had left, Rosa curled up into a little ball on her bed. Reaching under her pillow, she drew out her mirror and saw a sad girl looking back at her with large eyes bright with unshed tears. Rosa did not know if it was her normal reflection in the glass, or if the sadness was the sadness of her heart.

"They do not understand about the forest or my godmother," she sighed, and slipped her mirror in a pouch tied about her waist.

She wandered to the cloistered garden adjacent to the castle hall. It was enclosed by pillars and pointed arches, and, though most of the blossoms had long ago flowered and shed their petals, there were thick growing bushes and roses whose blooms lasted until the winter frost. With a pang she missed her godmother's garden and the magical wood she had left behind. Forlornly, she knelt under the bushes and pretended that she was back in the forest with her godmother and the Silver Wolf.

Rosa remained there with her memories until she noticed that someone else was in the garden with her. A boy, just a few years older than her, was lounging on a stone bench and observing her through the bushes with a mocking half smile. He was tall and pale, with thick, dark hair that curled around his neck.

Rosa recognized her cousin Edmund with surprise. She had not known he was visiting the castle and had only unpleasant memories of him. In the past, he had enjoyed teasing her to set her off on her wild tempers and would then laugh at her with the same mocking expression he was wearing now. But Rosa reflected that Edmund only knew her as the naughty princess she used to be and could not entirely be blamed for the bad memories. Besides, she wanted to make new friends, and here was an opportunity. So the princess crawled out from under the bushes and made her way to her cousin.

"Good morning, cousin Edmund," she said.

Edmund rose from his reclining position and returned a languid bow.

"Good morning to you, princess Rosamund. I see that you enjoy playing in the dirt." His smile grew larger and even more condescending.

Rosa felt mortified, but sniffed, "Yes, well, I'm having a nice time. I would suggest you try the same, but I am sure you wouldn't want to get your clothes dirty."

Edmund gave the princess a sharp glance.

Rosa pointed down to the bench. "Shall we sit down, so you can tell me why you are here?"

He sat down beside her, and she caught him giving her a sidelong glance.

"I came with my father on matters of state," he said after a pause, "but I think the real reason was that he was disturbed by the news of your disappearance. No one was supposed to know, but very little escapes his ears." Edmund gave Rosa his most disarming smile. "So where were you, Princess Rosamund?"

"Oh, I was staying with my godmother in her home in the forest... It was a very nice house," she hastened to add, since her parents had seemed to so object to her previous accommodation.

Edmund was silent for a moment and then became engrossed in a leaf he plucked from a nearby bush. When he spoke, it was in an offhand manner. "When you say that you stayed with your godmother, do you mean that you were staying with a faery?"

"Of course," said Rosa, "all of my godparents are faerie."

Edmund picked up a stick by his boot and became absorbed with drawing in the dirt. When he spoke again, it seemed merely an afterthought. "Did you see anything curious? Learn anything strange?"

"Oh, yes!" Rosa beamed with excitement. "I think that my godmother wished me to learn to care for myself. I've been doing my own chores, and made friends with the Silver Wolf, and danced with the faerie." She did not mention the fountain on the island; that seemed somehow harder to explain.

Edmund dropped the stick and looked directly at her. "A silver wolf... what do you mean? Chores and dancing? Is that all?"

"No," said Rosa, confused, "I'm supposed to learn about my gifts and make friends."

Edmund nodded slowly. "And have you?"

"Have I made friends?"

"No, learned about your gifts."

"Yes... a little... not really," she stammered.

"What about magic or spells? You spent a summer with the faerie. You must have seen some magic."

Rosa shook her head. "I didn't learn any spells. Faerie magic isn't like that. They simply *are* magic."

Edmund gave a dismissive laugh. "Well, princess, I can see that you only wanted to learn what you were told." He began to rise.

"Wait," said Rosa, "If you are so interested in magic I can show you my mirror, *it's* magic."

She drew the mirror from its pouch and held it out to him. Edmund's eyes latched onto its smooth surface, and he could not mask his fascination. He was about to take the mirror, but paused, his hand hovering over it, and whispered, "What does it do?"

"It shows you your inward self."

Edmund's hand recoiled. He gave the princess a hard stare and then looked away. He said in a sneering tone, "So you are trying to be good and make friends. What a little girl you are! No one thinks in that silly manner anymore. I'll wager that you came up to me because you wanted to be friends."

"Oh!" She sprang up from her seat. "Who would want to be friends with you?" She spun around, ran blindly back towards the castle, and nearly collided with her uncle, the king's younger brother, Prince Stefan.

"Princess! What a delight to see you." Prince Stefan beamed a smile down at her.

Rosa shifted nervously. Her uncle's smile was different from Edmund's, but it made her feel just as uncomfortable. Whenever Stefan visited, she felt that he was always watching her with calculating, grey eyes, and whenever she caught him staring, he smiled the smile he gave only to her.

Now he was saying, "It seems you and my son were engaged in an animated discussion. We should come to the capital more often, he and I, and you must visit us as well."

"Yes, indeed, but I am afraid I was just leaving," Rosa stammered before she stumbled inside.

Chapter Seven

The Mirror

THE NEXT MORNING Rosa woke early and dragged Alice down to the library to accompany her to her morning lessons. She was curious about the man her father had appointed as her tutor. When they arrived, he was already waiting for her by a table in an alcove tucked away near the bookshelves. Rose found his looks disappointing. He had a medium sized build, limp brown hair, and a short-sighted squint. He was the most plain and unremarkable looking man she had ever seen.

Clearing his throat, he gave a deep bow. "I am your tutor, Mercurius."

Rosa returned a curtsey.

"I hear that you can read and write and do simple geometry," he said.

"Why, yes, I had lessons when I was a little girl, and I found it easy enough." She couldn't keep herself from bragging.

Her tutor did not appear impressed. "It is no surprise that the princess is a quick study. But can you read that manuscript on the table?"

He motioned to the table on which were laid out pen, ink, and leaves of parchment. Above these was a rolled-up scroll, yellow with age. She unrolled it and saw that it was illuminated by bright blue and vermilion letters written in a long and elegant script, but the words were strange and made up of symbols she had never seen before.

"No." Rosa shook her head. "I cannot make it out. What language is it?"

"It is an old language, almost forgotten. There are few who can read this manuscript. I am one of them."

"Oh, is that what you are going to teach me," she asked, "how to read these old letters?"

Mercurius pried the scroll from her hands and replaced it with a sheet of parchment full of the same strange ink symbols.

"Copy these letters until the sheets on the table are full, front and back. And mind you make your letters small and neat," he instructed.

She gazed at the parchment in her hand. "You want me to copy these?" she asked, mystified.

Mercurius raised his eyebrows. "Yes, is that not what I just said? I am not in the habit of repeating myself."

"But wouldn't it be better if you taught me what the symbols meant first?"

"I want you to copy them exactly. And you have made me repeat myself for the third time."

"But it doesn't make any sense!" she exclaimed.

"Precisely."

She glared at her tutor and then glanced desperately about for help from Alice. She saw that the nursemaid had settled herself comfortably on a chair near the door and had nodded off to sleep.

"If you must, look at it as if you were practicing your penmanship," her tutor said unhelpfully.

Rosa bit her lip, but then thought of her godmother. She sat down and obediently began copying the symbols.

Mercurius soon looked over her shoulder. "No, stop!" he cried, "Did I not say small and neat? These are behemoths!"

"But it will take me forever otherwise!" Rosa wailed.

"Lazy creature, are you trying to avoid hard work?"

Rosa could hardly believe her ears. He dared call her, a princess, lazy! She bit back the retort on the tip of her tongue. She was not going to let her temper get the better of her, even though he was being terribly unfair. Clenching her teeth, she continued to copy the symbols. This time she wrote them smaller, but the copying seemed endless, and her hand started to cramp. She squirmed and fidgeted in her seat and looked up to find her tutor watching her, and his eyes darted back to the book he was reading.

Finally she finished her task and stood up with relief. Mercurius came over to her side and examined her handiwork.

"You may go. Your lesson is finished. But I expect you the same time tomorrow."

WHEN Rosa was seated at her desk the next morning, she was aghast to discover that her tutor had unrolled the old scroll full of unintelligible symbols on the table and that he expected her to copy out the entire manuscript.

"But I don't understand what I am writing. How will I learn anything?" she complained.

"It is not necessary for you to understand—yet. There are only two such manuscripts left on record. You would be copying it for posterity's sake. Is that not of itself a noble task?"

"But I will make mistakes if I do not know what I am writing."

"On the contrary, when you are familiar with something, you become careless. This way you will look at each symbol closely and carefully consider what you transcribe. Copy up to this point here," he said, pointing to a symbol that ended with a distinctive flourish, "and you will be finished for the day."

Rosa looked at her tutor with suspicion. She did not believe that this was what most people would consider lessons.

"The sooner you begin the sooner you will end," he said with catlike grin.

Rosa reassessed her opinion about her tutor. There was something distinctly unsettling about him. She dipped her pen into the inkwell and began to carefully copy the symbols. Her attention soon wandered, however, and Mercurius caught her nibbling at the end of her pen. The sharp rap of his rod against the table called her back to attention. She seethed at him.

After what must have been hours, Rosa finished the section allotted and was more than glad to leave. The princess, however, soon found that she was tired and bored. No one paid attention to her besides Alice, nor could she find Edmund, not that she wanted to see him anyways.

She climbed to the top of one of the tall towers and gazed through the window to beyond the city spires and out into the horizon. The castle seemed so small in comparison to the boundless freedom of the forest. Her old way of life in the castle seemed so empty. She wondered if she would be feeling the same ache of discontent in the pit of her stomach if she had never lived with her godmother and played with the silver wolf, if somehow she would be happy being who she used to be. She didn't know the answer to that question, but she did know that she was lonely.

THAT night, Rosa gazed long and deep into her godmother's mirror, as she always did, when Alice unexpectedly entered her room.

The princess dropped her mirror in surprise.

"I hoped you would let me brush your hair as you used to," Alice said softly.

"But I'm supposed to take care of myself…" Rosa stopped short at the look of entreaty on her nursemaid's face. Ever since she had returned from her godmother's house, Rosa bathed, dressed, and combed her own hair. Alice had stood aside, looking longingly at what once were her own duties, and Rosa wondered suddenly if her nursemaid did not feel a bit useless.

"Very well," Rosa sighed. "There will be no harm done if it is only once." She glanced down at the mirror. "Oh, that's funny!" she exclaimed.

"What is?" Alice asked.

"Nothing," Rosa said, as she tucked her mirror under the pillow.

While Alice braided the long strands of her hair, Rosa gazed at her nursemaid's reflection in the mirror. Alice seemed to glow in a joyful contentment. Afterwards she tucked Rosa into bed and blew out the candles.

When she had left, Rosa sat up and took out the mirror and gazed into it in the moonlight. Earlier, when she had let Alice have her way, Rosa's face had shone with the radiance of the Green Lady's fountain, but now her usual face stared back at her.

Rosa slipped the mirror again into its hiding place and lay awake in bed that night, trying to understand what had just happened.

AFTER another one of her boring lessons the next day, Rosa went for her usual walk in the garden. Her feet crunched against the autumn leaves as she knelt down to look at some late-blooming geraniums. Soon it will be winter, and we won't have any more flowers, she thought.

She heard more leaves crunching behind her and, looking up, saw to her surprise that Edmund was approaching her.

He must be bored too, she thought.

Her cousin was standing above her now and seemed to be having a hard time trying to keep himself from laughing.

"What is it, Edmund?" she asked crossly.

He tossed his head and then pointedly glanced down. Rosa followed his gaze and saw a large mud stain streaked across the front of her dress.

"Still a little girl playing in the bushes, Princess Rosamund?"

Rosa shot up. "Better that than an insufferable prig," she cried, storming out of the garden.

I could get as dirty as I wanted to in the forest, she fumed to herself, stomping up the tall winding staircase up to her room. She banged open her door, stalked across the room, flung open her trunk, and rifled through its contents, but she could not find what she was looking for. She could not find her blue dress from the forest.

Suspicion flooded her mind. She called for Alice.

"Alice, do you know where my forest dress is? I know I put it in the bottom of the trunk," Rosa asked with a hysterical note in her voice.

"Oh, that old, filthy thing? The dress was unsuitable, so I got rid of it while you were sleeping."

Something within the princess snapped.

"You got rid of it," she whispered. "You got rid of it!" she cried. "How dare you throw away my dress! Do you know what this means? You have ruined everything. Everything!"

"Tut, tut," said Alice. "You have many other dresses. Dresses much prettier than that ugly thing."

Rosa threw herself onto the bed. "I don't *want* another dress. I *want* my old one!" she shrieked, writhing and tearing at the sheets. She flung a pillow at Alice.

Alice raised her eyes heavenward and left the room. The princess thrashed and flailed until she lay in her bed panting from exhaustion, eyes smarting from hot tears. She slowly got up and pulled out her mirror from out of her pouch.

A sallow faced little goblin creature with gaping eyes grinned back at her.

Rosa shrieked, dropping the mirror. The goblin creature's features had unmistakably been her own. She shoved the mirror under the mess of twisted sheets.

"She ruined it," Rosa muttered. "It's all Alice's fault. I hate her."

DURING the next lesson with her tutor, Rosa was still in a black mood. She went down to the library, but slumped in her chair, refusing to copy anything. Mercurius peered at her from over his book.

She glowered at him.

"What, child, is the matter?" he asked.

"I won't do it. I will not write out these senseless words. You just want this manuscript copied out and are too lazy to do it yourself. Well, I will not."

"Is that what you think?" He gave her a crooked smile and returned to his book.

"I mean it," she cried, incensed. With a swift movement she knocked over the inkwell, so that ink spilled and entirely stained her work.

"Stupid child!" her tutor cried. Swift as an arrow he darted across the room and rescued his ancient scroll before the ink claimed it. "Did I not say that this was a rare manuscript? One of the last of its kind?" For an instant his eyes glowed, flashing quicksilver.

Rosa blinked, and his eyes were their normal brown shade. She must have imagined it.

"Well, it's your own fault. You shouldn't have ignored me. And if it is so precious, you shouldn't have left it with me to begin with," she said through set teeth.

"I can see that," Mercurius responded coolly.

Shamed and angry, Rosa felt herself flush and wondered if her goblin self was peeking out. "You are hateful, and I will not have you as a tutor anymore!" she screamed as she rushed from the library.

AFTER that, Rosa's anger was uncontrollable. She was back to her old self, but with a vengeance. She hated the little goblin creature inside of her, but now that she knew it was there, she intentionally brought it out. "See!" her insides were screaming, "See what I am! What you've made me be!

Edmund seemed the most gleeful whenever he watched one of Rosa's seething tantrums, so she flew at him at every opportunity. Her parents must have thought it best for Stefan and Edmund to return to their own estate in order to separate the cousins, so the two of them prepared for their journey home, though Rosa could tell that her uncle was disappointed.

When it was time for their departure, Stefan bowed deeply before Rosa and kissed her hand. "We will see you again when winter has passed. Perhaps we can convince my brother to let you stay the summer with us."

Rosa smiled weakly. As much as she wanted to leave the castle, she did not want to spend the summer with her Uncle Stefan and her cousin.

Edmund also smiled, but Rosa could detect the familiar tinge of mockery when he said, "We can become even better friends during your visit."

Rosa glared, and Prince Stefan looked down at his son sharply. Catching his father's look, the smile disappeared from Edmund's face, and Rosa felt positively smug.

ROSA went back to her room and took out her godmother's mirror. Even though she knew she was only growing uglier, she couldn't help but stare with fascination at her own reflection. She observed with a sort of grim satisfaction her goblin-self gaping back at her.

"This is what they all want me to look like. Mother, father, Alice, and Edmund," she muttered. "Well, I am just giving them what they want."

Her eyes widened in the mirror. Behind her, in the mirror's reflection, was the most beautiful person she had ever seen: a young girl glowing with a serene smile and a gentle beauty. Rosa whirled about in amazement, but the beautiful girl was gone. Instead, there stood a little kitchen girl, so plain and inconspicuous that she must often pass in and out of rooms without anyone noticing.

The kitchen girl curtseyed and said in a nervous voice, "Alice wunder'd if you wanted somethin' sweet brought up while she's in the kitchens, your highness."

A hot wave of anger flashed over Rosa. How dare this plain girl, this kitchen girl, be so beautiful when she, the princess, looked like a monster! Before she realized what she was doing, Rosa had flung the mirror straight at the kitchen girl's head.

The very instant the mirror left her fingers, Rosa wished she could take it back. She froze in dismay, watching the mirror fly through the air, its sharp corner gashing the kitchen girl's cheek.

Then it struck the floor behind her, shattering to pieces.

Chapter Eight

Mercurius

THE BLOOD WELLED, and a thin, long stream dripped from the jagged cut on the kitchen girl's face. A loud sob of horror burst from Rosa's chest. A sudden rush of wind stirred behind her. Rosa spun around. Her godmother stood before her, a grave look on her face.

The Green Lady glided over to the kitchen girl and brushed her hand over the girl's cheek. The blood disappeared, but there remained a long, red scar traced on the girl's face.

"Godmother," Rosa sobbed in relief. "Thank goodness you have come." Shame overwhelmed her, but she tentatively stepped forward. "I didn't mean to. Can you make the scar go away?" she pleaded.

The faerie lady looked down at her sternly. "No, princess. I am able to heal her wound, but I cannot undo what you have done. Her scar will remain."

"But the one with a scar should be me," the princess cried. "She is so beautiful, and I am so ugly. She doesn't deserve the scar. Can't you give it to me, or else give me one like it?"

"What're you saying?" The kitchen girl fell on her knees, flinging her arms around Rosa. "You dear princess, I'm all right. The scar won't bother me a bit. I am plain, and no one notices me. But you are the most beautiful princess I have ever seen. I would feel so much worse if you had a scar."

Rosa touched the girl's cheek and looked with wonder into

her eyes. "You are wrong," she said quietly. "You are more beautiful than I could ever be."

As the days passed, Rosa found out that the kitchen girl's name was Edwina. Though only a few years older than the princess, the girl had been working in the kitchens since she could first walk. Rosa took to following the kitchen girl about, casting wistful glances at her from the garden, loitering before the door to the kitchens, only to be shooed back upstairs by Alice or the imposing head cook.

Rosa's loneliness must have touched Edwina's heart, for, one day, when Rosa was all alone in the cloistered garden, Edwina snuck away from her duties to sit beside the princess and take her hand.

"Oh, thank you," cried Rosa. "You have forgiven me. You don't know how much I want to be friends. But I daren't, for I am afraid that you must hate me."

"But didn't I tell you, princess. I don't really mind about my looks."

Rosa shook her head in disbelief, but pressed Edwina's hand tightly. "We are going to be friends, you and I. I wish to make you my handmaid, would you mind?"

"Oh no, princess!" Edwina cried, "A kitchen girl can't be a handmaid. It's too much an honor."

"Oh, please," Rosa said. "My father does not refuse me anything I ask, so you can be my handmaid if you choose. I haven't a single friend in the castle besides Alice, and she's bossy."

Something in Rosa's eyes, in the insistent pressure of her hand, must have convinced Edwina that the princess truly did mean what she said.

"Very well, princess," she answered, "I'll be your handmaid."

Rosa threw her arms around Edwina and squeezed her so tight that she caused her to giggle in embarrassment.

From then on, the kitchen girl stayed with Rosa at all times. At first, the king and queen tried to convince Rosa that a kitchen girl was not appropriate company for a princess, but in the end they allowed Edwina to become her handmaid. Rosa suspected that her parents gave in so easily because they assumed that she would soon tire of her new friend. But Rosa did not tire of Edwina, and soon the king and queen begrudgingly admitted to her that she was better behaved since she had adopted her new handmaid. If Rosa was ever tempted to fall into a passion, the livid scar on Edwina's cheek was a constant reminder of the consequences of her rages.

Rosa also resumed her lessons with Mercurius and insisted that Edwina join her. Mercurius took on his additional pupil without comment and taught Edwina her letters, while Rosa began the task anew of copying out the ancient scroll.

Now Rosa transcribed without complaint and, after a few days, she began to find beauty in the mysteriously painted symbols, picking up patterns and relations between them as she painstakingly copied them out. She wished she could understand the story they told, for she saw that the symbols spoke, but she had no key to unlock their hidden meaning.

One day, while Rosa was patiently working, Mercurius' low voice whispered behind her, "You are ready now, Princess Rosamund, I will teach you how to speak the old tongue of the kingdom's founding."

In the lessons that followed, he taught her how to speak in the old tongue: a musical language that flowed like river-water. As the weeks went by, the elusive meaning hidden in the manuscript unfurled before her, and Rosa's heart skipped a beat when she spotted a tall figure wearing a large golden crown painted beside one of the large, introductory symbols in the manuscript.

"This passage," Mercurius was explaining, "describes the binding of the faerie guardians to the king during the coronation ceremony. They promise to forever bestow seven gifts to the heirs of the golden throne. Do you see the verb here? It implies reciprocity: both the king and the faerie are bound by the same promise."

"Is this the Golden King whose stories the Green Lady told me by the fireside?" Rosa asked in fascination.

Mercurius cleared his throat. "If by the Green Lady you mean one of your faerie godparents, I cannot say. The Golden King is a mythical figure, and many stories are told of him. Scholars speculate that the figure of the Golden King refers to the first three kings of Aurlia, and their stories are often confused. We do know, however, that, if we compare this manuscript to other early historical sources, we discover that it is with the third golden king, Lyr, that the faerie pact of seven gifts is made."

"You said that both the king and the faerie are bound by the same promise. What did the king promise to do?"

Mercurius dropped his eyes. "This passage does not say. Perhaps you will find out further along in the manuscript."

Rosa complained to Edwina when they left the library. "I wish he would just tell me everything he knows instead of making me wait until I read it in the scroll. It takes me so long to merely write out the manuscript, much less translate it."

"I don't think it's taking you long at all, princess!" Edwina exclaimed. "It's only been about a month, and you are already translating complicated passages in a foreign tongue. You must learn to be patient."

"Humph!" said the princess.

The next day was a great feast day and the longest night of the year. The outside was dark, with roaring winds and a heavy snowfall, but Rosa and Edwina were kept warm snuggled in their furs, playing a game of tokens and dice beside the great hall fire. Luck was favoring Edwina, when they were interrupted by a loud banging at the castle gate.

The girls watched the guard let a stranger into the hall. His brown hair was streaked with grey, the cloak wrapped around his form was damp and powdered with snow, and he bore a large strangely-shaped case on his back. The stranger spoke privately with the guard on duty, who directed him to the west side of the castle, toward the servants' quarters and away from the royal chambers.

As the stranger passed the two girls, he bowed deeply. Rosa saw that he had mournful brown eyes with a twinkle in them and a mysterious smile with the ghost of a frown.

After he was gone, Rosa asked who he was.

"He is a traveling minstrel seeking shelter from the storm," one of the guards replied.

Rosa turned with excitement to Edwina. "Oh, how lucky he has come! I remember there once were minstrels at the court when I was a very little girl, but they used to make my mother cry, and it has been a long time since any have visited us."

The two girls dashed up the stairs to tell Alice the news and prepare for the evening's feast.

THE princess and her handmaid sat together at the banquet table. Rosa dressed in the color of her namesake, and Edwina was in golden yellow. Near the end of the meal, the minstrel stepped forward, drawing the court's attention. He strummed his lute and bowed deeply to the king and queen, but, as he looked at the king, the twinkle disappeared from his eye.

"A tale of love," he announced, "to win the hearts of gentle ladies. I will sing of the Golden King when he was young and did not know he bore the burden of the golden crown upon his head, for his father had but just died, while he was away on a long journey. I will tell how he chanced upon a faerie garden and so won the hand of his faerie queen. I sing this song to you, O queen most fair."

The minstrel bowed before Queen Eleanor, and, as the firelight cast flickering shadows on the queen's dark hair, Rosa saw that her mother was still a beautiful woman. The minstrel's fingers plucked and danced over the strings of his wooden instru-

ment, and he sang in a voice as pure as water that tripped over
the mountain rocks.

A faerie lady sat in her silveréd garden.
The night called the soft breeze
that shook the silver apples in the trees.
In her silver pool shone the white moon.
She sighed because
everything rose and everything fell
and she always stayed the same.

A white lily grew in her silveréd garden
by her silver pool under the moon.
She cried because tomorrow it would wither.
The wind was cold and made her shiver.
She sighed because
everything rose and everything fell
and everything stayed the same.

The king found the silveréd garden
and rested from his long wandering,
seeking the song that sings unchanging.
He gazed at the moon in the silver pool.
He sighed because
everything rose and everything fell
and nothing stayed the same.

The lady saw the king in her silveréd garden
beside the pool under the white moon.
She saw the golden sun shine in his hair,
heard the stars sing their music in the air.
She sighed because
everything rose and everything fell
and she no longer was the same.

The king saw the lady in her silveréd garden
fair as the moon shining in the silver pool.
Their hands did reach, and meet, and clasp.
Nevermore did he wish to be free of their grasp.
He sighed because

everything rose and everything fell
and he found something that would stay the same.

The king and the lady left the silveréd garden,
left the silver apples in the trees,
Their laughter carried in the summer breeze.
They bid farewell to the moon shining in the silver pool.
They sighed because
everything rose and everything fell
and together they would be the same.

The minstrel's final note echoed into the silence. Unshed tears shone bright in the queen's eyes, and she ended the silence with her gracious applause. Rosa's gaze had never once left the minstrel, and she felt that his music woke a secret yearning deep within her.

The king rose. "Minstrel, tell us your name."

"Neirin. I have traveled far and wide to sing at your majesties' court."

"You have pleased us," the king said, "and you have a place at our royal table for as long as you so wish. And in return, you shall delight us with your music."

The minstrel bowed again, and the rest of the court musicians struck up their instruments as the king and queen began the dancing. Alice took Rosa and Edwina up to their rooms, since they were still too young to dance. Rosa cast a lingering glance back at the minstrel and saw that he was looking at her and that the twinkle had returned to his mournful eyes.

THE winter days passed hard and cold and with no new snowfall, but the chill was banished whenever Rosa, Alice, and Edwina gathered together before the fireplace in the great hall to listen to Neirin sing enchanting stories to them in a voice that made you remember things you never knew you had forgotten, a voice half happy and half sad.

Once Rosa drifted to sleep with her head resting on Alice's shoulder, and when she jerked awake, she glimpsed her mother watching her from the door. There was a strange expression on her mother's face. Rosa could not tell if it was wistful, or even a little sad. But the expression disappeared as soon as the queen became aware that Rosa had caught sight of her, and she left swiftly in a rustle of silks.

THE snow began to melt, and the spring thaw set in, though still the air smelled of winter. Rosa was summoned to her parent's chambers. She entered their rooms nervously, wondering if she had done anything wrong.

"How would you feel about going to the summer palace with your mother?" the king was saying. "It's a little early yet, but it has been a long winter. I cannot leave the castle or move the court as there is much here that needs my attention, but that does not mean that you and the queen cannot enjoy some quiet away from our royal affairs."

"Really, truly, mother?" Rosa asked. A blossom of joy flowered within her that made her so happy she could barely speak. She threw her arms around her mother.

"Now, Rosa, please don't carry on so. You know I don't like it."

Rosa quickly let go, frightened she might accidently threaten her sudden and unsought happiness. She had never spent time alone with her mother before, and she would rather die than do something to change the queen's mind.

Rosa counted each day that led to their departure. The royal carriage was outfitted with cushions and blankets, and an entourage of courtiers and handmaids were to accompany them. The only thing that marred her happiness was that Edwina was not going with them. Since Rosa was leaving for the summer palace, Edwina asked for permission to stay behind and help her mother, who had just had another baby. Rosa had felt that it would have been selfish to refuse, and she also wanted Edwina to be as happy as she was.

THE night before their planned departure, Rosa was called to the queen's rooms. Queen Eleanor was reclining on her couch with her hand to her head when the princess entered. The king stood gravely apart, and Rosa went up to him anxiously.

"Is mother ill?"

He patted her head reassuringly. "Don't you worry, dear. Your mother is all right. It is only that she will not be able to make the journey with you tomorrow. I want you to go on as planned, and your mother will catch up with you shortly."

Rosa felt her heart grow still. She approached her mother and knelt by her side. "Is it true?" she whispered.

The queen's voice was nasally with irritation, "Not now, Rosa."

"I will wait for you. We can go together."

"Do not disturb me, Rosa. You heard your father. I will join you when I am ready."

"No. You will not come at all."

The queen flushed and sat up among the cushions. "How dare you say that to me! Do you think you can call your mother a liar?"

The princess lowered her head. "I am sorry, mother. I did not mean to. But I think it is better if you tell me that you won't come than to have me waiting for you every day at the palace, and then never coming at all."

The queen gathered her long gown and sleeves together and rose with a smooth rustle of silk. "I am sorry, Rosa. I really did try, but I couldn't." And she disappeared into her bedroom.

Rosa felt a light pressure on her shoulder and she rose from her knees.

"Why don't you go to bed like a good girl," the king said, "You have a long journey in the morning."

ROSA did not feel like going to sleep and wanted to be alone, so that, instead of going to her room, she wandered down into the library, which was usually abandoned this late in the evening. She dragged her feet down the marble steps to the library. Now that her mother wasn't going to the summer palace with her, she realized that she was being simply sent away.

The thought sent a flash of anger piercing through her sadness. Why did both her parents think they could break their promises to her? Rosa clenched her fists. Well, she wasn't going to be sent away. She wasn't going anywhere. She would like to see them try to get her to do something she didn't want to do.

Rosa was startled from her building storm of anger by a flurry of sharp, scratching sounds and saw to her annoyance that she was not alone. Mercurius was at his desk, head bowed over a flickering candle, busy scribbling away at some parchment or other. She turned to leave, but his voice called out behind her.

"Tell me what is wrong."

Rosa glanced over her shoulder and saw Mercurius sitting up straight, his eyes glowing eerily in the candlelight. Something about those glowing eyes impelled her to tell him everything, and, when she was finished, her throat felt raw and her eyes smarted hot with tears.

"What if I told you that you *must* go to the summer palace."

"I would say that it isn't fair and that I won't go."

Mercurius gave her his catlike grin. Then a cloud descended on his face, and there were many faces lying hidden in its depths, all with darting, quicksilver eyes. His face shifted into one of the many faces, and Rosa found herself staring at a stranger with a curling, brown head, mischievous smile, and glittering eyes.

Rosa collapsed in a nearby chair in shock.

"You are of faerie kind!"

Mercurius didn't respond, but merely grinned wider. Rosa stared in consternation at his impish smile.

"Why did you become my tutor?"

He laughed. "So you could discover my gift, of course."

"Are you one of my godparents?"

The faery fell silent, but his eyes were still laughing.

Rosa lowered her head. "Yes, of course you are. I am sorry, but I did not understand. Edwina did say that I learned very quickly. Is what I am studying so very important?"

The faery nodded. "But there is much more that must be revealed to you. And for that to happen, you must go to the summer palace."

"But it isn't right! Why should I listen to my parents, if they are going to lie to me? My mother shouldn't have said she was coming with me if she wasn't going to."

The faery's smile disappeared, replaced by a grave expression. "Yes, but that was her choice, even if it was the wrong one. You must go to the summer palace now on your own. Will you go?"

Rosa breathed a deep sigh.

"Yes."

Chapter Nine

The Summer Palace

IT WAS WITH A HEAVY SPIRIT that Rosa watched the palace grow smaller and smaller from the jostling carriage window. She rested her head against Alice's shoulder. At least she wasn't entirely alone, she thought, though she did wish that Edwina was with her.

"They say misfortunes never come singly," Rosa murmured under her breath.

"What did you say, princess?" Alice asked, craning her neck to catch a glimpse of Rosa's downturned face.

"Oh, nothing, Alice."

Rosa peered out of her window and glimpsed Neirin riding on horseback beside the carriage. He had been waiting for her earlier that day, when she had stepped into the courtyard in the cool, morning air. "I asked permission to join your party," he had explained as they were departing. "I thought the princess would enjoy music on her journey, so the queen granted my request."

Rosa was comforted by his presence and his sad but smiling eyes. A crowd had gathered to bid her farewell. Mercurius was missing, but only Rosa noticed his absence. No one seemed to remember him ever being at the palace. Rosa said her goodbyes to her mother and father, but avoided meeting her mother's gaze.

They journeyed to the summer palace at a leisurely pace with many pauses for food and rest. When they stopped to make camp, tents arrayed with brightly colored flags, Neirin cheered them with his music. They traveled on for days, until they caught sight of the summer palace high on the cliff side overlooking the sea.

The carriage pulled to a halt, and the company admired the view of the gleaming white palace soaring up on the cliff above them. The sun was shining behind its brilliant, domed spires, and the waves churned white-crested against the rocks below. Rosa thought she could hear faint music drifting down from the cliffs, a piping high and melancholic that seemed to ride on seabird's wings. She was about to ask Alice if she could hear the music as well, when the carriage started up again and the horses' hoofs drowned out the sound. Rosa stuck her head out the window to see if she could still catch strains of the melody, but could hear nothing. She saw Neirin riding beside them. He also seemed to be straining after something, a yearning reflected in his face.

He heard the music too, she thought.

THEY arrived at the palace at midday and, passing the outer gatehouse, crossed the neck of land that connected the promontory on which the palace stood to the mainland. When she lighted from the carriage, Rosa was surprised to see her Uncle Stefan and Edmund waiting to greet her in the courtyard.

"Did not the king tell you?" her uncle asked. "Since neither he nor the queen could spare the time, I was happy to offer my services by joining the princess at the palace. You and my son will be pleasant companions, and I have often desired that we spend the summer together."

Rosa studied Edmund thoughtfully. It struck her as odd that, the second time one of her faerie godparents had sent her away, she had also run into her cousin.

"I also hope to be better friends," she answered, and Edmund lowered his eyes under her serious gaze.

Rosa then went to her apartments, made bright by large open windows that overlooked the water.

"Alice, may I go outside for a while? I would like to look at the sea."

The nursemaid, wanting a nap after the long journey, let the princess go without a protest. Rosa reached the cliff side, where the fresh wind whipped through her hair and wrapped her long skirt around her legs. Pulling her hair out of her eyes, Rosa peered over the edge and saw that the cliffs were not a sheer fall, but that there was a steep climb overlooking a white, sandy cove by the sea, and that the climb was riddled with natural trails which winded down to the bottom.

Then she heard the mysterious music she had heard earlier in the carriage, a piping, high and melancholic, that rode in the wind. The song stirred whispers of yearning within her, so she began her descent down the cliff side.

Rosa followed the ethereal music until she came upon the piper reclining against a tall, projecting rock that shielded him from the wind. The player had long, golden hair and his eyes were closed beneath a brow marble-white. Rosa stood enthralled at the beauty of the music and the beauty of the player. She no longer marked the passing of time, and the tip of the sun's rays touched the sea's horizon before the music stopped and the player opened his eyes. She saw that they were as serene as the sky in daytime and of faerie kind. His clear eyes gazed at her, and then, when he smiled, the sun broke forth from his face. Blinded by his brightness, the princess closed her eyes, and, when she opened them again, he had disappeared.

FOR the next few days, a certain listlessness draped over Rosa, and she would do nothing but gaze out the window toward the sea and the horizon. The same lethargy seemed to hang over Neirin as well. The minstrel would strum his lute in the corner of the room, but the smile had left his eyes, replaced by the yearning the princess had seen on his face during the carriage ride when they had first heard the melancholy piping. Rosa did not see much of Edmund and assumed he was avoiding her. Even though they sat together for meals, they remained uncomfortably silent. Rosa could never think of anything to say to her cousin, so she just let her Uncle Stefan and Alice chatter ceaselessly instead.

One afternoon, as the princess was walking down a corridor, she heard muffled voices from one of the rooms. She thought she heard Edmund's name and peered through the open door and saw two servants making up the room.

"He's such a dark and surly young man."

"Rather nasty and unpleasant."

"It's in his blood, you know. He's cursed. Per'aps he will vanish one day, like *her*."

The floor creaked as Rosa shifted, and the two servants stopped speaking, aware that someone was listening. Rosa hurried away, feeling guilty for eavesdropping. Were they talking about Edmund? What did they mean by a curse? She was filled with an unexplainable foreboding and searched for Edmund throughout the palace. Finally, she spotted him outside in the garden and raced toward him, but then she froze, horrified by what she saw.

Edmund stood rigid, eyes fixed on a serpent coiled at his feet. The serpent was white, the color of pale underground creatures that have never seen the sun. Both the serpent's and the boy's eyes were locked on each other, and Edmund sank to his knees, his face falling closer and closer to the serpent's flickering tongue.

"Edmund!" Rosa cried.

He jerked back, startled, no longer captivated by the serpentine gaze. The snake slid away into the underbrush, and Edmund rose to his feet, fear stamped on his features and in his wide, dark eyes. Slowly the color returned to his ash-white face, and he sharply turned away.

"Are you all right?" Rosa asked.

He kept his back toward her as he answered, "I'm fine. It wasn't anything, only a garden snake. Who asked you to interfere?"

The princess flushed, but then she remembered the fear in his eyes, and the word "curse" floated through her mind. Edmund was walking toward the palace, but she called after him.

"Don't go! I was looking for you. I wanted to ask you something."

This time Edmund turned and crossed his arms, the familiar mocking smile traced on his face.

"Well?" he asked after a few, silent moments of Rosa shifting about searching for the right words.

"You see," she began, "the servants were whispering. And I wondered if you would know what they were talking about... if you know something about a curse?" She whispered the last word, and the smile disappeared from Edmund's face.

"I think they may have mentioned you..."

"What, that I am cursed?" Edmund spat out.

Rosa was startled by the vehemence of his reply. "No," she said, shuddering, "only if you might know something about it."

"You really don't know anything, do you, princess? Protected behind castle walls and spoiled by your faerie godparents. You don't know what everyone else knows."

"What does everyone else know?" she whispered.

Edmund took a step forward, and Rosa stepped back, but he came nearer and brought his face next to hers and hissed in her ear.

"I'm cursed. It runs in my blood. And if you are not careful, I will curse you too. You never know how it might happen. I could touch you or whisper in your ear, and then you would wake up one morning with fire running through your blood. Or even worse, you could disappear, just like my—" he stopped and bit his lip. Rosa fearfully stared at him. Edmund grimaced and then walked away, leaving Rosa alone in the middle of the garden.

Rosa was confused and frightened. Edmund had always been mean to her, but never before had he mentioned a curse. Did he really have the power to do that? She thought of his ugly smile and the image of a forked tongue splitting through his lips came unbidden to her mind. She banished the thought quickly and fled to the edge of the cliff side to clear her head. The white palace rose majestically behind her, and the strong wind against her face drove the mysterious curse and Edmund's threats from her mind. She closed her eyes and drank in the wind for a long time, but just as she was ready to return to the palace, she heard the sound of a clear piping, a melody carried over the wind.

Rosa went searching down the cliff's winding path and found the golden-haired faery once again among the rocks. Settling down on one of the rocks, she closed her eyes to listen to his music. The piping stopped. When she opened her eyes, she saw that the faery was regarding her intently.

"Your heart is troubled," he said at last, "you cannot sing with me if your heart is so restless."

"There is so much that I do not understand," the princess said.

The faery put down his pipes and began to sing. Rosa could not understand his words, but his clear voice took her over the cliffs on the back of the wind and into the sky, and, when his song was finished, she found that her restlessness had disappeared. Then the faery held out his hand to her, and on his outstretched palm were three luminous pearls that shone a different color, a soft blue, a pale pink, and an ivory.

"Take them and keep them with you," he said. "They are a gift from my sister, young and fair as the moon."

Rosa took the three pearls and gently brushed her fingers over their smooth surfaces.

"May I meet your sister? Are both of you my faerie godparents?" she asked.

The Golden Piper nodded and said, "Yes, but I believe that

my younger sister is the last among us you will meet. But know that, even though you have not met her, you receive her gifts."

He then reached beside him and picked up a small harp and handed it to the princess. "Learn to play this," he said, "and then we will sing together."

Rosa gazed at the harp in wonder. Its rosewood frame was light and intricately carved, and, as she delicately plucked the strings, the purest notes rang forth.

The Golden Piper spoke, "Go back now to the summer palace, or you will be missed. We will meet again."

Rosa stumbled up the cliff side, carefully sheltering her gifts in the crook of her arm. She went directly to her room and found a small silver pouch for her pearls and tied it on a string about her neck. Then, still carrying her harp, she went in search of Neirin.

She found him tuning his lute in one of the many small, solitary rooms in the palace. "Can you teach me how to play this harp?" she asked.

"Where did you get this?" he asked in amazement. As he plucked sweet sounds from the harp, Rosa saw the yearning return his face.

"He gave it to me," she said. "The piper whose song you heard on the road."

"You heard it too?" His large, mournful eyes held hers. "I feared it was a dream and yet, at the same time, hoped it was a dream as well. No earthly creature can hear such music and not go searching for it." His glance fell reverently on the harp. "I will teach you how to play, though I am not worthy to touch such an instrument."

Rosa laid her hand on his arm. "Neither am I, but a gift freely given must be as freely accepted."

"Sometimes I wonder at you, princess. You are such a child, and yet have wisdom beyond your years."

Rosa ducked her head as she felt herself blush. "No, not I. It is just that I am surrounded by the wisdom of faerie kind." Then she laughed, "I am glad to learn even the smallest of things from them."

THAT night was the first night Rosa heard music in her dreams. Otherworldly and deep, it ebbed and flowed like the rolling waves outside her window. She would wake sometimes in the moonlight, draw down her thin sheets, and go to her window seat overlooking the sea. Watching the waves violently crashing on the craggy rocks below, she could almost hear strains of the song that disturbed her sleep in the swelling tumult. Sometimes she watched the waves until her eyes grew heavy and she would go back to bed, her feet pattering against the cold marble floor. Other times she would stay up till the dim in-between time, the sky tinged green just before the sunrise. Then she swore she could hear the melody awake, different from the piping, but still familiar. But then the glory of the sunrise, both in the sky and reflected in the water, would dispel her troubled night.

Rosa's lessons with the minstrel Neirin began. Her fingers felt at home among the strings, and she discovered that she had a gift for music. The minstrel and the princess spent many evenings together, and Neirin's eyes smiled again when he sang with her. During the day, she went down to the coast with Alice and danced to the music of the waves. She felt a humming on her breast and could hear the pearls singing along with the mysterious song of the ocean. Her dance was as entrancing as their song, and Alice never grew tired of watching her.

Another pair of eyes would also follow the princess from one of the windows in the palace. They would shine bright, and Edmund would swallow back unbidden tears and leave the window. But he almost always returned to watch the princess dance, and, sometimes, he would let the tears stream silently down his cheeks.

THE DAYS grew into weeks, and for Rosa the sea melody became a waking dream. During the daylight hours she could only hear the music faintly, but by dusk the music grew and grew, until one summer's night it was no longer enough to stare down at the waves from her window. The song possessed her, and she left her room, left the palace. In a drowsy numbness, she floated through the garden under the full moon. The heavy incense of sleeping flowers hung on the boughs of silhouetted trees as she made her way down the winding cliff trail to the cove. The melody rode low and sweet on the undercurrent of the waves and guided the princess' feet over the uneven and slippery ground where the waves lapped and pooled among the rocks.

Rosa knelt down, her hands plastered against the damp, dark rocks, and peered into the water. Under the dark rolling surface, a white face appeared, a strange woman's face with strange solid eyes and coral lips. The otherworldly music embraced Rosa and pulled her toward the face under the surface of the waters. The sea-green eyes beckoned, and, eyes and ears entranced, the princess slipped closer and closer to the waters. A white, luminous hand stretched out, then snatched the princess and pulled her head first into the salt sea.

Chapter Ten

The White Ruins

ONE DAY IN EARLY SPRING, Queen Sigrid was alone in the wood gathering toadstool, hemlock, nightshade, and other plants that grew in the deepest shadows. She spied movement in between the trees and stole upon the Erik casting Ninny Nanny's sticks in the middle of the forest. The prince was obscured by mist, and she sensed the whisper of a secret. She quietly stalked the prince through the wood as a hunter does his prey, but lost him as the forest gloom swallowed up his winding path. She lay waiting for him many an early morning from then on.

The queen knew how to walk softly amid the trees without making a sound, and Erik did not know that he was being hunted, but the queen always lost the prince in the mist of the forest. She came to understand that the prince could not be followed and that the mystery must somehow lie in the sticks.

Queen Sigrid of Lothene knew how to bide her time and wait for the right moment, like one waiting for the slow change in seasons, and her relentless patience became wholly absorbed by the prince and his enchanted sticks. Before, Erik had barely been above her notice as she grandly glided from room to room in her flowing furs, tall and imposing. She might call on him to fetch her things or silence him with a sharp word, but mostly she had simply ignored him. Now she invited him to share a drink or play a game, in which she always beat him soundly.

Erik was always tongue-tied in her presence, and now her smooth smiles and seemingly innocent questions seemed to only make him more awkward. The queen grew more and more frustrated as all her attempts to win the shy prince's confidence failed. She realized that she must devise another way of discovering his secret.

She called one of the serving boys to her room. While she never mingled with children, everything in the inner workings of the castle concerned her, and she had observed that this small boy was always alone.

The serving boy stood before her quaking, his eyes large and dark against his freckled, ashen face.

"What is your name?" the queen asked the trembling boy.

"Edgar," he said in a small voice.

"Edgar, you have nothing to fear," she soothed him. "You are a stranger here, are you not? The other boys exclude you because your father moved here from distant parts in order to make his fortune?"

The small boy nodded.

"Give me your hand, Edgar. Let me tell you a secret. I am a stranger too. I sailed from the northern lands over the sea on a merchant ship, and the king married me for my beauty. But I have no one I can call a friend. We strangers should help one another. What do you think, Edgar? Will you help me?"

The boy nodded as one mesmerized, and the queen gave him a smile that radiated warmth, kindness, and a little hint of loneliness.

"I am glad. Now this is what you must do. The prince carries at his side a brown pouch filled with sticks. I fear that whoever gave the prince those sticks wishes him harm. I want you to bring me that pouch and replace it with this." The queen rose and took out from a small chest another brown pouch filled with sticks identical to the one the prince wore on his belt. She handed it to the boy, saying, "The prince must not suspect anything. He does not trust me, you see. I am also a stranger and I cannot seem to earn his love, but I am so worried for him."

The queen looked so sad that Edgar reached forward and lightly touched her hand. She gazed at him, her eyes awash with unshed tears. "Will you help me, Edgar?"

"Yes, my queen."

"Good, we will be friends, you and I. Now go. Return when you have the prince's pouch of sticks."

Edgar left the room and the queen smiled, but this time there was no kindness in her smile. She knew that the prince kept the pouch on his belt at all times, but she also knew that young boys are careless and that, if she waited long enough, she would uncover the mystery of the prince's disappearances into the wood. Besides, she knew some magic of her own and had bespelled the false sticks. There would be a nasty surprise waiting for Erik once he used them.

ONE hot summer day, as the burning sun beat down on the land, a group of the castle boys planned a swim in the mountain river. Edgar saw that Erik was going with them, the usually reclusive prince also falling prey to the sweltering heat. Edgar joined the group at the main gate, where they all followed the heavily traveled path that led to the river. There the boys all stripped off their clothing and, with hoots and cries, plunged into the river's cold mountain waters.

Edgar saw his chance and seized it. Rummaging through the prince's clothes while he was swimming, he uncovered the pouch of sticks, replacing it with the pouch the queen had given him.

The instant he was finished, he sprinted back to the castle. In his haste he tripped and fell, and the sticks flew from the pouch, disappearing into a thick undergrowth of jagged thorns. Edgar gave a cry. The thicket was too sharp and cruel to search. Frightened over what the queen would do if she found out, he scurried around and gathered sticks from the forest floor to cram into the pouch. It was these that he presented to the queen when he made his way back to the castle. She thanked him with a smile and sent him away with a gold coin in his purse.

After Edgar had shut the door, the queen's smile was replaced with the furrowed brow of intense concentration. She muttered strange incantations over the sticks and turned them over this way and that, trying to uncover their magic, but found nothing. With a shriek she threw the sticks in the fireplace. The sticks were worthless, and the foolish prince was merely playing a child's game!

Queen Sigrid, irritated that she had wasted so much time over Erik and his sticks, ignored him when she next saw him and, when she did not ignore him, snapped at him. Soon she lost interest in him all together.

IT had been a while since Erik had visited Ninny Nanny. During his last visit, she had ended her story about princess Rosamund with the princess being snatched deep into the sea. He was itching to go back and find out what happened, but hadn't been able to escape the castle unseen. The queen had been making him nervous lately. He had felt her burning eyes boring into his back when she thought he wasn't watching. Then there had been Edgar, hanging about like a stray dog impossible to shake. But, to his relief, things had gone back to normal the past few days, and he finally felt safe enough to venture out to the woods again.

Erik stalked far enough out into the wood to where he knew no one would find him and emptied out Ninny Nanny's pouch. The instant his fingers wrapped around the sticks, they kindled into a red hot flame. He dropped them in surprise and immediately stamped out the flames on the ground. From the stick's charred remains rose a smoky cloud of ash that engulfed him, thrusting putrid tendrils of smoke into his mouth and nose, suffocating him. He darted out of the cloud, and clean air filled his lungs once again. Then he doubled over, coughing and retching. He wiped his smarting eyes and opened them. The forest was strange and terrible. Beady red eyes peered out at him through the darkness. Fantastic, lurid shapes clawed and snatched in the air. A high shriek tore through the forest, and then a low, thunderous crashing rumbled behind him. A wild fear seized Erik, and he ran, ran as fast as his terrified legs could carry him, deep into the wood.

THE prince trudged through the forest, his quickly beating heart slowing down to its regular pace. The vapors from the smoke had finally left Erik's clouded head, and the wood had returned to itself. Though he was no longer being chased by maddening screams and creatures from his nightmares, the forest was still gloomy and entirely unfamiliar. Erik knew with a sinking feeling that he was lost.

Erik hoped to reach the outskirts of the wood soon, or at least find a stream he could follow, but there was nothing but a wilderness of brambles and tall trees. Through his mind whirled questions: What had happened to Ninny Nanny's sticks? Why had they cursed him and lost him with a cloud of ash? Was Ninny Nanny dangerous after all? Erik shook his head, banishing the thought. He refused to believe Ninny Nanny wished him harm. The magic must have gone wrong somehow.

Erik shot a wild rabbit and cooked it over a fire for supper. He saw that it was growing dim and had to fight down a small stab of fear when he realized that he would have to spend the night in the forest alone. He had trekked overnight through the woods before, and Cynric had taken him on many hunting expeditions. But it was the feeling of being lost that made the thought of the dark woods at night so eerie. That night he took shelter in a tree to avoid the wolves and other wild animals that prowled about under the cover of darkness.

Erik continued on like this, wandering through the forest, for two more days, and the summer heat was stifling, even though he traveled under an overgrowth of shade. On the evening of the third day, he unexpectedly came to the wood's edge. Dusk was just spreading over the ground, and the prince saw that he was at the top of a gently sloping hill that led down eventually to the cliff side. The coolness of the wind and the sea swept over him, and he closed his eyes to drink in its freshness.

When he opened his eyes again, Erik saw in the distance the remains of what must have been a magnificent palace standing on a ragged promontory connected only by a narrow strip of land, with the sound of waves crashing against the rocks far below. There were many ruins littered about the kingdom left over from sackings and invasions. At first they had been looted and then burned, but now these ruins were left alone. Terrible stories were told of dispossessed ghosts haunting the remains of their destroyed dwelling places, jealous of those who now inhabited their land. But to Erik, the haunting ruin looked lonely, with its skeletal walls and jutting beams, a pallid ghost glimmering in the dusk washed bare by the waves of time.

Erik felt a tugging in his soul leading him toward the ruin and decided that it was the best shelter he could find for the night. Night had almost fallen by the time he crossed the narrow bridge of land and reached the pale remains of the palace. He did not have time to explore, but found shelter in a corner that guarded him from the wind. He curled up and listened to its howling and the waves crashing below him before he fell asleep.

ERIK woke to the cry of a seabird. He rose stiffly, stretched his limbs, and reassessed the ruin in the sharp clearness of the morning light. While it had shed its dreamy ghostliness with the night, the ruin still stood as a bleached monument to a forgotten past. Most of its ceiling was gone, though arches vaulted across the corners of stone walls, and there was rubble and tile scattered over the grass underfoot.

He peered round a crumbling wall and espied an entrance-way leading to a narrow room with its ceiling still mainly intact. Stepping through the archway into a room illuminated by wide beams of light streaming through the doorway and wide windows, he was amazed to find a brightly colored mosaic floor largely undamaged on the ground before him. There were sea-creatures swirling in intricate designs, dolphins and sea-animals, half-horse and half-fish, drawing chariots of sea-people holding aloft swords and tridents. Erik stared at the seamen's warlike features and the sharp teeth of their mighty steeds and recalled tales of sea-people, fish-men and women, who haunted the shores of the high cliffs and dragged enchanted sailors through the icy depths to their watery graves. Sailors bore charms against them and avoided certain parts of the coast.

Where am I? he wondered. It was almost as if he had stepped into one of Ninny Nanny's stories. The princess from her stories had lived in Lothene, when it had been the golden kingdom. Was she also real like the beautiful maiden from his dreams, and had she seen these very same ruined walls and towers when they were mighty and whole?

There was a door tucked into the corner of the room and the prince managed to pry it open. He saw that it led to a flight of steps going up. The steps led him to an open room overlooking the sea, and from the window he watched the white-crested waves smashing into the cliffs below. Had the princess ever looked down onto these same waves and cliffs? Perhaps she had even stayed in this room! An indescribable emotion possessed the prince, and he flew down the tower steps, dashing from crumbling room to crumbling room. The closest he could come to expressing this moment to himself was that he felt on the verge of stepping into another world that was much bigger and brighter than his own.

Erik came to a large room with tall walls and stone alcoves that protected it from sun, wind, and rain. There he stopped before one of the alcoves and saw that it had once acted as a bookcase—there were scorched and battered leather bindings in some of the shelves. He reverently opened one of the bindings and the moldy leaves inside crumbled into dust at his touch. Erik felt an overwhelming sense of loss. His people had done this, destroyed a palace that had once been beautiful and burned all these books so that no one could read their stories ever again. Ninny Nanny had once said that his own castle was built from the ruins of other castles, but he saw that his entire kingdom was built on the ruin of the kingdom before.

The prince's spirit felt heavy and sad as he wandered out of the ruin and looked up at the sun in the sky. He should start thinking about finding his way back home. In the silence and the stillness, he thought he heard a piping in the distance, a melody high and clear. The music was so faint he did not know if it was but his imagination.

A drowsiness washed over him, and he thought he would take a nap before he again began his journey in search of the castle. Lying down under a solitary fir tree, with the warm sun and the wind on his face, Erik fell asleep.

ERIK was startled by laughter. He was down on the coast by the seashore, and a golden-haired girl was standing at the edge of the waves. He recognized Princess Rosamund from his dream, but she was changed. She was older, gone was her unnatural paleness, and she was all smiles and brightly flashing eyes. There was something else too, something stirring within him that he was on the verge of remembering.

The princess spun about, dipping her feet in the water with

lightness and grace. Then she stopped smiling and seemed to be listening for something. Perhaps there was music in the sea that only she could hear, because she began to dance, and her dancing seemed to be all wind and water. Erik watched her, entranced, and forgot everything until his vision began to ripple and fade. He stepped forward, and the princess turned toward him, but, when he stepped again, he stepped into another dream.

Now Erik found himself in a dim room lit by firelight, where a minstrel was softly playing his lute. The princess was there too, and she was listening to the minstrel with her head resting against a pillow. She was even older now, and her face held a sorrow that the prince recognized, a sorrow that he had known when his mother had died. It was the princess' very sorrow which finally stirred the deep pool of his memory and brought to the surface the image of the sleeping maiden under the water. Her features and those of the princess blended into one, and the prince felt a wave of awe wash over him when he realized that the spoiled princess from Ninny Nannies' stories was the same beautiful maiden he had lost his heart to when he had first seen her in his dreams. He wondered that he hadn't recognized her before. Maybe her beauty itself had changed as her heart changed.

All the while, the minstrel strummed his lute, and it faintly recalled the melody the prince had heard on the cliffs by the seashore. Erik saw that the minstrel was also marked by sorrow, but it was of a different kind, as if his music set him apart from others, and that was his sadness, but also his joy. The prince's vision grew dim. Soon all was darkness, and all he could hear was the crackling of the fire, and then silence.

ERIK opened his eyes and saw that he was back in the ruin. He rose and drifted to the cliff side, where he stood overlooking the sea. The wind battered his face, and he spotted a path that led to the shore below and picked his way down the steep and winding climb.

When he made it down to the coast, standing upon the sands and watching the waves ebb and flow, he knew that this was where the princess from his dreams had danced. He could still hear the echoes of her golden laughter. Erik bent down and picked up one of the seashells scattered across the sandy beach and gave it a kiss. Suddenly he felt embarrassed and tucked the shell inside his pocket.

He turned and climbed the cliff side, debating with himself whether it would be better to spend one more night at the ruin or start on his way back now. When he reached the top, he was startled to find Mnemosyne sunning herself on a flat rock near where he had been sleeping. The sight of the cat was so unexpected that Erik let out a sharp laugh. Unperturbed, the cat yawned and stretched in a great arch before stalking away. Then she paused, looking back at the prince with a bored but eloquent look. Erik saw that he was meant to follow and trailed behind the cat through the ruin and back into the woods.

IN almost no time at all Erik was at Ninny Nanny's cottage. The prince stood before the cottage in confusion. He had wandered in the forest for days, and yet here was Ninny Nanny's cottage, merely a short distance away from his own castle. He gave up trying to wrap his mind around the mystery, however, when the old woman opened the door and invited him in.

Ninny Nanny fed him supper, and Erik realized he was famished. He was bursting to tell her about his discovery and talked between spoonfuls.

"Ninny Nanny, Rosa and the sleeping maiden are the same person!"

The old woman looked unsurprised.

"You already knew that, didn't you?"

Ninny Nanny gave him her secretive grin.

"Why didn't you tell me?"

"A storyteller does not reveal the plot 'til the time is right," she cackled.

"Ninny Nanny, the princess looked very sad."

"Yes, she lost something precious to her."

Erik was quiet for a while, but then said, "I feel the same way. And it isn't just that I lost my mother. I feel as if Lothene has lost something. When I was at the ruin, I understood that Lothene cannot make anything new, because it has forgotten the old, or worse, it destroys it. Why doesn't Faerie come to Lothene the way it came to the kingdom of Aurlia? Why are we so afraid of magic?"

"The northern people are conquerors an' take things by force. When magic is taken instead of given, it harms instead of helps. So Faerie left, and all that people remember is the harm and are afraid."

"But that's wrong!" the prince cried. "Can Faerie return?"

Instead of answering, the old woman recited in her sing-songy voice,

The wand'ring king tirelessly treads
The path of exile.
Alone unchanging in a fading world,
he waits for the time
when what was sunder'd is joined by
the coming of the crown.

"The western peoples still remember the old stories of the golden kingdom, and the one they keep closest and most secret is that of a sleeping princess lost in a dark tower. 'Tis said that, when the princess wakens, the wand'ring king will find his crown and bring back the golden kingdom."

"And the sleeping princess is Princess Rosamund," Erik whispered. "But Ninny Nanny, I am the crown prince of Lothene! If the Golden King comes back, what will happen to me and my father? Will the Golden King turn us to dust, as the old women say back at the castle?"

"Princeling, have you learned nothing from my stories?" Ninny Nanny said with exasperation. She hobbled over to her bubbling pot over the fire, muttering as she stirred. Erik caught the word "backwards" in her grumblings. She then shuffled back to her chair and heaved herself down with a grunt.

"The Princess Rosamund also needed to learn how to listen so she could face her curse," she said.

The prince curled up to the fireplace next to Ninny Nanny's chair and looked up at her hopefully.

"'Tis not time for stories," she said firmly. "They will be looking for ye back at the castle. And ye haven't explained to me yet how ye was lost in the first place."

The memory of the burning sticks returned to him in a flash. He had forgotten all about them in his excitement over the princess. Erik cautiously studied Ninny Nanny and realized that her eyes were also keenly studying him. He explained about the burning sticks and the cloud of ash, while Ninny Nanny listened in ominous silence.

"Someone must have replaced my sticks. They would not have misled ye so. Ye must go home, but be careful, princeling, someone wishes ye harm."

"Who?" he asked.

"That I do not know. You must be watchful, princeling."

The prince nodded reluctantly and stood up. "But how will I find my way to the castle and then back again, now that your sticks are gone?" He looked with worry at the old woman. It dawned on Erik that someone could use the stolen sticks to find Ninny Nanny's cottage.

His fear must have been plainly written on his face, for the old woman struggled to rise from her chair and then patted the young prince on the head.

"There, there. Ye will see me again. Follow ol' cat here and she will lead ye to the castle and bring ye back again and make sure no one follows. Only it may not be as regular as ye like. She has a mind of her own. And worry not over the stolen sticks. No one keeps my bones unless I give them to him."

Erik knelt down by Mnemosyne and stroked her smooth grey fur, scratching her behind the ears.

"I will meet you deep in the forest, friend cat. I would not have you at the castle grounds, where you might be caught again."

Mnemosyne purred, and the old woman grunted. "Now off with the both of ye. Ye will have to explain how ye got lost in the woods. Be watchful, princeling."

After the boy left, Ninny Nanny muttered to herself, "No wonder I felt my bones rattling."

Chapter Eleven

The Singing Pearls

THE SHARP COLD WOKE Rosa from her trance, and she writhed in panic. Strong, visor-like arms wrapped around her waist and dragged the girl down into the sea's depths. The plummeting speed froze the princess' heart, and she could not breathe. When they reached the bottom, two strong hands grabbed her face, and the strange woman kissed the princess' mouth with her coral lips. Rosa found that she could breathe again and gazed in awe at the woman before her and at her glistening tail, which undulated with the current in the water. A cloud of dark hair encircled the sea woman's face and breasts, and she was unclothed except for a girdle of coral and pearls wrapped about her waist. Rosa opened her mouth to speak, but nothing came out save unintelligible gurgling, and the sea woman simply stared at the princess with her unblinking eyes.

The sea woman then gently but insistently wrapped her arms against the princess' waist, and Rosa allowed herself to be pulled through the water. Her heart quickened in fear when she realized that the sea woman was pulling her into the gaping, black mouth of a tunnel in the underwater cliff side below the palace. She closed her eyes and clutched at the sea woman's girdle, but, when she finally worked up the courage to open them, she was amazed to find the walls bright with encrusted gems and the tunnels lit by flitting, phosphorescent fish.

Rosa saw that there were pictures glowing with an inner light carved into the tunnel walls. There were images of sea creatures and underwater chariots pulled by dolphins and sea-dragons, sea-palaces carved from coral reefs, with sea people swimming through their knobbly pillars. As they swam through the long tunnel, Rosa became gradually aware that the images were depicting a story, and not just of events in the watery realms, but also on shore under the sun. And, as they passed the pictures by, Rosa wondered if the stories depicted in these underwater tunnels had ever been told to the people above or if they would forever be unknown to those on the surface under the golden sun.

A shining golden figure caught her eye, and she pulled on the sea woman's girdle, begging her to stop. The sea woman halted before the picture, and Rosa saw that it depicted a battle, savage and cruel. Two massive forces clashed with shining swords and gleaming helms. The golden figure she had noticed stood with his men in the front ranks, wearing a crimson cape of coral and holding aloft a silver sword. The faerie were with him, riding chariots with swift archers, their showers of arrows carved from silver veins in the rock. Shining blue sea people were there as well, riding fierce dolphins to battle monsters of the deep or casting off their tails to join the fray on land. The golden figure's opponents were mortal men, led by a tall, dark figure wearing a silver circlet about his head that shone like a star. He held a leaden staff in his hand, and above the staff soared a dragon with red, ruby eyes. The dragon battled with a mighty gryphon streaked in gold, the two great beasts intertwined like two winged serpents in the air.

The princess could not tear her eyes away from the gleaming picture, so the sea woman put her hand on Rosa's shoulder and gently cupped her chin with her other hand. She opened her mouth, and her voice sang out low and sweet with the melody of the sea. Then she wrapped her arms about the princess, and they continued on through the gleaming tunnels, until they began to rise and their heads broke the surface of the water.

Rosa saw they were in an immense cavern with torches that

cast dancing shadows on the rocks. The sea woman lifted the princess out of the water and onto the cavern floor blackened by the wet. The princess nervously looked about the cavern and started shivering.

The sea woman then opened her mouth, and two sounds simultaneously emerged, one deep, the other high and crystal-line, and Rosa felt the pearls on her chest waken and hum in response. Leaning forward, the sea woman held out her hand, and Rosa pulled out her silver pouch and took out the luminous pearls and held them in her palm. The woman took the white pearl and placed it in the princess' mouth and motioned her to swallow. Rosa did so, and the sea woman cradled the princess' head in her arms and laid her down on the cold, wet rock. Rosa closed her eyes and fell asleep, listening to the sea woman's song.

ALL was darkness, and then there was a tiny flame. The tiny flame grew into a roaring fire, until Rosa realized she was staring into one of the fireplaces in the castle. She was not alone in the room. Her Uncle Stefan was sitting in a chair opposite her, though he looked younger and did not have his yellow beard. Next to him was a lady with dark hair and grey eyes, very beauti-ful, but also cold and distant. At their feet was a curly-headed, baby boy playing with his toy soldiers.

Stefan and the lady were staring right through Rosa and absently into the fire. The princess realized they could not see her, but still shifted out of the way, uncomfortable in their unsee-ing gaze. She sat near the little boy. Even though they were beside a fire, the boy seemed to be the only warm thing in the room.

Presently the lady spoke. "Did you invite her?"

There was a long pause, but then came "Yes," heavy and low.

Another long silence.

"What did you promise her?"

This time Stefan did not respond, and the crackling fire was the only sound in the room. The lady shifted, stood tall and straight as a column, and then sat on Stefan's lap, coiling her arms and legs around him.

"This is what you wanted," she whispered. "This is for our son. It curdled my blood with fury to watch the princess' christening in the cathedral this morning. Why should the barren queen dash all of our hopes with a child? Why should that fool of a king produce an heir? You are far more deserving." She spoke in a low whisper, and Stefan closed his eyes.

"What did you promise?"

He opened them again. "Something I cannot live without," he said hoarsely. "Iseult," he held his wife's gaze, "she promised our son the crown."

She flashed him a cold smile. "I would have spared you the promise if I could. But I do not have the blood of the golden kings to call her. The Dark Lady has never before stepped within the castle walls, though her influence has weakened them through the years. She will not give us anything for free, and promises are powerful. I ask you again, what did you promise her?"

He could not tear his eyes away from hers. "I cannot speak of it, or it will be undone."

She swiftly stood up and bent over to clutch the little boy in a fierce embrace, passionately covering the top of his curly head in kisses. "This head, my little Edmund, will wear the golden crown. The princess' christening is the birth of your kingship, and what should have been the door to new life will bring about her end."

Iseult left the room with her son. Stefan smiled grimly after his wife and heaved a great sigh. He too then left the room.

Rosa shivered and thought, That was Edmund's mother, and the baby was Edmund. This is a dream, but a dream of the past, and the day is my christening day. What does this mean? Edmund cannot become king unless, unless…

Rosa dashed out of the room, but instead of entering the hallway as she had expected, she was in the banquet hall. Her father and mother were seated splendidly in their ceremonial robes. Celebration filled the room. Minstrels played on the lute, mandolin, and the flute amid laughter and cheers. The table was heavy with roast goose and venison, and there was pile on top of pile of fruits and tarts, jellies and spiced cakes, and cups overflowing.

She saw the Green Lady sitting by the king and six other faerie seated in a row, some of whom she had met and some of whom she hadn't. They were dressed each in their chosen colors. The Lady of the Hawthorn Wood wore flaming red and the princess' faerie tutor wore a robe that shifted in the light. The Golden Piper was dressed as the sun and a silver lady sat beside him. There were two other faerie ladies, both tall and regal, one garbed in the royal blue and the other in a sober, grey robe, her eyes like diamonds.

As if on cue, the Master of Ceremonies beat the ground with his staff. When the laughter and chatter had died down, he announced, "Our Royal Princess Rosamund, firstborn child of King Aurleon IV and Queen Eleanor, heir to the seven faerie gifts, and the future Golden Queen of the Golden Throne of Aurlia."

Alice entered the banquet hall, bearing an infant dressed in white christening robes. The king rose from his seat, and the nursemaid handed the sleeping infant over to him. King Aurleon lifted the baby aloft, high over the festal table, crying, "Behold your princess!"

A loud cheer erupted throughout the court and drowned out the cries of the wailing infant. The king handed the baby to the queen, who soothed the child with gentle smiles and caressing whispers. When the baby calmed, the queen and king walked over to the dais prepared for the gifting ceremony. Rosa felt tears come to her eyes as she watched her mother smiling so radiantly at the infant lying at her breast.

The trumpets blew, and the Green Lady stood. "We will now bestow our gifts on the princess," she said. "May she ever rule in justice and peace according to the decree of the Golden Kings and fully recognize her role as protector of the kingdom and mediator between the faerie and mortal realms."

The Green Lady then walked up to the dais and smiled upon the infant with her youthful smile. She bent over and kissed her softly on the lips and whispered something in her ear. Each faery, in turn, rose and did the same, until it was the seventh faery's turn.

Tall and fair, the faerie lady's flaxen hair was almost white, and her gown rippled like silver water as she glided toward the baby in her mother's arms. She halted before she could give her faerie kiss, however, and grew pale. She held her hand to her throat and opened her mouth, but not a word could she speak. The room grew heavy with a silence that swallowed up sound. Nothing could be heard, not a breath, not the rustle of a skirt, or the shifting of feet. The Silver Lady turned, and, as she did, the gaze of the crowd followed hers.

A magnificent woman stood in the doorway at the other side of the hall, opposite the queen and her baby. She stood heads taller than the tallest of them, robed in black with a leaden staff gripped by her long fingers. Her face was chiseled and as bloodless as a stone, and her expression was as hard. Soundlessly she walked toward the princess, and everyone in the room felt their strength sapped by fear. The black robed woman stopped a few paces away from the queen, whose eyes were wide in terror, clutching the baby desperately to her breast.

"I am here to bestow the seventh gift to the child," said the Dark Lady, and her voice split the silence like a crack of thunder.

The six other faerie stood and the Green Lady spoke, her eyes blazing. "What claim have you on the seventh gift?"

The Dark Lady smiled, her lips red and cruel. "I have a claim in blood and sacrifice." She dropped her leaden staff on the floor, and the sound it made was heavy but muffled. "The seven of you combined could not stop me, and six of you have already used up your gifts."

Rosa shivered and hid behind one of the pillars as the Dark Lady stepped over the leaden staff onto the dais and clutched the baby's face in one of her long, powerful hands. "You, my golden princess, have been given six of the seven gifts due the Golden Kings, precious beyond measure. I now bestow on you the seventh and final gift,

> *The kiss I give claims ownership of the span of thine years.*
> *On the eve of the sixteenth year of your birth*
> *when you were twice born and gifted by faerie kind,*
> *you will prick your finger on the spindle of a spinning wheel*
> *and so receive your seventh gift.*
> *Death.*
> *Thus may you harden your parents' hearts."*

The Dark Lady bent down and placed her lips over the baby's mouth. The baby's face was stained red, and her chest heaved a silent cry, but nothing could break the heavy silence, nor could anyone move.

The Dark Lady smiled a cold smile and then withdrew to pick up her staff. She then unexpectedly turned toward the long banquet table and hissed, "I demand my price."

Iseult swiftly shot up from her seat, mouth opened in a soundless shriek. Her eyes, wide with terror, never left her husband's face. Rosa watched in horror as Iseult grew longer, thinner, and paler, until she stretched across the table and slithered across the floor, a white serpent. She glided over to the black faery and coiled herself around the leaden staff. Without another word, the Dark Lady departed.

A tumult of sound broke upon the banquet hall. Women screamed, chairs were overturned, and baby Rosa's howls carried throughout the hall.

"Silence," the Green Lady commanded. "It is not finished."

"Is there something that you can do?" the king cried, wrapping his arms around his wife and daughter.

"Can you undo the curse?" the queen pleaded

"That we cannot do," the Green Lady gently said. "A faerie gift once given cannot be taken away. But it can be transformed."

At this, the seventh faery once again approached the dais and looked sadly down on the little infant. "The gift I was to have given you has been stolen, but I will diminish the cruel curse laid upon you." She laid her hand on the baby's face, and the infant Rosa's wailing subsided.

> *The sweet blessing of sleep I grant unto thee,*
> *to soften the cruel curse of death.*
> *Akin to death, a hundred years*
> *of Time's turning wheel will you slumber.*
> *But Love's star will shine bright,*
> *and its kiss will redeem the kiss of death.*
> *And from enchantment will you waken*
> *to the glory of the sun and the moon and the stars.*

The queen's face crumbled as the slow realization of the spell's words pierced her heart. She buried the child in her breast and sobbed, "A hundred years."

Rosa watched behind the pillar and blinked back tears. Her sight grew blurry, and, when it cleared, everything was black. She stood high up on the castle parapet, and it was night, the stars shining brightly above her. Below the castle walls was a huge bonfire made up of wooden wheels consumed by flames in the darkness.

Rosa whispered aloud, "Spinning wheels."

About the burning pyre were women crying and wailing, clutching their children and looking up beseechingly at the king, who stood high on the parapet gazing down below on the flames. His face was stone and his lips set hard and straight.

Everything around Rosa again grew blurry and dissolved into darkness. Half-awake, Rosa was hazily aware that she was in the underwater cavern, but she felt warm and was dimly conscious that her head lay in a lady's lap. A dark face, out of which shone eyes as bright as diamonds, hovered over her, but she knew no more and fell into deeper slumber.

WHEN Rosa next awoke, she was in her bed in the summer palace. She sat up and pulled out her little silver pouch and dropped the pearls into her hand. There were only two of them.

"So it wasn't a dream," she whispered softly to herself.

Rosa got out of bed and dressed before Alice woke up and stole out of her room. She wandered through the hallway and saw the morning breaking through the tall windows and reflected in the long mirrors. She fell to musing over last night's vision and shivered as she thought of Iseult's metamorphosis into the pale serpent. Edmund! Should he be told? Rosa shook her head, banishing the thought. No! It was an unspeakable horror.

But as the day went by, her thoughts continued to return to Edmund. Surely she should tell him something. He was obviously haunted by the past, a dark and obscure past told in whispers and half-truths. He believed that he was the one who was cursed. But no, Rosa came to a startled realization. The one who was cursed was her! She let the thought slowly sink in. The curse was to fall on the eve of the sixteenth year of her christening. Somehow that felt far away, even though it was just in a few years' time. The princess wasn't frightened, for she felt in her heart that her faerie godparents were watching over her. Were they not taking special care of her even at this very moment, showing her the past that everyone else kept secret from her? Instead, she felt sorry for Edmund.

When she next dined with Edmund and her Uncle Stefan, Rosa kept glancing up at the both of them, sometimes leaving her fork hanging mid-air between the plate and her mouth. Stefan did not notice, but Edmund was becoming obviously irritated. He glared at her when his father left.

"You are being very rude, you know."

Rosa blushed and looked down at the table.

"Is there something you want?"

"No," she said, but then whispered, "Yes." She looked up and caught sight of the servants in the corners of the room. "No" she said again, hurriedly.

Edmund looked at her curiously, and, when Rosa left the room, he followed. "Well," he demanded when they were alone in the drawing room and Rosa had shut the door. "What is it that you want to tell me? This better be important."

Without looking at him, she said, "I've been thinking and thinking about what I should tell you, and how would be the best way. But I don't know if you will even believe me."

Edmund was quiet for a moment, looking at Rosa intently. He sat down next to her on the long bench. "Why don't you just tell me everything simply? It will be up to me whether to believe you or not. But I promise I will not get angry, no matter what it is."

"I daren't tell you everything, but I must say something."

"Well, get it over with," said Edmund, with growing impatience. "It is too late to back out now."

"Well, you know how I see my faerie godparents from time to time?"

"You mean when you went to live in the woods?"

"Yes," Rosa said slowly, "but other times as well."

Edmund looked as if he did not know, and found the newfound knowledge unsettling. "Go on."

"Well they teach me things, about my gifts, and how, I think, one should rule a kingdom. But this time they told me..."

"They told you something about my curse," Edmund finished for her.

Rosa shook her head. "Not exactly. You see, I had a vision of my christening day."

While that was probably not what he had been expecting, Edmund still looked interested. "Continue," he encouraged, "what has this to do with me?"

"You see, the curse that you think you are under, the one that you say everyone whispers about, the curse isn't for you. It is for me."

Edmund fell silent, and his face grew hard. Suddenly he sneered, "Of course, you would be the cursed one. Why not? Since you are already so gifted, so set apart, you must take everything for yourself, even the curse. Tell me this, then, why does everyone call me the accursed one behind my back? They have called me that ever since I can remember. They think I can't hear them, but I can."

"I do not know," said Rosa, her eyes brimming with tears, "but it might have something to do with your mother."

At her words, Edmund lost his mocking expression. "What do you know about my mother?" he hissed.

"Only that she was stolen. The faery who cursed me also took your mother away."

Edmund looked at her white face and shook his head. "No, there is something else. Something that has frightened you."

Rosa could not look at Edmund, but he insisted, saying hoarsely, "Tell me! It is worse not to know."

"She was turned into a snake," the princess whispered, and she quickly explained what she saw on her christening day. But she did not tell him about the part his father played.

Edmund sat by Rosa's side, unmoving. The princess took his hand gently into hers. "But one thing I do know, your mother loved you more than anything else. She would never have wanted to leave you. She was taken against her will."

Edmund buried his face in his hands, and then he quickly stood up and left the room.

For the next few days he avoided Rosa. The few times that she did see him, he seemed almost about to speak, but then would change his mind and leave. Rosa felt sad over the pain her cousin must be feeling, but no matter how hard she tried to reach him, he would not let her. Her only comfort was in her music lessons with Neirin, and the melodies they played were mournful, which suited them both.

ONE night, Rosa once again heard the sea melody and felt her pearls humming to its ebb and flow. Urged by the music, she went again to the seashore and stepped over the dark rocks. This time, when the sea woman raised her slender, pale arm out of the water, Rosa took her hand and was pulled back down into the sea.

They journeyed again into the underwater cavern, and, when Rosa was lifted onto its stone floor, she saw that they were not alone. A woman, tall and in flowing grey robes, stood in the shadows cast by the flickering torches. Her hair was dark, her skin the color of dusk dusted in silver, and her eyes were startlingly bright, shining like diamonds from her face.

Rosa gazed up into her strange, shining eyes. "You are my godmother. I saw you in my vision. You were with me the last time I was here, and I was half-asleep and half-awake with my head in your lap."

The woman held out an outstretched hand before her, and the hum of the princess' pearls swelled in response, so Rosa pulled out her silver pouch and placed the luminous pearls in the Grey Lady's palm. The lady selected the pink pearl and put it in the princess' mouth. Rosa swallowed the pearl as she had swallowed the white one before. There was only the blue pearl left.

The Grey Lady spoke. "Come, my princess, I must tell you a story. The last time you were in my cavern, you saw your christening day. Tonight I will tell you a story about the distant past."

The princess shut her eyes as the Grey Lady spoke, and she

119

saw the story unfold before her in clear images formed by the power of the Grey Lady's words.

In ages past, a young king and queen were separated from their company in the wood. To be lost in the wood is dangerous even now, but then it was even more so, for the faerie and mortal realms were one and the same and the boundaries between them were not yet in place.

When they were lost, the king and queen came upon a glass mountain, and it was brilliant, shining from a fire lit inside its deepest recesses. The queen was frightened and wished to return to the safety of her company, but the king was entranced by the wonder of the glass mountain and desired to understand the majesty before him and look upon its secret flame. He spent the day searching for a way to scale its steep walls, going without food and feeling no hunger, without drink and feeling no thirst, until, when the sun set and twilight hung upon the wood, he espied a narrow crevice which led deep into the mountain. He entered it without a thought, and the queen followed for fear of being left behind. They walked through the endless corridors of thick glowing glass until they came to the heart of the mountain. There the king and the queen fell upon their knees in terror, for beside his undying flame stood the Lord of the Glass Mountain, a powerful faerie lord, tall and resplendent, and in whose power the king and queen had fallen. The Lord of the Glass Mountain, heartless and cruel, declared their lives forfeit for daring to look into his secret fire. The king and queen begged to be spared, promising everything in their power to give. The faerie lord said he would spare their lives if the king gave him one night with his queen, for she was fair to look upon. The queen said nothing, but the king swiftly agreed.

The deal struck, the king was cast out of the mountain where he waited cold and alone all the night long until dawn stained the sky and the solitary figure of the queen emerged from the mountain. In the morning light they quickly found their company and returned to their castle. The queen spoke not a word to the king throughout the day and the night. And when she did speak again, she never once did mention the glass mountain or its faerie lord.

Soon it came to pass that the queen was with child, and the kingdom rejoiced in the news. She gave birth to twin sons, the eldest, fair as the golden sun, and the youngest, dark as night and the raven's wing. The king took great pride in his eldest born, for he was as magnificent as the day. Strong and brave, all things came easily to him by nature and by right. The queen preferred her youngest born, for, when she looked at her eldest, she remembered the Lord of the Glass Mountain and the wrong done to her by her husband, while, when she looked at her youngest, she saw her father and her mother and her husband's father and mother. The eldest's name was Auryn, and the younger by less than three heartbeats was named Aemlyn.

The boys grew into manhood, and a restlessness stirred in Auryn. He performed daring feats in the hunt, and it was whispered that he spoke the animal tongue, and he would seek after the most dangerous boar, wolf, or bear. Eventually he could no longer ignore the yearning of his heart and bid farewell to his father and mother to seek his fortune. His father the king gave him his own sword, and Auryn departed with a light heart and courageous spirit. He fought many battles and saw many marvels, and, if all were recounted, they would take many seasons to tell, and that which is known is but the half of it. Aemlyn remained at home and was a comfort to his mother.

Eventually the old king died, and Aemlyn went out in search of Auryn. He searched for a year and a day until he found his brother, and his heart was glad, for all who saw the golden prince loved him, and the dark prince was no exception, though he did not know the deepest secrets of his own heart. And Auryn returned to his kingdom with a faerie bride and bearing the standard of the Golden Gryphon. And the queen, who had ruled in her son's absence, welcomed her firstborn, and he was crowned king. The tales of Auryn's mighty deeds had spread throughout the kingdom and distant lands, and *many came and swore fealty to him, and the kingdom grew large and in magnificence.*

King Auryn ruled justly and lived many years, almost threefold the common lot of mortals. And when the time arrived, he left for the faerie realm with his bride, for their blood had mingled, and his life was joined to hers. The kingdom passed on to his son, Eirwyn, who was known as "the white" or the "the age-less," for he did not grow into old age as most mortals do, but instead his years were akin to Faerie. Tall and radiant, with hair of the whitest sunshine, Eirwyn loved music and peace. He did not desire adventure, as his father had before him, but desired instead to rule his kingdom. While his father had made the kingdom great and strong, he made it beautiful. He ruled wisely, and for the span of many mortal lives the kingdom pros-pered. Eirwyn loved his subjects, mortal things, and the green leaf that quickly fades. He fell in love with a mortal girl in his kingdom and was married with great celebration, and they were beloved of all their people. The king and his queen had a few years of much joy, but the young queen died in childbirth, and, from that point on, Eirwyn knew age and sorrow. Eirwyn reigned until his son grew into manhood and then departed to join his mother's people and was never seen in his kingdom again.

Lyr, son of Eirwyn, was a spirited young king and took after his grandfather in his love for adventure. He formed a band of young men, all noble and brave, who desired to prove them-selves in daring feats of arms, and each journey would take them farther away from their city. It was when Lyr was absent from his kingdom with his company of men that civil war broke loose.

This war was brooding many a year before Lyr was born. Its seed was planted in the days of Auryn and Aemlyn and by the jealousy between them. Aemlyn loved his brother, but was jeal-ous of his father's love; he buried his jealousy so deeply within his heart that even he did not know it was there. But it was passed from Aemlyn to his son, and then to his son's son, until the sixth generation. Finally Annwyr, great grandson many times removed from Aemlyn, led a revolt. But Annwyr did not only possess a great force of men, but a staff of lead that bent Faerie to its will. For, while Auryn was on his quest, Aemlyn would often walk in the shadowy wood and poured his jealousy into a deep hole in the earth and listened to the whispers of the dark trees and stared into pools of still water. He whispered his secrets to his son, who whispered his secrets to his son until the sixth generation, and then all the secrets came together and formed an artifact of great power and dominion, the Leaden Staff. Its might stirred through the land and shook the heart of Faerie. Feeling the earth shake and fearing the deep misgivings of their hearts, the faerie sent emissaries to bring Lyr back. And when Lyr returned, he found his city walls closed to him and his people divided. Those who could be bought by silver and promises of power joined Annwyr, but the noble and true joined the king outside the city walls.

Lyr knew better than anyone how impervious to attack were his city walls and how long they would last under siege. He would have despaired, but was able to call upon Faerie for help, his grandmother's people. The sea people came as well and cast off their tails to fight on the land, though many never returned to the water again.

The Leaden Staff cast darkness and mist upon the land, made the earth groan, and whipped the winds to fury. The staff brought many faerie lords to bended knee and bound even more to rock and tree. It shook the tallest mountain, and the power in the staff called forth a fearsome dragon who brought terror and fire from the sky. Great fear clutched the heart of Lyr's men and the faerie in their chariots, for the dragon was very old and nothing could withstand his flames. The men and women on both sides cried, as their young men and their fields were ravaged. But another piercing shriek shook the heavens, and the cries of sorrow changed to cries of hope. The legendary Golden Gryphon, servant to king Auryn, flew in from the east. Lyr held the gryphon's golden feather aloft and had called out his name.

The two great beasts clashed in the sky. At first, the dragon seemed to have the upper hand, and then the Golden Gryphon, and both wrapped their body around the other, rending and piercing each other's flesh with their talons, until finally the two flying beasts fell to the earth together, having slain each other. And with the fall of the dragon fell Annwyr's might. For the staff, though powerful, drew its potency from the bearer, and calling the dragon had exhausted the prince's strength. Annwyr was worn down, and Lyr's army prevailed, though not before his castle was ablaze and the white and gold city destroyed. A lament went through Lyr's army when they saw their city in ruins, and many a sorrowful song was sung in its memory.

Lyr spent the next ten years rebuilding his city, though it never regained its former magnificence. He was aided in this by the faerie. They set a boundary between themselves and the mortal realm, and the lead staff passed into their hands, and its power diminished, for they saw that their might was a temptation for mortal kind and that dark powers could use their own magic to bind them, and this they would not allow. They then bestowed upon Lyr seven faerie gifts to grace his kingdom and aid in his guardianship between the two realms. Lyr then named his realm Aurlia, after the Golden Gryphon who had given his life to defend the kingdom.

The Golden King Auryn was then cast out of the faerie realm, sundered from his faerie bride until the division between the two realms, first wrought when the king betrayed his queen in the caverns of the glass mountain, could be healed. He became known as the wandering king, a solitary witness to decay and the passing of time, but it has been long since any have seen him. Eirwyn remained in the faerie realm, for his blood was more of faerie than of mortal kind.

But the faerie did not abandon their mortal brothers entirely. For there are ways of crossing the boundaries, and those who are faerie friends find it easier to cross. The rulers of Aurlia became known as the golden kings and queens and act as guardians between the realms. They are able to call upon their faerie brethren for aid and sit in vigilance against those who would seek to use faerie magic for their own purposes. And in return, the faerie bless each first born child of the golden king or queen, bestowing upon the future rulers seven gifts to rule their kingdom.

The Grey Lady's echoing words lapsed into silence, and Rosa slowly opened her eyes, feeling as if she was waking from a dream, to find the Grey Lady gazing serenely at her.

"That is why I received faerie gifts, because I am a descendant of the golden kings who are friends of Faerie," Rosa whispered.

The Grey Lady nodded.

"And my father, did he receive seven gifts as well?"

The Grey Lady nodded again, and her diamond eyes glowed.

"What are his faerie gifts? He doesn't seem to know Faerie very well."

The Grey Lady spoke. "Your father received faerie gifts on his christening, but he has chosen not to use them and therefore lost them."

"But how did he lose them? Did he not have faerie teachers like me?"

The Grey Lady shook her head. "No, Princess Rosamund, we faerie are no longer as involved with mortal affairs as we used to be, for mortals desire to go their own way. You are different. You have been given a burden to bear that is not of the common lot, and we would not leave you to carry it alone, though carry it you must."

The princess whispered, "You mean the faery who cursed me. She carried a leaden staff. Is it the same one that Annwyr used to summon the dragon?"

"It is one and the same." The Grey Lady nodded. "When the staff passed into Faerie, it fell to the one whose nature is most like its own. The Dark Lady is a powerful foe, and she was called into the mortal realm by mortal kind. The power of her curse reaches as far back as the Lord of the Glass Mountain and the betrayal of husband and wife, the betrayal of blood against blood. You need to be very brave and strong, my child."

"But cannot I just run away? What if I hide so that the Dark Lady cannot find me?"

"You cannot run from the curse, for you carry it within you, and it will happen upon you wherever you would go. But it is time you return to the summer palace. This shall not be good-bye, for we shall meet one more time. There is still more that you must understand, for your story still unfolds about you." Then the Grey Lady took the princess by the hand and led her back to the dark pool which led out of the cavern.

The sea woman and the princess swam together to the shore, where the princess found the Golden Piper waiting for her, wrapped in a cloak of dusk, his radiance dimmed. He took her by the hand, and they walked under the stars back to the summer palace. The palace doors opened before him as he led her up to her room and stopped before her door.

"Soon, princess, you and I will listen to the stars and sing with them together."

Chapter Twelve

The Grey Lady's Spindle

THE NEXT MORNING Rosa lay in bed, her head full of the Grey Lady's story. *I wonder if I can discover something more about King Auryn and his descendants*, she thought. *After all, they are my ancestors, surely there must be records of them here in the palace.* Alice came in then, momentarily interrupting her musings on kings and their sons with the enticing smells of freshly baked bread and strawberries. After breakfast, though, her determination resumed, and Rosa wandered down to the library to see if she could discover anything there about the Golden Kings.

The library was bright and open, with high ceilings and tall windows that let in the morning light. Bookshelves lined all the walls, so Rosa started her search at the shelf nearest the door, looking for titles that might bear a clue to the Golden Kings. The only books she found had unenlightening titles like *The botanical classification of herbal remedies and their properties* and *Of plant life, toxins and curatives.* She moved to the next shelf, where she came across a book full of cooking recipes. She remembered Edwina with a sigh.

Moving on again, she was startled to find Edmund sitting in a corner near the window, watching her. He had a manuscript tucked under his arm. Rosa hesitated, but then decided to ignore him, not knowing if he would wish her to speak to him or not.

Her eyes were skimming over the title, *The folly of tyrants and the prideful fall of great princes due to vice*, when she was startled by a voice near her ear.

"What book are you looking for?"

Rosa glanced up.

"Do tell," Edmund said with a half grin. "I will help you look for it if you wish."

While unsure whether to trust this new and friendly mood, Rosa decided she did want to make up with him.

"Do you know the history of King Auryn and the Golden Kings? I want to find a book about them."

Edmund looked surprised. "King Auryn? I thought his stories were all myths and old wives' tales. My father says it's all nonsense. But still…" he fell silent.

Rosa wrinkled her nose at him and started investigating the next shelf.

"…still, I think I know where you can find something about him." He grabbed her hand and pulled an astonished Rosa to the rear of the library, stopping before a dusty, curtained shelf.

Rosa saw that the curtain had recently been disturbed, and, as Edmund pulled it back, he explained, "It's to protect the old books and manuscripts from the sun, though I also think it's because no one reads these books anymore and the librarian finds them embarrassing. There is a lot here which my father would call 'nonsense.'" The last he said with a sarcastic laugh. "But I think I have come across your king here once or twice. And if you wait a moment…" He ran his hand over the top of the shelf and pulled out a leather-bound volume. "I think you can find your answers here." Then he chuckled to himself. "But the book will do you no good."

He handed her the book with a mysterious air. It had a red binding and the simple title, "*The historie of the golden kings* by Galfridus de Osney," inscribed on the cover in the old tongue. Rosa opened the book and exclaimed over the brilliant picture on the first page. There was the Golden King Auryn, with his gleaming crown and the standard of the Gryphon fluttering behind him; on both sides were two birds, the heron and the kingfisher, and the opposite page was inscribed by hand, and the capital T was painted vermilion and embossed with twisted silver branches that bore golden fruit.

She translated the first sentence aloud. "Thus begin the records of the mighty deeds of King Auryn and his line down to the present day…" And then laughed at the shocked expression on Edmund's face.

"You can read the old tongue?" he exclaimed.

The princess nodded. "Yes, I had the best of tutors. Why don't we take the book out into the light, where we can read it more closely."

"I have a better idea," Edmund said. "Let's take it outside where no one can disturb us."

Rosa thrilled at the idea of their keeping a secret. She nodded and tucked the book under her arm. They left the palace through the double library doors, and Edmund led her in the opposite direction from the seashore toward the outpost before the narrow bridge of land that connected to the mainland. She was surprised to see that Edmund merely nodded to the guards, and they let them through.

"I hope you don't mind if we walk a bit in the forest," he said.

Rosa peered at him and then saw he was being serious. She laughed, "You of all people should know that I don't mind getting my dress dirty."

Edmund grinned at her. They found a perfect little mound of grass next to a large oak tree to sit under, and then Rosa opened the book and began to read aloud. The *Historie* began when Auryn was already crowned king and made no mention of the glass mountain or the faerie lord. Instead it recounted many of Auryn's adventures as he journeyed far beyond his kingdom and into the faerie realm. She skimmed many chapters concerning

King Eirwyn, not least because they contained long, boring lists of laws founded by the wise king.

"I'll come back to them later," she promised.

Edmund gave a short, disbelieving laugh.

The hours passed until they reached a detailed description of the great battle between Lyr and Annwyr. Edmund seemed particularly fascinated by the Leaden Staff.

"Prince Annwyr used the staff foolishly. He depended on it too much and let it control him. That is why it sapped him of strength and he lost the battle," he said.

Rosa widened her eyes. "Is there any way to use the staff that isn't foolish? It was made to control faerie kind. They are our friends!"

Edmund leaned against the oak tree and peered down at Rosa over his nose. "You are so serious, Princess. I was only speaking hypothetically. But not everyone trusts Faerie as much as you do."

"Well, you should," Rosa retorted. "You belong to the line of the Golden Kings as well."

He was about to respond, when they were interrupted by the sharp sound of crushed leaves and the whinny of a horse. Both Rosa and Edmund looked behind them and saw Prince Stefan approaching them on horseback.

The princess' uncle checked his horse, and both father and son shared a look. Stefan doffed his hat to the princess and then spurred his horse to a light canter deeper into the woods.

At the moment Rosa had first caught sight of her Uncle Stefan, her eyes had darted toward the ground, and she had shuffled a little closer to Edmund. She did not know how to look at her uncle knowing what she did about him from her earlier vision. Now that he was gone, Edmund glanced down at her curiously. "You really don't like my father, do you?"

Rosa didn't know how to answer.

"Well, that is all right. I don't care for him much myself," he

laughed, and his laughter had a bitter edge to it. "Come on, let's
go back."

It was early evening and they walked through the forest and
back to the palace in silence. When they reached the garden
door, Edmund said, "You know, I think it is pretty amazing how
much you have changed since you came back from wherever it
was you were with your godmother. You were hard to deal with
before, but you have grown a lot."

Rosa felt herself blushing. How nice it was for someone to
notice that she was trying to be different!

They were approaching the palace door now, and Edmund
said, "I would like to hear more about your godparents someday."

Rosa brightened. "I would love to tell you all about them.
They are so wonderful and have done so much for me!"

At that moment, Alice burst in on them from the garden
door. "I thought I heard the two of you! Rosa, where have you
been? I was worried sick over you. How could you leave me without a word? I had to send your Uncle Stefan out looking for you,
but he hasn't yet returned."

"Oh, I am sorry Alice." Rosa wrapped her arms around her
nursemaid. "I should have known you would miss me. I will let
you know next time I go beyond the outpost." She kissed her
nursemaid on the cheek.

Alice sniffed. "Oh, I suppose it is all right. Just don't do it
again. Now come inside, and I will get you ready for supper. Oh,
Rosa, your dress is dirty!"

The nursemaid dragged the princess indoors amidst further
scolding. Rosa flashed Edmund a bright smile before she was
dragged up the stairs.

Rosa felt quite content when she curled under the covers that
night, the final blue pearl tucked safely in the silver pouch round
her neck, humming softly with the waves outside. The last thing
she saw before she drifted off to sleep was the full moon outside
her window.

The next thing she knew, she was back at the castle at a great celebration in the banquet hall. Both her mother and father were at the feast, clad in the royal sapphire, their golden crowns gleaming on their heads. Toasts were given, and the air was full of music and laughter. Noblemen and women were garbed in fur and velvet, with glittering eyes and youthful faces. Rosa laughed along with everyone, infected by the excitement.

Then there was a wrong note, sharp and discordant in the music, and Rosa realized that the laughter no longer sounded joyful. She closely examined the faces before her. Their smiles did not reach their eyes, and they were no longer youthful, but rapidly aging right before her eyes. Rosa stood up, frightened, and searched for her parents. Catching sight of them, she saw that they looked as young as before, but their laughter also rang hollow. The sumptuous feast had been reduced to ash, but they did not notice. Rosa saw that the ash was choking them, but they continued to laugh their hollow laughter and they continued to eat and choke.

A wizened old man emerged from the shadows, bearing a chalice filled with clear water. Rosa knew he was from the world outside, for she smelled the sunbaked earth and the forest trees on him. He humbly knelt before the king and offered him the clear water.

"Drink," Rosa begged. "Wash away all the ash."

The king stood up enraged, dashing the chalice from the old man's hands, so that it clattered against the flagstones, spilling all of its precious contents.

"How dare you bring mud and filth before me! Guards, take the old man away and put him to death."

Rosa cried out in protest, but found that she was no longer in the banquet hall, but was instead in the blue and gold throne room. The room was empty except for her and her father. He was seated on his throne and looked magnificent and strong with his red-gold beard and his long, royal robes. The princess stood in awe before the kingliness of her father as she had never done before, but then her heart cried out for the old man, and she fell on her knees before him, begging him to spare the old man's life. But the king could not hear her, and a transformation took hold of the room. The walls lengthened and stretched, and the bright colors diminished to muddy browns and greys. Her father was seated on a throne of lead, and both he and the throne had grown with the room, tall and forbidding. Rosa's tears fell heedlessly as she clasped his knees, but the king's heart had withered, and he had turned to stone.

Rosa woke with a cry to see the sun shining brightly outside her window. The images from her dream were still fresh in her mind and did not fade in the morning light. Alice entered the princess' bedchamber anxiously, and Rosa threw back her coverlet and clung to her nursemaid.

"What is the matter, child?" Alice crooned, rocking the young girl in her arms and smoothing her golden hair.

"I had a terrible nightmare," Rosa said, burying herself further into her nursemaid's arms.

"There, there, my little one, it was only a dream," Alice reassured her.

THE memory of her nightmare troubled Rosa throughout the day. She wandered to the music room to see if she could find Neirin to confide in, but he was nowhere to be found. She reflected that she rarely saw him now, except during their music lessons, and even then his mind seemed far away. Her harp strings would call him back to himself momentarily, but then he would gaze beyond her, listening for a sound she could never play. Despite his distance, or maybe because of it, she felt that he would understand the terribleness of her dream and why she was afraid for her father.

Wandering out into the garden, she sat beneath a fir tree and watched the branches swaying in the soft breeze. Rosa closed her eyes. "If only Edwina were here," she sighed. Her eyes fluttered open as someone sank down beside her against the fir tree.

"You are looking thoughtful, everything all right?" Edmund asked.

Rosa felt an impulse to confide her dream to Edmund. He would tell her it was nonsense, and it *would be* nonsense, a terror dispelled by laughter and sunlight. She recounted her nightmare, shivering at the end, as she described her father turned into stone. She waited for him to laugh at her fears, but instead he was silent.

"You don't think there is anything to my dream, do you?" she asked anxiously.

He slowly shook his head. "I do not know. It is a strange dream, almost powerful; and I wouldn't dismiss the dreams of the faerie-gifted lightly."

"Oh! But it was a terrible dream. It mustn't come true!"

They both fell into silence, Rosa pulling at the grass at her feet. "One of my godmothers told me that my father has lost all his faerie gifts."

"Did she truly say that? Then this may indeed be a serious warning," he said.

Rosa gazed into his eyes, frightened. "Then what must I do?"

"Well," he said slowly, "we could try to understand your dream better. That way we could try to prevent it."

"Yes, I see that. But how am I to understand it? The dream is a riddle."

"Come with me, princess," he said.

Edmund led her to the library, back to the shelf where they had found *The historie of the golden kings*. "I've come across a book about dreams here," he said, as he pulled out an old, tattered book, small enough to fit in one's pocket, entitled, *A guide to discerning oracles, dreams, and portents*. He handed it to Rosa. She opened it and skimmed pages full of charts and symbols she did not understand.

"I don't see how this can help me," she said.

"Let me show you," Edmund said, and he could not suppress the eagerness in his voice. "There were obvious symbols in your dream, a chalice, water, an old man, and did you say ash and stone? Well, water obviously represents life, or possibly rebirth. So to sum up: an old man was offering your father life in a chalice. But what does the old man represent, or the chalice? If we look at the symbols in here..." Edmund flipped through the book. "Ah, here we have 'man,' subdivided into 'infant,' 'youth,' and 'old age.' And look! An old man can mean many things: approaching death, weakness, wisdom, and so forth. So now we have someone weak, but possibly wise, offering your father life. Now let us put more of the symbols together..."

Rosa put both hands up to her head. "No, stop," she exclaimed. "This is too much. I can't understand how strange symbols in an old book will help save my father."

Edmund sighed with exasperation. "I thought you of all people would understand. But never mind. I see this is too much for you." He stuffed the book back on the shelf, though his hand still hovered over it, and he seemed to be considering something. He removed the book again and gave it to the Rosa.

"While this seems confusing now, perhaps you can look at it later. Or..." and here he looked at Rosa intently, "do you think you could ask your faerie godparents about it?"

"I don't see why not," she said with hesitation, "though somehow I feel that they would find the book needlessly complicated, or perhaps too simple." She laughed. "They always seem to want me to work out things for myself."

"And that is exactly what you are doing," Edmund retorted. "But it's good that you feel like you can ask them questions. That means that they must give you answers."

"Er... sometimes."

"Then perhaps you wouldn't mind showing them something else?"

She lifted her eyebrows questioningly as Edmund bent over the bottom shelf, yanked out a heavy volume, and then, reaching his arm through the open space, pulled out a hidden, aged scroll, unrolling it on the ground.

"This manuscript is very old," he explained, "older than the *Historie* and the book I just gave you. It's in the old tongue, and I can't make it out. Do you think you or your faerie godparents could tell me what it's for?"

Rosa unrolled the manuscript on the ground and knelt down beside it, brushing her fingers over its cracked edges, inhaling the scent of aged parchment.

"This will take me a minute to work out," she said, as she pored over it line by line. "Hmm... there are many words here that I also don't understand... but this appears to be a summoning spell for faerie kind. This word here means 'calling,' but a very special kind of calling, like calling forth from another country or realm. The words 'heart' and 'blood' help make up the single word."

"Just who exactly was your tutor?" Edmund asked.

Rosa smiled and returned to the manuscript. "But it says that only those with faerie blood in their veins can use this summons."

"Only those with faerie blood?" Edmund asked sharply. "Does it say anything of faerie blood by marriage?"

Rosa glanced up with surprise. "What do you mean?"

"If you were married to someone with faerie blood, would you be able to summon the faerie?"

Rosa thought of Iseult. Did Edmund find this scroll among his father's belongings and hide it in the library?

"Where did you get this?" she asked him softly.

"On second thought, perhaps it would not be best to give this manuscript to your godparents after all." Edmund grabbed the parchment from her hands and rolled it back up. "Look, I have something else you could show them." He yanked another book from the shelf. "There is a spell here that requires mixtures and ingredients that I've never heard of. If you asked them about it, but didn't mention me, they might tell you where to find them."

"What are you saying, Edmund? How is this going to help my father?"

"It's not." He shrugged. "But who knows how much longer you will be able to speak to the faerie. You should make the most of the time you have with them."

Rosa became upset. "But I already told you that the faerie do not teach me magic. In fact, this sort of magic does not belong to them at all. I don't think I can help you."

"You mean you won't." Edmund's eyes flashed as he stood up. "How can you stand it? You find out that you are cursed and you won't even try to break it! Our parents take the faerie for granted. They are so used to them acting a certain way that they forget that the faerie are sources of great power. But you and I know better. Both of our lives have been touched by the darkness of faerie kind, and we should seek to protect ourselves!"

Rosa gazed into Edmund's burning, black eyes. Her heart fell as she suddenly understood. He did not wish to help her, but instead wanted to access Faerie through her. He wanted to learn more about magic and about the curse, and that was why he was acting like her friend. Her face must have shown what she was feeling, for Edmund looked down at the ground.

Rosa whispered, "I am sorry Edmund. I cannot help you. I have to look for a way to save my father from turning to stone."

She turned and left the library, and also the books of dreams and spells, behind her.

ROSA went to the cliff side to clear her head and found Neirin sitting by the rocks, his lute slung against his back.

She sat down beside him. "I was looking for you earlier. Play me a song."

The minstrel did not sing, but instead plucked clear notes that echoed the wind.

"All the songs you play since you came to the summer palace are sad," Rosa said.

"That is because I am searching for something I cannot find," the minstrel responded, gazing out into the distance to where the sky met the sea.

They both watched the waves crash against the shore, and she leaned her head against his shoulder.

Neirin gave her his sad smile. "You, my princess, are the only thing that calls my soul back from wandering forever."

THAT night, after kissing Alice goodnight, Rosa lay awake in her room fearing to dream again and brooding over Edmund, wondering if they would ever be friends. The hours passed slowly by, and she left her bed to sit by her window, realizing that she was not going to fall asleep. She grew aware of another presence in the room, and the Grey Lady emerged from the shadows.

Rosa stepped toward her and took her hand. "Are you going to tell me about my dream?" she asked.

Ignoring the question, or perhaps indirectly responding to it, the Grey Lady said, "Put on your shoes and something warm. I wish you to follow me tonight."

Rosa wrapped herself up in her soft, blue cloak, and the Grey Lady led her out of her room, out of the palace, and down the winding path to the coast. They walked silently along the shoreline, and Rosa gazed up at the brilliant stars overhead and the moon just past its fullness. The air around her shimmered, causing the moon to twinkle along with the stars. Now she knew she was in Faerie. The air tasted sweeter, she could see more subtle colors in the moonlight, and the wind that caressed her was gentle and warm.

After what could have been a few hours or a few moments,

they approached a tall mound in the earth in which were carved two gates, one of polished ivory and the other mother-of-pearl. They entered through the gate of mother-of-pearl down a long and narrow passageway, until they emerged into a high vaulted chamber deep in the earth. There, by low lamplight, Rosa saw the Grey Lady, sitting in the center of the room, surrounded by three wrinkled crones, spinning thread with something she was holding in her lap.

Rosa's eyes darted to her side in surprise. The Grey Lady had been just beside her, but now she was spinning in the center of the room. She wondered if the Grey Lady had been spinning the entire time.

"What is that you are holding in your hand?" Rosa asked.

"This is my spindle. It is sister to Time's turning wheel."

"Oh."

The shaft and hook of the giant spindle was made of lead, and the whorl was made of eight consecutive rings of many colors. Two crones whirled the spindle, while the crone on the Grey Lady's right fed in strands of fiber that turned into thread in the spinning. The crone in the middle spun the inner bands of the whorl, and the crone on the left spun the outer, and the three crones sang as they spun, their voices young and beautiful. Rosa observed the crone on the right feed a shining strand to the spindle and then saw the crone on the left pick up a large pair of iron scissors, which she used to snip at a lone strand that she mysteriously pulled from the thread. The Grey Lady held the thread with the spinning spindle in her lap, while the crones snipped, spun, and added shining strands.

Rosa felt a sudden, inexplicable impulse to grab the spindle and clutch it to her breast. "May I touch the spindle?" she whispered.

For an instant, it seemed as if the spinning stopped, and the princess and the Grey Lady were alone. Rosa was transfixed by the Grey Lady's piercing gaze. Then there was the sound of the crones singing, and the Grey Lady was working at her spindle and thread, spinning away.

"It is not right that you should desire to touch the spindle. No one may touch it but me and my three daughters. If I ever stopped spinning, then disorder would unwind our two realms."

The princess felt shame rise hot in her cheeks, but the Grey Lady motioned her forward. "Come to me, my child, and have a closer look at my thread. Tell me what you see."

Rosa approached with hesitation and saw that the thread was made up of a multitude of thin strands of silver and gold. Pooled around the bottom of the Grey Lady's feet lay coils of the thread that were made up of pure gold, but further up along and closer to the spinning, strands of silver and gold were intermingled, and the thread being spun now was mostly made up of silver strands.

Snap went the crone's iron scissors, and more silver strands were added to the thread.

"What do the silver and gold strands mean, godmother?"

"The thread with strands of pure gold shows the mortal lives that lived during the time when Faerie and the mortal realm were one. The silver thread shows mortal lives divided from the faerie realms. When the two threads are mixed, the golden thread belongs to those mortals still touched by Faerie. Now, there are very few of you left."

"These are mortal lives?" Rosa gasped and then stared fearfully at the iron scissors. "And you choose when someone is born and when someone dies?"

"I merely spin what has been given me," the Grey Lady answered.

Rosa continued to stare at the iron scissors in the crone's right hand. Rosa thought she heard one of the crones chuckle.

"My child," the Grey Lady spoke, "this spinning keeps the world in harmony, so that every life interweaves with the next as it should. All the different strands mingle into one beautiful and strong thread. There are those, however, who seek to destroy this balance. That is why you are here."

The fear that Rosa was fighting to keep down surged up. "So I am one of those strands? Is my strand going to be cut on the eve of the sixteenth year of my christening?"

The Grey Lady continued spinning. "Your future can go many ways. Your strand may be cut when you say. And if that is so, then there will be no more golden strands in my thread."

Rosa felt the blood drain from her face. "Then can't you stop it? If you see what is happening, can't you change it? You don't have to cut my strand, you can change the spinning."

The Grey Lady looked surprised. "Then you would not be free. Life and death may be given to you, but the shape your life takes is your own choice to make. I can see, but I cannot change. And when I spin, I spin betwixt joy and sadness over the choices made by the mortal race."

They fell into silence, and then the Grey lady spoke again gently. "But little one, was there something else you wanted to ask me, something from which my spindle has distracted you?"

Rosa remembered her dream. How could she ever have forgotten? "Will my nightmare come true? Can I do something to save my father?"

"Ah, my princess, your nightmare has the chance of coming true, for every day your father's heart is becoming a little bit harder and is turning to stone."

"How can I help him?" Rosa pleaded. "Please tell me."

"It is in your power to help him, for I have gifted you with an understanding spirit. Your father has forgotten that to be a king means that he must serve his people. The kingdom has grown old and weary under his care. You, my child, must look into his heart and remind him of that."

"How do I remind him?" Rosa asked.

"It will be made clear to you when it is time. But now we

must bid one another farewell. We may not see each other again, though I will think of you often when I am spinning."

Rosa bowed to the Grey Lady and then heard the rustle of the wind behind her. She spun around, and joy flooded her heart as she caught sight of the Green Lady shining bright as an emerald flame in the darkness of the cavern.

"Godmother!" she cried and threw herself into the lady's arms.

The Green Lady held the princess close and whispered in her ear, "You have endured an ordeal, but I will take you back to the palace, so that you can rest. You will be going home soon."

"Oh, thank you," Rosa whispered.

The Green Lady lifted the princess into her arms as she did on that day when she had first taken her from the castle and carried her away. Behind in the cavern, the Grey Lady continued spinning. But, instead of three crones, there were three beautiful maidens who lifted their voices in joyous song, and each strand of thread that was spun shone brightly in all the colors of the rainbow.

Chapter Thirteen

The Weeping Queen

THE NEXT MORNING, a herald arrived at the palace bearing a message that summoned Rosa back to the castle. They would leave in three days' time. That evening Rosa waited by the cliff side at the spot where she first had met the Golden Piper. She had brought along her harp, but the notes she played while she waited were lost in the wind. The second day she did the same, but still the faery did not appear. She awoke before the sun on the morning of the third day and again waited at the cliff side with her faerie harp.

The Golden Piper was there with the sunrise and held out his hand to Rosa. They strolled on the cliff path until they came upon a horse as pure and white as the first snowfall. The faery took the harp from the princess and lifted her up behind him onto the horse's back.

Away they flew, galloping along the coast towards the east and into the rising sun. The horse's hoofs thundered against the earth with such speed that Rosa knew the white horse was a faerie steed. They finally came to a tall mountain, but the horse did not stop. He clambered straight up the mountain, while Rosa clutched at his mane. Looking behind her, she thought she could glimpse wings out of the corner of her eye.

They climbed higher and higher through the clouds and the sky, until they reached the mountain peak. The arching sky was as dark as night. Both the sun and the moon and all the brilliant stars shone in the firmament. The Golden Piper also shone like the sun, and Rosa had to shield her eyes, but, when he lifted the hands that covered her face, she saw that he had dimmed and that she could look at him now without being blinded. He helped her down from the horse and led her to the center of the top of the mountain peak.

"Listen," he spoke. "What do you hear?"

Rosa gazed up at the moon, the sun, and the stars and strained her ears, but all she could hear was an unfilled silence.

"Nothing," she said.

Then the Golden Piper took the princess' harp and began to play, softly at first, but then the music swelled as she heard one new voice and then another join in the melody. She looked up at the sky and realized that the stars were singing and one by one she heard them join in the song, each voice singing its own part, yet in harmony with the others, blending into one song. Rosa realized that the stars had always been singing; it was she who only now had begun to listen. Then she saw seven bright lights, all of different colors, spinning and wheeling around the dome of the sky. She was looking up into Time's turning wheel, and it was beautiful. The princess continued to gaze and knew nothing but the song. Tears fell unheeded from her eyes as the heavens sang above her.

A new voice joined in the song and called the princess back to herself. The Golden Piper had stopped playing the harp and was singing with the stars. His eyes were closed, his face upturned, and he was shining brilliantly, but this time Rosa could look upon him. His voice was a white, hot light, thrilling with life. Rosa closed her eyes and joined her voice with his, and her heart sang its own song, and she was part of the great melody of the stars.

Rosa did not know how long they sang, or perhaps, since they stood at the center of Time's wheel, time had stopped. But there came a moment when she was finished and fell into a rich silence. The Golden Piper then took her hand and helped her onto the white horse, and they went back down the mountainside. Rosa saw that they had only been gone as long as the sunrise and that it was still early morning.

Neirin was at the cliff side, watching the rising sun's rays reflect against the morning waters. He seemed about to return to the palace, but froze when he saw the white horse and its riders. His face showed his wonder as the white horse trotted over to him, breathing into his face and allowing the minstrel to caress him. Rosa slid off the horse, while the Golden Piper fixed his gaze upon the minstrel.

"It's you," Neirin whispered.

The Golden Piper smiled and then rode away with his white horse into the sun. The minstrel and the princess watched him go until he was no more and then returned to the palace in silence.

WHEN Rosa and her company were ready to depart for the castle, she bade farewell to her uncle and cousin. Edmund couldn't meet her gaze, and Rosa realized with a pang that he was ashamed. She took his hand and pressed it, and his eyes fluttered to hers in surprise, but then he snatched his hand away. Rosa climbed into the carriage, sad that she and Edmund were still as distant as they ever had been.

They journeyed for days and sent a herald ahead of them to announce their arrival. When they reached the castle, Rosa was greeted by blaring trumpets, and her parents and Edwina were at the castle gate to meet her. For a moment, Rosa allowed herself to feel the simple joy of feeling her parents' arms around her and being reunited with her best friend, but all her happiness was quickly eclipsed by her desperation to speak with her father, to warn him in some way about her nightmare. But there was no time that day. She was rushed to a great feast in her honor and then ushered to bed.

A week went by, but the king was preoccupied with his cares, and the queen complained of headaches, refusing to receive anyone. Rosa sighed. This was more than mere busyness—they were avoiding her.

Late one afternoon she sat in the cloistered garden, her worry about the nightmare weighing down on her heart. She closed her eyes and softly hummed under her breath. She had not raised her voice in song since her journey up the mountain, when she had sung with the stars. She lifted up her voice, and it swelled with her memory of the beauty of the heavens, so that her music filled the farthest reaches and depths of the castle, flooding the vast halls and beckoning from twisting corridors. The daily castle hubbub fell silent, as slowly, one by one, courtiers and servants alike were drawn in by her song and filed under the arches and boughs of the cloistered gardens. Finally, the king and queen joined the crowd surrounding the princess. Tears glistened in the king's eyes, and the queen's face was a mystery.

Her song ended, Rosa lingered on the silence of the last note when she was startled by the thunder of exuberant applause. Her eyes fluttered wide open in surprise to see the entire castle cheering before her, and she battled the impulse to duck under the hedges and disappear. The crowd parted as the king and queen pressed forward.

"Beautiful, Rosa, beautiful." The king beamed. "I do not remember ever being so moved. I did not know that you could sing so exquisitely. Ask for a gift, any gift, and I will reward you, if it is within my power."

"Oh no, father," Rosa replied. "I do not need a reward for my song. It was a joy to sing it."

"Do not be falsely modest, Rosa," her father said. "What is the use of all my power and wealth, if I cannot shower those I favor with gifts? I miss your old, unreasonable demands. Do not tell me that your father has outlived his usefulness?"

Rosa shook her head and fell silent. The king's face darkened, and the queen's eyes darted toward the crowd surrounding them. She spoke sharply to the princess, "Do not be stubborn, Rosa. Do you not see that it makes your father happy to give you gifts?"

The princess felt chastened. "Very well," she said, "may I have some time to think about it?"

"Certainly, my dear." The king laughed, good humor returning to his features. "Take all the time you need. But do not devise a task too impossible to perform. I know how mischievous your mind can be."

"I know better now than to ask for the moon." Rosa smiled at the memory which had brought her into the Green Lady's care. It had the opposite effect on her parents. Their faces clouded, and they left without a further word. The crowd quickly followed.

Rosa lay in her bed that night with the burden of the unnamed gift in her mind. Her thoughts were interrupted by a low, muffled sound echoing from the hallway. It was the sound of a lady's weeping, and the weeping was so sad that it brought tears to Rosa's eyes.

She slid out of bed, put on her slippers, and followed the weeping sound through the long hall, down the spiral staircase, and into the throne room. There she saw a lady robed in the royal sapphire sitting on the golden throne. Her head was bowed, and she wore a crown of silver stars on her head. For a moment Rosa thought the lady was her mother, but there was a strangeness about her that whispered of Faerie, and, on a second glance, Rosa saw that the lady was too tall and her hair too dark.

She softly stole over to the weeping queen and whispered, "Please, why are you crying?"

The faerie queen ceased weeping and raised her bowed head, so that Rosa looked into endless pools of sky brimming with tears like the summer rain.

"I am weeping because a great evil will soon befall the kingdom," the faerie queen answered.

The princess knelt down before her and clasped her hands.

"Please tell me, gentle queen and godmother, for I know that you are one of my godmothers, how I can prevent this evil from happening, how I can save my father and the kingdom."

The faerie queen's fingers brushed against Rosa's cheeks as light as feathers. "I do not know how long the evil can be averted. And yet, love works mysteriously and its strength cannot be measured. You love your father and your mother, do you not, little one?"

"Oh, yes!"

"Do you love your kingdom as well?"

Rosa hesitated, for she wished to be truthful. "I do not know the kingdom," she said at last. "But I love my parents, Alice, Edwina, and Neirin, and they are part of the kingdom."

The queen's gaze turned sadder. "Should you not know the plight of your people?"

Rosa looked down at her feet and said in a small voice, "I never thought about it. Or at least, I start to think about it, but then I forget."

Again the queen touched the princess' cheek. "You love those who have entered into your life, and that is a good beginning, but the happiness of many rests on your shoulders, and you must not shrink from that burden."

"Please tell me what I should do."

The queen shook her head. "You are no longer a little child to only receive instruction. You must seek to understand the bond between a ruler and the people for yourself. When does the king see his people?"

"In his public audiences. The people come to him to ask for justice."

"Then you should attend them."

"But how?" Rosa asked. "I do not think that my father would wish it. I know he wants to set me apart from the rest of the kingdom, though I do not know why."

The queen gazed long into the princess's eyes.

"I can ask father if I can attend his audiences as a gift. He promised me a gift just this morning!" Rosa said, brightening.

The queen gathered Rosa's hands into her own. "This trial will be especially difficult for you, my princess. Only know that you have been gifted with a merciful heart, and it will guide you."

Rosa whispered, "And this will save my father?"

"There is still hope for your father. His heart is not yet stone."

The queen rose and led Rosa to the large double doors of the throne room and pressed the princess' hand. "Remember that you are not alone, my child, even if you feel alone. Ask for help when things feel darkest, for you never know from whence help may unexpectedly spring."

She kissed Rosa on the forehead, giving her a gentle smile of such tenderness that it put the princess' heart at ease. They both bid each other good night, and the princess returned to her quarters, bravely determined to face whatever tomorrow would bring.

The first thing Rosa did the next morning was to tell her father that she wished to attend his public audiences. He burst out into laughter and, taking both of her tiny hands into his very large one, said, "My little Rose has become too serious. Ask for something else. Believe me when I say that you would find the audiences very boring."

Rosa shook her head and said, "You promised me a gift, and kings do not break their promises."

His face flamed as he dropped her hands. "Once again you ask for the one thing that I would not have you do."

Rosa stood straight before her father's brimming anger, and it took all her courage to repeat, "You promised me a gift, and kings do not break their promises."

The king trembled in rage, but Rosa reached again for his hand and said, "Is it so strange that I wish to see how you rule your kingdom? Father, it is you most of all that I want to know, how you rule your people with justice and kindness."

The king's face softened as his anger dissolved, and he laid his hand on Rosa's shoulder. "You speak of justice and kindness, but people only understand fear. It is an ugly world, Rosa, and there is no reason for you to shoulder its burden."

"Why shouldn't I? Isn't that my duty?" she asked in surprise.

The king smiled sorrowfully, and Rosa's heart ached. She realized that he was thinking of the curse and that he thought that she wouldn't be awake long enough to be involved in the kingdom's troubles.

"I will let you have your way, my little Rose. You will grow tired of these audiences, and then you can ask me for something else."

That afternoon, Rosa attended an audience for the first time. A chair was placed for her a little to the side below her parent's thrones on the dais. She found the following proceedings bewildering. Many noblemen she recognized from her father's court were complaining over this or that petty dispute or the mismanagement of their estates. Her eyes strained past all the richly attired, self-important courtiers in the throne room to the throngs of people with lackluster eyes and ragged clothes waiting outside in the hall. Surely those were the people they were meant to help? she thought. But the king called the audience to a close before they were allowed into the throne room.

When the king kissed Rosa goodnight that evening, he asked, "Now, Rosa, wasn't that dreary? Don't you regret the waste of my gift? Name something else, and I will give it to you."

Rosa shook her head, "I will go to the audience tomorrow, father."

The king gave an exasperated huff.

FOR the next few days, Rosa attended the king's audiences. Each day, her father settled the noblemen's disputes in the throne room, and the poor in the hall were sent home unheard. Rosa suspected that her father was doing this deliberately, so that she would tire of the proceedings, but she waited patiently, knowing that speaking to him would only make him more resolved against her.

Finally the day came when, before the close of the audience, the king signaled the guard to let a few people in from the hall. Rosa was touched by the unlooked-for hope on their faces. A man past the prime of life limped forward to the center of the throne room and stood, without daring to raise his eyes up to the king.

"Please, your majesty. I do not have enough food to feed my family." He spoke so low that Rosa had to lean forward to hear him.

The king shook his head impatiently. "What is it that you would have me to do? How are you different from anyone else that I should empty the coffers of my treasury for you? You are not starving. I see that you have meat on your bones, your arms are strong, and you can work. Speak!"

The man did not answer; despair seemed to weigh down his dangling arms and bowed head. The king waved to the guards to lead the man away, but was interrupted by Rosa's cry as she leapt up from her seat.

"Wait!"

She dashed down the dais, pulled off her sparkling earrings, and thrust them in the man's hand. "Here," she said, "sell these so you can feed your family."

The man glanced at up her in surprise and then quickly looked back down toward the floor. He drew back, murmuring incoherent thanks, while the guards led him out of the throne room.

The king rose. "And so," he proclaimed, "the tenderhearted-ness of our princess tempers the king's justice with mercy."

The audience chamber broke out into cheers, and the royal family left the throne room amid thunderous applause.

Once inside their private chamber, her father rounded on Rosa in white fury. "How dare you cross my authority! How am I to maintain law and order in my kingdom, if I am undermined at every turn? I have put others to death for less!"

"What did I do wrong?" she whimpered. "I do not understand... I was only trying to help."

"You acted against my judgment." The king paced the floor in anger. "You made me look cruel. Now everyone will believe that my judgment can be swayed by a little girl. You are banished from any further audiences."

"No!" Rosa cried and fell on her knees. "I promise I will say nothing, do nothing from now on. But you gave me your word that I could attend your audiences."

The king stopped pacing and muttered to himself, "I do not want the people to think that I punished the princess for her act of kindness." He glared at her and spat out, "I will allow you to continue attending the audiences with the condition you mentioned—you may not speak or act in any way that seems to oppose my judgment."

He stomped out of the room, leaving Rosa and her mother alone.

Rosa turned to her mother. "Is what I did so wrong? I only wanted to help."

"You meddle in things you do not understand," the queen sighed in exasperation. "The kingdom's poor are innumerable, and you cannot help every single one of them. What happens when you run out of earrings, when the treasury is emptied? Then the bordering countries will attack us, when they see that we do not have enough money to pay our armies. And how do we know that what the man said is true? What proof did he have that he could not feed his family? He fooled your tender little heart, and you, in turn, made a fool of your father. He has every right to be angry with you."

Rosa's head swam with confusion, but then she thought of

all the suffering faces passed over in the hall and said, "How do we know that he was *not* telling the truth? We cannot dismiss those suffering so lightly."

"There is no reasoning with you, Rosa. You are fortunate that your father will still allow you to attend his audiences. I would not have been so lenient. Go to your room before you give me another one of my headaches."

Later that night Rosa went to the throne room, hoping to find the weeping faerie queen, but the room was empty. I hope I did right in promising not to speak, she thought.

THE audience the next day tested her promise, for the proceedings were so horrifying it was all Rosa could do not to cry out. Near the close of the audience, an old man with a tall, heavy staff hobbled to the center of the throne room.

Rosa's eyes darted up to her father and saw a look of genuine concern pass over his features. He leaned forward and asked, "What can I do for you, old father?"

"Someone has stolen my only treasure," the old man groaned.

"That is a terrible crime, to steal from someone of your years, who cannot defend himself. Tell me who stole from you, and he shall be punished."

The old man thrust out a shaking arm and his eyes rested on one of the noblemen in the court. "That is the man. He has stolen my little lamb, my only treasure. I ask you to have him give her back to me."

The king turned to the nobleman, storm clouds on his brow. "What does the old man mean by this? Why have you taken his only lamb?"

"I think he means his daughter," the nobleman said. "She was a fair maid and happy to leave her father's home."

The old man leaned against his staff, painfully sinking down on his knees. "See how he mocks me, your majesty. She was crying when he took her away. I beg you command him to give my daughter back to me, where I can care for her and dry her tears."

"She does not want to go back, my lord, and neither do I wish to return her," the nobleman spoke, and Rosa watched as he and her father exchanged glances. The nobleman's eyes contained a challenge, and her father visibly drooped before his gaze. She felt her whole body stiffen as she realized that her father was afraid of this man. She bit her lip and tasted the tangy salt of her blood. She had promised her father she would not speak.

The king sighed, his face growing suddenly weary with age. His shoulders sagged, and, when he spoke, his words were hollow. "You have heard the nobleman, old man. It is your word against his and I hold him in high esteem. Your daughter is fortunate in her present company, and you should be pleased that she is so well taken care of. I will, however, soften this unfortunate business and compensate you for her loss out of my own treasury, so that you will never feel her want in your old age. So speaks the generosity of the king."

"What?" the old man choked. "What is this I hear? I came to the court for justice, but instead encounter lies and false gold."

He clung to his staff as he pulled himself back on his feet. His body shook, and Rosa could not tell if he was shaking in anger or if he was crying. He straightened his spine and thrust away his staff, so that it landed with a sharp clang on the floor. His eyes grew into fiery wheels of rage as he stretched out both his arms as if to encompass the whole court as he cried, "You have taken away the prop of my old age, and I will never walk again. A curse upon your household!" His wild eyes rested on Rosa, and he pointed at her with a long, bony finger, "May you lose that which is most precious to you and feel the sorrow of this old man."

The king sprang to his feet. "Guards, remove him," he cried, and armed guards dragged the old man from the throne room.

Rosa's body grew numb in shock, and the throne room swam before her eyes. All she was aware of were the words of the old man's curse echoing in her ears. Did they not deserve it? she thought. They had all stood by and said nothing. Perhaps even without the Dark Lady her curse would have been inevitable.

ROSA could not sleep that night, but turned over and over in restless despair. She felt ill and, when the morning came, she could not drag herself out of bed to attend her father's audience. There was no point. She had promised not to speak, and her father would not listen to her anyway. She imagined her father, tall and strong, with his gentle smile. She buried her face in her pillow as the image of her beloved father splintered into pieces. Rosa refused to leave her chambers for the next two days. Nothing could rouse her, not even Neirin's music.

The third night, she stayed in bed and woke to the sounds of sobbing. Rosa did not want to get up, but the slow, steady persistence of the sobs grew unbearable. She dragged her feet to the throne room, where her queenly godmother sat weeping on the throne, her dark head bowed. Rosa waited dumbly beside the weeping queen, knowing that she had not done what she had been asked to do. The queen continued to sob, until Rosa could stand it no more.

"Please, please, godmother, please stop crying. I know that I have done wrong in not going to my father's audiences, but there is nothing I can do, and it is too horrible to watch."

The queen raised her head, tears streaming down her face. "Do you think I do not know how terrible it is? I can never stop watching."

The princess hung her head. "I am sorry, godmother. I did not know. But surely nothing very bad will happen because I did not go? There is nothing I can do after all, and it has only been a few days. I will go back tomorrow."

"A great evil will befall your kingdom," the faerie queen said sadly.

"Surely that is not my fault!" Rosa gasped.

"It is the fault of all those who stand by and do nothing." The faerie queen rose from the golden throne and began gliding away.

"Wait!" The princess called after her. "Tell me what I can do to change things. How can I save my kingdom?"

"The evil will come to pass." The faerie queen paused and said, "Too much blood has been shed and too much injustice done."

A wave of fear stifled Rosa's breath.

"But there is still a chance that you may save your father's heart," the faerie queen murmured.

"How?" Rosa cried faintly.

But the queen was gone.

ROSA sat in the audience chamber, petty disputes sapping her of her strength and the warning of the coming evil still ringing in her ears. She roused herself to pay attention when she saw the guards bring forth a frightened, wide-eyed boy, chains clanking around his small, thin wrists. Her heart reached out to him instantly, and it pitter-pattered in fear that once again she would be powerless to do anything to help. Next to the boy stood a hard-faced man swathed in furs with a large medallion hanging over his chest, his fingers studded with rings of gold and precious gems. Behind the man and the boy moaned a tear-stained woman, battling to hold back her sobs.

The king addressed the hard-faced man. "You have brought a complaint against this boy. What has he done and speak plainly. I do not like to see children in chains."

The man bowed and then spoke in a silky, persuasive voice. "This young boy is my indentured servant. His mother sold him to me for fifteen silver pieces to labor on my estate. All he does is cause trouble, and he has run away back to his mother's home.

She begs me to let her keep him, despite the fact that she will not return the silver she sold him for, and has gone so far as to incite the townspeople against me. They call out vile insults whenever I pass by, so that I fear for my life. I ask that you pass judgment in my favor and return the boy, so that the town no longer has the right to murmur against me."

The king turned to the mother. "Is what this man says true? Did you sell the boy into his service?"

"Yes," the woman sobbed. "But I had no choice. My husband died soon after my boy was born, and I have tried so hard to raise him on my own. But I cannot feed him, and he is always growing. I thought that, if I gave him away, at least he would be able to eat…" Her breast heaved. "But I did not know that my boy would be mistreated. The monster beats him, and my young boy goes almost as hungry as before."

Rosa heard an intake of breath behind her and turned to see that her mother's face had turned a bloodless white. She shifted her attention back to the boy and his mother, and her father was speaking. "But you took the fifteen silver pieces. Can you not give them back?"

The woman shook her head in despair. "I had to eat," came the hoarse reply, "and I had other debts to pay."

The king sighed. "Then I am afraid there is nothing I can do. I cannot bend the law for your sake alone. I will, however, decree that you shall be able to buy back the boy when you have the fifteen silver pieces. This is a favor, for the master is in no way obliged to sell the boy back to you, but I pity your case."

The woman's face was full of despair, and Rosa realized that there was no way for her to earn back the fifteen silver pieces. Rosa whirled back to face her parents, a silent entreaty ringing forth from her sealed lips. Both her parents were silent, and the queen's face was ashen, her eyes hollow like burnt out coals.

The young boy's voice rang out for the first time in the throne room. "It is your fault that we are so poor! My mother was a spinner. She could no longer work once you outlawed spinning and burnt all the spinning wheels in the kingdom!"

The king grew white, and Rosa froze in her chair.

"Throw him in prison," the king whispered. "Throw him in prison," the king roared. "Let the vile boy rot for his insolence. He dare presume to judge the king!"

The guards dragged the boy away amid the mother's wails and screams, and the king ended the audience in fury.

Rosa sat in her chair stunned and unmoving. Her father had outlawed spinning because of her curse, and for that people were going hungry, and the young boy would die in prison.

"It is all my fault," Rosa whispered.

Queen Eleanor whirled on the princess and asked, "What did you say?"

Rosa did not respond, and the queen grabbed Rosa's hand and dragged her from the throne room.

Chapter Fourteen

The King of the Wood

THE QUEEN TOOK ROSA to her private chambers. Ringing one of her servants for a small glass of wine, she then gave orders that they were not to be disturbed and thrust the glass before Rosa, ordering her to drink.

She paced up and down the room and muttered more to herself than to her daughter, "I knew that this latest fancy of yours would not bode well. You are not strong enough to endure the everyday hardships of the world." She turned back to Rosa. "Promise me that you will no longer attend the king's audiences."

Rosa felt like she was seeing her mother for the first time. She saw a nervous woman who hardly ever smiled or looked her in the eye. Even now the queen could not meet her gaze, but was instead looking nervously out the window.

"Mother," Rosa whispered. "Surely we cannot allow our kingdom to be a place that separates a mother from her child. These are the people that we are meant to protect. You must understand this! After all, you are a mother too."

"Why?" The queen's voice rang brittle, and she sharply thrust up her chin. "Many mothers endure separation from their children. Why should that mother be any different?"

Rosa rose and, taking her mother's hands, kissed them both. "Why must others suffer because we do? Our suffering should make us quick to pity the suffering of others. How could father burn all the spinning wheels for my sake? I am not happy that so many must starve so that I can live. And do you really think that such a measure will do any good? I do not think that faerie powers are so easily cheated."

Rosa's words finally forced the queen to look into her daughter's eyes. "You know?" she whispered.

Rosa nodded.

The queen crumpled in her chair. "You were not to know. We wished to spare you that much. Who told you, surely not your uncle?"

"The faerie showed me a vision of my christening. I saw it all, how happy you were when I was born and how you held me in your arms. And then the Dark Lady came... and everything changed."

"And then I knew I had to give you up," the queen sobbed. "You were no longer my child, but death's. You had been stolen from me."

"But that is not true." Rosa fell on her knees beside mother. "I'll fall asleep. Why, a hundred years could be different in faerie time! We could still meet again if we have hope."

"I don't believe you will sleep. The Dark Lady's power is too great. And even if it is true, you are still lost to me."

Rosa gazed at her mother sadly. The queen had lost all power to hope ever since the faerie had failed to save her daughter on that sorrowful christening day.

"Mother, I am right here," Rosa said softly. "Why don't you look at me?"

The queen stared long into her daughter's face, now wet with tears. "My precious child," the queen whispered, and Rosa felt her tender touch on her cheek. "We at least did not want you to know sorrow or to understand our loss. Not a cloud was to cover your sunny, little face during your short life. But it is all over..."

"No," Rosa said firmly. "I am still here and I am glad that I know. But my heart does hurt to see how sad you and others are because of me. Please speak to father and change his mind about the boy. Do you really want another mother to suffer the same way you do?"

The queen's face grew hard again, and a battle seemed to wage within her. The princess placed her hand over the queen's heart, and her eyes never left her hers, but held them in her unwavering gaze. And somehow, Rosa could sense her own calm acceptance passing over to her mother, giving her the strength to accept her own fate, at least for the time being.

The queen sighed. "You are right, Rosa. I do not want another mother to shed the same tears I do. I will speak to your father and see that the boy goes free."

THAT evening, the queen spoke with the king her husband, and, on the morrow, the boy was released from prison and given work in the castle stables. Then a wonderful thing happened in the audience chamber. Whenever the king's temper would blaze, a soothing word or a gentle glance from the queen would calm him. Whenever the queen made an entreaty on behalf of the people, the king would grant her request. Queen Eleanor, emboldened by her success, continued to mediate between the king and his people, and the kingdom tasted the sweetness of mercy.

Rosa was amazed by the change in her mother, and saw that her father was as glad of the change as she. When at supper together, the princess smiled whenever she saw the king look in sudden joy at his queen, but she often missed the look of sorrow they shared when she turned away and their gaze fell upon her.

The king repealed his law against spinners as a special favor to the princess. Soon Rosa forgot the words of warning spoken by the faerie queen as they passed the year in happiness and peace. And if Rosa did not completely forget, she at least put aside the memory, glad in the discovery that the queen, her mother, was her father's heart.

♔ ♔ ♔

MERCILESSLY shaken awake, Erik groggily sat up on his bed to see that it was still dark. He groaned when he remembered that he and Cynric were meant to set off hunting before the dawn, but he slid out of bed, put on his gear, and followed the hunter down to the courtyard. The cool, autumn air fully wakened him, and they went through the castle gate into the forest, two dark figures against the lightening sky.

The morning hunt was successful, and Erik and Cynric were cooking their game over the fire, when they heard a large rustling behind them in the trees.

"Get behind the undergrowth and lie still. This sounds like a large beast," the hunter whispered.

Erik quickly ducked behind the bushes and waited in tense silence for the approaching beast. A black bear emerged from the mist and gloom, a shadow materializing into solid form. Strength and power emanated from the beast, coiled in its sinews and flesh. The bear loomed over the abandoned campfire, dismissive of the flames. It reared majestically, and Erik held his breath as the bear's length and breadth seemed to blot out the sun and the sky. The great beast then lowered himself and crouched in a watchful stillness, an intelligent awareness discernible in its frame and its alert eyes.

Erik felt his muscles tense and his senses heighten. He knows that we are here, he thought. The stillness of the moment seemed to bleed across all tangible boundaries, and the prince held his breath in the fullness of its silence. Then the bear moved again and disappeared into the enclosing wilderness of the trees and woven shadows.

Erik found he could breathe again.

Cynric bounded to the spot near the campfire where the bear's presence somehow still lingered, almost as if its shadow had stayed behind and draped the forest in a thickening shroud.

He gazed into the veiled shadows of the forest with the keen appraisal of the hunter.

"You aren't going after it?" Erik whispered. It was probably safe to talk aloud now, but the prince felt that the air was thick with oppressive silence. He did not wish to go after the mighty animal. Not only would they be no match for its strength, but striking at the bear somehow felt like striking at the forest itself.

Cynric did not answer, but his eyes were still fixed on the spot where the bear had disappeared.

"You can't go alone," Erik said. "I'll go with you, even if that means slowing you down." He felt behind him for his quiver of arrows.

This seemed to break the spell Cynric was under, and he turned to the prince with a short laugh. "None doubt your courage, young prince, but to go after the bear alone would be suicide."

Erik sighed with relief.

The hunter again stared into the distance. "But have you ever seen such a magnificent beast?"

Erik shook his head and followed the hunter's gaze. "He seems to belong to the wood," he said.

"He is king of the wood," Cynric whispered.

Erik was startled, and then he realized that that was what he had felt all along, that the bear ruled over the entire wood.

"Let's go back," Cynric said. The two shifted their bagged game over their shoulders and returned to the castle in silence.

BEFORE the break of dawn the next day, the hunt for the bear began. The king led the hunt, and Erik was the only boy belonging to the hunting party since he and Cynric had had the honor of first sighting the bear. Cynric had described the great bear's magnificence to the king in the hall the night before, and the king's blood had boiled for the hunt, and so Erik found himself hanging towards the back of the company.

They went to the spot where the two of them had first sighted the bear and found its heavy paw prints indelibly marked in the brown earth. From there they tracked through the gloom of the forest and the cool dew, until they came to a wide stream. There they paused in the stillness and peered across the stream into the swirling mists. A dark shape on the other side, barely discernible in the early-morning haze, formed in a thickening of shadows. The still shape waited for them, silently watching, as the mists parted and revealed the great bear. Its eyes rested on the king.

The king and the bear observed each other from across the stream, the king rooted by the bear's inscrutable gaze. As Erik watched the two stare each other down, he desperately wished they would call off the hunt and that the mighty king and the great bear would return to their separate realms—the king back to his castle, the bear to his lair. The prince understood that to continue meant death, the death of the great bear or the death of his father.

The bear loosed the king's gaze and then dissolved back into the wood.

"Next time," the king promised darkly, and Erik understood that his father would not endure a force that could not be subjugated within his kingdom.

THEY set off again at dawn the next day, and in the dim shadows of the forest they lay in wait for the bear near the stream. Erik crouched in silence behind a boulder for what seemed a painfully endless amount of time. Then he heard a sound and felt the hunter beside him tense. The black bear emerged from the mist and the trees, lumbered over to the stream, and dipped its paw into the running water. An aura of wild kingliness wrapped around the bear like the mist, and Erik felt a fervent desire to warn the beast, somehow to make a noise, to slide in the rubble, but an inner battle waged within him, because to do so would be to act against his father and be disloyal to the hunt.

He hesitated.

One of the hunters saw his chance and loosed an arrow into the mighty beast's flank. The bear roared in fury and surged tall and immense on its hind feet. Arrows flew, and then the king stepped in with his hunting spear and faced the mighty bear maddened by pain and rage. The bear rushed forward to attack his foe, and the king plunged his spear with a powerful thrust into its side. It made a final mad sweep with its claws, but the king leapt out of its reach. With a great heave and a groan, the bear broke away to retreat into the wood, but the king took aim with his bow and loosed an arrow that struck the beast between his shoulder blades. The bear dragged itself a few more paces and then sank heavily onto the ground.

In a daze, Erik watched the hunters skin the bear and divide its carcass. He had not raised his arm against the beast, but he felt that his hesitation had been a blow struck against it.

The king severed the bear's head, holding it aloft on his spear, and the hunting party processed back to the castle gates in triumph. All hailed the might and strength of their king, who subjugated the wild beasts of the forest.

THAT night there was a great feast, and all partook in the king's kill. The king and queen were draped in robes of fur, and the royal bard sang songs of the hunt which pitted the mighty king against the powerful bear. Wine spilled over, and there was toasting and cheering long into the cold night. Erik felt hazy to the tip of his toes, and not a few of the warriors, glutted on meat and drink, were pounding their cups and fists on the table, so that the ringing echoed in Erik's ears. The king surveyed the feast with satisfaction.

The queen rose, magnificent and tall, her furs slipping off to reveal a scarlet robe. She was like a white lily kindled to a flame, and the king's eyes burned when he looked on her. She motioned to one of the servers, and he brought to her a large silver goblet worked with intricate carving. This she took and held out-stretched with both arms to the king and said, "Drink, my king. It is the blood of the beast you have slain. Take his power as you took his life, and the life of the forest that flowed in his veins will flow in yours."

The hall fell silent, and the king's eyes glowed with the challenge in the queen's eyes. His gaze never left hers as he took the goblet and slowly drained it of its contents, the bear's blood dribbling from his mouth and seeping into his beard. The entire hall rose and lifted their cups to the king.

"To the king of the wood," someone cried. "To the king of the wood!" the entire hall resounded, and everyone drank.

Erik also rose and drank to his father, but the wine tasted dry and stuck in his throat. He felt dizzy and left the hall, stumbling up the stairs and into his room, where he collapsed on his bed. His sleep was restless, and by morning he had a fever. He lay in bed for three days, sweating, his body racked by tremors. Nightmares painfully encroached on his consciousness and wrapped their piercing tendrils around him and choked him in his sleep, so that he never rested. If anyone visited his bedside, he never knew.

In the midst of his bewildered imaginings, he saw a woman bend over him. Her features were indistinct and dream-like, but her eyes were as light as the summer's day, and he felt himself drifting in the sea of their blueness. A vision of stars danced over her head like a crown, flashing brightly and spinning dizzyingly. Erik did not know if he made a sound or held out his hand beseechingly, but he felt the coolness of touch and water like tear-drops on his face as he floated in a white light.

That evening, his fever broke, and he fell into a healing slumber.

"THE young recover remarkably fast," the Captain of the Guard observed dryly when he discovered Erik outside in the training yard.

"You would be just as keen to leave if you had been cramped in the same room for days. I need to feel the wind on my face, and I will throw my bowl out the window if I am fed any more broth."

Kenelm grunted, "Very well. But I don't expect you training for a few days yet. I don't want you injured due to weakness."

Erik smiled to himself. That meant he could visit Ninny Nanny more often. When he stole away into the wood, he found Mnemosyne waiting for him at her usual spot near the blasted trunk of a tree. Ever since Ninny Ninny's sticks had been stolen, he would wait in the wood for Mnemosyne, and the cat would find him sooner or later; though sometimes the prince would grow tired of waiting and return home, grumbling over the unreliability of cats.

He grinned. "You knew I was coming today, didn't you?"

The cat stared at him with her unblinking, yellow eyes. She slinked away, and the prince followed her winding path to Ninny Nanny's cottage. There he knocked on the old woman's door, but received no answer. Strange sounds were coming from behind the cottage, so he made his way around and found Ninny Nanny bent over a wide patch of thorny brambles. A kerchief was tied around her head, and she was holding a large shovel.

"What are you doing, Ninny Nanny?" Erik asked.

"I'm a' clearing up this space before the ground grows hard," the old woman huffed.

Erik reached her side with long strides and firmly grasped the shovel's handle. "You shouldn't be doing such hard work at your age," he said, taking the shovel from her hands. "Here, let me help. How much do you want cleared?"

"All of it," the old woman wheezed. "I want to plant my garden in the springtime."

"All right, go inside and rest. I'll finish for you."

"You're a sweet boy, princeling. Here, take my gloves. You don't want to prick yourself."

Erik surveyed the tangled thicket, the thick, coiled ropes of wood digging into the earth and bristling with small but countless thorns. He gave a deep sigh, but then started the back-breaking task of cutting through the brambles and pulling up their clinging roots. Burning stings grazed his cheeks and arms from the prickly thorn bushes. His body was still weak from the fever, and sweat poured over his tired, straining muscles

When he paused from his labor to take a breath, he saw that he had barely made any noticeable progress. Shaking his head, he gritted his teeth and started again. Little by little he cleared away the thicket, though he paused from time to time, and Ninny Nanny brought him a cup of cool water or wiped the sweat from his brow. The old woman gathered the thorn bushes he uprooted into large bundles. "To burn 'em," she explained.

Erik found that, after a time, he entered into the rhythm of his work, and the dull, sick knot he had felt in the pit of his stomach ever since he had toasted the king of the wood slowly dissolved. When he finally finished, he threw himself exhausted onto the ground. It was growing dark. The days were becoming shorter and shorter, now that winter was drawing near, and the stars were coming out, one by one.

"Come inside, princeling. Ye must be hungry after all the hard work ye did," Ninny Nanny called from the cottage doorway.

When Erik entered the cottage, he saw that she had laid out supper for the two of them. He was so hungry it was not long before Erik was staring down at an empty plate.

The old woman chuckled, "Could ye draw me some more water from the well? Ye were so thirsty ye emptied my pitcher."

Erik grunted and took hold of the pitcher and went outside. It was so cold out that he shivered as he made his way to the well, where he drew up the water and heaved the bucket back to the cottage. Before crossing the threshold, he peered up into the night sky, and his eyes rested on the thin sliver crescent of the moon shimmering over the trees. Ninny Nanny was beside him, staring up at the stars.

"Later Mnemosyne will take ye back to the castle. She can see in the dark."

"Should I go back now? I don't want to be missed."

"They won't know that you're gone till much later," Ninny Nanny said.

"Won't they? How do you know?"

The old woman gave him her secretive smile, and Erik laughed.

"If you say so."

Ninny Nanny pointed up at the sky with her thin, bony finger. "See that bright star o'erhead in the north? It's the lodestar. It guides many wandr'ng feet by its bright and ever shining light."

Erik smiled to himself. Cynric had taught him how to navigate by the stars ever since the hunter had first put a bow into the small prince's hands. Erik had outgrown many bows since then.

"Already know all that, do ye?" The old woman chuckled. "The Princess Rosamund could 'ave used such a guide in the troubling times ahead."

He turned to the old woman. "Could she? What do you mean?"

The old woman chuckled again. "Let's go inside an' I'll tell ye. Ach! Don't spill the water in the bucket, princeling."

👑 👑 👑

TOMORROW WAS TO BE the first day of spring and Rosa's birthday, and she was looking forward to the upcoming celebrations. Stefan and Edmund had arrived at the castle a week earlier for the preparations, and she and her father had gone down to meet them at the gate.

The rich autumn and a long winter had passed since she and Edmund had last seen each other, and she saw in his eyes as he took her hand in greeting that he was glad to see her and that he thought her as fair as the summer's day. She in turn noticed for the first time that he was tall and strong, that his dark curls tumbled around his neck, and that, though his eyes were dark and sometimes sullen, they also flashed fire. But Rosa's heart was troubled, and she did not know what to do with these new thoughts.

The two often met in the following week, but always in company, and, when Edmund's eyes looked into hers, they whispered that he had a secret that he would tell only her, but not yet. She learned through their talks that he had spent the year at the woodland outposts at the kingdom's border, defending the people in their struggles against brigands and robbers, both from within the kingdom and from the outlying lands.

Rosa was quietly musing over her new feelings in the outer gardens far beyond the courtyard which lay adjacent to the outer walls. A slight chill still clung to the air, but the first flowers of spring were poking out their heads underfoot: the crocus, narcissus, and snowdrop that would be woven into garlands for her birthday celebrations.

"You will become cold standing so still," said a voice behind her, and strong arms wrapped a cloak about her.

She turned to see Edmund smiling down on her. "I was about to go in," she replied.

"Stay awhile. I feel as if we haven't really spoken since I've arrived. Too many banquets and too many parties have crowded out the times we could talk," he said.

Rosa nodded, so they strolled to the farther edges of the grassy grounds, where birch trees clustered by a still pool of water. Rosa spoke to break the silence that had grown between them and made her nervous. "You have been on many adventures since I last saw you. Your father was sharing with us your brave exploits in defense of our kingdom."

"Yes, well, he exaggerates. I am just like any other soldier on the borderland. And to be truthful, soldiery doesn't really suit me. I preferred the time I spent deep in the forest, discovering hidden paths to travel by. But enough about me. I have a gift for you, an early birthday present." He drew from beneath his cloak a miniature rose, its petals formed from the purest silver, while its stem, leaves, and thorns were wrought of twisted gold.

"It's exquisite," Rosa gasped.

"It goes in your hair. May I?"

Edmund tucked the flower into the many folds of her golden hair, and there his fingers lingered.

"We should be going in now," she said quickly. Rosa looked down at her feet the entire time they walked back to the castle.

THE next morning, while the men went out on the hunt for the princess' birthday feast, Rosa stayed with Edwina in her chambers. Would she be asleep this time next year? The thought fluttered unbidden into her mind. The revelation of the curse had somehow never felt real to her, but, from now on, every day would be the last of its kind before she fell asleep. She felt a pulse of fear and went to gaze outside her window. The sun shone brightly on the wings of the geese and swans, and not a whisper of a breeze ruffled their feathers in their tranquil bathing in the moat below. Edwina came to her side, and Rosa laced her fingers through her handmaiden's and said, "I try to imagine what it will be like this time next year, but all I see is blackness. I do not know what will come." Rosa had confided in Edwina everything about her curse and her time in the summer palace.

"Oh, Rosa." Edwina wrapped the princess in her arms. "Everyone's future is unseen, but I do know that we have this moment now together, and a whole precious store of moments to come."

"Yes, you are right. Only, you must promise to stay with me until the end," Rosa pleaded.

"There's no place I would rather be," Edwina whispered and tightened her embrace. The blaring sound of the horn and anxious dogs barking drew their attention to the courtyard below.

"They're back early," Rosa exclaimed.

"I think someone's hurt," Edwina cried, peering through the window.

The two girls rushed down the stairs and into the courtyard in time to see the court physician order an injured man onto a stretcher. The physician instructed that the man be brought down to the castle infirmary, and Rosa winced to see that his right leg was soaked in blood. The physician's eyes lighted on the two girls, and he sharply ordered for Edwina to come with him to minister to the injured man. Edwina took one look at the young man's pale face and his features withdrawn in pain and nodded hurriedly. She squeezed Rosa's hand and followed the physician.

Rosa went back inside to find her mother, and both waited anxiously for the rest of the hunting party to return. It arrived later in the day with bright trumpet calls and joyful cheers. Apparently the king had slain the monstrous boar that had injured the young man. The minute she saw that her father and everyone else were all right, Rosa whisked down to the sick quarters to check on injured man.

Edwina met her at the door.

"How is he?" Rosa asked in a hushed voice.

"He's very weak, but the doctor has high hopes he will pull through." Then she added sorrowfully, "I don't think he will ever be able to walk normally again."

"I have to go back upstairs to celebrate my birthday. It doesn't feel right to have a feast when he is lying down here injured."

"You must go," Edwina said. "The celebration is in your honor, and they will be expecting you. There's nothing that you, or really anyone, can do down here."

Rosa went upstairs with a heavy heart to prepare for the evening's feast. Edwina's words of the future being unknown echoed in her mind. That young man's life had changed in an instant. Nothing would be the same for him ever again.

"You are being very quiet," Alice mentioned while braiding the princess' hair into a coronet around her head. "It was a shock for you to see the young man, was it not?"

Rosa sighed. "Edwina said there is much hope he will recover."

"Well, that is something to be grateful for, isn't it? It is not uncommon for some hideous accident to occur during a hunt. We can rejoice in his narrow escape from death." She tugged at the princess' hair playfully, "...and in the joyous event of your birth."

But even though Alice was smiling, Rosa could detect a faint hint of sadness in her voice, and it was that sadness that made Rosa resolve to be cheerful for the rest of the evening. She knew she was not the only one thinking about the curse and her next birthday, and she would not allow unhappiness to cloud the little time she had left with her mother and father, Edwina, and Alice. She sprang from her seat and threw her arms around Alice. "Thank you for always taking care of me," she said.

"Oh, my little one, what else would I do? I have been looking after you since you were so very small." The nursemaid half-sobbed and wiped away a tear with her apron.

SPREAD out on the banquet table was an abundance of meats and cheese, spices and sweet wines, and at its very center was the head of the slain boar garlanded in flowers. The king sat at the head with the queen on his right and the princess on his left. Beside the princess sat Edmund. Edmund spoke pleasantly all evening, and Rosa smiled to herself, remembering their silent and awkward dinners at the summer palace. He had changed so much over the winter. When the banquet was winding down,

Neirin was called to sing before the court. He sang of the love between the golden king Eirwyn and a mortal maid, and the song was a sad one.

> The king had gone, the king was crowned.
> And golden were his gates and towers
> As golden as his father's crown.
> And he would climb the tallest spire
> And pluck the strings of his golden lyre
> And sing to the moon and the stars.
>
> His eyes beheld a maiden fair,
> Stars in her eyes, the moon in her hair.
> He shared with her his golden crown.
> And he would climb the tallest spire
> And pluck the strings of his golden lyre
> And sing of the moon and the stars.
>
> Gold and silver were the gates
> Which all passed through with untroubled brow
> Singing a song of the golden crown.
> And he would climb the tallest spire
> And pluck the strings of his golden lyre
> And sing with the moon and the stars.
>
> The Queen's eyes closed their final time.
> The king did mourn the blood in his veins
> Faerie blood that lengthenéd his days
> The blood that gave him his golden crown.
> Grief plucked the strings of his heart's lyre
> And he climbed down the tallest spire
> And disappeared under the moon and the stars.

By the last lingering note a tear lay in the corner of every eye. But, when the song was finished, the time had come for dancing. The mood changed as the court musicians struck a lively tune and the king took the princess by the hand and led her to the center of the room. Rosa danced gracefully on her feet, radiant with every step. It was the first time she had danced before the court, and she drew all eyes to her. The princess saw that her father's eyes were bright with unshed tears, and with the closing of the dance he pressed her hand against his heart.

The music started again, and Edmund claimed the next dance, and, when it was over, he drew her to one side.

"That was a sad song the minstrel sang, was it not?" he said.

Rosa nodded. "Neirin's songs are often sad, but I think sadness is what he sings most beautifully."

"Still," he said, "I would have chosen a joyful song for your birthday celebrations."

"Would you?" Rosa laughed. "I am surprised. I would have thought a sad song more to your liking."

"Not necessarily," he murmured. Then he looked straight into her eyes. "I would not have your song be a sad one."

Rosa felt a surge of warmth toward her cousin. "Thank you, Edmund, that is kind." She pressed his hand and made to move away, but he kept a firm grasp on her hand.

"And I would say more, if I may be so bold. I would like to be the one who ensures that your song is a happy one."

"What do you mean?" she asked in surprise.

But before he could speak again they were interrupted as the princess' hand was eagerly sought for the next dance. The rest of the evening was full of dancing, as everyone wished to partner with the beautiful princess on her birthday, and Rosa did not speak to Edmund again that night, but she stayed up late in bed thinking of his words and fought to banish a thought from her head. That thought was that Edmund loved her, and it made her heart beat faster, but she did not know if it beat in hope or in fear.

Chapter Fifteen

The Engagement

WHEN ROSA JOINED her parents for breakfast the next morning, she noticed she had interrupted a disagreement. They looked at her strangely throughout the meal, and she wanted to ask them what was wrong, but their stern glances forbade any talking. Later that day the king took Rosa aside.

"Tell me what you think of your cousin Edmund," he said.

"I am not sure," she stammered. "I am glad that we are friends, but he confuses me." She did not say that at times she felt a darkness about him and did not know if she could trust him.

The king paced up and down and then turned again to Rosa. "Would you be averse to marrying him?" he asked.

"Marriage!" the princess burst out. "I've never thought of marriage!"

"And why not," the king demanded. "You are of age."

"Why, because!" the princess responded, and then she spoke of that which she had never spoken of before with her father. "Because of the curse."

The king grew white about the lips, and his face turned the color ash. "Even more of a reason," he said in a low voice, and then motioned her to leave.

Rosa left with her heart pounding. She realized now that Edmund had spoken to her father and that he intended to marry her. All of a sudden, a sharp image of Edmund mesmerized by the white snake's gaze back in the summer palace flashed in her mind. She thrust the image away. She would not believe that Edmund wished to marry her to secure the throne, and he was not to blame for his father and mother.

She climbed up to the top of the castle parapets to clear her head, but unexpectedly happened upon Edmund speaking to one of the guards. She froze, poised as a bird about to take wing, but Edmund saw her, saw her hesitation, and came striding towards her. Rosa overcame her desire to run away, knowing that it would look foolish.

"You have spoken to your father," Edmund stated when he reached her.

She nodded.

"What did he say?"

"He asked if I would mind marrying you."

Edmund was silent for a moment and then said, "That is not how I would have had it. I merely asked if he could find out what you felt about me. Testing the waters, so to speak."

"But you do wish to marry me?"

"Yes."

"Why?" Rosa asked, meeting his eyes.

"I would save you from the curse," he answered.

"And you think marriage will accomplish this?"

"What else would?" he asked earnestly. "How else will you find the love required? Do you believe that you will meet someone in your dreams? Or that someone will simply gaze on your sleeping form and fall madly in love? How is it that you expect to break the curse?"

"I had not thought about it," Rosa said, running her fingers over the rough, stone crenellations.

"How can you be so maddening?" Edmund exclaimed. "You should be fighting against this curse with your very last breath."

"I only found out about the curse last summer. Besides, my faerie godparents will protect me."

"How can you trust them? The faerie never fully reveal their true intentions to mortals." He lowered his voice. "I know what it is like to live with a curse hanging over your head. Now I know you bear the brunt of it, but I am still cursed through my mother, through my blood, through the part she played on your christening day. I would not have this evil befall you, not while there is breath in my body or my heart beats against my breast." The last he spoke hoarsely, bringing her finger tips to his lips.

Rosa gazed at him, captured by the fire in his eyes. Then she slowly pulled her hand away. "I will think on it," she whispered before she fled the castle walls.

ROSA went searching for Edwina down in the infirmary with the hope that her friend could soothe her confusion, but stopped at the doorway. Edwina was dressing the young man's wound and smiling at him gently. The young man's eyes lit up at her smile in a way that made Rosa's heart ache. All at once Rosa felt all alone and left without disturbing the two of them.

She went up to her room and sat on her bed. Had Edwina left her? Had she found something that they could not share? The princess shook her head. "Don't be selfish, Rosa," she muttered, clutching a pillow to her chest. She wanted Edwina to be happy, particularly after she was gone. "But not now," she whispered. "I don't want to be alone now, I can't be alone now."

THAT night, Rosa began having nightmares. She was standing alone at the top of the castle parapets. The air was brittle, the ground below hard, as dense snowfall engulfed the entire kingdom. A staff of lead, heavy and cruel, thrust in a tall mound of snow, appeared below her. It radiated a dull heat, and from its source the snow slowly melted, leaving the earth barren and the trees withered. Darkness fell, and one by one the stars peeped out their heads to move in their song and dance. But then the staff throbbed, disturbing their harmony, so that the stars began singing on their own accord regardless of the overarching melody. The song was broken, and the notes became piercing cries, until, one by one, the stars fell silent and became cold flames in the sky.

The silence of the stars woke Rosa from her nightmare, and she rushed to her window. The moon was full, and the stars were twinkling merrily, and it was all a dream. Still, Rosa was filled by a sense of foreboding that her dream was no ordinary dream, but something that might come to pass, though she did not understand what it meant.

IN the morning, her father again called her before him and asked if she had thought over her marriage to Edmund.

"I don't know what I think," she said quietly. "But if I am unsure, I would rather not."

The king shook his head. "No, Rosa, that is not good enough. If you have no serious objections to Edmund, I will announce your engagement."

"Why!" Rosa cried. "Can you not wait until I have thought it over more? What if it is a mistake?"

"What if it is a mistake to do nothing!" the king cried. He clutched her by the shoulders. "Rosa, do you not understand how powerless I feel? You are my treasure, my only child. There is nothing that I can do for you to save you from the Dark Lady's curse. But if Edmund can save you, if there is even a breath of hope, then we must fight your fate with all that we have." He tenderly caressed her cheek. "I will not lose my little girl by doing nothing."

Rosa's eyes brimmed with tears, and she clutched her father's hands. "I will think on it, father. Please give me some time before you announce anything."

"I will do as you ask, Rosa, but know that, in the end, I will announce your engagement."

IN THE music room, Rosa was plucking the strings of her harp at random until she realized that she was playing the song the stars had sung in her dream. Her fingers recoiled from the strings as if they had burned her fingers. She sensed another presence and looked up to see Edmund watching her from the doorway. He came in to sit beside her and said, "Something has disturbed you, tell me."

Rosa bit her lip and began to play again, but this time a well-known and familiar tune. Edmund listened for a while and then said, "You know, I love watching you play."

Her fingers once again fell away from the strings, and she opened her mouth to ask the question that was building up inside her so much she might burst.

"Edmund, you say you want to marry me to save me from the curse. But do you love me?"

"Rosa," he said, taking her hand, "we share a darkness, you and I, the darkness of the curse. Yet you remain untouched by it and serve as a light to my own. How could I not love you?"

Rosa saw the pain in his eyes, and knew he was speaking the truth. "Edmund, I am not sure if I love you," she said sincerely. "At least, I know that I care for you, but I don't know if I love you in the way that you want. How can I be sure of my own feelings?"

"Let my certainty be enough for the both of us," he exclaimed, and Rosa's hand was squeezed in his tightening grip.

"Rosa, I want you to marry me, I want you to marry me soon. The one thing we do not have is time. Our love must be strong enough to overcome the curse, so that, when you fall asleep, I can wake you. I will not have you condemned to an eternal sleep! You are too bright, too beautiful, the shining star in my life." He leaned forward to kiss her, but his words recalled to Rosa the stars in her dream. She felt a pang of fear and snatched her hand away.

"Rosa, do you feel nothing for me?" he cried.

"No, it isn't that, but this is too much, too quickly. Marriage, the curse... this is all too important. Oh, I don't know." She wailed, standing and wringing her hands. "Thank you, Edmund, thank you so much. I will think about your proposal. I will think on it long and hard."

She was gone, and Edmund sat alone in the music room staring at the harp she had so recently been playing.

ROSA'S continued nightmares and anxiety over Edmund's proposal left her desperate to confide in Edwina. She felt that her parents and Alice wouldn't understand her misapprehensions about Edmund, knowing as she did that they would grasp at any means to save her. But she hardly ever saw her handmaid anymore as all of Edwina's time was given over to tending to the injured man, so it was with surprise that when she went for a walk in the castle grounds, she glimpsed Edwina in a secluded spot in the distance, sheltering under the boughs of an ash tree.

Edwina's back was toward her, but she must have heard Rosa's footsteps, because she turned to face the princess with a brave smile. Rosa, however, wasn't fooled; she saw that Edwina's eyes were red, as if she had been crying.

"Edwina dear, what is the matter?" she asked.

Edwina's smile fell. At first, she tried to deny that anything was wrong, but then finally she broke down and sobbed against Rosa's shoulder.

"Giles says he loves me."

So that is the young man's name, Rosa thought.

"Oh, Rosa, I can't believe it's true. He's wonderful, so kind and so gentle. I can't believe he could ever care for someone like me."

"Silly Edwina." Rosa smiled, shaking her friend by the shoulders. "Is that all? Of course he loves you. He cannot help himself any more than I can. You are so good and so true. Dry your tears and tell me, do you feel the same way about him?"

Edwina lowered her face. "I know he loves me if he says so. But Rosa, I'm a nobody, a common kitchen girl. His love for me can do nothing but harm him. His family can't accept me, and neither would the court. Someday he will tire of fighting the world for me. And... and... I'm not beautiful..." Edwina made an unconscious gesture toward her scarred cheek, but caught herself just in time. Rosa, however, noticed her movement, and a wave of sadness and regret washed over her. Edwina had never reproached her for the scar, but Rosa could only feel sorrow over her past cruelty and thoughtlessness that had forever marred her friend's face.

Rosa threw her arms around Edwina and kissed her on both cheeks, once over the scar. "Edwina, no one who knows you could help but love you. That Giles wants to marry you shows his worth. Now answer me plainly. Do you love him?"

Edwina clutched the princess' arm. "I love him so. I don't want to let him go."

"Nor should you!" Rosa cried. "You are my dearest friend, and you are no longer a kitchen girl, but my handmaid. I can speak to my father and mother and arrange the match, and we can give you such a dowry and hold your place in the court with such high esteem, that nobody could object."

"Oh, no, Rosa, I couldn't ask for that. I wasn't going to tell you. Only you caught me by surprise."

"And I am glad that I did. Otherwise you would be breaking your heart for no reason. Do you think I would let my dearest friend suffer when it is in my power to make her happy?"

Edwina threw herself in Rosa's arms. "Oh, my dear princess," she sobbed, "I'm so unbearably happy."

Rosa went straightaway to her mother and poured out Edwina's story, and the queen kept silent until Rosa had finished. The princess was seated beside her mother and looked earnestly into her face. "Mother, do you not think that they should marry if they love each other?" she asked.

Her words pulled the queen from her reverie, and she smiled at her daughter. "Yes, I do," she admitted. "What strange magic you work, my little rose. I would have thought differently not so long ago. But now I see that nothing could be simpler. Do not worry. I will take the matter in hand and speak to your father. Only..." And here she softly caressed Rosa's cheek. "You must weave the same spell for yourself, my dear. I would trust in your own heart when it comes to love and not let other cares and fears overwhelm what you know to be true." The queen tucked a gold strand of Rosa's hair behind her ear. "I am sorry that I was lost for so long, but I will never leave your side again."

As her mother embraced her, Rosa felt that a burden was lifted. Rosa now understood that if she refused Edmund's proposal, her mother would be at her side, and she rested in her mother's arms for a long while.

EDWINA and Giles were married with great festivity, and, for once, the princess did not outshine her handmaid. Joy so transfixed Edwina's face on her wedding day that everyone in the castle glimpsed the girl whom Rosa saw in the mirror when they first had met. After the wedding ceremony, the king danced the first dance with the bride and then handed her over to her new husband. Giles moved stiffly on his injured leg, but it did not seem that either bride or groom minded. They had only eyes for one another, and he glowed when he held Edwina in his arms.

Rosa sighed with happiness as she watched them, and Edmund met her eyes from across the room. She gave him a bright smile, and the question flitted in her mind. "Could Edmund and I ever love one another the way Edwina and Giles do?"

Edmund strode across the room, took the princess in his arms, and they danced. The entire court watched, and, for the first time, Rosa could imagine herself marrying Edmund. Then she saw her father gazing at them intently, and, when she caught his eye, he gave her a nod. Her eyes darted away, and she saw that her Uncle Stefan was also watching them.

"What is it, Rosa? You seem distracted," Edmund asked.

Rosa shook her head, but then sighed, "Oh, Edmund, I wish you were asking me to marry you without the curse. Then I would not feel as if my decision was being forced."

"Rosa, I promise that I will not marry you if you do not wish me to. If you say no, I will withdraw my claim, and then neither your father nor mine could force you into marriage."

"Truly?" she whispered.

Edmund nodded. "Yes," he said and drew her closer to him, "I want you to feel perfectly free."

They spoke not another word as they linked arms and spun in a tight circle. Then, even though he passed her on to the waiting partner next in line, Rosa felt her fears dissolving in the hope that he loved her and would do all that he could to rescue her.

ROSA fell asleep happy that night, but her dreams were yet again disturbed by nightmares. This time the night sky shone brilliantly with stars, but then the stars were no longer in the sky, but woven in a tapestry. There they danced among the threads, singing in gold and silver waves. Then the heavy, ominous thud of shearing scissors rent through the air, and, one by one, the golden threads snapped, dissolving into inky blackness. The magic was snuffed from the tapestry, and the stars were nothing but woven threads, grey and lifeless.

Rosa woke in a cold sweat; terror beat in her temples and shortened her breath. "No, I won't let the stars die," she whispered hoarsely. "Edmund and I will fight the darkness together."

She threw on her cloak and desperately went out in search of him, but somehow, to her mounting dismay, she found herself lost in her very own castle. Tall shadows fell from forbidding arches. All the corridors twisted in a maze that inevitably led her to the thick oaken door before the high tower stairs. Every time she found herself at the door, she turned around in a rising tide of panic, searching for another path, but, no matter how many times she took a different way, her feet always led her to the high tower door. Her churning emotions settled down into a determined resolve. She knew that she must climb. She firmly grasped the cold, iron handle and heaved open the door.

The climb up the dark, winding stairway seemed endless. A hushed silence seemed to muffle even her own footsteps, so that all she could hear was the rapid pitter patter of her own heart until she finally reached the top of the tower. There, bathed in the moonlight shining from the open window, stood the Green Lady.

Rosa hesitated. Before, she would have immediately thrown herself straight into her godmother's arms, but now she wavered, a reproach forming at the tip of her tongue. The Green Lady smiled softly, and the smile drew the princess to her.

"I had a nightmare," Rosa said. "The stars had gone out, and the golden threads were cut."

The Green Lady nodded.

"Of course, you know all that. You know everything that happens to me. You know what I must do."

The Green Lady smiled more softly still.

"Tell me what I must do to keep the stars from going out," Rosa demanded.

The Green Lady held out her arms. "My princess, you are full of doubts, come and I will comfort you."

Rosa shook her head. "No, that will not do any good. I am not a child any more to be soothed and kept in the dark. Tell me what I must do."

"Princess, if I told you now what lies in your path and what you must do to overcome the Dark Lady's curse, you would not believe me or doubt that it could ever come to pass. You will do what your heart wishes either way. But if you choose wrongly, it would be much worse for you to do so fully knowing than only half- knowing."

"But I will not do nothing!" Rosa cried. "I know that you want me to discover my gifts, but I do not understand what use they will be if I fall asleep. My father is right. I cannot wait for the curse to fall. Edmund and I will fight my fate together. We will marry, and he will save me from my sleep. Can you think of a better way?" Rosa lifted her chin defiantly.

The Green Lady still spoke softly, but the smile left her. "You would marry Edmund to escape your sleep? Do you love him?"

"Yes." Rosa's voice faltered. "At least, I think I might." She shook her head and said in an agonized voice, "How is one supposed to know? I felt that I could, in his arms tonight. I know that he loves me and that he wants to save me."

Her godmother's voice was stern. "And you would use his love out of fear?"

"No!" Rosa cried, stung by the accusation. "It is not like that. Edmund cares for me, and I care for him. We will marry, and he will wake me from my sleep because he loves me. Then we will rule the kingdom in peace, and my father and mother won't have to suffer anymore. If you have a better plan, you must tell me what to do. Otherwise I will marry Edmund."

"You wish to bargain with me?" The Green Lady's tone was hard and forbidding. She seemed to grow taller, blocking out the moonlight, her shadow stretching ominously long across the room.

Rosa shrank and clutched at her head. "You won't tell me anything! You warn me about the curse, but you will not show me how to break it. Then why do you come here?"

The Green Lady remained silent.

"How can you say nothing? If what you truly want is for me is to fall asleep with no hope, then I cannot do that. Just leave me be."

The Green Lady spoke. "Beware of what you say, Rosa. You belong to the line of the Golden Kings, and your words have power. If you send me away, then I will not come back to you until the trial has come to pass, and you will have need of me before long."

"Will you tell me what I must do?"

The Green Lady said nothing.

"Then go."

For a long moment her last words hung heavy in the air. Then the Green Lady spoke. "As you wish, Princess Rosamund. But I leave you with this final word of warning: If you do not take care, you will bring about the very fate you seek to escape." With those parting words, the Green Lady was gone.

Rosa felt a dull, heavy ache inside. Had she really just sent her godmother away? Why wouldn't her godmother tell her things like she used to?

Her head throbbing, Rosa managed to stumble down the tower steps. She no longer wished to see Edmund. She did not wish to see anyone. Rosa found her way back to her room and collapsed in weariness on her bed.

WHEN she awoke the next day, the events from the night before seemed shrouded in a mist and Rosa could barely believe that they had happened, except for the dull ache in the pit of her stomach that was her fear. The days passed, and, though Rosa slept fitfully, she no longer had any nightmares. She resolved that, for her parents' and Edmund's sakes, she would fight the curse. If Edmund truly loved her as he said, then she would wake up when he kissed her.

But does he? A little voice that she tried to banish whispered in her head. Does he love you enough to wake you? And do you? Do you love him enough to wake up when he calls?

She shook her head. This was her only chance, and that was why they must marry, so that their love would be strong enough when the time came.

The princess did not confide in Edwina her fears or her plan to marry Edmund. If she did, she feared the little voice would become stronger and cause her to waver in her resolve. Edwina noticed at times that Rosa was troubled and would grasp her hand, begging her to tell her what was wrong, but Rosa would shake her head, smile, and say that it was nothing, so eventually Edwina let the matter drop.

ROSA'S engagement to Edmund was announced. Her father did not ask her finally if she would accept the engagement, but she did not try to stop him from announcing it either. It is the only way, she thought.

Edmund stood beside her as the king proclaimed their engagement before the entire court. He grasped the princess' hand as the court broke into a ringing applause that thundered painfully in the Rosa's head. All she could see was a whirl of bright colors from the ladies' gowns and she suddenly felt sick to her stomach. The engagement made the day of her curse feel so much nearer. Was she making a mistake? Edmund must have seen that she was in a daze, so he kissed her hand, which made the court cheer even louder. One by one, the lords and ladies filed up to congratulate the newly engaged couple. Stefan was the first of all to approach and kiss her hand, but Rosa avoided his gaze.

After the engagement ceremony, Edwina accompanied the princess to her room. Rosa could see that Edwina felt hurt that she had not told her of the engagement beforehand, and an unnatural silence hung between them. The queen was waiting for them at Rosa's bedroom door. "I will put the princess to bed," she said, so Edwina departed.

Rosa could not remember a time when her mother had ever tucked her into bed and burst out crying. The queen held Rosa's hand and smoothed back her hair until her sobs subsided. "My dear," the queen said, "do you regret your engagement?"

Rosa dried her eyes and shook her head. "No, it is not that," she said. "The day has just been weary and long. I will feel better after I rest."

The queen remained at the princess' bedside until finally Rosa whispered. "If you spoke with father, do you think he might call off the engagement?"

After a long pause the queen spoke. "You father believes that your engagement will save you from the curse. I do not know if even my words could sway him."

Rosa gazed long and hard into her mother's eyes. "What do you believe? Do you think that Edmund can break the curse?"

"I do not know, my dear. I hope he can. But I have misgivings, since you heart is so full of doubt."

"No, there is no doubt," Rosa said quickly. "You and father do not need to worry anymore. On the eve of my christening I will fall asleep, and Edmund will wake me on the morrow, and it will have been just like any other sleep."

The queen bent over and tenderly kissed her daughter on the forehead. "I will pray that it is so," she said.

THE weeks passed by, and a seething tumult of cooks, chambermaids, gardeners, and servants invaded the castle in preparations for the wedding festivities. It was only a few days away when, without warning, the queen fell ill.

Rosa was at her mother's sick bed day and night, and the king was with them too. Both watched in horror as the queen grew weaker and weaker.

"Godmother, where are you?" Rosa cried to herself, but then she remembered that she had sent her away. She was not sure if her godmother had the power to heal her mother, but she could have used her strong arms of comfort now.

Alice and Edwina stayed with Rosa to make sure that she ate and slept, though the princess never felt hungry and could only sleep fitfully for a few hours at a time. The court physician shook his head and declared that there was nothing he could do. Then, unexpectedly, the queen seemed to recover, falling into a peaceful slumber. The king and princess clasped hands in hope, but then a shadow trembled over the queen's face, and she awoke.

"Aurleon," she cried, not seeing him.

"I am here, my heart," he said, reaching for her outstretched hand.

"I had a dream," she gasped. "Promise me…"

"Anything, I promise you anything," he said fervently.

"Our Rosa, if she chooses not to marry Edmund, do not force it upon her. Promise me."

Rosa's blood ran cold. Her father sobbed into his wife's hand. "I promise, but you will stay with me and can see to it yourself."

The queen stretched her other hand out to her daughter. "Rosa, my love, how silly and meaningless were those years I spent trying not to love you because I knew you would be leaving me, and now I am the one to go first. Can you ever forgive me?"

"Do not speak of leaving." Rosa sobbed and kissed the queen's hands over and over again. "If there is anything to forgive, I do it gladly. I love you so much."

The queen fell asleep, and then she died, both her hands clasped by her husband and daughter.

THE kingdom went into mourning, the wedding preparations forgotten. The king was inconsolable and the princess could not spend time with her own grief as she was needed to comfort her father.

Rosa was taking a rare moment alone in the garden, leaning against a tree whose leaves had just burst into the flames of autumn. The sky was a thin blanket of cloud, and its faint mist sprayed a thin layer of wetness against her skin.

Someone settled beside her, and she knew it was Edmund.

He did not say anything, but waited silently with her. She slowly opened her eyes and let in a wash of brightness. There was something she needed to say to Edmund, but she did not know how to start. When she turned to speak, she saw that she did not need to, that he had already read her words in her glance. It was so easy for him to understand hidden looks, to spy secrets.

"You do not wish to be married," he said.

She nodded.

"Why? Is it because it is so soon? I can wait. I will wait as long as you need."

"Are you willing to wait, Edmund?" She reached for his hand. "Are you willing to wait until after my sleep?"

A veil fell over his face. "I do not understand. Why do you not wish to get married? Have you given up?"

"No, Edmund, I have not given up. I have realized that we are trying to trick magic, to control it by our marriage, and we are sure to fail that way. My godmother tried to warn me, but I sent her away."

"Your godmother again," he cried, rising. "Will you ever be free of those meddling faerie? You would rather depend on them than on yourself. It is not that you are afraid. You are no coward, Rosa…" And here his voice took on a pleading tone, "…It is just that you are too childlike, too trusting. Rosa, cannot you see it? What deeper love is there than between man and wife? You would be mine to claim by human and by faerie law. What curse could stand against that?"

Rosa shook her head. "No, Edmund, you always try to control magic, and that is why it eludes you. Words and deeds are nothing if they do not come from the heart."

Edmund's face drained to a ghastly shade of white, and his eyes burned. He gave a short laugh. "You have all the answers, don't you, princess. None of this is your fault. It must be my love that is not strong enough. Very well, reject all those who wish to help you. Sleep eternally if you wish."

He spun away from her, but she sprang up to grab his hand. "Wait, don't go away angry. It is not only my godmother, you see, but my mother as well. This was her last gift to me: my freedom. She saw that there was something wrong with our marriage, that it was built on fear and not on love. We must wait for the curse to be broken. It cannot hang over our heads, forcing our marriage. Edmund, if you love me and believe that you can wake me from my sleep, then you will. After that, we will know that we truly love one another. That is what my mother saw, and the gift she gave me with her dying breath. How can I reject her wish? Do you see now, can you understand?"

"All I see is that you are choosing the wishes of a woman who abandoned you as a child. Whose last gift of love, as you call it, is to condemn you to the curse. You choose her over someone who loves you and wishes to save you. I see that you put your faith in everyone except for me. You are the one who doubts my love, who thinks me incapable of love, but it is your own love that falls too short. I take it back. You are a coward. Tell me plainly you do not love me. You would rather be cursed than marry me."

Rosa dropped Edmund's hand. "If that is what you believe, then go. I will tell my father my decision on my own."

EDMUND leapt on his horse and rode long and deep into the woods, the pounding of his horse's hoofs drowning out the raging in his head. In the dark of the wood, he finally dismounted, when unexpectedly his horse shied away, breaking from him in blind terror. Edmund muttered curses under his breath as he watched it gallop away back toward the castle. He turned and saw what had set his horse affright. A white snake slithered deep in the undergrowth. Edmund stared at it in fascination as it glided nearer and reared its head, so that he stared deeply into its strange, slitted eyes.

Back in the garden, Rosa felt the chill in the air around her. It will be winter soon, she thought, and I will not be awake to see the spring.

Chapter Sixteen

The Spinning Wheel

ERIK AND CYNRIC RETURNED from one of their morning hunts to find a large gathering in the great hall. The prince left the hunter's side and ducked through the assembly until he was in view of his father. King Mark sat rigidly in his throne with a look on his face that Erik knew well enough to fear. The queen sat by his side as tall as a spear shaft, her lips drawn in a straight line, her eyes kindled embers. Before the king and queen stood a messenger in a livery Erik did not recognize, but he knew was the royal blue of the west.

The king was speaking to the messenger in a voice smooth with suppressed anger. "If Lord Biron of Westhane refuses to pay fealty to his king, then let him answer for his treason with cold, hard steel... Lord Clovis!" he called.

One of the lords of the hall stepped forward. He was a tall man, with a cruel set to his mouth, known as a ruthless man by friend and enemy alike.

"Yes, my lord." He bowed.

"Take a contingent of soldiers and crush this rebellion before Westhane has time to draw the other western lords to his cause. Send me news as soon as it is over," the king commanded.

Lord Clovis stiffly inclined his head and strode out of the hall.

When he was gone, the king barked, "Imprison the messenger. We cannot have him warning his treasonous lord."

"Your majesty, please hear me," the messenger protested.

"Lord Biron does not wish to start a rebellion, though he will defend the western lands to the last man. We cannot allow our lands to be ravaged and our people starved."

The king's eyes flashed, and he signaled to the guards. They surrounded the messenger in a clatter of armor and bore him away. The king rose, spitting out further orders before he also strode out of the hall to oversee the dispatch of Lord Clovis' troops. The rest of the lords of the hall dispersed, but Erik stayed behind.

Erik felt solemn. There had been tenuous peace with the west ever since the king had married his mother, but now it seemed that the peace was over. Was a civil war about to break out that would pit his mother's and father's peoples against each other? Erik hoped that such tragedy would not come to pass, that the Lord of Westhane would acquiesce to the king's demands when he saw the might of the Midlothian troops.

The prince turned and saw that he was not alone. Cynric stood quietly in one of the shadowy alcoves lost in thought, an unreadable expression on his face. The huntsman looked up, noticed that the prince was watching him, and, with echoing footsteps, left the hall. Erik followed him out into the courtyard and through the main gate, catching up with him at the steep, rocky mountain path, where their paces fell together as they journeyed through the wood in silence.

When they reached the hunter's lodge, Cyrnic let him inside without a word. Erik sat on a wooden bench draped with a red fox skin pelt. More pelts were spread across the floor, and branching antlers hung from the walls, with the tree-forked antlers of a mighty stag adorning the fireplace. Cynric poured Erik and himself some wine.

Finally Erik spoke. "Do you think there will be civil war?"

Cynric shrugged. "It's hard to tell. Until recently, the west was continuously starting uprisings that didn't amount to much."

"Does the west hate my father that much?"

Cynric gazed at the prince thoughtfully. Erik felt that a bond had been forged between them ever since they had encountered the great bear together in the wood, that they could speak their minds to each other without fear. The hunter must have felt the same, for he said, "There are many in the west who do not believe the Midlothian kings are the rightful heirs to the Lothian throne."

"They are waiting for the sleeping princess to wake and bring back the golden kingdom of Aurlia," Erik whispered.

Cynric stared at the prince. "Where did you hear of the old legends?" he asked in surprise.

Erik evaded the question. "Do you believe that my father is a usurper?"

Cynric cocked his eyebrow at the prince and laughed. "What makes a king a king? Powerful men battle over the throne, and the one left standing is the ruler."

"But that is no way to keep the throne. Whoever rules that way lives in fear that it will be stolen when someone else grows even more powerful. To keep that from happening, he oppresses the land."

Cynric studied the prince. "Sometimes I cannot make you out. You are not like your father or other Midlothians. I often wonder if it will be different when you are king."

"Now *you* don't sound like a Midlothian."

Cynric laughed and then leaned over to ruffle the prince's hair. "Me? I don't call myself anything. The forest is my home."

BEFORE the week was out, a rider thundered across the castle drawbridge with a message for the king.

"We were betrayed," he cried. "The Lord of Westhane knew we were coming and ambushed us at the pass. Lord Clovis retreated, but lost over half of his men. He asks for reinforcements and awaits your orders."

Eric's attention fastened on the king, who remained ominously silent and then waved the messenger aside. He turned his burning eyes to the queen and whispered, "Discover who betrayed me."

Queen Sigrid met the king's eyes with an unflinching gaze, and her voice was smooth with a hint of laughter. "How would you have me do that, my king?"

"I do not know how you accomplish many things, and I do not want to know. Just do it."

The king stormed out of the hall.

THE next morning, Erik was in his room when he heard noises ringing from the courtyard through his bedroom window. Leaning out, he distinguished three guards escorting a prisoner.

Erik gasped. The prisoner was Cynric.

He flew down to the king's war room, bursting through the door. The king was plotting out a route for his fighting men over a large map of Lothene with the queen and the other lords of the hall at his side. Everyone fell silent and fixed their gazes on the prince. The king's brow darkened, but Erik was past caring.

"Why is Cynric under arrest?" he asked.

The king and queen exchanged glances. "Cynric is a spy and a traitor. We discovered that it was he who sent a messenger and warned the Lord of Westhane of our attack," the king answered.

"How do you know?" Erik asked with a sinking heart.

The king's face grew darker and even more forbidding.

"Missives from Lord Clovis were found in his lodge. He admitted to sending a warning to the western lord under questioning." This time it was the queen who spoke, her eyes never leaving the prince's face.

Erik shivered. "What will happen to him?" he asked in a small voice.

"He will be executed as befits a traitor." The king looked

down at the map, effectively dismissing the prince. Erik could not move, so the queen rose to take his hand and then led him from the war room.

"When?" Erik asked in a dull voice. His heart had turned to lead in the pit of his stomach.

"Tomorrow."

Queen Sigrid regarded Erik, her eyes searing into his. "You cannot be seen to have sympathy with traitors. You must not forget who you are. You will stand beside the king at the execution and you will not turn away."

Erik bowed his head.

IN the courtyard, the stark morning light was so bright Erik needed to shield his eyes. The executioner's block loomed in the middle of the yard, bleak and foreboding. Kenelm called the guards to attention, and Cynric was escorted to the courtyard.

The huntsman walked with his head held high, resolutely staring straight ahead as the Captain of the Guard read the sentence aloud. Erik could not tear his gaze from Cynric's defiant form, and, for an instant, their eyes met, and they shared a look that seemed to say that this was not how the world was supposed to be, but then the hunter gazed at the king and his face grew hard.

Cynric's head was roughly thrust on the block, and the sun gleamed on the keen edge of the upraised axe. The axe fell swiftly. Erik turned his face away and heard five heavy strokes. At each stroke, his heart split in two. Then the crowd broke into wild cheers, and when Erik looked up, the executioner was holding Cynric's severed head high up in the air. He scanned the crowd of men and women of the castle cheering over the death of one whom they so recently had called friend and saw the queen watching him, her lips curled in disdain.

THE queen called Erik to her chamber that evening. "King Mark will leave tomorrow with his men to free the traitorous lord of his lands of Westhane. You will leave as well, but not to battle. Instead you will depart for Castle Wallstone in the northeast to stay with your uncle, Lord Denis."

An ice-cold hand gripped Erik's heart. His first thought was for Ninny Nanny. Would he no longer be able to visit her?

"Why?" he burst out. "Wouldn't it be better for me to stay here with you while the king is gone?"

The queen shook her head. "No, I will be riding with the king. It does not suit me stay behind and wait. That strength, young prince, is something that you lack. You looked away at the traitor's death."

Erik stared down at the floor. "He was my friend."

"He betrayed the king, you, and all of Lothene. The kingdom will be yours one day. If you show such softness, it will be wrenched from your weak grasp."

Erik felt miserable.

The queen grabbed his chin, her nails digging into his flesh like sharp thorns. She stared at him long and hard, a small smile blossoming on her face, and Erik shuddered.

"Fear not, young prince. I will always be here to look after you and Lothene. But go…" She released him. "Prepare for your departure."

ERIK ran madly into the woods, searching for Mnemosyne. Where was that blasted cat when he truly needed it? If he didn't see Ninny Nanny today, then he would have to leave without saying goodbye. He gulped down the sob growing in his throat. He continued searching desperately for Ninny Nanny's cottage on his own until it grew dark and he realized with a heavy heart that he would have to give up.

Before dawn the next day, Erik was sitting astride his horse, blinking back sleep. Kenelm was at his side; the sword master was to travel with him to Castle Wallstone. Erik feared that Kenelm resented losing his post as Captain of the Guard to watch over him, but, if the stoic guardsman felt a grudge, he did not show it.

Soldiers filed into the courtyard with gleaming helms and shields. King Mark rode at the head, mighty and strong. The queen rode beside him, the glow in her eyes rivaling the brightness of her armor as she blazed with the ancient fire of the warrior queens of the north. Gazing at them both made Erik instinctively sit taller on his horse.

Before his departure, King Mark spoke to Erik. "You are to go to your uncle's castle. It is constantly under threat from northern raiders who pillage our coastal cities. Perhaps there you will finally learn how to use that sword arm of yours."

Erik did not speak, but his spirit grew grave within him.

"You will look after the boy," the king said, turning to Kenelm.

"I will guard the crown prince with my life."

The king returned to the head of the army and gave the order to march. The soldiers thundered past Erik, the light of the sunrise glinting off their helms and shields. Erik waited until the resounding clash of armor was a dull roar in the distance and then he looked up at his sword master. "Shall we depart?"

Kenelm shook his head. "No, I have things to take care of. Meet me here at midday."

The unlooked for reprieve kindled a newborn hope in Erik's breast, and, as soon as Kenelm was out of sight, he dashed into the wood, hoping against hope that Mnemosyne would be waiting for him at her usual spot.

There she was, watching his approach with her unblinking, yellow eyes. At the sight of the cat, Erik let out a sound that was a mixture between a sob and a laugh. Mnemosyne led Erik straight to Ninny Nanny's cottage as if she knew that there was no time to waste. The old woman met Erik at the door.

"I've come to say good bye," said Erik as he threw himself into her arms.

"There, there, princeling, don't be so sad. Ye will come back to the castle one day, and Mnemosyne and I will be waiting for ye."

The prince burrowed himself further into the old woman's embrace. Then he whispered. "Cynric is dead."

The old woman tightened her arms around him, and Erik remained quiet a few moments more, but then he withdrew and peered up into her face. "Why did he have to die? Why did Cynric betray my father? I thought he was my friend."

The old woman brushed the prince's hair out of his eyes and then shook her head sadly. "Cynric was your friend, but his heart's loyalty was divided as the kingdom is divided. He could not see his people die."

"Were the western people his people?"

"Yes, princeling, and they are your people, too. All the people in Lothene are your people."

"I don't think my father and the queen see it that way. The west is strange to them; they fear it. Yet those they fear are my mother's people. How am I to decide whose side I am on? My father is the king, and I cannot betray him."

"Princeling, it is right that ye be loyal to your father and still love your mother's people. Ye have both old blood and new blood in your veins an' the strength and weakness of both. Ye are a strong and courageous lad, and that comes from your father. Ye are gentle and love the things of old, and that comes from your mother. It is by being both that ye will unite the kingdom one day."

"Ninny Nanny, what am I to do without you? Am I really not going to see you when I am gone?"

Ninny Nanny shook her head, and Erik felt his hope extinguished like a burnt out candle. "I had hoped that somehow… since your cottage seems to move… that I would still be able to visit you," he whispered.

"I am sorry, princeling, but my cottage belongs to this wood. Ye must be strong and patient, and ye must remember all my stories."

"I will never forget your stories. Nor will I forget the princess."

The old woman smiled sadly. "Most of all, ye will have to be brave, even though you don't know what might happen, princeling. It was the same with Princess Rosamund when she had to face her curse."

"Tell me what happens to the princess, Ninny Nanny. Tell me how she falls asleep."

"That I will do, princeling. Though ye don't have much time left, ye have just time enough."

👑 👑 👑

THICK SHEETS OF RAIN washed the snow away from heavily traveled roads and byways. The thaw had set it, but the cold wind and wet days still brought a damp shiver to limbs wrapped in wools and furs. It had been a long and tiring winter. The king was still stricken by his wife's death, and Rosa even missed his bouts of fiery temper. Though they dined together every evening, she could not draw him from the cloud he had wandered in to. He was irritable if she was ever late, but was silent for as long as the meal lasted. She did know that he needed her, that she was, in fact, indispensable, so she sat in audience with him every day, gently intervening in his judgments, and the people grew to love their golden princess.

The king no longer forbade Rosa from leaving the castle, and she took to visiting the poor and sick in the city, distributing loaves of bread to the beggars at the gates. She never felt unsafe. Not only did she trust in her people's love, but she felt that the impending fatality of the curse also draped over her like a mantle, shielding her from harm. She had the stirring suspicion that, whenever anyone looked at her, they also imagined her body laid out lifeless in her chamber, her voice silent, fallen prey to the curse, and she realized that sadness mingled with all the joy she brought.

THE day before the curse was destined to fall, Rosa had asked to be left alone for a time in her chamber and was surprised to see her Uncle Stefan at the door when she looked up from a letter she had been writing to Alice. Various letters were neatly sealed with wax and lined up on her table, final farewells to all those she loved.

"Can I do anything for you, Uncle Stefan?" she asked politely, but without any touch of warmth. She was no longer afraid of her uncle. He was so much smaller than the curse and smaller than her mother's death, but that did not mean she wished to spend any more time in his company than was strictly necessary.

"Can I not simply desire to enjoy the princess' company?"

"No," she said.

"No? You do not wish me to stay?"

"No, you would not seek me out merely for my company. May I ask you what it is you wish from me?"

Stefan chuckled. "How very straightforward, very different from the blushing princess who hid behind Edmund that summer day I surprised the two of you in the forest. Can you believe that was two summers ago? Time's wheel turns relentlessly on, doesn't it, princess?"

Rosa refused to reply, so he continued, "You liked my son then, if I may be so bold to say. What causes you to refuse his offer now?"

"I would not be trapped into marriage in a futile attempt to avoid the curse."

"Poor princess, of course you are wise. That is no way to go about overcoming faerie magic. I admire your strength in facing the facts. You will succumb to the curse and sleep. You have no choice. But have you thought about your kingdom and your duty as the heir to the golden throne? Will you leave the kingdom without a successor? Civil war will break out, and many lives will be lost when the heir to the crown is unclear. As your husband, Edmund would be the natural choice to rule in your stead. Think of your people, princess. Surely you do not wish your last act before you sleep to be a selfish one? Who knows, perhaps Edmund will be able to wake you. There is always hope."

Rosa shook her head. "I do not understand why you wish me to marry. Edmund is the natural heir to the throne when I am gone, whether he be my husband or no. You are afraid and do not wish to leave anything to chance. You need not worry, Uncle Stefan. The curse will be fulfilled. Edmund will be king as the Dark Lady promised you long ago on my christening day."

Stefan's face sank into a lifeless grey. "How do you know?" he said hoarsely. "Out of all people, how is it that *you* know?"

"I was shown by the faerie. I know the part you played in my curse and in your wife's disappearance."

"How long have you known this?" Stefan asked.

"Since the summer palace."

"Why have you told no one?"

"I would not deprive Edmund of his father when he has already lost a mother. That and you have no more power. You will not interfere with the curse because you know it will do no good. Nor do you have any strength. The curse took everything away from you, didn't it?" Rosa asked, thinking of Iseult.

Stefan's shoulders sagged, the strength seeming to visibly seep from his frame. Watching him, Rosa realized that there was still something that she did not understand about her christening day. "I have always wondered why it was that no one knew it was you who summoned the Dark Lady. Surely only you could have done so?" she asked.

Stefan muttered bitterly. "They have all forgotten how Faerie and magic is tied to our blood. Iseult was turned into a serpent, so they blamed her; it was the easiest thing to do. And I have often thought that perhaps the curse protects me and clouds the minds of those who would look deeper."

Rosa felt a flutter of pity for her uncle. He was nothing more than a weak-willed man whose ambitions had claimed higher stakes than he had been prepared to pay. "You are afraid, afraid of the curse and afraid that it is not done with you yet, but you have nothing to fear from me, uncle. I will tell no one." She reached out to touch his hand, but Stefan drew away as though her touch burned him. He gave her a glance of horror mingled with guilt before he left.

THAT night Rosa lay in bed and wondered, as she had many times before, how the curse would inevitably fall. She could not imagine any scenario in which she would ever willingly prick her finger on a spindle. Would it be as simple as an accident? Would she fall into a trance, be without a choice? She was still angry at the Green Lady for choosing not to tell her how to overcome the curse, but she was even more angry at herself for sending her godmother away. She knew her godmother had been right about her only wishing to marry Edmund because she was afraid. She could admit that to herself now. But what was left for her to do? The Grey Lady had told her that, if she ran, the curse would still find her. There was nothing to do but wait and face whatever would come. Rosa buried her face in her pillow and cried herself to sleep.

THE sun rose glorious and bright on the morning of the eve of her christening. Rosa woke to birdsong, a song sparrow chirping in joyful anticipation of spring. The princess lay in her bed, drinking in the moment, the warmth of the sun against her skin, the pillow soft against her cheek, the beautiful silver thread of the stars woven on her canopy. Alice and Edwina entered, and Rosa leapt out of bed to throw her arms around them. Alice clutched the princess to her breast, and Edwina battled back tears.

Rosa went to her dresser and solemnly handed Alice her comb one final time. Edwina placed a crown of the first flowers of spring on Rosa's head. The flowers had been sheltering under the castle eaves away from the heavy spring rains and were carefully woven into a crown of crocus, snowdrop, and celandine. Alice drew Rosa close to her and kissed her, whispering, "Now go and say farewell to your people. You stole so quickly into their hearts."

ROSA spent the day among her subjects. She gave away every single thing of worth that she owned to the poor children of the city. The townspeople had prepared a large garland of flowers for her. "For your birthday," they said, unable to say out loud that it was a farewell present. Rosa was fighting back her tears, when a tall man wearing a long brown cloak parted through the crowd to stand at her side.

Rosa sniffed and looked up at the tall stranger. At first she had thought that the robed man was old, for his hair was as white as the whitest of snow, but, as she looked closer, she saw that his face showed no age, as if he were of faerie kind, but that his deep, black eyes reflected pain and loss in a way that only a mortal's could. An air of awe and solemnity settled around Rosa as she gazed at this strange man that was neither completely faerie nor completely mortal, and then he reverently took her hand and kissed it before turning away and disappearing into the crowd without a word.

WHEN Rosa returned to the castle, the sun was setting, and Neirin greeted her and Edwina at the gate. He held the princess' harp in one hand, his lute slung over his shoulder. Rosa word-lessly took the harp, and together they sang a song of farewell to the sun. When its uppermost rays left the horizon, their song was finished, and Rosa knew it was time to say their final fare-well.

"I shall resume my wanderings." Neirin spoke first. "And wherever I go, I shall sing of the princess who sleeps like the moon, whose beauty is like the sun, and who sings with the stars in her dreams."

The minstrel knelt, and Rosa, finding herself unable to speak, bent over and kissed him on the forehead. He gave her one last smile, half happy and half sad, and departed.

Edwina took Rosa's hand and clasped it tightly, as if she was daring the world to separate them.

"I must go dine with my father now," Rosa said. "Is Edmund still avoiding me? I would like to say farewell."

"He's a selfish boy, my princess. I'm glad you did not marry him," Edwina said.

"Well, see if you can find him when I am with my father and tell him I would see him if he is willing."

"I will." Edwina nodded and went in search of Edmund.

When Rosa entered the king's chambers, she found her father already sitting down, the dinner laid out for them. She slipped into her chair, but the king gave no sign that he noticed her and lifted his fork to his mouth. Rosa sighed and tried to eat as well. He still seemed to wander as if in a dream ever since the queen's death. She did not know what he would do without her to take care of him, and the thought of it broke her heart more than the thought of being unable to wake up from her sleep.

"Father, I love you," she said.

The king paused, but he still did not meet her gaze.

"For my sake, and for mother's, please promise me that you will be happy and that you will look after the kingdom. The peo-ple need you."

The king finally gazed into his daughter's face. "Your mother is gone and so are you, and there is nothing."

"I am not gone yet!" Rosa cried and sprang from her chair, throwing her arms around him. He sat immobile as she spent her tears, so she gently kissed him on both cheeks before returning to her seat. There was a knock at the door, and a servant slowly opened it. Outside stood Edwina and Edmund. When the king saw the two of them, it almost seemed, if only for a moment, that a flicker of life passed through his face.

"Promise me," he said hoarsely, "promise me that you will not leave the princess alone tonight. That if you can say anything, do anything to protect her, you will."

Edwina rushed to Rosa, clasping her in her arms. Edmund fell on one knee before the king. "I will not ever leave her side, I swear it," he promised.

"Take the princess to her chambers and keep watch with her in the night. There are guards around the castle and posted at her door. We will see if steel and iron are of any use against Faerie," the king said grimly. "Now go."

The three walked silently through the long stretch of the torch-lit corridor to the princess' chambers. Edwina gave Rosa's hand a reassuring squeeze, and the princess was glad to have her and Edmund by her side. She looked up at her cousin's inscrutable profile. Even though he was disappointed over her refusal, he was with her now, and he had sworn to her father that he would stay at her side. She was glad that they were able to make peace at the end.

They were just turning the bend of the corridor where the door to the high tower entrance stood when Edmund grabbed her arm, wrenching her from Edwina's grasp. He thrust her through the open tower door and pulled it shut behind them with a heavy, resounding slam. Rosa could hear Edwina beating on the other side of the thick door with her fists, though the sound was muffled and growing fainter. She turned wide, questioning eyes on Edmund, waiting for him to speak. The stairs were dark, but moonlight streamed in through the window slits in the tower and illuminated Edmund's face, ghastly and white.

"She can scream and pound all she wants, but it will not disturb us," he said.

Rosa turned back again to the door only to discover that it was gone, replaced by a dark and empty space.

"There is nowhere to go but up," Edmund said.

Rosa's fear was replaced by a calm sense of inevitability. So this was how it was going to happen. She was ready to face her trial.

"Then let us go up," she said.

Edmund bowed and began the long climb up the winding stairs. Rosa followed him without wavering. The rooms and corridors attached to the tower were gone, replaced by a seamless wall of grey, leaden slabs. The moonlight let through the window slits only lit up the immediate steps before her, so that she could not see Edmund's back ahead of her, but could only hear his steady footfalls. The darkness grew oppressive, the winding steps dizzying, and fear woke in her heart, setting it to a rapid patter, the only sound she could hear besides Edmund's relentless steps.

Rosa froze, unable to go on, and even the sound of Edmund's echoing steps faded away. Would she stay here forever, lost in the darkness? If she turned back, would she fade away into the formless nothingness behind her? She stood alone and abandoned. Letting out a broken whimper, she sank down on the steps. She did not know how long she stayed there in the darkness, but then a small seed of hope blossomed, she did not know how, and it dawned on her that she could not be more lost than she already was. With that realization, her despair lifted, and an unexpected lightness entered her heart. She felt the strength returning to her legs and she slowly rose to continue her long climb. The stairs went on and on, and time seemed to end before the stairs did.

When finally Rosa knew she could not climb another single step, she reached the top of the tower.

Edmund had opened the door ahead of her, and Rosa stepped into a fire-lit room. The room was dark and windowless, and in the center stood the spinning wheel, its great wheel slowly turning, spun by invisible hands. Rosa had never seen a spinning wheel besides the broken wheels in the pyre of her dream, but she recognized it for what it was. She saw the spindle mounted on the wheel's frame, and a sudden urge tugged her toward the spindle. She was pulled closer and closer to it, drawn forward by the same invisible hands that spun the wheel. But she stopped before she got too close. She realized that the fascination did not overwhelm her. She did not have to prick her finger. Her desire to do so was something that she could resist and subdue.

Was that it? Was her trial over? She looked about for Edmund and saw that he was still by the door, but that he was not looking at her or the wheel, but at the darkest corner of the room furthest from the door and the fire. She followed his gaze, and the darkness in the corner took shape and a figure emerged.

A lady stepped into the firelight, tall, her face white, her lips blood red, and Rosa recognized the Dark Lady who had cursed her on her christening day. She was dressed in black, but the black was not so much a color, but an absence of light that drew in the firelight and annihilated it. Around her neck she wore a necklace in the shape of a serpent as white as a skull. Rosa stood unmoving and unspeaking, not wishing to put herself in the power of so terrible and fearsome a faery. The faery gazed at Rosa for time immeasurable and then smiled softly, but there was no kindness in her smile.

"The time has come for you to receive your final gift, Princess Rosamund. Some may call it a curse, but many call death a blessing." The Dark Lady spoke in a whisper, but the whisper filled the room.

"I do not think they mean your kind of death," Rosa replied.

She did not whisper and, though she tried to speak firmly, her voice sounded very small. "And in case you have forgotten, it is sleep, not death, that is the final gift."

The faery let out a small laugh, and its very smallness was frightening. "Do you think that your faerie godparents have any power over me and over death? Their promise of sleep was to save you from despair, and it is a weak promise, as are all such false hopes. Know the truth: there is no sleep, only death."

Rosa stood rooted in fear. Was everything her godparents told her a lie? Was she such a child that only she had believed in Faerie. No one else had been fooled. Edmund, her father and mother, Alice; they had all known that she would never wake up. The princess backed up against the wall, her hands clutching each other behind her back. She would not touch the spindle!

The faery uttered another low and small laugh. "Do you truly believe that if I wished you to touch the spindle that you could resist me? I am here to offer you a choice."

Rosa eyes darted wildly. A choice? Was her sleep not inevitable, then?

The Dark Lady laughed at the emotions plainly visible on Rosa's face.

"I will let you go back to your father, your friends, and to your kingdom, if, in return, you give your hand in marriage to Edmund. It is a simple choice really, death or marriage to one whom you might have chosen for yourself. I am not as cruel as others would have you believe, am I, Princess Rosamund?"

Rosa could scarcely understand what the Dark Lady was saying. Was it truly so simple? What was she missing? Why was this marriage so important to the Dark Lady, and was it a coincidence that she had been tempted by this same marriage to avoid the curse? She looked over to Edmund for help, but realized that he could not see her, nor had he moved since she first entered the room. Rosa's gaze returned to the faery, and she saw that the skull white serpent around her neck was undulating. It was not a necklace in the form of a snake, but was instead the white serpent that had once been Edmund's mother.

"He knew," she whispered, "he knew that you would offer me this choice."

The faery said nothing.

"What did he promise you in return?"

In the silence Rosa's voice grew stronger. "If I married Edmund, he would forever be in your debt because you gave me to him. He would be yours, and, if he is yours, then so would I and the kingdom for accepting the condition."

"Make your choice, Princess Rosamund," the Dark Lady said in her relentless whisper.

Rosa did not move or speak.

"You must choose. You are in Faerie, and time will not start again until you make your choice."

Rosa looked again at Edmund, frozen and ensorcelled to the Dark Lady. She listened to the whirring of the spinning wheel, turning and turning, and then faintly she heard the melody that the stars had been singing in her dream and, before that, on the top of the mountain. The melody grew louder, and she reached deeper into her memory and recalled that it was the same song that the three sisters had been singing as they spun the Grey Lady's spindle, singing of the past, present, and the future. The songs were one and the same, only she had not realized this until now.

Rosa bravely looked into the Dark Lady's eyes. "I would rather die than be enslaved to you, and my death would save Edmund and the kingdom. But I do not believe that I will die. I have faith in my godmother's promise. She loves me, but you have every reason to lie." Rosa stepped forward without fear. Her finger floated over the spindle only for an instant, and then she pricked her finger.

Rosa crumpled down to the ground, but did not land on the

floor, however, but in the Green Lady's arms that caught her as she fell.

The Dark Lady laughed, but her eyes could barely contain the fury that blazed within them. "So you did not save her after all, but left her to her sleep. No wonder so few mortals seek your aid, if this is how you treat them."

"You know nothing. Though you imagine yourself crafting a web of fate, you belong to the same pattern that we all do. Moreover, you have no more power here. Be gone," the Green Lady ordered.

"I will go. But do not think that you have saved the princess. She has escaped my power, but Time's turning wheel will complete its cycle, and a new age will dawn with the next revolution of the wheel, and it will be an age that does not know Faerie, nor will it love and know what the princess loves and knows, and it will crush what does belong to it. How do you think this new world will treat the princess when she wakens?"

After her terrible warning, the Dark Lady departed, and time re-entered the room. Edmund woke from his daze and saw the Green Lady and the princess, lying in her arms. He let out a cry. "No! Why did she choose death? I could have saved her!"

"Poor Edmund, striving so hard to fight the curse, you became the very one to bring it about."

The Green Lady's pity rent through him like a knife.

"You," he snarled. "You are the one to blame. If she did not have such blind faith in you, she would not have made such a desperate choice. Otherwise, why would she have chosen the curse over me?"

The Green Lady spoke softly. "She did choose you, Edmund. She did this to save you. That is why you will let her go."

Edmund let out another cry, this time full of pain and disbelief, and rushed out of the room. The Green Lady gathered the princess in her arms and kissed her pale forehead. The room returned to its natural state, and a stream of moonlight shone full and bright through the window. The moonbeam shimmered, and a young maiden, tall and with flaxen hair as white as pale silver, stood where the moonbeam was before.

She approached the princess and also kissed her forehead, "The time of madness is approaching, but the princess shall be safe and have peaceful dreams in my soft light until the time ordained when she shall waken."

The shadow of night cloaked the castle, and the moon shone gently upon the princess who not so long ago wished to wear the moon as a necklace, but who now belonged to the moon in her sleep.

Chapter Seventeen

The Prince's Homecoming

TWO YOUNG MEN on horseback paused on the high ridge over-looking a valley, with the mountains rising in the distance. They wore simple tunics that did not draw attention, though, if one looked closely, one could tell that both were battle-hardened and noble in bearing.

More noticeable were their two magnificent horses. The tall, dark-haired, young man was astride a horse of midnight black with a white diamond that shone like a star on its forehead. His fair-haired companion rode a chestnut stallion whose coat gleamed red in the sun. Both horses shifted and snorted, pawing the ground, and the fair-haired young man absentmindedly rubbed his horse's neck, as the other gazed across the valley at the castle nestled in the mountains' rocky depths.

The prince said with a deep breath that was almost a sigh, "It is hard to believe that it has been four years."

His companion grinned. "Well, let's not add another day to your absence. We should move on, or we shall not reach the cas-tle until nightfall."

Erik swung about his horse—named Lodestar, after the northernmost star in the sky—and began his slow descent into the valley. He was lost in thought, but his fair-haired companion drew him out of it.

"Erik, thinking about that pretty little thing at the inn last night? I saw you eyeing her. Don't deny it. If I had known you liked them fair and blue-eyed, I would have introduced you to a few girls I knew back in town."

"I was not eyeing anyone," Erik said dryly and then, after a pause, "She reminded me of someone."

"Who? Someone at the castle? Could you introduce me?"

The prince smiled and shook his head. "No, she is not at the castle."

"Oh, that explains it."

"Explains what?"

"Why you didn't even look at the girls at Wallstone castle. Some tragic tale of unrequited love, I warrant. It's written all over your face. Something about your dreaming and lost expression draws girls in like moths to a flame, and you never notice. Waste, really."

"Don't be ridiculous," Erik snorted. "Some of us don't have time to go running after skirts all the day long, Dunstan."

"Well you know what they say about all work and no play."

"Not really," said the prince as he set off at a gallop.

THE two made good progress, and, as they neared the castle, Erik reflected on the years he had been away. With the onset of the civil war, which was now long over, he had been sent to stay with his aunt and uncle up at Castle Wallstone on the northeastern coast of Lothene, which was constantly under attack by raiding ships from the north. Castle Wallstone was the first line of defense against pirate raiders, but there was not much fighting to be had when he and Kenelm first arrived. Winter was just beginning, and the pirate raiders would not harry the coastline until spring. So instead, his aunt, the Lady Elisenda, schooled him in manners—a subject which she declared had been rudely ignored in his upbringing. She was born overseas from the southeast, where she claimed that the people were more civilized, and had brought with her a tutor under whose care Erik had studied foreign languages, history, and philosophy. The prince learned about the wide world and discovered that Lothene was only a small part of it.

It was during the long winter that Erik had met his friend Dunstan. The fast-talking and fun-loving boy had not been put off by the prince's reserved manner and had recognized the shyness at the root of it. He slowly drew out the quiet and more serious prince, and they became close companions, fighting by each other's side when spring came and the pirate ships arrived to plunder the coast and raid the villages. In the years that followed, Erik learned the boldness that came from leading men.

Erik had most recently conceived and executed a successful night raid on the enemy ships, and he wondered if his father had heard of his success and if that was the reason he was being summoned back to the castle.

The prince pulled his horse to a halt and Dunstan reined in beside him.

"What is it?" Dunstan asked.

"I am not sure. I thought I saw something."

"A wild animal?"

Erik smiled to himself. "Perhaps, shall we go on?"

THE two young men reached the castle well before dark. They were greeted by King Mark and Queen Sigrid in the great hall.

"Father, it is good to be home," Erik said, kneeling before his father.

King Mark lifted up his son and, placing both hands on Erik's shoulders, gazed into his eyes. The king seemed pleased at what he saw there. "Welcome home," he said, pulling Erik into a tight embrace.

The queen looked at the prince with visible interest, and he wondered cynically if the news of his exploits had raised him up to her notice. She no longer seemed the terrifying figure she had been when he was a young boy, and he presented his friend to her with ease.

"This is my close friend and companion, Dunstan. We have fought side by side through numberless battles, and he has saved my life not a few times. You could not ask for a truer friend."

Dunstan bowed. "What the prince fails to mention is that he has saved my life more times than I can count. He is the best swordfighter at Castle Wallstone."

The king's eyes gleamed at Dunstan's words, when they were interrupted by a ringing voice calling out from behind them.

"He should be after all the training I put him through."

As he turned, Erik exclaimed. "Kenelm! When did you arrive?"

"A full day before you, my prince. You must have dallied on the way."

"Or you traveled a short cut known only to you and bribed the innkeeper to hold us back with his best beer and ale. Your ways are forever devious, Kenelm," Dunstan retorted.

"None of your lip, pup. You are in the presence of the king and queen, not in a tavern brimming with wenches and brigands."

Erik chuckled at the familiar exchange, but the queen interrupted. "Enough of this talk. The young men should go to their rooms and wash off the stain of travel from their clothes. There will be a feast in the evening in honor of your return, Prince Erik."

The prince bowed. "My gratitude, my queen. We will see you shortly, then." He and Dunstan departed to refresh themselves.

WHEN time came for the feast, the queen made room for the prince to sit beside her at the feasting table. She was all smiles and graciousness and plied him with questions about his life away from the castle. "You have come back a great warrior." She smiled, and the candlelight glittered off her rings, and her eyes sparkled.

Erik shrugged. "Hardly, I play but a small part in the defense of the kingdom. You must go to the king if you wish to hear heroic tales."

"Lady Elisenda may have taught you the virtue of modesty, but a warrior's prowess must be celebrated, particularly if he is to one day be king."

Erik inclined his head.

"Not only must your deeds evoke respect and even fear from your subjects, but you must think of marrying to produce an heir. The king and I have been discussing this, and that is why you were called back from Wallstone Castle. You are of age, and I can think of a few young ladies who would be suitable."

Erik's usual self-possession deserted him, and his eyes widened in alarm. This he had not been expecting.

The king broke into their conversation, "What have you been saying to the boy, my queen? He looks as if you had challenged him to single-combat. Erik, my boy, are you discovering that my queen is as dangerous an opponent as any armed warrior?"

Erik stared down at his plate to compose himself. He had a pretty fair idea of what sort of suitable lady the queen had in mind: one obedient only to her. Not a single word would pass between him and his wife that would not also be whispered in his step-mother's ear.

The queen turned to her husband. "Not anything so frightening, my king. I merely mentioned to the prince that it was time for him to consider a bride."

The king laughed. "I can see why his blood froze within him. Such news should not be suddenly sprung on a young man."

"The prince has proven his valor, but life is dangerous on the battlefield. We must consider the throne."

There was an awkward silence. Queen Sigrid had borne no

children, and Erik was the only direct heir to the throne. Erik wondered if the queen would still be as considerate of his well-being if she had also produced an heir.

"You know that we have discussed a bride of the old blood for the prince, in order to placate the clans in the west," the queen continued.

King Mark had defeated Lord Biron and subjugated the western lands under his iron rule. He had appointed Lord Clovis as the new Lord of Westhane, so that the western lands were now nominally loyal to him. Biron's son Gavin, however, had escaped and was still in hiding, stirring up trouble and civil unrest in the western lands. So his own marriage was to be another maneuver in their game to subjugate the west, as had been his father's first marriage before, Erik realized.

Turning to the king, he said, "I understand the political advantages of a good marriage, but surely you will let me have some say in the choice of a bride. After all, you and the queen are living proof to the happiness of a marriage of your own choosing. You would not deny me the same happiness?"

The queen flashed a hard smile. "The prince argues well. He wishes to score a point through flattery."

"What are you afraid of, my boy?" King Mark laughed. "Do you think I would match my own son to a hag? The girl will be pretty, never worry. But enough! We are here to celebrate your return. We have time before we settle you with a bride."

Erik pretended to be cheerful for the rest of the evening, but, inside his head, his thoughts were awhirl with many questions that needed answers, and he knew he would find no answers in the castle.

EARLY the next morning, Erik went out to the margin between the castle grounds and the forest. The air was chill and damp, and a faint mist still clung to the forest floor. There sat Mnemosyne waiting for him by the stump of the blasted tree. The grey cat blended in with the mist, and Erik would have missed her if it had not been for her yellow eyes.

The prince stilled, feelings surging within him that he had not experienced since he left the castle many years ago. Erik knelt, caught between belief and disbelief, as he rubbed the cat in the usual place behind her ears.

"It was you I saw yesterday in the forest, was it not? You witnessed my homecoming," he murmured. "I did not know if you would still be here."

The cat purred and rubbed up against him, wrapping her tail around his legs. He followed her on the winding path to Ninny Nanny's cottage, and each step seemed to him to be a step farther back into his past. When he knocked against the door, Erik felt that he was a child again, visiting the cottage for the very first time.

"Come in," came the familiar voice from his childhood.

Erik opened the cottage door, and there she was, sitting on her chair by the fireplace, the old woman who had rescued him from loneliness and given his starving heart the love it had cried out for in its need. He reached her in a few strides and kissed her cheek.

"Ye have grown, princeling, ye almost fill the cottage now."

"And you haven't changed at all," Erik said. "You are the same Ninny Nanny that I remember."

"Humph! Ye have learned a flattering tongue while ye were away."

"But you *are* the same," the prince protested. "I felt like a young boy the moment I walked into your cottage. Time stands still here in the forest."

The old woman cackled. "That is your nostalgia speaking. But it is good of ye to remember your old friends and pay me and Mnemosyne a visit. Four years is a long time for one your age, and I feared ye may have forgotten us."

"How could you say that, Ninny Nanny?" Erik asked in reproach. "You found a sad, little boy and made him smile again with all of your magical stories. I was very unhappy when I was sent away. I used to cry at nights missing you and I am not ashamed to admit it."

"Ach, bless ye. But ye have done well. Ye have returned a strong and handsome man."

Erik saw that the old woman's eyes gleamed with pride and bent over to kiss her again. Then he sat down at the table, resting his chin between his hands. "It would be an even sweeter homecoming if the queen wasn't already plotting to marry me off." The prince peered at Ninny Nanny through furrowed eyebrows, but the old woman did not say anything and continued to knit by the fire. "They say that the west is grumbling again, and apparently I am a bone to throw at them to silence them for a while."

The old woman smiled. "I wouldn't dismiss the power of bones."

Erik was confused for a moment and then smiled at the memory of the old woman and her sticks.

"That's true." He laughed, but his laughter had a troubled edge to it. "So you think I should do as they say and marry the woman they choose for me?"

"I didn't say that."

Erik bit back words of exasperation.

"Here it comes," the old woman said.

"Here what comes?" he asked.

"The question your eyes have been asking me ever since ye stepped into my cottage."

"Very well then... Those dreams I had of the princess as a young boy, all those stories that you told me, are they true?"

Ninny Nanny fell silent, and all that could be heard was the crackling of the fire. Then she spoke, "I already told ye that they were. Why do ye need to hear me say it again?"

"What you say to a little boy is different from what you say to a grown man," Erik responded.

"Do ye? I don't."

"Do not what?"

"Speak differently to men than to little boys."

Erik raised his eyebrows and then shook his head, his mouth twitching at the corners with a suppressed smile. "Ninny Nanny, you never did answer questions clearly."

"If the answers were clear, ye most likely wouldn't be asking the question."

Erik tried a different tack. "I know, in a way, that all stories are true, especially your stories. We are supposed to find the moral in them. What I want to know is, are your stories real?"

Ninny Nanny snorted. "What, have ye turned philosopher? Only one of them would come up with such a ridiculous question."

Erik ignored her comment. "Take the princess sleeping in the tower for one hundred years. It has been more than a hundred years since my father's people came from the north in their ships. More than double that time, in fact. How could that part of the story be true?"

Ninny Nanny's eyes flashed. "Are ye a man of science as well? All the young men of your time are so literal. The curse meant not a hundred years as ye count it. It meant until the time was ripe, the completion of Time's turning wheel. Words are used in different ways in different times. They uncover the thinking of all those behind 'em."

"So you are telling me that the princess is still asleep in her tower?"

"Waiting to be wakened."

"But such things don't happen. They are only stories," Erik protested.

"Look at me, I come out of a children's story, but here I am."

"But you are different."

"Am I?"

Erik scrutinized the old woman. All of a sudden, her familiar figure appeared strange to him and his old questions resurfaced. Who was Ninny Nanny exactly? This strange old woman with a mysterious past that sat by the fire in a cottage that never stayed in the same place twice. Erik blinked, and her figure was made familiar again. He buried his head in his hands.

"Ever since I saw her sleeping in the river, the princess' face has been ever before me. I used to dream up adventures where I would rescue her, and she would be the princess from my dreams, a little spoiled, but beautiful and kind. And very, very brave. Her bravery made me want to be brave, and her kindness made me want to be kind. What choice did a small boy have but to fall in love with the princess who appeared to him in his dreams?"

"An' would ye deny all that now that ye have grown? Would ye cast that all aside?" Ninny Nanny asked.

Erik lifted up a face, feeling worn and tired. "No! But how can I pin my hopes on her either? Dunstan teases me for not noticing other women, and he is right, for how can they compare to her? The king and queen want me to enter into a political marriage, and they are right, for it would be good for the kingdom. How can I put all of that aside for a woman who may only be a dream?"

"Ye did not have these doubts as a child. Ye were wiser then."

"Children do not have responsibilities."

"Ye promised ye would save her, that you would risk your life for her."

Erik leapt to his feet. "Give me a dragon to fight, a monster to defeat, and I would do it gladly. But all of this waiting, not knowing..."

"Requires more strength," Ninny Nanny finished for him.

Erik felt himself flush and then stiffly bowed. "Good day, Ninny Nanny. I should return to the castle before I am missed. I will find my own way back."

Ninny Nanny stared at the door after he left and then said to Mnemosyne, "He's developed a bit of a temper."

LATE that night Erik was quietly staring at something in his hands by candlelight. It was a shell, a white scallop shell worn ragged round the edges. He traced its shape gently with his thumb and then carefully placed it in a small wooden box. Blowing out the candle, he threw himself down on the bed and gazed up into the formless darkness.

He wished he could find something to cling to, a light to reveal the princess, or, if she was but a dream, something that would make her vanish in the cold, hard, daylight. He felt an anxiety he had not known while he was away. Now that he had returned, Erik knew that he must act, but he felt lost in doubts that he did not know as a child, the doubts of the growing man who questions what he had once taken for granted.

THE weeks passed by, until, one day, the prince and Dunstan were out by the river fishing. They had been angling with hook and line all morning, and Erik was feeling irritated, since he hadn't caught anything. Dunstan had long since given up and was napping comfortably on the bank.

Erik heard a rustling in the bushes, and a white stag burst through about a stone's throw away from him. It was a beast of nobility and purity, its coat as unbesmirched as newly fallen snow, its limbs lithe and graceful. For an instant, the prince's eyes met the startled golden eyes of the white stag. Then it was off, bounding swiftly into the trees behind it.

"Wake up, Dunstan!" Erik yelled as he sprang onto his horse and immediately gave chase. The prince could formulate no reason why he need ride after the stag, but, when he had looked into its eyes, he had felt that the stag had drawn his soul from his body. He had no choice but to chase the wild creature if he wished to find it again and be made whole.

The stag led the two young men on a winding chase, Erik following the stag, Dunstan following Erik, until Dunstan fell behind and was lost in the forest.

Erik rode on to the thunder of Lodestar's hooves. There was a moment when the prince thought the stag had evaded him. He scanned the forest frantically and spotted it. It had stopped running and was staring at him with its eyes of liquid gold. It took off again, and Erik once more gave chase. He gave no thought to what he would do if he caught the stag. Shooting the beautiful animal was the furthest thing from his mind. But if he did not give chase, he knew that he would forever be lost.

Then Lodestar stumbled, and Erik lost his seat and fell. He hit his head, and all the greens and browns of the forest swirled together and turned black.

ERIK found himself lying in a field of silver grass. He sat up in amazement and discerned the dim blue form of a mountain in the distance ahead of him. When he turned, his heart pounding in his ears, he saw the riverbank shaded by the purple trees he had known he would find there.

The gentle wind rose, and the purple leaves and the silver grass rustled in the breeze. Erik knew he was dreaming, but he could feel the wind on his cheek, and, as he closed his eyes, he could feel the tranquility of the field seeping into him. He opened his eyes and made his way to the river bank, with his heart trembling over what he might find there.

When he reached the riverbank, Erik knelt, staring into the river's clear waters. There she was, still lying at the bottom of the riverbed, the beautiful maiden he had lost his heart to as a boy. She was more beautiful than his memories, and this time he knew that she was also the princess from Ninny Nanny's stories.

He gazed down on her sleeping face. "If only you would open your eyes," he whispered again, as he had when he was a child.

Then he knew he must be dreaming, for the princess slowly floated up from the bottom of the river bed, and, as she rose to the surface, the water gently deposited her onto the bank opposite him. He saw her eyes softly flutter from a distance and realized that she was waking up. With his heart in his throat, he waited as he watched her sit up and look about her in confusion.

Her eyes fell on him, and she smiled. Erik thought he saw the breaking of the dawn in her smile and wished that she would look that way at him always. Then, as the drowsiness slowly lifted away from her, the princess' smile was replaced by an expression of alarm.

"Don't be afraid, I will not harm you," he called out reassuringly.

"Where am I, and who are you?" she called back across the river.

Erik noticed that the princess spoke with an accent. It was similar to the dialect used by the people in the west, who proudly claimed that their language had not changed with the times. It also had a lilt similar to Ninny Nanny's, but that was where the comparisons between the princess and the old woman ended.

"My name is Erik, and you have been asleep in the river and have only just woken up."

"Can you say that again? I didn't understand you."

Erik repeated himself, and the princess looked even more confused.

"How can I have been asleep in the river if my clothes are not even wet?" she called out again.

Erik saw that what she said was true. Her dress and her golden hair were completely dry.

"That is because we are dreaming," he explained.

"What do you mean?"

"The last thing I remember is falling off my horse, and then here I was, and you were in the river." Erik saw that she was thinking hard about what he was saying, so he continued. Since it was all a dream, he had the feeling that he could tell her anything anyways. "I used to dream of you when I was little. I saw you sleeping here once before and then, at other times, I saw bits of your life when you were growing up."

"What did you say?"

He threw up his arms half in laughter and half in frustration. "I used to dream of you as a young boy."

"Well, you may be a dream, but I am not," she called back.

Erik felt a large grin spread across his face. "All this shouting is ridiculous," he said, "I am going to cross the river."

"Is it safe?" the princess called back in alarm, but Erik had already pulled off his tunic and was removing his boots. The river was shallow enough, and the current seemed gentle. He dived in, but, the instant he touched the surface of the water, tumultuous waves overwhelmed him, and he found himself struggling frantically to keep his head above the water. The churning river dragged him away from the princess, and, after he had swallowed more than enough mouthfuls, it spat him back on his side of its bank.

The princess had been running down her side of the riverbank and called out to him, "Are you all right?"

Erik spat up water, then nodded, and the princess sat down on the bank and cocked her head to one side. "My name is Rosamund."

"I know," Erik said.

"Because you have dreamed of me."

"Yes."

"What have you dreamed?"

Erik thought for a moment and then called over the river, trying to slowly and carefully enunciate each word. "I first dreamed of you sleeping in the river and then I saw you as a little girl who wanted the moon. Once while you were dancing by the seashore and then after your mother had died. Finally I saw you climbing the tower to confront the curse. I have heard stories of you besides. I know all about you, Rosa... I mean, Princess Rosamund."

Rosa was silent for a while, seeming to take it all in.

"That doesn't seem fair," she called back finally. "I don't know anything about you."

"You are right," he admitted. "What do you want to know?"

She shook her head in frustration. "I don't know. Everything? But it is so hard with me over here and you over there."

Erik agreed wholeheartedly. "I will tell you everything once I rescue you."

Rosa turned pink. "Are you going to rescue me?"

"Of course."

The princess turned her head away. "Well I would not assume... Wait! Don't go!"

Erik found that the whole world was dissolving away.

"I can't help it," he cried. "But I promise I will find you and wake you."

Then he was gone.

THE prince woke with Lodestar's muzzle in his face. "Ow, stop that, I'm alive. You dragged me away from the princess, you stupid horse."

He sat up, his head pounding from the fall. Erik felt the back of his head. "That is going to leave a bump," he muttered. "Now let us have a look at you." He turned to his horse and examined Lodestar's back legs and forelegs. "Looks all right, thank the heavens." Erik mounted Lodestar and rode only a little ways before he burst out laughing. "Of course that would happen."

The stag had led the prince right up to Ninny Nanny's cottage. He quickly dismounted and tied Lodestar's reins around the post at the front gate. Then he bounded up the path and rapped on Ninny Nanny's front door. "Ninny Nanny, let me in! I saw her! I saw her!"

The door opened with a crack. First Ninny Nanny's nose appeared, followed by the rest of her head. "Stop that racket! I may be old, but I'm not deaf. Now what nonsense are ye spouting?" Ninny Nanny's eyes were twinkling.

"I saw the princess and I spoke to her! You glorious Ninny Nanny, she is real!" The prince scooped up the old woman and spun her around.

"I could have told ye that. Now put me down!" she squawked.

Erik lowered her gently. "I have you to thank for everything. I am so sorry that I ever doubted you."

"Come round to the back, princeling, I want to show ye something."

Erik followed Ninny Nanny to the back of the cottage and stopped in wonder. Spread out before him was a rose garden of every bloom and shade, bushes and climbing roses spilling over trellises in a profusion of color. Erik looked at the old woman questioningly, and she nodded. "Yes, this is the thorn patch ye cleared away. I planted a rose garden when ye left. Now that ye have seen the blooms, the time is ripe for ye to seek the princess."

"Then I must go to the Shadowood?"

"Aye, but more than that I cannot help ye with, for ye must discover your own path."

Erik took Ninny Nanny's hand and pressed it. "I cannot wait for Princess Rosamund to meet you. You are like a mother to me."

Ninny Nanny gave him a sad smile through all her wrinkles.

"What is wrong?" he exclaimed.

Ninny Nanny shook her head. "'Tis nothing." The old woman pointed to the rose garden. "When ye return with the princess, bring her here and deck her in these roses for her bridal flowers. They will be my wedding present."

"Of course, Ninny Nanny, nothing would make me happier."

"Now off with ye. Ye must make haste to depart. Start tomorrow by daybreak. Brook no delays."

Erik embraced the old woman, and Mnemosyne came and rubbed up against his legs. He bent over and scratched her in her favorite spot behind the ears until she purred.

"Farewell to you, mysterious Mnemosyne. You have ever been my faithful guide."

Erik straightened and said farewell for the final time, then the old woman and the cat watched him mount his horse and ride away.

"'Tis the last time the prince sees us and knows us, Mnemosyne," Ninny Nanny said to the cat, and then the old woman sighed.

WHEN Erik returned to the castle, he immediately began preparations for the next day's journey. He packed his saddlebags and was laying out an extra tunic, when Dunstan walked into his room without knocking.

"Aha! I knew you were up to something."

"I am just laying out my clothes for tomorrow," Erik said wryly, which strictly was true.

Dunstan grimaced and looked pointedly at the bundle next to his bed. "You can't trick a trickster. Ever since you returned from chasing who knows what in the forest, you've barely spoken two words, and there is a traitorous glint in your eyes. You are planning something, but what I don't understand is why you haven't told me what!"

Erik looked at his friend curiously. "So you didn't see the stag earlier in the woods?"

Dunstan shook his head. "I saw *something* streaking through the forest, but you had nearly disappeared by the time I mounted my horse."

The prince was silent for a moment and then said, "If you are a loyal friend, you will not hinder me."

"Hinder you? Certainly not. I will join you! Though I have to say I'm a bit offended you haven't trusted me with your secret. Where are we going?"

Erik shook his head, a small smile playing on his lips. "I will tell you when we are on the road tomorrow and not before. You will think me mad, but I have never been more serious about anything in my life."

Dunstan studied his friend. "I can see that. What would make our serious prince even more serious than usual, I wonder? Have you heard of another rebellion breaking out? Shouldn't you tell the king?"

"No nothing like that, this concerns me alone, and you must not breathe a word of this to anyone, particularly to the king or the queen. I have a feeling that my stepmother would expend all her powers trying to stop me."

Dunstan whistled, "Well, this is a mystery. But I see that I must wait until tomorrow for it to be revealed."

"I'll meet you at the gates at break of day."

Dunstan nodded.

"Break of day, do you hear? Otherwise I will leave you behind."

The prince's friend waved at him dismissively and walked through the door.

"Dunstan," Erik's voice stopped him.

The fair-haired young man paused and looked over his shoulder.

"I am glad that you are coming. This will be a hard journey, and it will be lighter with company."

"You're welcome." Dunstan grinned and then left the prince's room.

Chapter Eighteen

The Grey Hawk

THE MORNING BROKE on two dark figures on horseback riding against the sunrise. Lodestar and Embermane bore their masters westwards like great comets streaking across the heavens. The two young men rode until the rosy-golden hues of the sunrise dissolved into the clear morning light, and, while they rested their horses, Erik told Dunstan about the princess, his dreams, and Ninny Nanny and her stories. Dunstan did not speak throughout the entire explanation and kept his silence when the prince finished.

"You think I am mad, don't you?" Erik asked.

Dunstan answered with hesitation, "If anyone else told me that story and expected me to believe it, I *would* say that he was mad and laugh it away. But since it is you…" Dunstan shrugged.

"Well, you can turn back now if you do not believe me, but you must swear on your sword that you will not tell anyone."

"I am not going anywhere," Dunstan said firmly, "and I did not say I did not believe you." Then he threw back his head and laughed. "Whoever would have dreamed that I would see the day that the serious prince would fall in love? It only stands to reason that she would be no ordinary woman, but a magical princess under a curse."

"I would rather you stay behind than have to endure your mockery throughout the entire journey," Erik said through gritted teeth.

"I am profoundly sorry. I know you are a delicate soul, and it will not happen again."

Erik smiled in spite of himself. He knew that such a promise would be impossible for his friend.

"Now onward! We journey to rescue a damsel in distress!"

"That is enough, Dunstan."

THE two rode for days without mishap, staying at inns overnight. They did not expect pursuit, for Erik had left a message behind to the effect that he and Dunstan had wearied of the castle and were leaving for the hunting lodge a few days south. They shouldn't be missed for weeks if fortune smiled upon them.

As they approached the western marches, Erik asked those he met on the way for stories of the Shadowood. Most were too frightened to talk of the cursed wood, though a few would tell him wild stories of men lost in mazes of thorn, or of wolves larger than men gleaming silver in the night. More often than not, however, innkeepers and their customers would fill their ears with the more mundane complaints of the Greyhawk and his band of men. They were bandits who roamed the western highways and forests preying on Midlothian travelers. Erik and Dunstan made note to be watchful on the road and took care not to reveal their identities.

They reached the river marking the boundary between Westhane and Midlothia on the morning of the fourth day of their travels, but saw no bridge by which to cross. Erik espied an old, white-haired man standing knee high deep in the river, holding a net, his coracle landed on the bank nearby. Erik dismounted from his horse and called out to him, but the old man gestured for the prince to be silent. Both Erik and Dunstan stood patiently by as he remained motionless, waiting for his catch. He must have captured something in his net, for soon he let out a victorious laugh and slowly waded ashore, dragging his net up through the water. Erik reached out and gave him a hand back onto the shore.

Now that the he was near, Erik saw that the fisherman was not as old as he had thought. Though his hair was bone-white, his face was unlined, and the prince could not make out his age.

"Look at my beautiful fish." The man laughed as he dumped his catch into the coracle. "They glimmer and dance so gracefully."

"Is the river shallow enough to wade across? We need to cross to the other side," Erik asked.

The fisherman shook his head. "No, she dips in the middle and becomes too deep for horses. There was a bridge here, but it was washed away in the spring floods. You will have to travel a few hours north to find the next one."

Erik nodded. "Many thanks, but we must be on our way."

"Why don't you share a meal with me? I have more than enough fish to share among three."

"No, we would travel a few more hours before resting. We are making haste."

Erik would have turned to go, but the fisherman caught sight of the silver pendant that he wore around his neck. It had slipped over his tunic when he had helped the man ashore. The fisherman exclaimed as he reached forward and caught hold of the pendant and then examined it closely. "It has been many a year since I've seen a piece so old in my wanderings. Do you know what this is?"

Erik shook his head. "It was given me by my mother, but, other than that, I do not know anything about it. Does it hold any significance for you?"

The fisherman stared at Erik keenly and then said, "This pendant is called a *symbolon*. They are always made in matching pairs and contain a secret. See how this ridge in indented?"

The prince nodded.

"This is where it interlocks with its matching pair." He

turned it over on its back and paused, running his thumb over the cross hatching on the back surface. He flipped it over again to the engraving of the bird clutching the fish.

"This bird is a kingfisher, a friend to all fisherman. Guard this pendant well, and perhaps one day you will unlock the key to its secret."

Erik gazed at the man with curiosity. His eyes were as deep as still black pools and as inscrutable. He certainly did not speak like an ordinary fisherman. Erik wondered if perhaps he would know more about the Shadowood than those they had encountered on their travels so far.

"Would you know any tales that would be helpful in navigating the Shadowood?" he asked.

"One does not navigate the Shadowood. The wood either chooses to reveal itself or it does not. But I will tell you that what you seek is lost within a labyrinth, and you will not find the true path until you have journeyed the labyrinth of your own heart."

The fisherman fixed his eyes on Dunstan, who had dismounted to join the both of them. "The wood tolerates no doubt. It weighs those who enter it and casts away those who are unworthy. Once you walk into the wood, your step must not falter."

Erik felt his blood run cold and then he looked at his friend with troubled eyes. Dunstan merely gave a light laugh and shrugged his shoulders.

"Thank you for your warning, mysterious fisherman, but I'm a little too old to be frightened by old wives' tales. Shall we head off, Erik?"

The prince nodded and thanked the fisherman, who had returned to the coracle to look after his catch.

"Next time," the fisherman said, "we shall share a meal, you and I."

Erik waved, and both he and Dunstan mounted their horses and followed the river up north until they came to the bridge and crossed it into Westhane.

BOTH Erik and Dunstan had intended to be on their guard against the Grey Hawk and his band of brigands, for, though they were dressed simply, their tunics were finely woven, and no one could mistake Lodestar and Embermane for anything other than noble steeds. But partly because they were both dwelling on the fisherman's final words of warning, and partly because of the great stealth of the Grey Hawk's band, Erik and Dunstan were completely taken by surprise when they were ambushed on the solitary road.

Erik had barely drawn his sword when it was knocked out of his hand, and soon both he and Dunstan were unhorsed and bound as brigands rifled through their belongings, lifting them of their money pouches.

"Now these are a fine pair of steeds," said one of the men addressing the one who appeared to be their leader. "I say that we keep them instead of selling them."

The leader, who could only be the Grey Hawk, nodded. He was a tall man dressed in a grey tunic, with an angular face possessing a sharp nose and deep-set, piercing, grey eyes. He held up his hand, and one of the men tossed him the money pouches. Opening one of them, he peered at the gold and then glanced sharply at Erik and Dunstan. "Now what may be your errand in these parts, boys?"

"What's it to you?" Dunstan retorted. "We are traveling to Castle Westhane, where I am sure the Lord Clovis would be displeased to learn that you are manhandling his guests."

The Grey Hawk's face turned hard at the mention of the Lord of Westhane. He gave Dunstan a dangerous smile and then bowed low to him and the prince. "Forgive me, where are my manners? Any guest of the Lord's is a guest of mine." He barked out orders to his men, who brought him the horses and then unbound the prisoners.

"I am afraid I must relieve you of your fine steeds and your gold," the Grey Hawk continued. "You see, I and the Lord of

Westhane have a little game that we play. Both try to outdo the other in generosity towards our guests. If I take your horses, then that only means he will have to supply you with a pair of his own. He helps me out in the same way."

He threw Erik and Dunstan's swords out into the middle of the road. "I'll leave these here with you. Perhaps next time, Midlothian boys, you will think before you travel the western roads alone. I hear there are dangerous men abroad."

The brigands rode off, and Erik took up his sword and sheathed it. Dunstan did the same, saying, "Curse those vile outlaws and horse thieves! I know what you must be thinking. Why couldn't I have kept my large mouth shut and not mention the Lord of Westhane. You know I always say the first thing that comes to mind… I wanted to make him think twice about robbing us."

Erik shook his head. "No, they would have robbed us either way. I should have noticed them waiting in ambush. It is my own carelessness that brought us here."

"Well, you are not the only one with eyes and ears. I should have noticed them as well. What now? Shall we go back to the nearest inn and send word to the castle?"

"No, I am not giving up. We are going to get our horses back."

"What!" Dunstan exclaimed. "Why don't we take the Grey Hawk's suggestion and instead get a fresh pair from the Lord of Westhane?"

"And lose Lodestar and Embermane? You should be ashamed!"

"Better than losing our necks," Dunstan grimaced. "Now, you know I am as eager for battle as the best of them, but there were at least fifteen men here on ambush, and there will be more at the camp. I do not think that they will let us go a second time."

Erik felt for the hilt of his sword. "They left behind our swords. I do not think they will kill us. Besides, it will take us days to get to Castle Westhane by foot, and I am not sure if the Lord of the castle may not try to detain me until he gets word to my father. No, we will just have to not get caught."

Dunstan grinned. "Well, I *was* getting bored. Let's go then!"

IT WAS easy enough to follow the trail left behind by so large a band as the Grey Hawk's, so Erik and Dunstan pursued Lodestar and Embermane by foot. It was dusk when the prince and his friend finally reached the outskirts of the brigands' camp. There was a watch posted about the camp, so the two hid in the undergrowth and waited for the darkness to completely fall before they stole past the watch and, when near enough to observe the camp, hid in the bushes.

A large fire blazed in the center of the camp, with a boar on a spit roasting above it. The men were seated about the fire, and one of them made the rounds, pouring sparkling liquid into outstretched goblets like a royal cupbearer. The men were seated tall and straight, and the Grey Hawk himself sat lordly in the midst of them. This was no common outlaw's feast. The trees rose tall in a leafy canopy around them, and they appeared like lords of a forest hall.

The Grey Hawk seemed far away from all the laughter and the talk, watching the flames dance with a somber brow. He waved to one of the men, saying, "Aymer, sing us a song of the wandering king. I am in a melancholy mood tonight."

A thin young man picked up the lyre that lay beside him and, after plucking a few chords gently, tightened a few of its strings before he began his song.

The wand'ring king tirelessly treads
the path of exile.
There is none left among mortal kind
to whom he dares speak.

There is none left to unburden
the treasures of his thoughts.

The monuments of old have crumbled
into the ocean.
Branches shake against the bitter cold
where once the bird sang.
The ruined earth lies waiting for
the renewal of the rain.

The shadows lengthen in the dark night.
The moon shines above.
Sorrow returns at old memories
of love won and lost.
The wounds of his soul are sore with
the longing of lament.

The wanderer cries:
Time the destroyer of cities
who cuts short the breath of men,
how long will your wheel fall relentlessly downward
and fate follow its predetermined path?
All glory is fled
buried with the dead.

The wand'ring king tirelessly treads
The path of exile.
Alone unchanging in a fading world,
he waits for the time
when what was sunder'd is joined by
the coming of the crown.

As the last notes faded into stillness, Erik was lost in the images of the sorrowful king wandering through the bygone ages. A quick nudge from Dunstan brought him back to himself, and his friend pointed out where the horses were being kept. They were at the rear of the campsite, a far enough distance to be stolen back without alerting the main band of men. The prince nodded quietly, and the two crept softly and gently toward the horses. A guard was on duty, but Erik disabled him without a sound and then untethered Lodestar and Embermane while Dunstan stooped over to relieve the fallen man of his bow and quiver.

They stealthily led their horses from the camp, but the fallen man and the theft of the horses must have been discovered, for a sharp cry echoed through the forest.

Erik and Dunstan leapt on their horses, all attempts at remaining hidden abandoned. They fled the inevitable pursuit, but the sentries up ahead on horseback diverted their flight, and the rest of the Grey Hawk's band rushed the two young men with their swords drawn. As they were surrounded, the prince unsheathed his sword, which glimmered in the torchlight, and Dunstan drew his bow.

"I recommend that you lower your weapons," rang a voice in the darkness, and Erik recognized the Grey Hawk's commanding tones. "You are outnumbered and in the sights of our arrows. If you lower your weapons, I promise you your lives."

Erik saw no choice other than to heed the Grey Hawk's warning and sheathe his sword, and, following his lead, Dunstan lowered his bow. Two of the men rode up with torches, and the fire cast its light upon the intruders, revealing their features. One of the men laughed.

"If it isn't the two boys we met on the road. They must enjoy being soundly fleeced."

"Quiet, Corwin," the Grey Hawk snapped. He stared at the two young men with a thoughtful expression. "You are welcome to sit with us at our fire and partake of our food as our guests. But you will have to lower your weapons and, of course, return the horses to us."

"I am afraid we cannot do that," Erik spoke firmly. "I will not leave Lodestar behind and I am on a journey of great haste. You will have to slay me where I stand."

Dunstan started, and the Grey Hawk looked at the prince intently.

"You are not traveling to Castle Westhane," he said.

"We are not."

The Grey Hawk came to a rapid decision. "You will return with us to the camp, and we will reach an agreement. I promise you will not be worse off than you are now."

The last the Grey Hawk said with an ironic smile that Erik did not like, but both he and Dunstan agreed and followed the men back to the campsite, where the Grey Hawk offered them food and drink.

"I hope the meat and drink is to your liking. We do not partake of the sumptuous fare I am sure you are accustomed to. We have music, however, to rival even the bards of the king's court."

"Indeed," Erik acknowledged. "Your bard sings songs of the wandering king."

"You know the old legends, then?"

Erik recited softly,

The wand'ring king tirelessly treads
The path of exile.
Alone unchanging in a fading world,
he waits for the time
when what was sunder'd is joined by
the coming of the crown.

"I had never heard the full song before." Seeing the Grey Hawk's questioning eyes, he continued. "My mother was a westerner."

The Grey Hawk nodded. "Yes, you have that look about you. But your speech is that of a Midlothian. Tell me your name and what has brought you to my woods."

Dunstan snorted. "Your woods? Surely these woods belong to the Lord of Westhane."

"Quiet, Dunstan," Erik said. "This man has a claim. If I am not mistaken, we are sitting before Gavin, son of Lord Biron, the dispossessed lord of Westhane."

The Grey Hawk threw back his head and laughed. "You are a perceptive young man. I did not expect a molly-coddled boy from Midlothia to know me."

"Watch your mouth," Dunstan retorted, causing the men around the campfire to grumble and eye him dangerously.

"Don't, Dunstan. We are this man's guests."

The Grey Hawk laughed again. "You have an unfair advantage over me. You know who I am, but I am still in unhappy ignorance of your identities. I gather that your hot-headed companion's name is Dunstan, but whom do I have the honor of addressing?"

"You may call me Erik, though I would not say that we are in an advantageous position."

"Erik?"

"Just Erik."

"Well, then, 'Just Erik,' why don't you tell me of the pressing errand that drives you to sneak into an outlaw's camp and steal their horses?"

"We were not stealing anything, but simply taking back what is rightfully ours. I may ask you by what right you have, true lord of Westhane or no, to waylay innocent travelers on the road and commit other similar acts of wrong-doing, if the stories are to be believed."

"Silence, Midlothian boy," cried the man called Corwin. "Or I will slit you from the navel to the throat where you stand."

"No, that is all right, Corwin," said the Grey Hawk. "These young men have a vested interest in the answer. My acts of 'wrong-doing,' as you call them, depend greatly on from which side of the river you hear the tale. I do prey upon the false lord's men, as well as unsuspecting, self-important Midlothians such as yourselves; though I grant that I may have misjudged in your case, but you owe that, in part, to the fine lad Dunstan there."

"You still have no right to waylay innocent men from Midlothia," Erik said, "and your father lost the western lands through disloyalty to the king. You will have no recourse to the law if you act like an outlaw, nor will you have your rights restored to you."

Some of the men cried out and leapt to their feet, their hands on the hilts of their swords.

Dunstan whispered furiously to the prince, "Erik! Even I know you've gone too far."

The Grey Hawk's eyes had grown hard, but Erik's gaze never left his, and the dispossessed lord lifted his hand, and his men settled back down.

"You speak of loyalty and of the law, but a Westlander knows better than to expect justice from a Midlothian. I claim that we uphold the law against the false lord and his unjust thievery of our lands. My father's disloyalty, which you refer to, was his refusal to let the king bleed his land and his people dry, though he was a fool to make a stand on his own. Yet someday our injuries will strike too deep into the heart of our land, and we will rise up with one voice and throw off our northern oppressors. That is what the king fears most."

Erik spoke abruptly. "I would see firsthand this injustice of which you speak."

The Grey Hawk raised his eyebrows and said in a low voice, "You are hardly in a position to make demands."

"You know that you have done us an injury by waylaying us on the road. We are not the Lord of Westhane's men, nor are we in any way involved in your struggle. We are not leaving without our horses, so you are left with the difficulty of what to do with us. You claim that there is injustice being committed in this land by the current lord, and I would see this for myself. It is the least that you can do, and, despite your outlaw ways, I can see that you and your company are honorable men."

"Your request is a strange one, but I will grant it. You will ride with us tomorrow. But this one," the Grey Hawk motioned to Dunstan, "will stay behind to ensure you do not attempt escape."

Dunstan began to protest, but Erik assured him, "Do not fear, Dunstan, these men will treat you well, and you know that I will not leave you behind."

Dunstan mumbled under his breath to the prince, "Forgive me if I am not as assured of their good intentions as you are."

Erik patted his friend's back reassuringly, and they were both led to a tent where a man kept watch over them outside. The two of them lay down on the hard ground, and Dunstan whispered in the darkness, "In all seriousness, Erik, these men are just as likely to slit our throats as the northern raiders were up at Castle Wallstone. And their hatred is more personal."

"Don't worry so much, Dunstan. We have the Grey Hawk's word that nothing will happen to us. He would not command the loyalty of so many men if he did not keep his word." Then the prince added in a more thoughtful tone. "If there is injustice being committed in the kingdom, then I want to know of it. Not to mention that I want the Grey Hawk to let us go with our horses."

"I don't know how you expect to convince him to let us go... and if he finds out who you are, you may as well have signed your own death warrant. The best thing to do is to make plans for escape. Do you hear, Erik? Erik? You aren't asleep are you?... Incredible!"

Erik had rolled over onto his side and fallen fast to sleep. Dunstan mumbled under his breath, then tried to do the same.

THE next morning, Erik joined the Grey Hawk's band as they journeyed down one of the many long roads cutting through the farmlands and the woods. The area was deserted, but Erik got the sense that every man was ready to dissolve into the forest should a party appear on the road. A lone rider emerged on the horizon, galloping toward them. It was one of the men the Grey Hawk had sent to scout ahead.

"I sense trouble," one of the men muttered as the rider reached them. The scout reported that there was a company of men headed toward the nearby farm and that the Lord Clovis was riding with them.

"Is it not unusual for the Lord Clovis to visit a farm?" Erik asked the Grey Hawk.

The man's eyes gleamed hard. "The tax collector was there last week and probably told tales of the farmer's pretty, new wife."

Erik looked warily at the men surrounding him, swords in their hands. "If the Lord of Westhane falls into your power, will you slay him?"

The Grey Hawk grunted. "Nay, for I do not have the power to defend against the king's reprisal, which would be swift and merciless, and the country folk would suffer alongside my men. There has been many a time when I could have thrust my sword into that false coward's belly, but better judgment stayed my hand. However, talk is idle. Come and witness, 'Just Erik,' what royal oppression does to my people."

They rode onward and took the narrow byway at the crossroads that led to the farm. Dismounting near a cluster of trees, two men were set to watch the horses, while the rest moved stealthily through the wood until they reached the nearside of the farmhouse overlooked by the trees. There they took cover, with Erik at the Grey Hawk's side. They observed the farmer and his wife at the gate, exchanging heated words with a burly, heavily armed man, whom Erik assumed was the tax collector.

The Grey Hawk pointed out five armed men on horseback further up on the road, and Erik recognized Lord Clovis' sharp features. He hadn't changed much since Erik remembered seeing him in the throne room receiving orders to quell the western uprising all those years ago.

"We can give you no more and paid you in full last week. I still do not understand why you are here." The farmer's words called Erik and the Grey Hawk's attention back to the scene closer at hand.

"A farm your size should have yielded a greater crop. All you farmers are cheaters. You better deliver unless you wish us to seize the farm."

The farmer ran his hands desperately through his hair. "I swear we have held nothing back. Search yourselves."

"Oh, we can do that if you insist, greedy lying swine that you are. But then, I cannot guarantee what could happen. One of the soldiers might accidently set your fields ablaze… you know how clumsy those brutes are."

The farmer groaned, and the tax collector smiled with his teeth. "I have another proposal for you, one that meets with the Lord of Westhane's approval. Why not have your pretty little bride pay off the debt? The Lord is a generous man and will let you off with such a trifle. Who knows, you may even get her back."

The farmer's wife started sobbing even louder and clutched at her husband's sleeve.

"This is an outrage," Erik whispered in repressed fury and turned to the Grey Hawk. "I am going to stop this. Will you give me a show of men if I need them? This should not turn into a fight, but I am not afraid of a skirmish if need be."

The Grey Hawk narrowed his eyes and curtly nodded his head. With that sign of approval, Erik moved rapidly through the wood. When he reached the line of trees, Erik sprang forward, swiftly drawing his sword and knocking the blade out of the surprised tax collector's hand. Erik saw that the sound had alerted Lord Clovis and his men and that they were rapidly approaching.

The prince pointed his sword threateningly at the tax collector's throat. "Halt! You are close enough! Do you recognize me, Lord Clovis of Westhane?"

The sharp eyes of the lord appraised the youth. "Indeed, Prince Erik, you bear your own likeness. But I am at a loss to understand why you threaten one of my men and interfere in my affairs."

Erik released the tax collector and sent him back to his master with the flat of his blade. "Are your affairs to extort unjust taxation and defile women, my Lord? Your affairs stink with corruption."

Lord Clovis spoke coolly. "Your highness is naïve if you believe that rebellious provinces can be governed with other than a rod of iron. What would the king think if he knew you were overstepping your bounds and interfering with my governance?"

"What would the king think if he knew how harshly you were oppressing the western peoples? He wants peace in Lothene, not a land pushed to its breaking point. How do you know he has not sent me to look into your affairs?"

The lord gave Erik a knowing smile. "Alone? I think not. Why don't you come with me and we can both send word to your father."

He signaled to the guards, but suddenly the wood came alive with men as the Grey Hawk and his band emerged and, with their weapons drawn, took their places around the prince.

"You take a stand with my enemies!" Lord Clovis hissed in outrage.

Erik spoke sternly. "Go back to your castle, my Lord, and leave this farm in peace. I will hear of it if you continue your outrages against my people. I swear to you that my father and I will uphold the laws of Lothene."

Lord Clovis glared at the prince in rage and seemed to be calculating if he could pin the blame on the Grey Hawk and his men if the prince was slain in battle. The Grey Hawk must have read his mind. "We outnumber you three to one," he said, "and the prince and my band are all battle-hardened men. Can you say the same of your soldiers? Or do they only raise their arms against the weak and defenseless?" Apparently the lord was not confident in the odds, for he shot a single venomous look at the Grey Hawk and then turned his horse back in retreat, his men following after him.

The prince and the Grey Hawk returned to their horses at the top of the hill with the farmer and his wife's abundant thanks still echoing in their ears. They rode side by side back to the camp, and, after they dismounted, the prince turned to the Grey Hawk. "Lord Gavin of Westhane, will you let me and Dunstan go now that you know who I am, or will you hold us for ransom?"

The Grey Hawk's eyes sparkled, and Erik saw that his use of the Lord's title was not lost on Gavin.

"Do you think I would have let you have your way and ride with us and then take your stand against the false Lord of Westhane, if I did not know who you were?" the Grey Hawk asked.

Erik felt mystified. "How did you know?"

The Grey Hawk gave a short laugh. "First this." He reached into his jerkin and pulled out the prince's money bag and took out a single golden coin. He flipped it in the air and caught it, revealing the stamped profile of the king. "Your coloring may be of the western peoples, but your profile bears a certain family resemblance. Secondly, no one could mistake in your bearing other than what you are. You are a little imperious, my dear prince. You need to do more to disguise yourself than simply change your apparel."

Erik felt ruffled.

"Yet you show concern for your people and a love for justice that bodes well for the Western Lands. It may be that fate led you to my camp so I could do you the courtesy of aiding you in your journey."

"So you will let us go?"

"Do us the honor of spending the night with us as our royal guest, and your horses will be supplied with provisions for your journey tomorrow."

THE knowledge of Erik's identity quickly spread throughout the camp, and many startled glances were directed toward the prince and the Grey Hawk, but the men followed their leader absolutely and did not question Erik's presence among them. Corwin went so far as to approach the prince and stiffly bow. "My apologies to the prince for any rudeness I may have committed."

Erik returned the bow. "Do not mention it. You had no way of knowing who I was. It is all in the past."

The Grey Hawk joined them. "Corwin is a gem of a man, the first to blaze to anger, but also the first to reproach himself if he has done wrong. I would count my life safe in the hands of any of my men."

"That is a treasure, indeed," Erik agreed. "When such nobility is outlawed, then the foundations of a kingdom must crumble."

"I counselled my father against civil war. I knew failure would be the only result. But my father was a rash man of the old way, while I and my men are weary of bloodshed."

"I too have lost many precious to me. If I restored justice to the land, Lord Gavin, would you follow me?"

The Grey Hawk's eyes gleamed. "The line of the old kings died out long ago, and all of the western clans vie each other for leadership. If you defend the Western peoples and bring them peace, then you would be a king I could follow."

"Then you must stop waylaying innocent travelers on the road... though this time it may have fallen to the advantage of us both."

The Grey Hawk smiled and left to tend to things in his camp. Dunstan came over to Erik and pulled him aside. "Don't you think your father will question your loyalty if you side with the Grey Hawk instead of the lord he appointed? The Lord of West-hane will have tales to tell the king, and you should return to the castle before he turns the king against you."

Erik gazed at Dunstan. "I cannot go back," he said softly.

Dunstan shifted uncomfortably. "But surely this matter is

more pressing than your dream princess. We can always set out again once things are settled."

Erik shook his head. "You may go back and bear a message for me, if you will. But I must go on."

"Go back and say what?" Dunstan exploded. "The prince is not really inciting revolutionaries in the Western Lands, but is too busy searching for a princess he saw in his dreams to tell you so himself? Someone has to go with you to help you search for your lost wits!"

Erik gave a quiet laugh. "I admit that this is difficult, Dunstan, but, if I turn my back on the princess now, then the quest will never be fulfilled. I feel it. I would be condemning Princess Rosamund to eternal sleep, and I would rather die first."

Dunstan shook his head in disbelief. "Do you hear yourself? What has happened to the reasonable and serious prince?"

"If you believed what I believed, my friend, you would know that I am being very serious. But enough of this." He clapped Dunstan on the back. "I see food is being prepared. Shall we feast on venison and ale as honored guests?"

Dunstan grumbled and then nodded. "The least we can do is get a decent meal out of all this. I'm famished."

THEY all enjoyed a hearty meal by the glow of the campfire. Toasts were made, music played, and a newfound hope stirred in the heart of the Grey Hawk's band. The Lord Gavin leaned back and said to the prince, "Now tell me of your journey and with what I can assist you."

Dunstan looked down in his cup, but Erik spoke to the Grey Hawk with an unwavering voice. "We are seeking the Shadowood. Can you lead us there?"

An uneasy murmur rippled through the men, and the Grey Hawk looked troubled. "What is it that you hope to find, young prince, that is worth traveling through the accursed wood?"

"I wish to find the sleeping princess of legend and wake her."

Someone laughed, but Erik's gaze did not falter, and the Grey Hawk must have seen the conviction in his eye.

"I will not deny that I dislike what I hear. I know many stories of the Shadowood, a few ancient, many new, and I cannot help you, for I do not know the truth behind them. The sleeping princess is merely an old tale meant to keep the west from losing hope and to foster the dream of a return of a golden age. I do not believe in such tales, and I also do not wish to lose the newfound friendship we have forged by chasing myths and legends. Yet I see that you are resolved and that nothing but force will move you, and friendship does not move by force. Aymer, do you have anything to tell the prince?"

The minstrel shook his head. "After the fall of the kingdom of Aurlia, the minstrel Neiren, ancient father of the golden tales, wandered throughout the fallen land, singing of the sleeping princess and how her wakening would bring back the Golden Kingdom. His songs kept hope alive in the hearts of the fallen, and many in the west wait for the princess still. But nowhere in his songs does he say how to wake the princess, or where she is sleeping."

A somber silence had settled on the camp at the mention of the Shadowood and the princess. The men looked at the prince as though one dead, and even the prince began to feel a chill in his blood.

The Grey Hawk spoke again. "We should rest, for you have a long and dangerous journey ahead of you. Tomorrow I will show you the entrance into the accursed wood."

Chapter Nineteen

The Shadowood

BOTH ERIK and Dunstan had a restless night troubled by dreams, for the Grey Hawk's warning brought home to them the danger they were about to face. They awoke at dawn, and the men had already saddled their horses and furnished them with provisions.

Lodestar was straining to depart, and Erik soothed him and stroked his mane. "You have been well-cared for here. I wonder if you would be so eager to leave if you knew where we were headed?"

"Horses are loyal creatures," said the Grey Hawk, riding up beside him, and then he looked down at Dunstan. "So are friends who would follow you into unknown danger. But come, I will bring you to the edge of the Shadowood. It is not far."

They journeyed a few hours southwest, passing fields full of blooming trees that grew thicker with elms and linden trees as they rode, until they came up to a wall of stone and slate, ancient but kept in good repair.

The Grey Hawk spoke. "This marks the boundary to the Shadowood. Those who live near the edge of the wood built it to ward off the unwary and have been tending it for generations. If you continue following it southward, you will find an opening that will let your horses through." He turned to the prince. "Is there nothing I can say that will dissuade you?"

"No, Lord Gavin, but I thank you for leading me thus far."

The Grey Hawk inclined his head. "There may be something

working in this that I do not understand. Perhaps only one who faces myths and legends will have the strength to unite a troubled Lothene. I would that you return to be my king."

The Grey Hawk bowed, and Dunstan, watching him ride away, said, "If his allegiance is the only thing that comes out of all this dream-chasing, it will have been worth it."

Erik glanced at Dunstan. "You know, you don't have to come... you can still go back."

Dunstan rolled his eyes and spurred his horse to follow the wall due east. Soon he and Erik found an opening and stared into the gap in the wall that led into the dark wood before them. Without a word, Erik rode into the Shadowood.

THE two companions traveled through the forest, tense and alert. The trees were broad and ancient, and there seemed to be an almost oppressively thick silence in the air. Random shafts of light pierced through the dense canopy above and momentarily dispersed the gloom, but then were inexorably swallowed by the shadows. Erik shivered, feeling stifled by the cloud of silence.

"Erik, which way are we going?" Dunstan broke the silence. To Erik's ears, Dunstan's voice sounded harsh in the hushed wood, even though he had spoken in little more than a whisper.

"Forward."

"Not exactly the specificity I was looking for, but what more did I expect?" Dunstan mumbled to himself.

They rode deeper into the forest and spoke little, for their voices too were swallowed by the almost tangible thickness of the wood. They stopped a few times to rest their horses and consume their provisions, and Erik tried to speculate how many days they could travel before they ran out of food. He did not relish the idea of hunting in the forest and secretly wondered if the wood might retaliate if they shot down one of its own, then he dismissed the thought as ridiculous.

In this manner, the first day passed. They encountered nothing, neither wild beast nor anything magical, only eerie silence. The second day, they continued their journey into the heart of the Shadowood and noticed the undergrowth growing more rampant, the hawthorn burgeoning and intertwining with the trees. It became more and more difficult to pick their trail, until they finally came to a spreading morass of thickets that impeded their path. Erik looked ahead and saw that the thicket amassed into an incredibly dense natural barrier, an impenetrable wall of thorns, sharp and jagged, that only seemed to grow taller and thicker the further it went.

Erik pondered the thorns before him. "This wall is as tall as trees. Let us see how far this growth travels."

They rode along the thorn wood for a good hour, before the growth lessened and they were able to round the corner. Erik then saw that the thorn wall continued deep into the wood as far as the eye could see.

Dunstan whistled. "Well, we are not going to be able to investigate this ungodly large briar patch. I've never seen thorn bushes grow so tall. Shall we go a different route?"

"No… There is something unnatural about this, almost as if the wood is hiding something. I say we continue alongside this hedge, or what is more like a thorn wood, and see if we can spy a pathway or opening."

Dunstan did not speak, but his look voiced his skepticism.

Erik led them alongside the wall of thorns, until he exclaimed, "I think I see something!" He dismounted and carefully picked his way up to a narrow gap in the thorns. "I see a way in!" he called back. "Watch the horses until I return." He ducked into the wall before Dunstan could protest.

After he had pierced the outer wall, Erik saw that narrow pathways riddled the thorn wood like a maze. Choosing a path at random, he followed it until it stopped before another impassible wall of thorns, cruel and forbidding. Hacking at it with his sword did no good, for the thorns were unending, and he felt a sting as a hacked piece flew against his cheek. He turned back and began again, trying to keep track of the many branching paths so as not to get lost.

The riddled paths were narrow, and long, piercing thorns tore at Erik's flesh and ripped into his cloak. He wiped away the blood, but continued onward, his path leading him to yet another dead end. The prince turned back for the entrance to begin his path anew, but he must have miscalculated somewhere, for, when he thought he should have reached his old trail, he came upon a new path. Erik retraced his steps, but found that yet again he came upon the wrong turn. Looking up at the sky, he saw that he had been in the thorn maze for over an hour and knew that Dunstan must be worried, but, when he called out to his friend, he could hear no response through the thick, tangled walls of thorn. He slashed again at the impenetrable walls with his sword, but could make no dent in the thick growth.

Realizing that he was hopelessly lost, Erik stopped trying to count his steps and turns, but instead struck at random, hoping to either return to the entrance or reach the mysterious heart of the maze. He lost all track of time, and it was not until it was growing dark that he stumbled from out of the maze back to where Dunstan was waiting for him with the horses. Dunstan looked visibly relieved when he saw the prince, scratched and torn though he was, limping back towards him.

"Thank the stars, you've come back," he said. "I could find no way into the maze, no matter how hard I looked."

Erik did not say anything, but merely took the water flask that Dunstan offered and drank deeply of the cool, refreshing water.

"I have to go back," he gasped, when he had quenched his parched throat.

"Go back where?"

"Into the thorn maze."

Dunstan looked at him with concern. "I thought you just explored in there. What did you find?"

"Nothing. That is why I have to go back."

A combination of worry and frustration gave Dunstan's voice a sharp edge. "What makes you think that there is anything to find? It is nothing but an unnaturally large thorn patch."

"Dunstan, she could be in there," Erik said.

"Who, your sleeping princess?"

"Yes, we have to explore the Shadowood thoroughly."

"No wonder you want to rescue your princess so desperately. She can't be sleeping very comfortably in a thorn patch."

"Dunstan, you aren't helping," Erik said wearily.

"No, of course not, far be it for me to point out the lunacy of the situation. You have just wasted the entire day getting lost and torn to shreds in a thorn patch, and you have to go back because you found nothing. Which of course you interpret to mean that *something* must be in there after all, instead of what most would deduce from the situation, which is that there is *nothing* to be found."

Erik ignored Dunstan and scrutinized the top of the thorn walls. "We'd be able to see it over the walls if it was there, wouldn't we?" he murmured to himself.

"See what?"

"The tower?"

"What tower?"

"The princess is sleeping in a tower," Erik snapped. "Don't you listen to anything I tell you?"

"Oh, yes, of course, how could I have forgotten? I just thought you said she was in a thorn patch," Dunstan retorted.

"A tower *in* a thorn patch."

"A tower in a thorn patch," Dunstan repeated stupidly.

The prince stared hard at his friend and then burst out laughing, "I'm sorry Dunstan. It does sound ridiculous if you put it like that. Why don't we camp for the night? We can decide what to do in the morning."

Relief spread across his features, and Dunstan broke out into a grin. "Well, you haven't been making any sense this entire journey, so why should I expect you to start making sense now? Only, this wood *does* things to one. I've been feeling uneasy ever since we entered."

Erik nodded sympathetically, and they both rode a little ways from the thorn wood, so they could find a comfortable ground that wasn't riddled with thorns to set up camp. They were gathering fallen boughs from the forest floor for a fire, when they heard a howl deep within the wood that set their horses affright. Erik and Dunstan shared a look.

"Do you think they've caught our scent?" Erik asked.

"Well, they've caught *something's* scent," Dunstan said testily. "I knew things had been going too well."

"Let's finish building the fire. Hopefully that will keep the wolves at bay."

Erik and Dunstan quickly set the fire blazing, and it burned strong and bright. They sat around the campfire and watched and waited as it grew dark, their hands resting by their bows. They did not have to wait long, however, before they saw pairs of gleaming, yellow eyes glaring at them in the dark. Both Dunstan and the prince stood and strung their bows taut. Dunstan loosed an arrow, and Erik heard a thump and a sharp whine as Dunstan swiftly restrung his bow.

"It seems they won't come too near the fire," Erik observed.

Dunstan grunted in response, but the prince had spoken too soon, for there came a howl, and then the air around them was full of clamor and the sudden onrush of springing wolves. They were the largest wolves the prince had ever encountered, silver, mammoth, but lean with ferocious power, and deadly. Both of them dropped their bows and grabbed the thick branches they had prepared and thrust them into the fire. They swung the fiery brands with one hand and hacked at the wolves with their swords with the other.

"We have to protect the horses," Erik yelled.

The horses had been tied up to tree branches to keep them from fleeing, and they were screaming and rearing in blind terror. Erik managed to reach them and fight the wolves away, but he saw that the pack was instead gathering around Dunstan. With a cry, Erik saw them overwhelm his friend, and Dunstan went down under the pack.

Erik struck at the wolves from behind, blind with fury, his heart sore afraid for his friend. Then he heard a sharp call, and the wolves pulled back. He saw Dunstan lying on the ground in his blood and rushed to his side.

Erik whirled back to face the wolves and saw the tall figure of a woman, dark before the firelight, with the wolves gathering by her side and then disappearing in the woods behind her. The woman's face was shrouded in the shadows, and all he could see was the redness of her hair in the light of the fire. She lifted her arm, pointed, then turned and followed the wolves into the darkness. Erik almost cried in despair. Ripping apart his tunic, he tried to staunch the blood flowing from Dunstan's side. He managed to lift his friend and lay him astride his horse, and then he led them in the direction the woman had pointed.

It was with a mixture of relief and disbelief that he found that they had come before a strange cabin in the deep of the wood. He rushed to the door and pounded on it, crying for help. The door opened by a crack, and an old woman peered fearfully at him.

"Please," Erik pleaded, "my friend is gravely injured."

The old woman nodded and opened the door wide, and Erik carried Dunstan inside. There was a young woman in the cottage as well, and she helped Erik lower Dunstan onto the only bed in the cottage. The old woman began to bathe Dunstan's wounds, while the younger one went outside to see to the horses.

The young woman returned indoors and went without a word to the old woman's side and helped her tend to Dunstan.

Erik stood by feeling helpless. He could see that both women were skilled at treating wounds, and Dunstan remained in semi-consciousness as they cared for him, only murmuring as they gave him a draught of something out of a small bottle.

"That should help him rest and deal with the pain," the old woman explained.

The girl smoothed back Dunstan's yellow hair, and her touch seemed to soothe him.

"We've done all that we can, and the boy must rest. Why don't you tell me what you are doing so deep within the Shadowood?" the old woman said.

Erik was staring with worry at Dunstan's slumbering form and answered distractedly, "Yes? Oh, I am looking for someone… Do you know if Dunstan will live?"

The old woman also gazed at Dunstan's recumbent form. "Yes, I expect he will. His wounds are strange, bloody, but not life-threatening. Nothing vital has been damaged. With enough rest, he should be walking in a week or so."

Erik buried his head in his hands, overcome by emotion. "Thank the heavens! I would never have forgiven myself if he had perished following me. He never wanted to come and only followed me because he is my friend."

The old woman did not say anything, but the younger one pulled up a chair and gently sat Erik down. She then joined the old woman beside the fireplace, and both remained silent. The prince looked up at them after a moment and thought again how strange it was that there should be a cabin in the middle of the Shadowood and that these two women should live all alone in it.

He voiced his surprise, and the old woman replied, "My daughter and I are left in peace here, far away from the strife which troubles our land, far from the conflict between Westerners and Midlothians. Those who live in the wood follow the old ways, and the wood shelters us."

"There are more of you?"

"Some. Not many."

The old woman fell silent again, and Erik realized that he had not properly answered her question about what he was doing in the wood, nor had he explained who he was. These two women had helped him and Dunstan without question and had opened their home to total strangers, and yet he was the one asking questions.

He rose to his feet and bowed low. "You must forgive me for my rudeness. Excuse my thoughtlessness in my distress for my friend. I am the Crown Prince, Erik of Lothene. I have come to the Shadowood to find the sleeping princess of legend, though very few have heard of her. Do you know of anything which might aid me in my quest?"

The old woman pursed her lips and said, "What would you do with the sleeping princess when you found her?"

"I would wake her, of course."

"What makes you think you can? You are a Midlothian, the prince from the line of invaders. Why should I help you find our princess?"

The prince said softly, "The invasion happened a long time ago."

"We in the west have long memories."

Erik felt troubled, and the thought occurred to him that the princess might feel the same way, but then he said, "I have dreamed of the princess since I was a young boy and have heard stories about her my whole life. I wish to wake her because I love her and will marry her if she will have me."

The old woman snorted, "You, a Midlothian have dreams of the princess? What makes you think they are true dreams, if you even dreamed at all, as you say? I come from a line of women loyal to the princess. My mother's grandmother's great-grandmother was her loyal handmaid. 'Tis from her that the art of healing has passed down from generation to generation, as my mother passed it to me, and I to my daughter. Why would the princess appear to you in a dream, and not to me, who has lived my entire life keeping faith with her memory?"

The prince looked at the healing woman with compassion. She was also one whose life was touched by the princess, and that was why she lived alone with her daughter in the Shadowood. If anyone could help him, this woman could, and yet he would first have to convince her of his trustworthiness. He thought for a moment. "The princess' handmaid, I've heard of her from the stories. She was once a kitchen maid, was she not?"

The healing woman started visibly and then grew pale. "How do you know? No one outside our family has ever heard of her, let alone known that hidden detail of her life. How do you know?"

Erik knelt before her and took her hand. "I know because I am meant to find the princess. Because I have met with her and spoken with her, even though it happened in a dream. I must find her and awaken her, or she will forever remain asleep. You must help me. Why else would the forest have sent me to you?"

The healing woman shook her head in disbelief. Then her daughter spoke for the first time. "Mother, he speaks truly. He must know of the princess. The wood has protected him thus far and sent him to us. Surely it's not up to us to choose who should or shouldn't rescue the princess, but to accept and aid the one who *is* sent."

The old woman tore her eyes away from Erik's earnest gaze and looked down at the floor. "Do you know the story of how the kingdom fell in the northern invasion and what happened to the castle when it fell?" she asked.

Erik shook his head. "Only what has been recorded in history."

"Recorded by Northerners," she said sharply. "Sit down, Crown Prince, and I will tell you the story as it was passed down to me by my mother, and by her mother's mother before her, back to when Edwina first recounted the story with tears in her eyes."

The healing woman's face took on a faraway look, and, as she told her story, each word she spoke was thick with the weight of memory.

After the curse had fallen and the princess was in deep slumber, she was laid to rest in the tower on her faerie godmother's orders. The king had her put there in ceremony and spent a night all alone by her bedside. No one knew if he had shed tears when he said farewell to his only little one, but, after he shut the door behind him, he never returned to see her.

Her cousin Edmund stayed away from the tower as well. He never looked toward it, nor spoke of the princess, yet he could not force himself to leave the castle, even though his father had gone long ago. The servants whispered that at night there could be seen a dark-hooded figure circling the tower and falling on its knees before the door, its hand outstretched as if begging for forgiveness.

The once great kingdom fell into confusion, and the weariness that before had threatened the king now overcame him. He sat all alone on his golden throne and banished all his noblemen from the castle. Every evening he ate in his chambers, alone and unspeaking, though he had three place settings laid out on the table. And every evening the servants would take back three plates fully laden to the kitchen, for the king rarely ate and would only take a little bread and wine to sustain him.

Thieves and brigands overran the lands, and the lords did not watch o'er those in their care. So, when raiders in ships from o'er the northern sea came, they found a country unresisting. They burned and pillaged and their numbers grew, until a large force came from o'er the sea and broke like a great and mighty wave against the castle walls and battered down the gates.

Then the king was roused and returned to life to face his death like the Golden Kings of old. He slew many northern warriors, with his sword stained red and flashing silver. But finally he fell before the great numbers, and, with his death, Edmund

became king as the dark faery promised. But like all such prom-
ises, no joy came from it.

Edmund called the last of the soldiers to defend the princess in
the tower. The soldiers fought bravely, but fell, one by one, until
Edmund was the only one standing. He too finally fell and lay
down on the pile of broken bodies of foe and friend alike.

The invaders swarmed through the castle searching for gold
and treasure and left the tower undisturbed, for the door to the
tower was missing, and they strangely never thought to be curi-
ous about what was inside.

But Edmund was not dead yet and lay facing the cloudy grey
sky with his body on fire and his mind in even deeper agony
o'er the princess' fate. A cool shadow fell o'er him, bringing
relief and the scent of the spring morning. Eyes of dawn and
dusk stared into the fading eyes of the dying king.

Edmund reached up to the Green Lady. He gasped the princess'
name with the last of his strength, and the faery clasped his
hand before it fell.

"Rest peacefully," she said. "Your sacrifice has saved the prin-
cess."

Edmund died from a sword wound that had pierced his heart.
The Green Lady took three drops of his heart's blood and bur-
ied them deep in the earth. From the blood sprang a bush that
grew speedily with sharp, clawing thorns. It grew o'er and
claimed the bodies of the dead men surrounding the tower. The
thorns crept o'er the castle, digging into its foundations and
scaling its walls, until they severed the tower from the rest of
the castle, and the castle crumbled, leaving a solid wall of thorn
wrapped around the tower. The invaders fled in terror from the
tumbling castle, though many fell and were impaled on the
sharp thorns, and their blood was mingled in the ground with
the heart's blood of Edmund. Edwina was a witness to all this,
for she was with the Green Lady.

From that day onward, the northern men avoided the woods round the tower. Time passed, and the tower was forgotten as more northerners came from o'er the sea and settled on the land. But there are still those who whisper among themselves of the dark tower in the heart of what is now known as the Shadowood, and little children are frightened into being good by tales of fearsome creatures inhabiting the wood.

So the Golden Kings and the Golden Kingdom were forgotten by most. Seasons passed, and years passed. How many years I could not say. But those with long memories remember the princess and the promise that she will one day awaken, and with her sleeps the hope that her awakening will bring back Faerie and the Golden Kingdom of old.

When the healing woman finished, Erik was silent for a long time, lost in thoughts that made his brow knit in worry and his heart grow sad.

The old woman drew him away from his reverie. "You should sleep now. We will discuss what you must do in the morning. If you will sleep on the floor? The patient has our only bed, but I have spare blankets."

Erik rose to his feet. "Bear no thought for me; make yourselves as comfortable as you can. I have slept many a night on the hard earth under the stars."

The woman's daughter brought the prince an extra blanket, and he lay down on the floor beside the wall near the door. The events of the day played through his mind, the thorn maze, the wolves, the old woman's story that brought ancient memories to the very present. He did not know how he could ever fall asleep, but he must have been tired, because the next thing he knew was that he was no longer in the cottage, but in the silver field near the river, shaded by purple trees from his dreams.

The weariness lifted from him, and Erik went to the river's edge, hoping to catch sight of the princess. Only this time his feet were not as eager as before, for he knew that there was something he needed to tell Rosa, and he wished he did not have to do so.

But the princess was not at the other side of the river bank, nor was she in the water. He heard someone calling his name and turned to find the princess standing in the field from where he had just come. His heart leapt at the sight of her. There she was, and this time there was no river separating them. She was still a distance away, so he rushed back up to the field, but, when he came near her, Rosa held up her hands in warning. It was too late, however. He had stepped too close, and the ground shifted, so that a wide expanse of the field separated them and the princess was but a speck on the horizon.

Erik cried out in surprise, but he plowed across the field back toward the princess, and he soon saw that she was doing the same. In fact, it did not take long to reach her, as she was closer than she had appeared, as is the way in dreams. They both stopped walking when they were a few arm spans away and looked at each other.

The prince felt struck dumb, as he always did whenever he first saw the princess. She was so lovely.

"We should probably stop here," she spoke. "I do not think we are meant to be near enough to touch."

Erik shook his head and then, confused, he nodded.

Rosa laughed her bubbling, mirthful laughter, and Erik thought her laugh wonderful.

"Shall we sit down? We could talk more comfortably."

"Yes, of course," Erik said, embarrassed by his stupidity. "Would you like to sit on my cloak?" He held it up and then looked at it critically, "...though it is quite dirty and torn."

Suddenly, he wondered about his appearance. He must look very travel stained, with a torn cloak and Dunstan's blood on his tunic. The princess, however, stood before him as fresh and radiant as ever, looking the same as when he first saw her.

The dreams are different for her than for me, he thought. Is it because she is always here and I come and go, or is it because this is my dream and she is not really... the prince did not allow himself to finish his train of thought.

"No, it is all right," the princess was saying. "My dress doesn't get dirty, and I wouldn't mind if it did." She sat down and so did Erik. The princess peered at him shyly and said. "It seems like you have been through an ordeal."

Erik explained how he and his friend were attacked by wolves. Rosa gazed at him and then said simply, "Because you are looking for me?"

The prince nodded.

"Tell me."

So Erik described everything that had happened since he had last spoken with her, but he failed to mention the old healing woman in the wood.

She looked deep into his eyes and said, "Thank you." Erik felt that all of his difficulties had been repaid.

They both fell into an awkward silence, Erik because he kept pushing away that thing which he did not want to say. Whatever Rosa was thinking made her blush and she was the first to speak.

"You are right that I am in a dream."

He looked at her questioningly.

"I don't have to eat," she explained, "and I spend most of my time sleeping."

"You crossed the river." He stated the obvious for something to say.

"Yes, I wanted to be on this side in case you came back." She continued hurriedly. "I guessed the waters would let me cross when you were gone. So I wandered about the fields waiting for you, but most of the time I just felt sleepy. Then, a short while ago, I felt less tired and hoped that meant you were coming back, and now I don't feel sleepy at all."

The prince smiled softly at her. Rosa's eyes darted down, and she began pulling up tufts of silver grass. Then she raised her head and said shyly, "Last time you said you would tell me all about yourself."

So Erik recounted his past to her. He told of his mother's death and how he met Ninny Nanny in the woods, of the old woman's stories and his dreams, how he left the castle and doubted the princess' existence, and, finally, how he chased the stag and found out that she was real. Yet somehow, as he told his story, he managed to avoid telling the princess that he was the crown prince and that Lothene had once been Aurlia long ago.

Rosa stared at him with shining eyes, and Erik saw that she understood more about him than he had meant her to. When he was finished, she said, "Erik, I wanted to ask you if you knew anything of my father and the Kingdom of Aurlia. Do you know if he is still alive?"

The prince's heart grew heavy. The moment that he had wished to avoid had arrived. He had hoped that he would not have to tell her, but he knew it had been a vain hope.

"Rosa," he said gently, "it has been hundreds and hundreds of years since you fell asleep. Everything you know is gone."

There was a dreadful silence, and Rosa's face grew pale. "I feared that might be the case." Her voice trembled. "Do you know how he died?"

Erik nodded miserably. "I just found out. Soon after you fell asleep, the kingdom fell to northern invaders. Aurlia is no more. The kingdom is called Lothene now."

The princess' eyes grew wide and wet with unshed tears, and she asked in heartbreaking tones, "My father?"

"He fell with the castle. You don't know how sorry I am, Rosa," he said sorrowfully.

"Edmund?" The tears were streaming down her face.

Erik shook his head. His heart ached because he could not put his arms around her. "But your handmaid survived," he said, trying to send a ray of comfort to her. "I met one of her descendants in the forest. She is the one looking after Dunstan, I just couldn't tell you before."

"Oh." Rosa laughed a pitiful and sad laugh. "I am so glad to hear that... so Edwina survived to have children."

Each of the princess' tears wrung Erik heart, but he knew there was something else he had to say. "Rosa, there is one thing more. I told you that my name is Erik, but I did not tell you that I am the crown prince of Lothene."

He saw the realization of his words slowly sink into her face. The princess did not say a word, and her tears stopped flowing.

"Rosa," he whispered, "do you think that you could ever forgive me? For being who I am and not telling you sooner?"

The princess leaned her head against her hand and closed her eyes. "I don't know, Erik. I am too full of grief to think properly."

Erik gazed down on Rosa sadly and could think of nothing that he could do or say to comfort her. He came to the wrenching realization that he was really nothing more than a stranger to the princess, while she had been all that he had truly loved since he was a boy.

"Do you think you could leave me alone for a while?" she asked.

Erik nodded, mute and miserable, and Rosa rose and reached her hand out to touch him. His heart was torn as he realized that she was reaching out to him not to be near him, but to send him away, and he was hurtled backwards, whipping through the fields and fading from the dream.

Chapter Twenty

Barden of the Winds

IT WAS ALREADY late morning when Erik woke up in the cabin in the woods and saw that everyone was already awake. The old woman was outside, and Dunstan was sitting up in bed, eating some broth that the healing woman's daughter fed him with a spoon.

The prince stood, raked his hand through his hair, and then pulled up a chair beside Dunstan's bed, his sorrow over his last encounter with Rosa momentarily dispelled by his joy at seeing Dunstan so well.

His friend gave him a large grin. "Didn't expect to see me again, did you? I thought those wolves would have finished me. I suppose I don't taste very good."

Erik laughed, happy and relieved to see Dunstan back to his old self. The girl hid a smile and said, "I'll join my mother out of doors and gather more herbs for the poultice. I'm sure there is much that you would like to say to one another." She rose and left them alone, and Dunstan followed her with his eyes.

"Both the girl and her mother are taking good care of you."

"Hmm?" Dunstan's attention returned to Erik. "Oh, yes… probably would be dead otherwise."

"I do not think I would have ever forgiven myself if you had been killed following me on my quest."

Dunstan gave Erik a serious glance. "Emma told me how the wolves attacked only me, and that none of the wounds were grievous."

270

"Emma?"

"The girl's name is Emma."

"Of course it is." Erik suppressed a smile.

Dunstan continued. "I was thinking about the fisherman's warning—the one we met on the river at the border of Westhane. He said that the forest doesn't tolerate doubt and that it would cast out those it found wanting. I am sorry, Erik, but I don't believe in your sleeping princess."

"I know, Dunstan. I did not expect you to. There is nothing to forgive."

Dunstan brushed Erik's assurance aside. "But I pretended to believe you. At least, I didn't say that I didn't. That is why the wolves attacked us. The forest doesn't want me here, Erik."

The prince clasped his friend's forearm and said, "Yes, I know. That is why I am going on alone."

"That's what's so frustrating!" Dunstan exclaimed. "I don't want you to go on this harebrained journey on your own. I didn't believe that there was anything to your dreams before, but now I am not so sure. What if someone wishes to entrap you, Erik? Have you thought of that? The westerners know magic. Their forests are full of witches. Perhaps they wish to kidnap the crown prince?"

"I wouldn't have thought you the sort to believe in witchcraft."

"Yes, well, perhaps this forest has changed my mind," Dunstan mumbled.

"I have to go on, Dunstan."

"I knew you'd say that." Dunstan scowled, clenching his fists. "I just wished that I understood the madness that has seized you."

Erik smiled a little sadly at his friend, but they were interrupted by the healing woman and her daughter entering the cottage. The healing woman went over to the fireplace and stirred whatever was bubbling in the cast-iron pot. Its scent wafted to

Erik's nostrils and set his stomach growling. He realized that he hadn't eaten since lunch yesterday.

Emma came over to check on Dunstan, whose scowl immediately disappeared. The prince observed that Emma was a very pretty girl, with dark hair and red lips. He raised his eyebrows at Dunstan, who gave him a sly wink, and then left the two of them to go and speak to the old woman.

"I must depart soon. May I leave Dunstan in your care?"

"You may."

"Is there anything more that you can tell me to aid me in my quest?"

The old woman continued to stir the pot. "I have learned that it is not for me to decide who the forest chooses and who it casts aside, but there is actually very little that I know which can help you. Stories alter over time. Some things change, some things remain the same. 'Tis said that the Dark Tower stands in the middle of the thorn wood and that the princess sleeps inside, but the thorn wood is a labyrinth, and no one knows the true path."

"Then I will go back. I have already wandered the thorn wood and will discover its secret path. Otherwise all has been for nothing."

The old woman shook her head. "That I wouldn't do. You've already been in the thorn wood, and it cast you out. You cannot enter the labyrinth the same way twice."

"Then what would you suggest?"

"You must speak with Barden of the Winds. There're some who say that he has faerie blood, though how far back it goes I do not know, but he deals in the secrets of the wood. He can speak to the trees and to the winds. If anyone knows the way through the labyrinth, it would be he."

"Where might I find him?"

"That I *can* tell you. Barden's Hall is about a day's ride from here. You must travel north until you come to a wide stream; follow the stream westwards and you will reach a steep incline; when you reach the top, you will have a view of the house below. Tell Barden that the healing woman of the thorn wood has sent you, and he will help you. I tended his eldest boy through a sickness, and he owes me a favor."

Erik thanked the old woman, and she ladled her stew into a bowl. "Eat this, Erik, Crown Prince of Lothene. You have a long journey ahead of you, and you will not fail on my account. But beware of Barden. Those who deal in secrets have secrets themselves, and they do not reveal them without a price."

When Erik was ready to depart, he bade farewell to Dunstan, who gave him a grim look.

"If I didn't know I would be a hindrance to you, nothing would keep me from accompanying you. But as it is… Swear you will come back."

"I swear, Dunstan."

"You have to," said Dunstan, smiling weakly. "Your father will have me flayed alive if I return to the castle without you."

Erik clasped his friend's hand and then bade farewell to the old woman and her daughter. He mounted Lodestar and began the day's journey to Barden's Hall. It was early evening before he reached the top of the ridge the old woman had described, and he was just able to discern the large, timbered hall through the trees a far distance below.

During his journey, Erik had spent hours reflecting on his last encounter with the princess. The fear gripped him that she might never see him as anything other than a usurper to the throne and the murderer of her people. What had happened hundreds of years ago was new and present to her, but he resolved that it did not matter if Rosa returned his love or no. It was enough that he loved her and that he saved her. That was all.

Dusk was creeping in by the time Erik reached the hall where lived Barden of the Winds, and Erik wondered what sort of man would dwell deep in the Shadowood. A large iron knocker hung

on the door, engraved with the image of a boar with two projecting tusks. He gripped the handle and gave three heavy knocks,
then waited. Presently the door opened to a narrow crack, and a
small pair of eyes gleamed up at him from below. The prince saw
that they belonged to a young boy.

"A fair evening to you." Erik smiled down at the boy. "I have
come seeking Barden of the Winds and shelter for the night. May
I come in?"

The heavy door was slammed shut, and Erik was considering
knocking again when it was opened, and a tall woman, her dark
hair streaked with grey, stood before him. The prince bowed.

"You come seeking my husband?"

"The healing woman by the thorn wood sent me. She said
your husband could aid me on my journey."

The woman stared at him hard and then let him in without a
word.

"I have a horse outside."

She sent the boy to tend to Erik's horse with a wave of her
head and then led the prince to a spacious hall lit by a large fire.
Seated at the head of a long table heaped with food was a man
with iron grey hair and a face set as hard as steel. Down one side
of the table sat three young women, two dark and one fair, and
on the other side was one boy on the cusp of manhood.

Erik bowed to all, saying, "My apologies for disturbing your
evening meal. I was sent by the healing woman by the thorn
wood to request your aid. May I have shelter for the night?"

Barden of the Winds gave the prince a searching glance and
gestured to the table. "Would you join us? We have a place set for
you at our table."

Erik looked down in surprise and saw that there was indeed a
place reserved for him by the eldest boy at his host's right. He
took his seat, and the woman sat opposite her husband. The
youngest boy, who had finished tending to Erik's horse, had just
slipped in as well to sit at the other side of his elder brother.

"Now that we are all here, we can begin," said Barden, and they all helped themselves to the food before them in a clatter of platters and silverware.

"Aelwyn, why don't you serve our guest some wine?" Barden said.

The young woman sitting opposite the prince rose and took the flagon from the middle of the table to fill his goblet with a dark ale.

"As you can see," Barden continued, "we have simple manners and simple fare in our home. You must be used to grander meals, Erik, Crown Prince of Lothene."

"You know who I am and knew to expect me. How is that?" Erik asked.

Barden smiled enigmatically. "The trees whisper secrets, and the winds carry their tales to me. They told me you were coming, but did not tell me what you are seeking. We will discuss that after our meal."

Erik nodded to the others at the table. "Are these your sons and daughters?"

"Indeed." Barden smiled and showed his teeth. "You see my three daughters and my two youngest sons. I have two more sons, but they have left the woods and travel abroad to make their fortune."

The prince glanced at the three women and thought with pity that they must find it a lonely life in the wood. Barden seemed to read his thoughts, for he said, "My daughters will also one day leave the wood, when they have found husbands. Are not my daughters beautiful to behold, Crown Prince of Lothene?"

"They are indeed, good sir," said Erik, speaking the truth, for Barden's daughters were as lovely and regal as the women in his father's court.

"My daughter, Aelwyn, is particularly beautiful and will be the first to be married."

Aelwyn did not speak, but merely crumbled the bread on her

plate. Erik did not know how to respond, so he simply nodded. Then he turned to his host's wife. "You have my thanks for this meal. I was surprised when the healing woman told me that there were others living in the Shadowood. Those living by the outskirts of the forest tell many dark tales of its danger. I, too, have seen glimmers of strange things."

The woman remained silent, and her husband answered for her. "Those dark tales, as you call them, were spread by those new to the land, who found that the wood resisted their invasion and withheld its secrets. These tales are also an attempt to stamp out our old way of life, though it is also true that a dark wildness was loosed after the kingdom fell, and it gathers thickest in the Shadowood."

"And you do not find it dangerous to live here?" Erik asked.

"There are always dangers, my prince. But at least here we live in peace and can live by the old ways undisturbed." He smiled at the prince, but his smile was not friendly, and Erik saw that he stood on a razor's edge before his host. Erik fell silent, and Barden stood. "I see the prince has finished his meal. Why don't the others leave us, and you can tell me of what you seek and how I can best assist you."

Barden's wife and his children all rose and filed through the large double doors, leaving Erik alone with his host.

"More wine, my prince?" Barden gestured to the flagon, and Erik poured himself and his host another glass. But Barden did not touch his wine and said, "Now tell me what it is that you seek."

"I am seeking the Dark Tower that stands in the heart of the thorn wood. The healing woman said that you would know if there is a secret entrance to the labyrinth and how to find the way through it."

Barden was silent for a moment and then asked softly, "And what does the prince seek in the Dark Tower?"

"The sleeping princess."

Barden strode to the fireplace to stare into the crackling

flames, then turned to the prince, his eyes dancing with the light of the fire, and said, "The old stories are silent and confused with regards to the sleeping princess. No one knows if she is real, or if she can be wakened."

"She is real," Erik said firmly.

"What will you do when you find her?"

"I will wake her."

Barden waited for Erik to say more, but the prince remained silent. Barden turned away and said, "You should retire for the night. A room has been prepared for you. Tonight I will speak to the winds and find out what they know of the thorn wood."

Erik inclined his head. "You have my thanks for your hospitality and assistance. I am in your debt."

Barden's eyes gleamed. "It is no small thing to be owed a favor by the crown prince. I am sure that he repays his debts with honor."

Barden's wife entered before the prince could respond, and Erik followed her up the stairs to the room she had prepared for him. He was half-way undressed when he heard a soft knocking at the door. He opened it, and there stood Aelwyn, her unbound dark hair tumbling down to her waist.

"I have come to help the prince ready for bed."

Erik shook his head and said firmly, "Thank you, Aelwyn, but I do not require any assistance. Why don't you go to sleep?"

Aelwyn did not leave, however, but asked, "Does the prince desire company?"

Erik looked at the girl and saw that she was beautiful. Her dark eyes were large and her neck was long and white, and he saw that her lips trembled. The prince spoke softly to her. "Did your father send you?"

Aelwyn nodded.

The prince took her hand and kissed it. "I thank you, Aelywn, but my heart belongs to another, and I would never do anything to dishonor her or you."

The girl's eyes filled with tears as she snatched her hand away and fled from the prince. Erik sighed and closed the door. As he lay down on the bed, he feared what Aelwyn's visit would bode for him and her father in the morning. Barden had named his price, and Erik had just refused to pay it.

When Erik greeted Barden the following morning, the iron-haired man made no reference to any of the events that had occurred the night before. He greeted the prince with an amiable smile, and they shared a meal alone together, but the prince felt that Barden was like the wise, old wolf, waiting to strike when the time was right.

When they finished, his host said, "Last night I sent the four winds to the four corners of the wood. The north and south wind returned without any secrets to tell. The east wind came next and bore secrets, but nothing to do with the sleeping princess in the tower. The west wind came last and whispered softly in my ear and murmured of a tower and a hidden way, dark and secret."

"Will you tell me that secret way?" Erik asked, trying to hide the misgiving in his voice.

"Gladly, my prince, for what use could this secret be to me? I cannot waken the princess. Ride due west. The west wind shall accompany you and reveal the secret way to you when it is time."

"Due west," Erik pondered, "but is that not further away from the thorn wood?" The prince gravely studied the man who spoke with the winds, who was tall and lordly, but whose face was as unknowable as the Shadowood itself.

"Do you doubt me, crown prince? Do you fear that I would lead you astray? It is true that I bear no great love for Midlothians, but to you, at least, I have shown nothing but my most generous hospitality. Spurn that gift at your peril... but you may believe what you will."

Erik bowed low to his host. "My apologies if I appear hesitant. It is against my nature to leap blindly, though that is all I have been doing since I began my quest. I will do as you say. Is there anything I can do to repay you for your kindness?"

Barden shook his head dismissively. "To see a legend come to life again would be repayment enough. There is nothing that I require."

The prince felt a nagging doubt over his host's seemingly selfless generosity, but he didn't see how following Barden's advice could leave him any worse off than he was now, so he bid farewell to his host and rode due west with the sun rising behind him.

BY the time the sun reached its noonday zenith, the forest air was thick and sweltering despite the canopy of leaves, and Erik's sweaty tunic clung to his back. He dismounted to give Lodestar a break and dig into his provisions. There was no hint of leaves stirring or the faintest breath of wind, and, as he wiped his brow, he wondered if the west wind would come to guide him as Barden promised. His doubts about Barden were mounting, and he was readying his plans to return to the thorn wood and navigate the maze on his own, when a sharp gust of wind suddenly ripped through his hair and clothes, sending Lodestar's tail and mane flapping and whipping the dry leaves into a crackling whirlpool that encircled them.

Erik leapt onto his horse and galloped with the wind lashing him onward, a surging roar pressing him from behind, nipping Lodestar's ankles and leading him through the wood at a mad pace until he reached the foot of a tall hill. It pressed him up the steep climb, Lodestar's hoofs stumbling and scraping over the loose rocks. When he reached the crest of the hill, the wind instantly quelled, a hushed silence replacing the wind's vast roar. It took Erik a moment to catch his breath and regain his bearings, but, when he did, he saw that he had a prime view of the forest below. Craning his neck, he scanned the landscape, catching sight of a distant, dark form so enveloped in mist that he could not clearly discern its shape.

"Is that the tower?" he whispered and strained against his saddle for a better look. There was a sudden roar and a blast of wind, and the western wind engulfed him, plucked him up from his seat, and thrust him over the edge of the ravine below. Erik twisted with a cry, straining to grasp the earth beneath his fingers, but the wind mercilessly buffeted him, and he tumbled through a gaping fissure at the bottom of the ravine.

Erik lay with his face against the cold dark. Stirring, he realized that he was lying almost vertically and strained his head upward to see the light peering through the fissure high above him. Feeling about himself, he realized that he was lying precariously lodged against some projecting rocks, which kept him from plummeting further down into the abyss below. The prince warily shifted his weight and found the rocks would hold. Slowly and painfully he began his ascent, hugging the ground with his knees, straining and digging his fingers into the earth. It was slow going, and he barely managed to pull himself a few body lengths up, when the ground steepened and the earth again crumbled in fingers. He scrambled, desperately trying to maintain his hold, but he found himself sliding and scraping, carried down by the tumbling earth into the darkness and over a ledge, and then he knew no more.

Chapter Twenty-One

The Underground Labyrinth

ERIK WOKE in deep darkness and sat up with a groan. Tasting the salt of blood in his mouth, he felt his head and found it wet and sticky to the touch. He hoped the cut was a shallow wound, for there was nothing he could do about it, lost as he was in the underground depths. His arms and legs were aflame and bruised, but he found that nothing was broken and tried to count himself lucky, though his heart was sinking faster with every second he spent in the absolute darkness.

Erik weakly attempted to rise, but a sudden dizziness over-powered him, and he sat down again for a few moments, waiting for it to pass. He peered about him, trying to pierce the thick cloak of darkness. Mounting panic and despair threatened to overwhelm him, but he savagely thrust them down. He let out a few calls into the darkness, but heard no response. He had not expected there would be. Nothing or no one would be there save the wild beasts that made their home in the murky underground.

The prince cursed himself having foolishly trusted Barden. The Lord of the winds had had his revenge for the spurning of his daughter. Finally Erik found that he could manage to stand, so he took a few blind steps, groping ahead. Discovering a wall to his right, he pressed his body against it, the cool damp rock against his cheek soothing his throbbing head. There was no use going backwards. He had felt himself drop from an unclimbable height.

He would go forward hoping that fortune would place his feet on a path that would lead him out of the dark.

Erik crept slowly on, fearful of stumbling over crevices. He did not know how long he walked. Sometimes the wall on his right would disappear, and he would find himself at the mouth of another tunnel, having to decide on which path to choose. Other times he would reach a dead end and have to retrace his steps. The prince made so many twists and turns he knew not if he walked the same path twice. But all the paths he chose were by chance, and he only pretended to have hope. His weary limbs weighed down every step he took, so that he had to battle the desire to sit down and give in to despair.

Erik's heightened senses became aware of a new sound other than his own footfalls. He paused, and the sound ceased. He started again, and the sound started up again as well, an almost imperceptible soft padding dogging his steps in the darkness. The prince froze, his heart beating quickly. He was being followed!

Slowly Erik turned around and peered into the inky blackness. Rounding the bend behind him there materialized a pair of yellow eyes, unblinking in the darkness. Terror seized him. He had held his ground before many mighty beasts and warriors, but the darkness, the helplessness of being trapped underground, and, most of all, the unknown nature of the beast, were too much for him to bear. He fled blindly into the dark tunnel ahead of him. He could hear the heavy breath of the beast chasing him, gaining on him, and he knew he could not escape. He grabbed the hilt of his sword and turned to face the animal, but his foot caught on a rock. He fell and so he lay there waiting for the beast to spring upon him and shred him from limb to limb.

But no beast came.

A small voice in his head told him he should muster his strength and rise, but it was drowned by the throbbing in his head. He would never be able to rescue Rosa now, and she would forever sleep believing his love too weak to withstand the sorrow and uncertainty of their last meeting. But it was impossible to escape the deep underground, and he did not have the strength even if he knew the way. The worst of all was how achingly alone he felt, lost in the darkness, with the earth between him and the sun.

Erik did not know how long he lay there, when he felt the coolness of touch on his face, and his head being lifted and placed on a soft lap. Gentle hands softly brushed his hair from his eyes and caressed his cheek.

"Who is it?" he murmured.

"Shh, rest for a little while," a woman softly spoke, and Erik recognized the voice.

"Rosa," he whispered.

"Go to sleep, and I will keep watch."

Erik felt that there must be many questions he should want to ask her, but he could not think of a single one. His eyelids closed in weariness, and he slept. When he awoke, Rosa was still there, and he still lay in her lap and felt her cool hands on his cheek.

Am I dreaming?" he murmured in wonder.

"Most probably." He could tell by her voice that she was smiling.

"But I can feel your touch."

"I am glad. I did not know if you could."

He lay there silently, comforted by her nearness.

"Rosa," he said at last, and his voice broke with despair. "I don't know if I can rescue you! I don't know if I can find my way out of this darkness."

The princess continued to stroke his hair and then said firmly. "Erik, you cannot stay here. You must get up and continue searching. If not for my sake, then for your own."

Erik reached and clasped the hand against his cheek. "All that I do is for your sake."

Rosa spoke, and her beautiful voice trembled. "You must get up. I will not have you die."

Erik smiled. "Does this mean you have forgiven me?"

"Oh, Erik." The way she spoke his name made the prince's heart flutter in hope. "I do not know what it is I have to forgive, but, if there is anything, then I forgive it freely. I am sorry that I ever pushed you away."

"Let me remain here a little longer, and stay with me."

"Of course."

He lay there drawing strength and comfort from the princess. He spoke again after a while.

"They both died well, your father and Edmund. They died in battle defending you."

He then told her of how Edmund had protected her to the last. He felt that he owed it to the tortured, young man somehow, even though, in a sense, he considered Edmund a rival. Rosa did not say anything, but he felt a teardrop fall on his face.

"Did you love him, Edmund, I mean?"

She spoke after a pause. "Yes… but not in the way you mean. Edmund needed me to rescue him. He had not the strength to rescue himself."

"We all need to be rescued, Rosa. You have rescued me since I was a small boy."

"Yes, but he would only take. He could not give. When he learned how to give, I was already gone. We cannot always save ourselves from what the world thrusts upon us, but our strength is measured by how we face our fears."

Erik pondered this and then said, "Do you think you can help me stand?"

For an answer, she put his arm over her shoulder and helped him rise.

"Rosa," Erik said with his arm still about her, "I was in despair before you came, but now I believe that I can find my way. My princess, you are still rescuing me."

She laughed and then brushed his cheek. "I am glad, and you are right. We all do need to be rescued." Then she clasped both of his hands and said urgently, "Erik, you must search for me. You must find me."

Then she was gone, and Erik felt her absence like a great hole in his heart.

He steeled himself to begin again his search for the way out. He peered around, hoping against hope to discern something in the inky blackness, and was startled to find the pair of yellow eyes looming again in the darkness before him. They had been silently watching him all this while.

Erik calmly drew his sword and waited, but the eyes did not move, and slowly the darkness around them was faintly illuminated, as if light was emanating from the yellow eyes. He could just make out the shape of a cat as large as a leopard sitting there watching him. It rose and slowly slinked over to him. Erik gripped his sword, but did not strike, for the beast did not appear to be threatening, but only walked around and past him, then it looked back. Erik sheathed his sword and stepped forward, Immediately the large cat began its loping walk.

So the prince followed, and, as they journeyed, the cat's eyes cast a light on the path before them. To their left were large pools of water darker than the darkness of the tunnels. They passed by the gaping mouths of many intersecting tunnels. Erik followed warily, trying to discern all he could in the gloom lightened by the cat's eyes, but mainly all he could do was distinguish one dark shape from another and the lithe figure of the black cat moving steadily forward.

Finally they reached the end of the tunnel, and a white light emanated from it. The prince stepped into a wide and spacious cavern, where in the center stood a woman holding a silver lamp shaped like a globe, which shone with the soft radiance of the moon. It was from her lamp that the white light came. She was tall and straight, robed in silver, with long flaxen hair that was almost white.

She stood before two pedestals behind which were the

entrances to two more tunnels, each leading to somewhere dark in their mysterious depths.

The woman waited for Erik to approach and then spoke. "Tell me what it is that you seek."

"I am seeking the sleeping princess in the tower," he answered.

"And why seek you a tower in the dark caverns of the underground?"

"I was betrayed and fell into the dark."

The woman studied Erik slowly and then said, "It is the strange way of fate that many bring about what they wish to prevent. For it is true, Erik, Crown Prince of Lothene, that Barden of the Winds wished to betray you to death and oblivion. His heart has become dark and twisted, searching for answers to secrets he should not know, and, when he finds an answer, he does not understand that it is merely another secret. He thought that a secret would lead to your death. Instead it has led you to me, and I bring before you a choice."

She cast the light of her lamp on the two pedestals behind her and illuminated the objects on top of them. The pedestal on the left bore a silver crown, set with diamonds and a large, red ruby; the pedestal on the right bore a simple leaden casket.

"If you choose the silver crown," she said, "you will take the path on the left and it will lead you back to your castle. There your father waits, suspicion darkening his brow over your disappearance. You will allay his doubts and become King of Lothene after him, ruling the kingdom with justice and bringing it peace and prosperity. If you choose the leaden casket, your path will take you to the dark tower."

"The choice is simple," Erik said.

"Hold." The woman's voice echoed throughout the cavern. "You would choose the leaden casket that leads to the dark tower, but know that, once made, the choice is irrevocable, and I would that you know your heart."

"I have sworn to rescue the sleeping princess."

"What would you find if she is not there?" she countered, her words heavy leaden drops reverberating throughout the cavern.

All of a sudden, questions Erik had been avoiding flooded over him. When had he ever seen the princess but in his own dreams? Could his dreams have simply been wishful thinking? Then there were Dunstan's own disbelieving questions. What if a witch from the west sought to entrap him to revenge herself against his father? What could Ninny Nanny be, if not a witch?

He stared at the beautiful and impassive face of the woman before him. *What would he find if the princess was not in the tower?*

Nothing but despair.

He had placed all his hope, all his belief in love in his stark, hollow world, on Rosa. Would it be better for him to live his life with the hope that she might be there in the tower, always waiting, ever sleeping, a promise? His dreams of her would be untarnished. Would that not be better than to find out that she was not real and have all his dreams shattered. If he chose the silver crown, he would rule his people justly. The obligation he owed his kingdom weighed him down. Could he really throw that all over for what might be a selfish dream?

Yet, as he thought of all this, Erik knew that he could never condemn the princess to a life of eternal sleep merely because he was afraid. Had she not just spoken to him and told him that strength is measured by how one faces one's fear?

"I have made my decision," Erik said.

He stepped up to the leaden casket and opened it. Something silver glimmered inside, and, as he took it out, he saw that it was a half-moon pendant on a silver chain. On it was engraved a heron with a delicately arched neck and wings outstretched. He pulled out his own pendant from around his neck and fitted the two pieces together. The symbolon became as whole as the full moon. He turned to the woman beside him.

"You were testing me."

She gave him a small smile. "It was only by making such a

choice that you will have strength to face the ordeals ahead. Do not think that all will be simple after you have found the princess. But go. Take the path on the right that leads to the dark tower. You now have all that you need to help you find your way."

Erik nodded, gazing at the woman and the large cat beside her. The cat's yellow eyes were unblinking, and then a low rumble issued from its throat that was its purr. Erik felt a flicker of recognition stirring within him, and his eyes moved from the cat to the woman and he saw something there he could barely believe.

"Ninny Nanny, is that you?" he asked in amazement.

The woman smiled and then laughed, and such a cheerful, tinkling laugh had never bounced off the cavern's walls before. "You mortals are ever surprising. Erik, I did not think that you would recognize me."

Erik stared at the beautiful woman in awe, wondering how she could be so like Ninny Nanny and yet so unlike her at the same time. There was something in her laugh, her smile, and something in her eyes, which belonged to the old woman who had raised him. The prince knelt before her and kissed her hand.

"To think that I almost did not know you."

The woman's eyes softened, and she caressed Erik's cheek. "Your heart sees truly, princeling. Remember to trust it when all seems to darken before you."

"Ninny Nanny, why have you appeared before me as an old woman all this while, if this is your true form?"

The Silver Lady smiled a little sadly. "My kind left the kingdom long ago, although occasionally you may catch a faint trace or a glimpse, if they wish to reveal themselves. But you mortals no longer look for us and would destroy us if you could, so we dress ourselves in guises that you can understand and hope someday to change your hearts. Besides, Ninny Nanny was more fun than I thought she would be." The Sliver Lady's eyes gleamed full of Ninny Nanny's mischief. "Now it is time for you to go. Princess Rosamund has been waiting long enough, think you not?"

Erik nodded happily and, springing to his feet, entered the tunnel that led to the dark tower.

The Silver Lady watched him go with her large cat beside her. "You helped him recognize me, did you not, Mnemosyne?"

The large cat purred.

"I should be angry with you, but I am glad."

ERIK traveled through the dark tunnel at a steady pace. It inclined upwards gently, and it was not long before he saw the daylight up ahead of him. When he emerged from the tunnel, Erik blinked at the brightness of the early morning and realized that he had spent the entire night underground. He saw that he was in the middle of the thorn wood and recognized the same twisting corridors winding inside the maze of thorns that had so baffled him before. The underground tunnel had brought him to another entrance in the thorn maze, one that would lead him to the princess. But, as he stood before the many paths extending before him, he recalled the Silver Lady's words: *You now have all that you need to help you find your way.*

Erik lifted the full moon pendant from around his neck and studied the image of the two birds. Then he turned it over and looked at the cross hatchings on the back, those seemingly random scratches that had held the strange fisherman's interest that now seemed so long ago. With both pieces fitted together, he saw that the scratched marks were not as random as he had originally thought, but instead resembled a map of some sort. Erik smiled as he realized that he held a map to the labyrinth of thorns in his hands. Two round notches on the silver surface marked where he was and where he was going, and parallel scratches were the pathways in the maze.

Erik found the path on the map and followed its twists and turns through the maze until he emerged into a clearing. In the center was the tower. It loomed high with rubble and large chunks of stone strewn about its base. Before the prince stepped toward the tower, he heard the crackling of a fire, and the scent of cooked fish hovered on the breeze. He turned and saw a man with bone-white hair sitting on a large boulder amid the rubble and broken fragments of rock. The man was grilling fish over an open flame, and, as he looked up, Erik saw that it was the fisherman he had met before.

"Come and share a meal with me," the fisherman called.

Erik joined him by the fire, knowing that this strange fisherman was more than what he seemed. He handed the prince a fish, and both ate together.

"Who are you? Did you know that the piece of the symbolon I wore about my neck was half of a map to the thorn maze?" Erik asked.

"That indeed I did," the fisherman said, "for I have been many things in my time, and one of them was a silversmith. I made the symbolon you wear about your neck and carved the map on the back by my lady's instruction. She gave a piece away and kept the other until the time came for the two pieces to be drawn together again."

"Your lady is Ninny Nanny?" Erik asked in surprise.

The fisherman's dark eyes twinkled. "Is that what she goes by these days? I will have to remember that."

"May I have your name? For though you know of me and even more than I do, it seems, of my quest, I know nothing of you. Besides, I hope that you are a friend."

The fisherman's eyes took on a faraway look, then he spoke in a voice with the low round tones of the old tongue of the west. "Some would know me as Lothene, and, before that, they would know me as Aurlia. But even before that, long ago, I was called by the name Auryn, and I was a Golden King of old. After the battle between Lyr and his brother Annwyr, I was cast out of Faerie and parted from my faerie bride. I am cursed to wander the broken kingdom, mourning the diminishment of its glory, unless the rift caused between Faerie and mortal kind, planted in the dark night in the hall of the Faerie Lord of the Glass Mountain, is healed."

The fisherman fell silent, and Erik sat in awe before the ancient Golden King cursed to wander all these years.

He rose and bowed deeply. "My lord, I pray that your hope is granted, and that the two worlds may be joined one day as they were of old. But I beg you give me leave, as I would go and wake Princess Rosamund, who has also been waiting this long while."

The fisherman laughed. "Go, Prince Erik. Fulfill your quest and wake your sleeping princess. Bring healing to your divided kingdom."

Erik set off for the tower and found the wooden door at its base. It was so heavy and rusted with age, it took him a few minutes to pry it open. Stone steps spiraled up before him. Shafts of light shot through the narrow windows as he steadily mounted each step. A hushed stillness entered him. When he finally reached the uppermost room, he found it flooded by light from the morning sun streaming through the open window, and there before him lay the princess. Erik went to Rosa's side and gazed at her for the first time anew. She was real, no longer a dream, and as beautiful as the northern star.

He stooped down and softly kissed her. Then he quietly waited, watching the gentle stirring of her features as slowly her eyes opened. Rosa's eyes shone with the joy they had first held when she beheld him on the riverbank in their dreams. Only this time, their joy did not diminish, but turned into the gentle radiance of recognition.

The princess seemed as if she wished to speak, so Erik gently took her hand, but she must have forgotten what she wanted to say. Instead they both simply gazed at each other without speaking. Rosa laughed, then she burst into tears, and the prince held the sobbing princess in his arms.

After a while, her tears subsided, and she said in an embarrassed tone, "Please forgive me. I couldn't help weeping."

Erik thrilled at the sound of her voice. "Rosa, don't be sorry." He gently wiped each tear away, and then kissed one eye and then another. When he had finished, the princess had turned bright red and she ducked her head in his shoulder.

He gave a delighted laugh. "Rosa, what are you doing? Don't hide your face from me!"

Rosa only shook her head and buried herself in further, so he contented himself with holding her tightly. Then he recollected himself. "Rosa, we should leave this tower. I must get you somewhere safe. Are you hungry?"

Rosa extricated herself from his embrace. "Now that you mention it, I am famished. I suppose I haven't eaten in hundreds of years." She looked up at him shyly and softly traced the scratches on his face with her finger. Erik held his breath at her touch.

"You suffered all this for me," she whispered.

Erik did not say anything, but tucked stray golden strands of her hair behind her ear. Rosa then tried to rise out of bed, but, when she got to her feet, she wobbled, and the prince had to catch her.

"I suppose I haven't walked in hundreds of years either," she sighed.

Erik helped her down the stairs and into the sun. The wood and the fresh breeze welcomed them when they stepped outside. A wave of wonder and of shyness washed over him as he gazed at Rosa standing before him, a miracle of flesh and blood, not the wisp of a dream. Rosa was looking thoughtfully about her, and Erik realized that she was observing the ruins of her old castle. He felt a twinge of the old fear that Rosa might not ever be able to look at him without thinking of the loss of her family and kingdom. He pressed her hand in comfort, but was interrupted by a rustling sound behind them.

"Lodestar," Erik cried, as he sprung forward to greet his horse, who was making its way through a gap in the thorn hedges.

Rosa laughed and caressed his handsome mane, while Erik went to explore the strange, new gap.

"I don't know how this opening came to be here," he said, turning to Rosa. "I wonder if the fisherman made it."

They both mounted Lodestar, the princess sitting before the prince, and made their way to the healing woman's cottage, where they found Emma tending the herb garden outside. The dark-haired girl stared in amazement when she saw them, then dashed indoors to call her mother. By the time Erik and Rosa had dismounted, both of them were back outside, and the old woman's eyes brightly threatened tears as she cried, "To think that I have lived to see this day!"

Rosa approached her and Emma shyly, but then held out her hands to them. "So you are both the distant children of my dear friend and handmaid, Edwina. It brings me much joy to see you, particularly since all that I know is gone."

"So she is real," came a voice from the doorway, and there stood Dunstan wrapped in bandages, leaning against the door-frame, gazing with wonder at the princess. He knelt down on one knee and bowed his head. "Please forgive me for my disbelief."

Erik sprang to his friend's side and lifted him up. "Now, none of that, Dunstan. You have been faithful throughout the journey."

Rosa approached Dunstan and clasped both of his hands. "Erik has spoken very warmly of you, and I love you for the love you bear him."

Dunstan did not respond, mesmerized by the beauty of the princess before him. Erik coughed and clasped his friend by the shoulder. "How are you? You seem to be recovering well."

Dunstan tore his gaze away from the princess and smiled, then looked at Emma standing quietly a little bit away. "Thanks to my ministering angel over there. She has been tireless in her care for me these past two days."

The dark-haired girl went up to Dunstan's side and said, "You should go back and lie down. Your wounds have not yet healed."

Dunstan turned to Erik and said in mock despair, "Do you see what a tyrant my angel is? She won't let me rise from my bed. Yesterday your horse returned riderless, and I was determined to set out in search for you. But she insisted and tearfully pleaded that I wait until my wounds were healed. I would have set out tomorrow, though, if you had not returned. Now tell me everything that has happened since we parted ways."

Despite his complaints, Dunstan let Emma lead him back to bed, and the others followed, and they spent the evening recounting the prince's adventures and how he had come to wake the princess.

Chapter Twenty-Two

The Rose Garden

THE NEXT DAY, Erik and Rosa set off for the castle, while Dunstan stayed behind as Emma declared him still not well enough to travel. When Rosa bid the girl farewell, she begged her to come to the castle and be her handmaid, as Edwina had been before her. Rosa knew that she would be a stranger in the castle and that it would be comforting to be near someone connected to her old way of life, no matter how indirectly. Emma promised to come, saying that it would be an honor to wait upon the princess. Dunstan was looking at Emma as she spoke, but she studiously avoided his gaze.

Erik and Rosa entreated the healing woman to come with her daughter, but she shook her head and said that she wished to remain behind in the woods and practice her healing craft on those who managed to stray in and lose themselves in the forest. She had a premonition that the wood would let more wanderers in, now that the princess' curse was lifted.

As Rosa and Erik rode through the forest, Rosa's spirit reveled in the wind, the sun, and the birdsong. She was reborn, still waking up to the world around her, everything new and strange. She felt all things at once, joy, delight, and also sorrow, loss, and a tinge of fear.

She was surprised to spy a huddled figure waiting for them at the edge of the forest like a bump on the stone wall. She felt Erik tense up and then relax behind her.

295

"Corwin!" he called out. "What are you doing here?"

Rosa saw that the man called Corwin was as surprised to see them as they were to see him, and he stared at the both of them in amazement as he explained, "The Grey Hawk has posted a man here every day and every night on the chance that you would return. But none of us did expect to see you again. Come back with me to our campfire and introduce this fair maiden to us."

Rosa had been curious to see the Grey Hawk ever since Erik had spoken of his nobility and was glad when they followed Corwin to the camp. They were greeted with cheers as Erik presented her to Lord Gavin, and she noticed that the disinherited lord looked thoughtful as he observed her with Erik.

They feasted that evening, and, near the end, Aymer asked Rosa if she would sing some of the old songs of her kingdom, songs that had long since been forgotten. She took the outstretched lyre and, as her fingers hesitantly skimmed over the strings, she called forth ancient melodies not heard in hundreds of years. She softly hummed, and then the music in her throat swelled into song. She sang along to the melody of the stars, the melody that had been vibrating in her blood and her bones ever since she had awakened.

When she finished, a solemn hush fell over the campsite, and no one dared speak for fear of disturbing something blessed. Then the Lord Gavin bowed before the princess, and each of the men did the same in turn. Erik knelt before Rosa, took her hand, and kissed it. Rosa touched her cheek and felt that it was wet. She had been crying, but hadn't even realized it.

THE next morning, Erik and Rosa bade farewell to the Grey Hawk and his men and began their journey to the castle. They galloped across fields and farmland, the green valleys and sloping hills of the kingdom, and some of the land Rosa recognized, but most of it she did not. As they journeyed, Erik murmured in a low and quiet voice about the history of the kingdom since his people had come and the strife that it still endured, and she soaked in every word he said.

They stopped at an inn that night, and Rosa woke early before dawn, ruefully realizing that she needed very little sleep after her long enchanted slumber. She threw on her dress over her shift and thought she might take a stroll on the dew-filled grass, but, when she opened the door, she found the prince sleeping propped against the door frame, guarding her room. Her heart fluttered at this unexpected sign of his care for her, and she knelt down beside him, taking the opportunity to study his features unobserved. How gentle his face is when he is asleep, she thought. His raven hair had grown long and unkempt, tumbling over his eyes, and she could not resist brushing it away from his forehead.

Erik woke at her touch, and they both froze, their eyes locked together. Rosa found that she could not break away from his gaze. His eyes were so bright, like the clouded grey skies of the morning. She tried to speak, but her throat went dry, and she could not form the words. Erik seemed to be encountering a similar difficulty. One of them might have broken the silence if they had not been interrupted by a door slam from the depths of the inn.

Erik sprang up and exclaimed at being found in such an unseemly position before her door. Rosa ducked back into her room in embarrassment. She felt a hot blush overspread her features, but she was also annoyed that they had been interrupted.

LATER on that morning, Erik helped Rosa up onto his horse, and she noticed the strength in his arms and was aware of his nearness as he sat behind her. She wondered what she should do to make him speak what he had been on the verge of saying earlier that morning, but, the more she thought on it, the more tongue-tied she became. The unusual silence became almost painful as she felt that she was sinking further and further down into a boggy marsh of embarrassment.

Erik spoke behind her, breaking the awkward silence. "We are entering the woods near my father's castle, but, before I take you there, there is something I would show you. I hope that I can find it."

Curiosity stirred through Rosa's shyness, though she did not speak, still not trusting her voice.

"Ah, here we are. I knew that we should find it as she wished me to bring you here."

Rosa heard the note of triumph in Erik's voice and glimpsed the stone walls and the thatched roof of a cottage between the trees and the pines. When they were nearer, she saw a picket fence and the gate that now swung open.

"This is Ninny Nanny's cottage," she whispered.

Erik nodded while they both dismounted.

"May we go inside?"

"Yes, but I fear it will be empty."

Erik opened the cottage door, and the interior was bare and the fire was out. The cottage possessed the particular stillness of a dwelling that has been abandoned.

"I wish you could have met her," Erik said.

Rosa clasped his hand. She knew he was referring to Ninny Nanny.

He cleared his throat. "This is not what I wanted to show you. Come, let us go back outside."

Rosa followed Erik to the back of the cottage, and there before them was a rose garden in full bloom. She gasped at the deep, rich blossoms, the vibrant, overflowing wealth of flowers that grew in abundance both in shade and in the sun. She ran to the center of the flower garden and gazed her fill of them and drank in their sweet smelling scents.

"This garden is yours. Ninny Nanny said these roses were a

gift to you... and that you would wear them on your wedding day."

Rosa turned to the prince, and his eyes spoke a question in their cloudy depths, and there had been something in his voice that made her heart grow too full to speak. She plucked a perfect blossom from a bush, a rose rich and red and deep, and kissed its petals and gave it to him.

Erik clasped both of her hands. "I have loved you since I first saw you, and, when I grew from a boy to a man, so did my love grow. Every time I saw you, every time I discovered something new, how you smiled, how you cried, your joys and your pains, I fell in love with you all over again. And now that you are here before me... Rosa, I have to know if you love me."

His gaze was so bright that Rosa had to look down. She whispered to him with a waver in her throat, but the more she spoke, the steadier grew her voice. "When I first saw you... my heart recognized you. But I was afraid and did not want to vainly hope. The more I saw you, the more I wanted you to find me and, when I sent you away, I was afraid that you would stop looking... and I knew that I loved you. I have been wondering all this while why you did not speak..."

She said no more, however, for Erik had stooped to catch her downcast face and kiss her. The kiss was so sudden that Rosa could not help but laugh. He kissed her again, and her heart beat faster. He kissed her a third time, and she clung to him.

Rosa lay in Erik's arms in the brilliance of the rose garden, and he whispered to her, his lips touching her hair, "Rosa, we must be married this instant, before we enter my father's castle. I cannot allow him or anyone the power to part us."

She nodded happily against his chest and reluctantly withdrew from his embrace. She gathered an armful of roses, and they rode Lodestar to a little church at the outskirts of the wood to which Erik's mother had once taken him when he was small. Rosa was dressed in no finery beside the blue dress she had woken in and the armful of roses picked from the faerie garden, but their own beauty was enough, and nothing could have added to the radiance of her joy in marrying the prince.

Before nightfall, Erik brought Rosa to his father's castle. The herald announced them to the throne room, and both Rosa and Erik faced the cold, silent stares of the king and queen. Rosa observed that King Mark thawed slightly when he gazed at her, and she gave him a deep curtsey.

Erik took a step forward, his arm protectively shielding his new wife. "Father, allow me to present to you my bride, the Princess Rosamund. She has lain under an enchantment for hundreds of years, and it was with the purpose to wake her that I set out on my journey."

The king waved his son silent and gazed with sharp, appraising eyes at the princess. Then he rose and, in an unexpected gesture, greeted Rosa with open arms. Queen Sigrid followed suit, and Rosa felt the queen's cold cheek against her own.

When she withdrew from the queen's embrace, she saw that the queen was all smiles, graciousness, and courtesy, though there was something lurking hidden in the majestic woman's eyes that Rosa could not quite fathom. The queen was speaking, informing her that she would personally prepare for the princess and the prince joint rooms upstairs and that the princess must be tired from the long journey. Did she have any gowns? No, then she would lend her some until new ones could be made. Before she could resist, Rosa was guided upstairs by the pressure of the queen's firm grip on her arm, and she knew that the queen had engineered for Erik and his father to be alone.

Erik calmly endured the king's calculating gaze. There was much that he needed to explain to his father, and he suspected that there was something hidden behind their warm reception. He waited, wondering what direction their conversation would take.

"There were troublesome rumors of your journey through the western marches," the king began.

"You speak of the Lord of Westhane?"

"Indeed. I heard you fell in with the Grey Hawk and his band and sought to incite a rebellion against my crown. It was said you were gathering forces to act against me."

"No, father," Erik said sharply. "I would never act against you. You can count on my loyalty. I fell in with the Grey Hawk by chance on the journey to the Shadowood... He stole my horse."

"Cursed bandits." The king grimaced. "We shall rout that band of outlaws for good."

"Nay, father, for we came to an understanding, he and I. The Grey Hawk aided me on my quest, and he has much reason to be aggrieved. There is evil done in the western lands in your good name that must be remedied."

The king fell silent, a curtain overspreading his features, and Erik felt with uneasiness that he had not said something that the king wanted to hear.

"There were other rumors as well," the king continued, "tales of a mysterious stranger and his companion seeking the sleeping princess and then finding her, whispers of the western peoples' hope in her golden lineage. Such a union would finally unite Lothene once and for all."

"You heard of Rosa before she arrived?" Erik said in surprise.

"Don't think that two such unusual companions can pass by without comment, particularly when they stop at inns. Why did you not tell me of your plans?" the king asked.

Erik weighed his response. He knew that the king would never believe that he had had dreams of Rosa and that she was actually who she said she was. He suspected that his father thought Rosa was a ruse steeped in myth and legend to gain the west's support, that he had fabricated the princess' past so that he would have the freedom to choose his own bride.

"I was afraid that you would try to stop me... I met her long ago... and I love her," he said finally.

The king peered at his son shrewdly. "Ha! And here I was,

doubting your manhood, and you were keeping this pretty face secret all the while. It is well for you that you returned with a bride. I can forgive a lover's weakness, but not treachery. Do you think the princess can stand to scrutiny?"

"In what way?" said Erik, startled.

"Can she prove that she is a princess of Aurlia, enchanted sleep or no?"

"She is who she says she is," Erik said softly.

The king gave his son a knowing smile. "Then all is well. Her authenticity must not be questioned, so we must have her identity acknowledged by the lords of the west. Make sure she is ready."

Erik bowed stiffly and left his father's company to seek out Rosa and warn her that her identity was going to be tested before the lords of the west. She received the news with a shrug of her shoulders and assured him that her own people would recognize her. Erik found her lack of concern maddening, but she laughed and then banished away his worries with a kiss.

THE next day the king dispatched heralds to the four corners of the kingdom, summoning the lords of the major provinces to a royal conclave. Such a conclave had not been called in many years, and, while the purpose of the assembly had yet to be announced, rumor carried tales of the sleeping princess, so that nobility and the common folk, those invited and those who had not, all streamed in droves to the capital.

Dunstan and Emma arrived at the castle during the flurry, and Dunstan chaffed the prince for marrying the princess so quickly. His teasing did Erik good, for the prince was anxious about the conclave, though he tried to hide it, especially from Rosa. It had not escaped his notice that his father had called in militia from his outposts and that there was double the guard at the castle. He wondered through gritted teeth if the conclave was really an excuse to threaten the lords of the west with a show of force and arms rather than extending the olive branch of unity and peace. He wondered if the guard's glistening silver swords would shine red if the proceedings turned sour.

Finally, it was the evening of the conclave. Erik and Rosa glided into the throne room, their entrance causing a hushed stir among the crowd as the two of them took their seats beside the king and queen. Erik stole a glance at Rosa seated beside him. She was dressed in a gown of the royal sapphire studded with the golden stars of the old kingdom. Both she and he wore a piece of the silver symbolon around their necks.

For a moment all was silent. Then one of the lords from the west stood up to be acknowledged. He bowed to the king and queen and then spoke to the princess. "My lady, we would not do you the indignity of besieging you with questions, but we do desire to hear your story from your own lips."

Rosa smiled graciously and then told the story of her sleep in accents more ancient than their own, with an odd word or two unknown that had to be repeated and explained. Erik observed with relief that her language, the unhesitating simplicity with which she spoke, her regal bearing and grace, favorably disposed those who listened to her. He was then asked to tell his own part in the story, which he did, aware the entire time that his father's watchful eyes were on him.

When he finished, the assembly stood as one divided. The lords from Midlothia, the east, and the north had no qualms about accepting the princess; as Erik could have predicted, they would cast their vote whichever way his father wanted. It was the western lords that hesitated. They would demand further proof of the princess, since with her rested their hopes for peace and justice for the west.

An elderly man, doubled over with age and wearing the long robes of a scholar, asked for permission to approach the princess. With a slow stride, he reached her, then, pulling out an ancient scroll from one of his voluminous sleeves, he held it before Rosa with a deep bow, his white beard almost brushing the floor. Rosa took the scroll with a puzzled look on her face, which then transformed into an expression of wonder as she unrolled it.

"Do you recognize it?" the old scholar asked.

Rosa nodded, her eyes brimming with tears. The old man signaled one of his clerks to bring him a writing case containing vellum, quill, and inkwell, which he then offered to the princess. She dipped the quill in ink and copied the first line of the scroll onto the fresh piece of vellum. The old scholar's eyes lit up as he examined first her writing and then the manuscript, and, when he spoke to the princess, he spoke in words that none in the room could understand. Rosa laughed and then spoke to him in the same unknown tongue. Murmurs traveled round the assembly, and the king asked the old scholar to explain what they had been saying.

The old man gazed at Rosa in admiration. "The princess speaks the old tongue better than I do. I asked her if she liked the prince and wished to be our princess. She said that she liked him very much and would be our princess if we would have her."

The assembly buzzed with excitement and had to be silenced with the pounding of the royal staff. The king then asked the scholar, "What is the scroll you brought with you?"

The scholar cleared his throat. "The scroll is an ancient manuscript that the last princess of Aurlia transcribed with her own hand, telling the old story of the faerie gifts to the golden kings. It was taken from the castle library when its inhabitants fled the invasion and has been safeguarded for generations as one of our ancient treasures. It would never have been brought out again to the open if such a claim to the princess' identity had not been made. The Princess Rosamund's hand and the hand in the manuscript are the same. I for one am satisfied that this is the true Princess Rosamund, last in the line of the Golden Kings of old and heir to the throne of Aurlia."

The assembly erupted into thunderous applause, and it took several resounding thumps of the king's staff to bring it back to order. The conclave was quickly brought to a close as the old man's opinion held great weight amongst the western lords.

After the proceedings were over, the king drew Erik aside. "Was that silver pendant truly given to you by your mother?" he asked thoughtfully. When Erik nodded, the king laughed. "Even I am half-convinced by your story."

"Father, everything that the princess and I have said is true," Erik said earnestly.

King Mark shook his head. "I am no believer in legend, though I do admit its power over the common mind. Be grateful that you have convinced the western lords, but...," and here his voice became as hard as iron, "never forget, my son, who holds the true power in Lothene."

"Father, please, I will ever be your faithful son," Erik said, trying to hide the hurt from his voice.

The king merely nodded and signaled that they should both join the rest of the court for the feast.

The throne room was empty save for the queen, who remained immobile in her seat. Throughout the entire conclave, she had been as cold as snow on the mountaintop and, while the assembly had thawed before the princess, she had only grown colder. She had not spoken or moved during the entire proceeding, but, when the princess had spoken in the old tongue, her long fingers had clenched, and, now as she unfurled them, she saw that she had drawn blood.

She rose and made her way to the feast, the majestic folds of her red cloak trailing behind her as she walked. She was patient, and she would bide her time.

THE days that followed were some of the happiest that Erik and Rosa knew. They both found a home in each other's arms, and the kingdom was balanced on the fine edge of peace. Rosa saw that Lothene did not only need healing from civil discord, but that its spirit needed renewal as well. A forgetfulness had settled over the land, diminishing the memory of its former glory. Rosa longed to reach out to the people, so she confided in Erik hopes for a royal library that would also house a school for children, where scholars would gather and where children would not only learn how to read and write, but also learn the history of Aurlia and Lothene, all its legends, and its founding myth.

They brought their plan before the king, and he sanctioned it. Erik oversaw the building of the royal library at the foot of the mountain, and, when news of its erection spread by word of mouth and proclamation, many came forward with gifts for the library, old books that had been salvaged from pillage and flame. It was completed before the year was out, and there was a ceremony that installed the books into the library, and the princess' ancient manuscript was the crown of the collection. Rosa considered each book an unexpected treasure and, if she ever did mourn for all that had been lost, she also marveled over the fact that her life had been spared from destruction and considered her time a gift.

Erik, patiently and with slow counsel, advised his father in the governance of the western lands. Though he could not convince his father to return to the Grey Hawk his old title of Westhane, the disinherited lord was given new lands in the western provinces, and he became Lord Gavin once again. This took skillful maneuvering, however, for the queen never failed to point out to the king that the Lord Gavin's loyalty would lie with the prince, not with king. But the aureole of peace that had descended on the kingdom swayed the king's heart, and he eventually gave in to his son's request. The queen saw that she had lost her control over the king, and the serpent of envy that had coiled in wait in the shadows sank its sharp fangs into the secret chambers of her heart.

THE months went by, and one day Erik and Rosa joyfully announced that they were expecting a baby. The queen greeted the news with smiles, and her words were all flowers and sunshine, but the fang of jealousy bit even deeper. She sought out the princess alone in her chambers to congratulate her on the joyful news.

"The birth of your child will be the final seal guarding the peace of Lothene. You and Erik must be overjoyed," she said.

Rosa smiled. "That we are, for the kingdom's sake, but mostly for ourselves."

"Of course it will be a child of both the old and the new kingdom. I must admit that I have often wished to read your ancient manuscript, but, of course, I do not know the old tongue."

"I can teach it you!" Rosa exclaimed, and the queen perceived with disgust that Rosa was reaching out to her, trying to find a way for them to become closer.

Queen Sigrid smiled bitterly. "It is admirable that you do not desire to keep such knowledge to yourself. Many believe that knowledge is power and are loath to part with it."

Rosa shook her head. "There is nothing of the old kingdom that I wish to keep secret, and hope that all may someday love the memory of it as I do."

The queen waved her hand impatiently. "I would take care, princess. Too deep a longing for the past is dangerous, and things not understood are often feared. Not everyone approaches knowledge with the same purity of heart that you do."

Rosa fell silent, so the queen spoke again. "You related that the manuscript you transcribed tells the story of seven faerie gifts, does it not? Do you also bear such gifts?"

"Yes, they were given to me by the faerie to aid in the governance of the kingdom. They are meant to mediate between the mortal and the faerie realms."

"Do you believe that your first-born child will also receive such faerie gifts?"

Rosa seemed startled by the question. "That I do not know. Faerie seems so far from this world, and I do not know how to call it back."

"But if you could, would you?"

Though Rosa did not speak, her translucent features betrayed the happiness she felt at the thought, and the queen felt her heart constrict with fear. The queen swiftly rose. "I wish you and the crown prince the greatest joy."

Queen Sigrid went to her bedroom to brood over what she had just discovered. The queen was content with the balance of power: the king was feared by the people, and he let her have her own way. She had never considered the prince much of a threat. Perhaps she had been unwise to overlook him, but alone he could do nothing. The princess was different. Her presence alone drew love and adoration from the people. If the princess did manage to bring back Faerie, then a new age would dawn, and she, the queen, would be consigned to the shadows of forgetfulness. Queen Sigrid laid her hand over her barren womb and wondered if she should also bear a child, but that would mean dealing with Erik as well.

The queen endured many sleepless nights wrestling with her helpless fury. She fell ill, and Rosa herself tended to her, but this did nothing to stem the queen's silent hatred for the princess and only stoked her venom further. She writhed in unbearable agony, until one night she fell asleep and dreamed a dark dream. At the end of her dream, she saw a dark woman with blood red lips and a pitiless smile, who held out to her a leaden staff. The queen wrapped her fingers around the staff and, when she woke, she smiled the same pitiless smile as the dark woman in her dream.

The queen began collecting plants from the thickly shadowed regions of the forest and laid them to dry in a cottage she had had the king build in the wood only for her. She mixed concoctions seeped in gentle poison, slow acting drugs that could only lull one to sleep in large doses. And the sleep could be as deep and as still as death, or filled with nighttime horrors and tormenting dreams. Or they could be dreams that unhinged the mind and made the sleeper walk in a waking sleep. Those were the drugs that she dried and aged in the slow simmering of time. They would be ready in nine months, just when she would need them.

Chapter Twenty-Three

A Flight in the Shadows

EMMA WAS IN the castle kitchens preparing a light meal for the princess when Dunstan's head popped through the door. When he caught sight of her, the rest of him followed.

"Emma, I've been searching for you. I've barely caught a glimpse of you these past few days."

The dark-haired girl ignored him and continued slicing though fruit, her knife thudding sharply on the wooden counter.

"Is that for our pregnant princess? You will be running many like errands in the months to come, I warrant."

"I'd prefer that you didn't refer to Princess Rosamund in such a manner."

"You know, Emma, I cannot help but notice that you have been very cold of late."

She did not say anything, but was busy pouring a drink into the princess' goblet.

"Will not my ministering angel tell me why she is being so unkind?"

Emma spilled some of the drink onto the napkin and had to get a new one.

"Emma, an angel should not frown so."

The handmaid glared at him with frustration. "I saw you flirting with the kitchen maid the other day."

"I am innocent." Dunstan held up his hands. "She was the one flirting with me."

"And you were flirting with the serving maid before that."

"Jealously does not become you, Emma. You know that all that means nothing and that my heart lies at your feet."

Emma's eyes flashed. "Where your heart lies is no matter to me. If you will give me leave, I must bring this to the princess." She shoved past him with an indifferent air.

DUNSTAN made his way to the prince's study, where he found Erik sealing some papers, and the fair-haired man slumped in a chair with a groan. He looked up at the prince and then shielded his eyes. "Would you wipe that idiotic grin off your face? Your happiness is blinding."

Erik glanced up at his friend. "What has put you out of temper?"

"My angel is falling to earth."

Erik shook his head. "With the way you carry on, it is no wonder. She is only human, Dunstan."

"Not you, too," Dunstan groaned. "It is not as if I were married to the lady. All of my flirting is harmless anyways. But I should have known better than to come to you. You've only ever had eyes for one woman, and fatherhood is going to make you even more unbearable. I am going to take myself off to find a more sympathetic ear."

"If your ear wears skirts, Dunstan, I warn you. You may lose Emma."

"I am going to see the princess!" Dunstan said, rising indignantly. "She understands me better than you do, I believe."

"And she can whisper words in your favor to her handmaid. So you see, I do understand you." Erik's voice was grave, but his eyes were laughing.

"Such suspicions I would not believe in one who calls himself my friend," said Dunstan with wounded dignity. "I leave you to your papers and your fanciful dreams of joy in approaching fatherhood, and I console myself with the thought that soon all your dreams will burst at the bitter truth of sleepless nights and endless crying." He stalked out of the room to have his ruffled feelings soothed by the princess.

THE months passed, and a little girl was born. The prince and princess named her Oriana, after the golden dawn, for she was like the morning sun rising upon their hearts. Early one morning, the sun shone through their high tower window and Erik woke to its pale light bathing the sleeping form of his wife beside him. She stirred at his side, woke, and then smiled at him sleepily.

"I never tire of watching you wake up," he said, kissing the tip of her nose.

She stretched and climbed out of bed. "Little Oriana has been quiet all through the night."

Erik was watching his beloved wife stoop to lift their baby from the cradle when she suddenly uttered such a terrible cry that all his drowsiness instantly fled and he sprang out of bed to her side. What he saw struck him dumb with horror. The swaddling clothes had tumbled open at Rosa's touch. Its contents spilled over, covering everything around them, including the cradle and the princess, in a thick layer of ash. There was no baby in the cradle.

Erik ran to the door and called the guards, who were immediately ordered to apprehend anyone carrying a baby, but there was no one to be found in the castle. As the days went by, no one could find baby Oriana in the towns or villages or throughout the entire kingdom.

The search continued as Erik and Rosa waited in agonizing silence, faces pale and eyes hollow with sleepless nights. The weeks went by, weighed down with dread, and they heard no word of their missing baby. Rosa rarely left her room. At first, she sobbed by the cradle inconsolably, but, as the days went by, she merely sat in silence, waiting for the news that did not come.

Erik yearned to aid in the search, but he could not leave Rosa, and there was no lead, no hint or whisper, ransom note or motive, only loss. Doubt and rumor whispered throughout the castle walls, but Rosa and Erik did not hear them, so wrapped up were they in their grief.

Erik observed in a half dazed state that the queen remained by Rosa's side, gentle and comforting. She ensured that the princess ate the little that she did, taking great care over her meals, allowing no one but herself to prepare them. Erik was grateful for the queen's unexpected kindness and felt that he had misjudged her, that her coldness was a shield she hid behind, and that she stood true in times of hardship.

A FEW months after the baby was stolen, Queen Sigrid drew Erik aside to her chambers and said, "You and I must protect the princess from the rumors that have taken hold and ensure that she never hears of them."

Erik gazed at her questioningly.

"Then you do not know? It is said that the princess is cursed. That she is a witch from the Shadowood and that she turned her daughter into ash, which is why we cannot find her."

Anger surged up in Erik's chest. "Who dares speak thus of my wife? Tell me, and I will defend her honor," he cried, reaching for the hilt of his sword.

"Peace, Erik," the queen said, laying her hand over his. "That is not how one goes about dispelling rumors. They are intangible and not something silenced by the sword." She spoke in a soft and coaxing voice. "You and I love the princess and know that she is incapable of such a crime. But can you honestly hold the people to blame? What does anyone truly know of the princess? She is a stranger among us. The kingdom fears the witchcraft of the old kingdom, and terrible things haunt the wood, seeking revenge for past bloodshed."

Erik shook his head. "Rosa has nothing to do with that."

"I know," the queen said soothingly. "I only repeat what others have said. But I do believe that there are hidden forces at work." She studied his face carefully. "Do you know that one time, when you were a little boy, I feared that you were prey to a dangerous magic in the wood and sought to keep you away from it? I did not say anything because I thought I was mistaken. Was I mistaken, Erik?"

The prince thought of Ninny Nanny's stolen sticks. "You were mistaken, my queen," he said firmly.

She held his gaze. "Very well, then," she said at last. "Go now to your princess and comfort her in her grief. Keep her away from others in the castle, so that she does not discover what is being said. She has enough sorrow to bear. Here, take this to her..." The queen went over to her bureau and poured a piping hot drink from a silver decanter. The smell of warm spices wafted over to Erik on the other side of the room. The queen extended the goblet to him.

"Have a taste," she said.

The drink was sweet and pungent, sending a warm glow down to the tip of his toes.

"It's to help settle her nerves," the queen explained. "Dwelling too long on grief can unhinge the mind."

"Thank you, stepmother. I don't know what Rosa and I would do without your care."

Her red lips broke into a gentle smile full of sympathy.

IT was soon after his conversation with the queen that Erik accepted in his heart that his daughter was most likely dead. His main concern was to watch over Rosa, shielding her from rumors, comforting her in her sorrow and embracing her during the nights.

At first, he did not notice that anything was wrong with

Rosa, only that she slept later in the mornings and had difficulty waking up. Then, one morning, he awakened to the princess sleeping by his side fully dressed. He shook her awake, but she had no recollection of dressing in the night.

The next morning was the same, only this time her dress was stained with dirt, but again Rosa did not remember waking. She did not seem bothered by the strangeness of it, but merely floated about in a daze. Erik questioned the guards near his room, but they said that no one had come in or out of the bedroom.

Erik resolved to stay awake that night, but nothing unusual occurred, and Rosa slept by his side all through the night, though shadows crossed her faced, and she shed silent tears. The same occurred the next night, and, by the third, his eyes were so heavy that he could not keep them open. He woke abruptly in the middle of the night and saw that the space beside him was empty and that Rosa was gone.

He dashed out of the room in his sleeping tunic. The guards posted outside swore that they had seen no one leave the room. Erik had no time to argue, but resolved to look into that mystery later and immediately went outside the castle to search for Rosa. Recollecting the dirt, he sensed that she might be in the woods, though he feared what that might mean. He found the postern gate open and unguarded, another mystery he brushed aside to worry about later.

As he stepped beyond the castle walls, he heard a strange keening song faintly floating through the trees, a weird mixture of lament and lullaby. He followed the sound, until he reached a glade of woven shadows illuminated by the pale and ghostly moon. There kneeled the princess with her breasts unbound, rocking a little bundle as if she were feeding it and singing it to sleep.

Erik's heart sank to his feet, and he softly approached Rosa so as not to surprise her. The little bundle she held was nothing but a sack stuffed with earth and twigs and leaves. Her eyes were open but unseeing, and he saw that she was still asleep. Gently removing the bundle from her groping hands, he shook her softly, trying to waken her. Rosa began to scream, piecing ear-splitting shrieks, as she thrashed and flailed wildly. Erik restrained her as gently as he could, speaking soothingly to her all the while. A tremor passed through her body. She fell on his breast, heaving broken sobs, and he held her against him and wept. Then he lifted her up and cradled her in his arms and, covering her with his tunic, carried her back to the castle.

He put the princess to bed and watched over her until the sun rose. Then he swore the guards to secrecy so as not to reveal that they had seen him and the princess in the night. From then on he kept close watch over Rosa, and his worry over her and his grief drained him of his strength.

THE sun was setting in the prince's study. He sat alone, clutching his head in his hands, snatching a brief moment of stillness before he returned to Rosa's side. Looking up, he saw Dunstan's figure outlined in the doorway.

"Dunstan." He rose swiftly. "What is it? Any news?"

Dunstan shook his head, and Erik sank back down again in his chair. His friend stepped into the room and went to his side. "Erik," he spoke in an earnest tone, "it is not good for the princess that she stay always in her room. She needs to go outside. The people need to see that she is all right."

"The people!" Erik exclaimed. "Do you know what the people say about her?"

"I do," Dunstan said softly.

"And you would have me expose my wife to such slander?"

"Erik, it is precisely because of what is being said about her that the princess must no longer be hidden from view."

"Dunstan, you do not believe in these mad rumors?"

"Of course not." Dunstan laid a steadying hand on Erik's

shoulder. "There was a time when I disbelieved in the princess, but she appeared miraculously despite my doubt. I will never disbelieve her again."

Erik bowed his head, weighed down by emotion.

"But others must look upon the princess, taste her grief, feel the grace of her presence. Secrets only breed more secrets, my friend."

Erik wearily passed his hands over his eyes. "I am so clouded by sorrow that I do not know what to do. I am only trying to protect her."

Dunstan's eyes shone with sympathy. "Let the people see their princess."

So Erik led Rosa from her rooms, and she would sit in the garden for hours, basking in the peace and the quiet. At the royal banquets she barely spoke a word, but her features were so stricken by sorrow that the rumors began to quieten, until they were only an echo in the wind.

ROSA and Erik sat alone in the garden one hushed night. As she laid her head on his shoulder, she whispered, "I have endured much loss, my parents, my kingdom, my own time, but somehow I feel that the loss of a child is an emptiness that can never be filled."

Erik held her tightly. "But this is a loss that you do not have to bear on your own. I am here with you, and, though we will never forget, time may soften the wound."

They wept together, and from then on, Rosa began to slowly heal. The days passed, and Emma and sometimes Dunstan would sit with Rosa in the garden and draw a smile or two from her face, though her laughter was no longer heard ringing in the castle. Erik stayed by her side as she poured herself into the new school at the royal library, telling stories, and teaching young children their letters. He watched her look hungrily into the children's faces and knew she was thinking of the child she had lost.

Erik was surprised one day to see Kenelm, his old sword master, sitting with Rosa in the garden. The old soldier's rough visage softened as he spoke quiet words to the princess and, when Erik joined them, he rose and departed.

"He often comes to keep me company when no one is around. I believe he has endured much suffering and loss, for he knows what words will comfort me, and when silence is best," she explained, responding to his questioning glance.

Erik clasped her hand and turned to watch the receding figure of the retired Captain of the Guard disappear into the castle barracks. He reflected that Rosa's sorrow had drawn forth kindness from a heart that he had always thought as hard as the mountain rock.

THEN the time came when Rosa found that she was expecting another child. Erik felt a stab of joy mixed with fear. He did not know if he or Rosa could endure another loss. Rosa smiled more often now. He could hear her singing to herself when she walked in the garden. A heaviness that he didn't know he had been carrying lifted from his shoulders, and Rosa clasped his hand and together they made promises to keep unceasing vigilance over their new child.

Autumn came with its golden harvest, and a son was born. They named him Lucien, for he was like the light that dispelled the darkness of their mourning. The baby received love in double-portion, for his own sake and for the love that could not be given to his sister. Rosa's laughter could be heard echoing through the castle as she cooed and kissed her lovely one. She never left her son alone, and Erik stayed protectively by their side. Guards were stationed directly outside their door, and both he and the princess took turns staying up with the baby tucked between them in their bed. One night they both started awake, Erik realizing that he had fallen asleep on his watch. He breathed a sigh of relief when he saw that little Lucien was sleeping peacefully between them.

A FEW more months passed, and the castle, which had held its breath when the baby was born, began to feel that all was well with the princess and her child. Then the queen smiled her red, pitiless smile. She saw that Rosa and Erik had relaxed their vigilance, becoming just a little less cautious, a little less watchful. This was the moment for which she had been waiting. Queen Sigrid stirred her potions and mixed for the second time that soporific concoction whose cloudy vapors had lulled Rosa and the prince to sleep and enabled her to steal the first child away from her loving parents. She placed the glass vessel in their room as they slept and fanned the billowing clouds until their tendrils wrapped Rosa, Erik, and little Lucien in heavy slumber.

IN the morning Erik woke from his stupefied sleep, his head throbbing. The ache was immediately forgotten in horror: Rosa lay sleeping at his side, smeared in ash. Their baby was gone.

Suspicions that he had not even known he harbored in his mind stirred awake, and it was at this moment that Rosa opened her eyes and saw the bed cloths stained with ash. She sat up with a cry, her face a mirror image of the prince's horror and pain.

She reached out to her husband. "Our baby," she moaned, but Erik recoiled at her touch.

"Erik?" the anguish in Rosa's voice took on a new tone.

The prince sprang out of the bed and looked at his wife. "Rosa, he was my son," he said hoarsely.

Rosa stared at him in mute amazement.

Erik went to the door, immediately ordering a search for their missing child, and the guards cast dark and suspicious glances on the princess. After he shut the door, Erik gazed at the tear streaked trails on his wife's ashy face and then, with a groan, buried his face in his hands.

The princess rose and went to him. "Erik, you don't think that I...?" Her sentence trailed off.

Erik looked up at his wife and could see that she read the doubt in his eyes. "Rosa, I don't know what to think."

Rosa turned white beneath the ash and flinched as if he had struck her. Erik moaned at the look of betrayal on his wife's face. "Rosa, please forgive me. I just have to be alone for a while." He left the room and Rosa stood alone, rigid with disbelief.

ERIK was in his study, bowed in grief, when he felt the light pressure of a hand resting gently on his head.

"Erik, forgive me, but I must ask. Has the princess done anything strange that you can think of? Anything that bears the stamp of witchcraft?" The queen's soft yet insistent words hovered ominously over Erik like a thundercloud.

The prince peeled his clammy hands away from his face. He thought of the dark night he had found the princess in the moonlit glade, madly suckling a false baby to her breast. He did not say anything, but his silence was a confirmation.

The queen wrapped her arms around him and whispered softly, "Erik, I am so sorry. Some women are unnatural mothers, like a cat eating its young. I am sure that she could not help it."

The prince gave a low groan and burst from her embrace. He ran madly down the stairs through the castle to the stables, where he leapt onto Lodestar's back and rode blindly into the forest.

WHEN Erik had rushed out of his study, the queen had smiled to herself and then went to join Rosa in her room.

"Come, let me wipe the ash off you," she said.

The queen ordered a tub of water brought to her and wiped the princess clean. Then she changed her into a simple woolen dress and tied her golden waves into a knot on the back of her head. When she was finished, she took the unresisting princess into another, smaller room of which only she had the key. "Remain in here until I give word," she commanded.

Rosa gave no sign that she had heard, and the queen locked the door behind her with the key that she wore about her neck.

Erik galloped through the forest, fleeing thoughts that were relentless demons chasing him down. He rode on and on, until the shadows lengthened and the trees seemed possessed by the very furies he sought to escape. He would have ridden Lodestar to the breaking point, if an inhuman cry in the wood had not startled the horse, so that he reared and cast Erik off. Lodestar turned faithless and fled, leaving the prince in the wake of his thundering hoofs.

Erik lay in the dust and the withered leaves, and the gloom settled over him. The tall black boughs wove a canopy of leaves above him, and he lay unthinking in the darkness, until the sharp cry of a bird of prey brought him back to his senses. Starting, he realized that he was leaving himself vulnerable in the dark of the wood. He had left hunger and other human desires behind him at the castle, so he built a fire and kept a waking vigil. Sleep eluded him, and he did not wish to dream.

He set off at dawn, his steps aimless, searching for some-thing, but he knew not what. He trekked through the day. At first, he thought that he was searching for Ninny Nanny's cottage, but after a while he knew that he was not, for the cottage would be empty, and, if he did find the witch or faery, her answers would be hollow. Was not Ninny Nanny herself cast into doubt? Would her riddles lead him on the true path, or were they traps in a labyrinth of lies? The very foundation of his belief was shaken, and he kept savagely pushing down dark thoughts. He did not yet dare think of *her*.

Again he did not eat or sleep, but the next day he found an animal caught in a hunter's snare and ate it, for still he clung to life. Yet he disliked that he was near other human trails, so he went deeper and deeper into the forest. Erik still did not know where he was going, but, if anyone had asked, he would have told them that he was heading toward the Shadowood. What he did not know was that the Shadowood had already come to him and had entered his heart.

At last he thought about the princess. Better never to have found her, better to have gone to the tower and discovered it empty, than to take her home with him, love her, and find out that she was the lie. He had thought that, when he chose the lead casket during his trial underground, his choice to believe in her was final and irrevocable. He had not understood that he would have to make that same choice again and again every day of his life. And yet, even now, though he did not know the truth, he loved her still. But his stepmother had planted the seed of doubt in his heart with all the whispers and all the rumors and all her seemingly well-meaning words. The old question returned to haunt him: was Ninny Nanny a witch and the sleeping princess a subtle trap to ensnare the crown prince with a dark magic? He could not believe it of Rosa, with her musical laugh and the light of the sun in her eyes. Then the images of his two beloved children's faces floated before him, and he fell to his knees with an anguished cry.

The days blended into one long span of darkness, and the doubt gnawed at his heart, driving him mad. He wandered until he stumbled upon a large, grey pool of water shrouded in mist. Casting himself upon the ground, he stared into the still waters, which reflected the grey skies and the shadows of the trees above him, but the dark waters revealed nothing of the secrets below. He gazed through the fathomless depths into nothing. He saw nothing itself and wondered what it would be like to sink into nothing.

ROSA stared blankly out her window, the horrible events of the morning settling into their places in her mind. She shuddered. Erik thought that she was responsible for the loss of their children. This thought kindled a flame of anger within her. She had not been the only one left alone in the room with their son, and she had never once doubted Erik!

Still, Rosa realized that there were other elements at work, those that had stolen away her children and turned her husband against her. She would not think on the loss of her son. She must put away that grief for later. Deep within her heart was the hope that her children were not dead, but were being kept alive by whoever was plotting against them.

She rose and paced the room. She must see Erik, convince him that they were caught in a trap, show him that someone meant them further harm in a way that they could not yet foresee. She understood this so clearly now and, if she could but speak to Erik, she could persuade him of her innocence. But Erik did not come, and, when she tried the door, she found that it was locked.

Rosa sank impatiently in the chair and waited, but, when the door finally did open, it was not the prince but the queen who entered, bearing a tray of food.

"Where is my husband?" Rosa demanded.

"He is in his old rooms, he does not wish to see you," the queen said coldly.

"Tell him I wish to speak with him."

"I will."

The queen put down her tray and sat down on the bed, the only other place to sit in the small room. "Would you confide in me what you wish to say to him? It may help me convince him to see you."

Rosa did not speak, so the queen took the princess' hand into her own long and beautiful hands, gleaming with gold and shining gems. "Confide in me, Rosa. I can help you. I know you are innocent of all the evil that is said of you."

"Do you?" Rosa asked, searching the queen's eyes with a long, discerning gaze. The queen must not have liked the power behind the princess' deep and clear eyes, for she looked away and said, "If you will not let me help you, then I am afraid you will remain here until the king decides what to do with you."

"My husband will protect me. Will you tell him that I wish to speak to him as I asked?"

The queen gave Rosa a small, secretive smile that the princess could not interpret, and, after she had left the room, Rosa began to pace about again in agitation.

Erik still did not come.

The queen returned in the evening with more food and the simple message that Erik would not see her.

Rosa sank deep into her chair. Had Erik abandoned her? Surely he would not. But then she recalled the doubt in his eyes and felt a shiver run through her body. He could not be so convinced that she murdered her own children? What sort of love did he bear if he could believe that of her? The princess felt ill at the thought.

THE queen barred everyone else in the castle from Rosa's room, turning a deaf ear to Emma's persistent requests to see the princess. In despair, the handmaid went searching for Dunstan. When she found him, he visibly started at the distress that must have been stamped on her face.

"Emma, what is the matter?"

She clutched his outstretched hand. "Dunstan," she gasped. "You don't believe the terrible lies that are being told about the princess?"

"No, Emma," he said soothingly, "I could not believe that of her."

"Then you must go find Erik and bring him back. The queen has the princess locked in a room and will not let anyone see her."

"I thought the princess had hidden herself away so she could grieve alone," Dunstan exclaimed in surprise.

"And there is more," the handmaid whispered. "Yesterday, Erik left in secret. I heard the queen speak to the king against him. She said the princess is a witch and that she's ensorcelled the prince to plot against the king with the Lord Gavin and the rest of the western lords. That's why he left the castle."

Dunstan turned white. "I shall leave this instant."

Emma did not let go of his hand. "Take care," she whispered.

Dunstan gave her a reassuring smile. She released her grasp, and he left.

ROSA sat alone in her room. Gone was the fire of indignation from her eyes at being innocently locked in a cage. Gone was the conviction that she could sway Erik to her side if she could but speak to him. Despondency and hopelessness traced her figure and left their outline impressed on her sunken limbs. At her side was the empty tray of food and drink that the queen left behind her after every visit. That morning, the queen had held the goblet of spiced wine before Rosa's lips, whispering suggestive words of despair and loss, of the meaninglessness of the princess' life, now that her children and her husband were taken from her. She would not leave until Rosa had drained the goblet of its contents. In her cloudy state, Rosa wondered why the queen would not leave her alone, but any stirring of suspicions was silenced by the lethargy that pressed over her like a heavy pillow, suffocating her.

Rosa weakly rose, staggered to the open window, and leaned through. Nothing was left for her, no husband and no children. She was alone in a strange time, in a place where she did not belong. Why had she survived alone of all her family? Her mind turned to her godmother as it had many a time before. Why did she not come? Was Faerie so irrefutably banished that she could not rescue her? Or did her godmother choose not to come? Either way, she was alone. Surely it was right for her to die and join her father and her mother and her two children in their graves?

Rosa's vision sank down to the ground far below, but then a tree, whose branches rose up almost to her window, fixed her gaze. Every veined leaf stood out sharp and distinct, each edge crimsoned as if red flames of fire licked it and would later transform it into a full blaze of brilliance. Even now, the world was still beautiful.

Every fiber in Rosa's being thrilled with a sudden burst of life. How silly, the thought floated across her mind, to lock her up when there was this tall tree beside her window. With the thought of escape, the princess hastily withdrew from the window, shuddering. What had she been about to do? The very life force within her vibrated in outrage over the fact that she had been contemplating her own death. Her very being gloried in each waking day after so long a slumber in her tower.

Her head cleared, and she had one thought: she must flee the castle. There was nothing to tie her here. Erik had abandoned her, and she must escape the queen's poisoned words.

Rosa stared grimly outside the window. The queen must think so little of her that it never even crossed her mind that she would attempt escape. She must think her so helpless.

ROSA waited until dark and, when the queen came in to check on her, she pretended to sleep. After the door closed she waited silently for a few moments, then she slipped out of bed, opened the casement window, and climbed onto the narrow ledge on her hands and knees. The dark outline of the tree loomed before her, and Rosa took a deep breath, then leapt from the window. The slender bough tremulously shook under her weight, but she managed to wrap her arms around it and swing her leg over the bough, and then climbed down to the lowest branch to drop onto the soft grass below.

Rosa knew that most of the castle guards were all stationed further out at the outer gate, so she was easily able to slip into the garden under the cover of darkness. There she climbed up the trellis and the ivy that led over the wall and thanked the stars that the walls were there to keep those outside from coming in, not those on the inside from going out.

Once she reached the top, she saw that the wall joined with the mountain rock and was able to find firm handholds to lower herself down the mountain side. Soon the mountain smoothed into a sheer drop, however, and Rosa realized that there was nothing for her to do but to leap down to the ground below.

She lowered her hanging body down as far as she could, and let go. Rosa stifled a cry as she landed, and a sharp pain flashed up her side from her ankle, but she had no choice but to go on, limping painfully into the forest with her bare feet. Her shoes had fallen off when she dropped, and she could not find them in the darkness.

Rosa crept slowly and painfully through the dark wood. She knew she had to find shelter in the morning. By then her flight would be discovered, and she would not be able to travel in the daylight.

The ghostly half-light of the early dawn seeped through the forest, and, as she journeyed through the morning mist, she hovered at the outskirts of the woods until she came upon a farm. The farmer and his son were at their early morning chores, and, when she called out to them, they dropped their hoes and rushed to her side and then almost carried her to their farmhouse, where the farmer's wife, a stout woman with a white kerchief tied neatly about her head, was just putting her loaf of bread into the fireside oven.

The woman exclaimed at the sight of Rosa, sat her down on the nearest chair, then shooed the men from her kitchen. The farmer's son cast one last admiring look at Rosa over his shoulder before he returned to the fields. Then the farmer's wife placed on the table a heaping bowl of steaming porridge. Rosa fought back the tears that were threatening to fall over the woman's kindness.

The farm woman took Rosa's bleeding feet in her rough hands and began to wash and bind them. "Now why don't you tell me of your trouble, you poor, little dove?"

Rosa shook her head. "No, you are being very kind, and I do not want to endanger you for helping me."

"Is it very bad?"

"I am fleeing for my life."

The farmer's wife clucked and then shook her head. She must have observed that Rosa was struggling to keep awake because she gently said, "Ah, poor, little dove, you want some sleep. Why don't you rest in my bed?"

Rosa insisted that she rest in the barn. She did not want these kind people harmed if she was discovered, and she could always claim that she had snuck into their barn unawares. She hoped she had had enough of a head start to catch a few hours of sleep, and the pain in her foot was worse, almost burning.

It seemed to Rosa that no sooner had she fallen asleep when she woke to loud oaths, horses clamoring outside, and rough hands seizing her, pulling her up, and yanking her to the barn door. She was dragged outside past the farmer's wife, whose face had hardened to implacable granite.

The woman's eyes narrowed, and she spat out, "We don't hold with witches or murderesses."

Rosa pulled herself straight, queenly and tall. "I am not any of those things of which you say. I forgive you, because you do not know any better, and for the kindness you showed a stranger before you were deceived."

Doubt stamped the woman's face, her lips turned white, and she turned away. Rosa was lifted onto her horse by the guard who had dragged her from the barn. She looked down and caught his gaze. She saw that the guard was young, his eyes wide and dark against a freckled, ashen face.

Rosa was taken back to the castle, to another cell in the tower, this time without a window. The only light was the little that came through the narrow slits in the stone walls. She wondered if at last Erik would come to see her, or if he was being prevented in some way, or if it was true that he had abandoned her.

She had no way of keeping track of time without a window, and the oppressive darkness drew the seconds into hours. Finally, Rosa heard the jangling of keys outside her cell, and, as the door swung open, Rosa's heart leapt with the hope that Erik had finally come to see her, but that hope was quickly dashed as the queen, bearing a lighted torch, stepped into the room.

The torch cast long and eerie shadows on the stone walls and the ground, illuminating the queen's pale face with a hellish glow. Queen Sigrid did not speak at first, but only looked coldly at Rosa, though the fire flickered in her eyes. "I did not expect you to flee, but that does not matter, for your flight has served the same purpose as would have your death. You have confirmed your guilt."

Rosa remained silent, and the queen leaned over her, triumph blazing forth from her face. "Do you have nothing to say to me? I, who have engineered your destruction?"

Rosa met her gaze without flinching. "It is you who took my babies. Are they dead?"

The queen did not answer, but she smiled, and her smile was cruel.

Rosa closed her eyes.

The queen stood tall and raised her torch high up into the air. "You are to stand before the king for judgment tomorrow. What will you say?"

Rosa's eyes remained shut, but she whispered, "The truth."

"No one will believe you, and you will be burnt at the stake as a witch. The people live in dread of the old kingdom and a magic they have never known. In their suspicion, they have twisted all into darkness beyond recognition. But I do know...," and the queen leaned over until her face almost touched the princess' own, "...I know that our two worlds cannot exist together and that the old magic would banish my own. When I first saw you, I knew you and I hated you, but even now, if you admit that you are a witch and that you ensnared the prince, I will save you and you will be forgiven."

Rosa opened her eyes. "If the truth kills me, then so be it." Her voice was sharp and cold.

The princess refused to say another word, so the queen departed, leaving behind her the darkness and the echoes of her triumphant laughter.

Chapter Twenty-Four

The Faerie Company

ERIK LAY ON the dry and hard ground, gazing into the still waters of the grey pool. He gradually became aware of a low, plashing sound and looked up to see a boat emerging from the mist, the figure within only a silhouette in the darkness.

The boat reached the shore. The dark shape did not step out, but only sat motionless, as if ominously waiting. There was no sound except the ghostly stirring of the branches overhead.

Erik approached the boat, and, when he reached the shadowy figure, it looked up, thrusting back its hood to reveal an old man with strangely shifting eyes that changed from grey to liquid gold. The eyes bid him come, and Erik stepped onto the boat behind the old man, who then cast off, rowing back through the mists. Erik soon realized that what he thought was merely a small grey pool was really a lake, and, as he strained his eyes to peer through the mist, a dark shape slowly solidified into a small island in the middle of the lake. When they reached the dark island, Erik stepped out from the boat, and the old man wordlessly signaled that the prince should continue deeper into the island's veiled darkness.

Erik walked through the low, clinging growth and the pines until he came to a small clearing in the mist. In the center stood a tall woman robed in grey, and the mists wrapped so thickly around her feet that he could not tell where the mist ended and her robes began. Her eyes were like diamonds, their brilliance shining forth from a face as dark as night. A dart of fear stabbed him. This strange lady was old and powerful, and here he was, already weakened by hunger and sleepless nights and even more, he knew, by doubt.

The women spoke, and all the riddles of the deep earth were contained in her voice. "What has led you to the Grey Isle?"

Erik's throat became suddenly dry. His tongue cleaved to the roof of his mouth. How could he answer the lady's question, if even he didn't know what he was searching for? Finally he said in desperation, "I seek the truth."

"That is not what brought you here, for you possessed the truth, and you did not believe it."

"Then doubt brought me here."

"What do you wish to change for this doubt?"

"Certainty." He spoke barely in a whisper.

The woman's shining, inscrutable eyes observed him silently. Then she said, "Follow me."

Erik obeyed and followed her to the edge of the island, where she pointed to a small pitcher standing on the shore.

"Fill the whole lake inside this pitcher."

Erik tried to make sense of her words. What she asked of him was clearly impossible, but, nevertheless, he grasped the earthenware pitcher and, kneeling by the shore, he dipped it in the cold, dark waters. When he drew it back up, the pitcher was heavy and already full of water. He tried again a second time and then a third, but every time he drew the pitcher from the lake, it was full, and the water in the lake was no less in any distinguishable way than before.

"It is impossible," he finally said. "The pitcher is too small and the lake too great to fit into it."

"And so it is with you," the woman said. "You seek to understand the truth with certainty, but you are too small to contain it. Do you think that the truth is something that you can measure, that it is something that you can hold? Its height and breadth and

332

depth are something that you cannot fathom and you can but glimpse a small part, but it can fill you in your entirety."

"Then how can I go on," the prince asked, "if I know nothing?"

The woman pressed her hand over his heart. "When a man speaks some secret thing about himself, how do you know he speaks the truth?"

Erik thought for a moment, "Because I trust him."

"Why do you trust? How do you know, how do you ever truly know, that anyone is who they say they are?"

Erik searched deep within himself. He knew from growing up in his father's court that it was so easy to say one thing, but do another. There were very few people whom Erik trusted without question, and, even then, it was conceivable that those he trusted might betray him. Yet he did know, he did trust in others. Who were those people he did believe?

"Love bindeth all things," the woman whispered.

Erik stared into her shining eyes and saw. Another person's heart was a mystery, and only one who loves can behold another truly as they are and as they are meant to be, and it was on this love that trust rests. Then it was as if the morning sun broke and dispelled the dark night of his doubt.

He loved Rosa, and that love was enough.

The woman bent down and picked up the pitcher. "Drink and renew your strength. The princess' life is in danger as we speak. You must make haste, for, if you delay, it will be too late."

Erik felt the blood draining from his face. He gripped the pitcher and drained it. He knew now that, if he lost Rosa, all the love would go out of his life.

Then the woman took him to the ferryman, who once again wordlessly rowed him to the shore. There Lodestar was waiting for him. Grim and determined, he did not question the horse's presence, but saw the purpose in it.

The prince and his horse galloped through the wood, leaving

the wind behind them. Their course was straight, and they did not falter. Bursting forth from the wood, they galloped across the plains, picking up speed. A dark speck materialized in the distance, and another rider rapidly approached. Erik would have shot past him, but, upon seeing that it was Dunstan, he pulled up tight, and his friend reined in beside him.

"Erik!" Dunstan exclaimed. "I have been scouring the countryside for you. We must go back. Rosa is in danger and the queen plots against you both."

"I know. We have not a moment to spare."

ROSA knew it was morning, because she could hear the birdsong. As the princess sat alone in her prison cell, the lapsing moments lengthened, and Rosa held every one of them deep within her breast. She thought on her time with the faerie, her time with her mother and father, and of Edmund's sacrifice. She thought on her slumber and the curse, her brief happy moments with Erik, and on her children's beautiful faces. Rosa did not know where Erik was or why he did not come to her, but she knew he was trapped like herself. Only she wondered if his prison was one of the mind and spirit, while hers possessed physical walls.

As she continued to reflect, Rosa could not but feel that this morning was familiar, that she had experienced this all before on the eve of her sixteenth birthday, only then she was going to her sleep, and now she was to go to her death.

She heard the keys turn in her cell door, and the guard opened it.

"Follow me," he ordered.

The guard did not bind her as they both knew that another attempt at escape would be in vain. He led her down the long twisting stairs and into the throne room with its timbered arches. The lords of the hall gathered to hear the sentence pronounced, and any who might have been the prince's supporters were absent from the courtroom. Their faces were grim; not one doubted the outcome of the trial.

Rosa's eyes fluttered over the hard faces. Erik was not among them. She did not know if she felt relief, or if his absence made her heart grow colder. It no longer mattered. She turned her full attention to the king.

"You have been charged with witchcraft, murder, and treason. How do you respond?"

She met the king's gaze. "I am innocent." The white flame of her innocence blazed within her. Her voice rang the clarion call of the clearest purity.

A shifting murmuring echoed in the court. Rosa stood alone and defenseless yet was unafraid. The king's face was as hard as stone, the queen a dart of ice at his side.

"We took you into our kingdom and wed you to our son. Yet you turned him against us with your witchcraft and murdered your own children. Tell me why we should not burn you at the stake?"

"The prince has ever been faithful to you."

"Then tell me where he is now," the king commanded.

"I do not know, but, if he were here, he would defend my innocence."

"He is not here because he is plotting with my enemies. Where else would he be unless...," and the king looked at the princess coldly, "he fled because he was convinced of your guilt."

The fire within Rosa abruptly extinguished. A film passed over her eyes, and all she could see was the dark. Then the conviction of her innocence welled up within her, and she once again blazed forth. "I do not know where Erik is, but why do you not ask the queen what she did with him and what she has done with my two babies?"

An awful silence filled the courtroom, then it was shattered by the queen's piecing laugh. The king's knuckles grew white as he gripped the arms of his throne.

"You dare?" His voice was the smoothness of the deepest of rages.

Rosa continued in ringing tones. "I am not afraid to die, for I am innocent and bear no stain of guilt upon my soul. Yet for the truth's sake and for the kingdom's, I will speak. The queen is a deadly poison that pollutes the kingdom. She has already tainted the love you bear your son and turned you against him, and, as she divided you from him, so she will divide you from the kingdom. Though you will not heed me now, remember my warning when you stand before your undoing and hope that you will still have the strength to save yourself, for her poison already lies deep within you."

"Burn her." The two words weighed hard and heavy as lead.

The guards surrounded the princess, roughly gripped her by the shoulders, and thrust her out into the courtyard. The crowd followed, and the king and queen sat on the elevated dais to watch the princess burn.

She was tied to the pyre, the ropes cruelly biting into her wrists. The herald proclaimed the decree of her death, and the flaming torch was brought forward. Rosa's eyes fixed in fascination on its roaring fire, and she could already imagine the heat of its blaze consuming her into ash.

Cries broke from the crowds in a confused tumult, then Erik burst upon the courtyard on his night-black horse.

THE crowd thronged ominously silent around the courtyard. The heart in Erik's chest hammered with the fear that he was too late. He burst through the crowd and in an instant took in the scene before him.

"Hold!" he cried.

The torchbearer stayed his hand, anxiously looking up to the king. Lodestar snorted, and Erik directed him over to the dais, calling up to the king, "Father, you must not harm my wife. She is guiltless of all wrongdoing, and I am here to defend her innocence."

The king raised his hand, and his words were pitiless, his voice unyielding. "The sentence has been given and must be carried out. Stand aside or be proclaimed a traitor to the crown and share the traitor's common fate."

Erik spun Lodestar around and cantered up to his wife strung up on the pyre, a stark white figure in her wool dress against the dark wood. He spoke so that only she could hear him. "Rosa, can you ever forgive me for my doubt?"

Rosa's translucent features lighted in radiance and love. Her voice murmured low with the gentle strength of joy safeguarded by peace. "Yes, my love. I am so happy that you have come back to me that nothing else matters. Erik, please stand aside. There is nothing more you can do, and I would not have you die."

Erik drank in the sight of his wife, and her courage strengthened his own resolution. Rosa's eyes widened, and he saw their flicker of terror as she read the determination in his gaze.

"Erik, no!" she cried.

But he had already lunged forward and snatched the flaming torch from the surprised hands of the guard. He swerved his horse around, unsheathing his sword. "Whosoever wishes to harm the princess must pass through me first."

"And me as well!" Another voice cried as Dunstan pushed through the crowd on Embermane, his sword also held aloft.

Riding up to the prince's side, he said, "You didn't think I would let you take all the glory, did you?" Their eyes locked, and Erik understood that this might be their last and greatest battle together, and he was glad that Dunstan was at his side.

Both turned to face the king, and King Mark looked down on them from his elevation and said without a single tremor shadowing his face, "So be it. Guards, execute the crown prince and his companion as traitors to the crown."

The guards surged forward with gleaming swords and battle

cries. The ringing clash of steel echoed through the mountain castle. Erik and Dunstan were mounted, while the guards were on foot, so they were able to defend themselves and disarm a fair number of soldiers. Then, out of the corner of his eye, Erik saw something streak past him towards Rosa. It was the queen, and she held a dagger of twisted iron.

Erik urgently spurred Lodestar forward, and the prince and his horse burst through the circle of guards surrounding them. The queen reached the pyre, her arm lifted high to bury the ugly dagger in Rosa's breast. Erik leapt from Lodestar's back and ran her through the heart with his sword.

The queen crumpled at the foot of the pyre and lay dead. Erik and Rosa locked eyes in horror. Their horror was echoed by the sharp cries of the crowd.

Erik had no more time to reflect on what he had done and wheeled around to face the oncoming guards, incited to a greater ferocity by the queen's death. He saw that Embermane had been brutally cut down from under Dunstan and that both he and his friend now had to fight on foot. They would soon be overwhelmed, and Erik steeled his heart to face his death.

As he darted aside to dodge a blow to his head, he saw Dunstan go down out of the corner of his eyes. A fire coursed through his arm as his sword was knocked from his grasp. He was shoved to his knees beside Dunstan. His head yanked back by his hair, he felt cold steel rest against his neck.

"Hold!" The command rang through the courtyard.

It was Kenelm. The authority in the sword master's voice stayed the guard's hand. He called up to the king through the crowd. "Your highness, I beg of you mercy. Enough blood has been spilled! Show mercy and spare the life of your only son and heir!"

An unnatural silence fell over the courtyard as the lords of the hall held their breaths and the guards waited for the king's decision.

But no word came.

There was a stirring up in the dais and someone exclaimed, "The king is dead!"

Shouts and cries erupted madly from the crowd, and the guard loosed Erik's hair. Everyone gazed up at the king on the elevated dais, his unseeing eyes staring opaquely before him.

The king's physician ran up the elevation's steps, and the crowd hushed to a murmur, waiting apprehensively for his verdict. The physician turned to the crowd. "The king is indeed dead. There is no wound, no blood. There is no obvious cause of his death."

The tense silence of horror settled over the crowd. Kenelm seized the opportunity to dash up to the top of the dais. He raised his right arm, and his voice projected through the crowd. "An awful judgment has been passed. The princess was clearly innocent, and the king was struck down in his guilt." He grabbed a horn from the nearest herald and blasted a loud trumpet call, then cried. "The king is dead, long live the king!"

The crowd erupted into cheers, while the guards nervously released the prince.

Erik blinked in shock. He was king.

Bending over to pick up his sword, he laid his hand on Dunstan's shoulder. "Are you all right?"

Dunstan groaned, "I'll live."

Erik then stumbled to the pyre, cut Rosa loose from her bonds, and she fell into his arms. They held each other wordlessly, his dark head bowed over her fair one, and Erik could not believe how near he had come to losing her. Slowly he loosed the tightness of their embrace and looked down on the dead queen.

"I would have spared her, despite everything, but she left me no choice," he said.

Rosa shuddered and looked away. "Come, let us go down. Your people are waiting."

They stepped down from the pyre, his arms still wrapped

around her, and they walked up to the crowd, which parted before them. Erik climbed up the dais and knelt before the dead king, gazing at him sadly, and then closed his unseeing eyes.

By the time he returned to Rosa's side, Kenelm had dragged forward the current Captain of the Guard. Erik recognized Edgard, the young boy others had laughed at as a child. Rosa clutched Erik's wrist, whispering, "He is the one who captured me at the farm." Erik felt a stab of guilt and wondered what else Rosa had suffered because of his doubt.

"I saw the captain attempt to make an escape and I bring him before your highness to question," Kenelm spoke.

Erik looked at his old sword master, his heart filled with gratitude. Both he and Rosa would most likely be dead if it hadn't been for his unwavering loyalty, a loyalty that Erik did not even know that Kenelm had felt until now.

Edgard dropped to his knees before Erik. "I beg your mercy, my lord. Death has marked all those who acted against you, and I am next on his fatal list. I beg you to spare me and I will confess my wrongdoing."

"Speak! I will not take your life no matter what crime you confess," Erik promised.

"It was at the queen's bidding. She stole away your children with her sorcery and gave them to me. I and a few others under my direct command were posted outside your door."

Rosa gave a cry and knelt by the guard, grasping his hand. "My babies, are they alive?"

Edgard avoided her gaze and stared down at the ground. "Forgive me, princess, the queen did not want their blood on her hands, so she had me take them out to the forest and leave them to the mercy of the wild beasts. Since they have not been found, I can only presume that they are dead."

Rosa's sobs strangled her cry, and Erik knelt down by her side and took her in his arms, his heart also weighed by grief.

"Your highness! Look!" one of the guards cried.

A most wondrous and strange procession was riding through the castle gate. Two lords and five ladies on horseback were richly attired in the most brilliant hues. They were tall, high-featured, and serene. Their limbs carried grace, and their eyes shone like lights from the sky. A tall woman with flaming red hair was at the front, and by her side paced a large, silver wolf. The rest followed two by two, and their horse's bridles tinkled with small, silver bells. At the rear of the company rode two ladies, one dark and one light, one draped in the flowing green of springtime, the other in the lightest silver, and they both bore a little child in their arms.

Erik and Rosa stood in amazement, and Rosa could not tear her eyes away from the two children, the smallest merely an infant in the Green Lady's arms. Rosa sprang with a cry and ran to her godmother, who gently lowered the sleeping infant into his mother's outstretched arms. Behind her, the Silver Lady handed Erik a little girl with dark curls and eyes as blue as her mother's. Both Erik and Rosa smothered their little ones with kisses and then threw their arms around each other, and laughter mingled with the tears they tasted on the other's lips.

In his joy, Erik gazed at the noble company before him. Some he recognized and some he did not, but he felt as if all were familiar somehow, as if each one had touched his life in some faint and elusive way. One of the Faerie Lords rode up beside him, and Erik looked into eyes swirling and shifting in color. The prince had a sudden vision of the old man in the boat on the Grey Lake, and the Faerie Lord gave the prince a mischievous grin.

Erik turned to the Silver Lady. "Ninny Nanny, how is it that you have our children?"

The golden-haired lord beside her said with bemusement, "Sister, is that the name you went by when you stayed behind in the Lothene wood? Surely the time has come for you to choose another?"

"If you will, brother, it is the name I am most fond of." Her eyes twinkled as she looked down at Erik, and they both smiled.

"To answer your question, and this time I will speak clearly as the time for riddles is over, Mnemosyne has always watched over the margin between the castle and the wood. She saw the guard leave your children behind and brought them to me."

Erik looked about for the cat, but the Silver Lady said, "She is not here today, for she does not like large crowds. You will have your chance to thank her later."

Then a somber mood settled over Erik, and his voice took on a hard edge that caused little Orianna to duck her head in his shoulder.

"Ninny Nanny, how did my father die?"

The Silver Lady's eyes gleamed in sympathy. "When the king had sentenced his only son to death, his heart turned to stone and burst his chest. The queen knew this and was not surprised, for she had been slowly turning his heart to stone since their wedding day."

Erik nodded soberly and turned to Rosa, who all this while had been throwing her arms around each of her faerie godparents, raining kisses down on the Silver Wolf, and somehow managing all throughout not to disturb the baby safely nestled at her breast.

Just as he said to Rosa, "I want you to meet Ninny Nanny," she turned to him and said, "I want you to meet the Green Lady."

They both burst into laughter.

Rosa smiled up at the Silver Lady. "Are you one of my godmothers?"

"I am, though I was not able to give you a gift on your Christening Day."

Rosa reached out and took the Silver Lady's hand. "I know you. You made it so that I would sleep and not die and you gave me the gift of the singing pearls." Then she said softly, "It is to you that I owe my many dreams, is it not?"

The Silver Lady nodded. "Yes, I am the Lady of the Moon, and dreams are under my governance."

"You have watched over me, brought Erik to me, and saved my children. Oh, dear godmother, I can never thank you enough."

Erik gave Rosa and the Silver Lady a moment and turned to the Green Lady. As he gazed into those ageless eyes of dawn and dusk and all the time between, his heart grew hushed, and he knew that he stood before a great lady, very old and very wise.

He knelt down before her, but he heard her say, "Erik, arise." As he stood up, he saw that she was smiling and that her smile made her as youthful as a maiden.

"O wise lady, you are ever welcome in my kingdom, and you will always possess my heart's gratitude for keeping Rosa in your loving care."

The Green Lady laughed, and her laughter was like a singing brook and the wind rustling through wildflowers, and it made Erik laugh as well.

Rosa joined him and took his hand.

The Green Lady spoke. "You both bear our thanks as well. For you have undone an old curse that was cast long before the princess was born, back at the founding of the kingdom in the dreaded hall of the Lord of the Glass Mountain. At that time, a young king feared the powerful faerie lord and betrayed his wife unto him, and, ever since, the seeds of jealously and discord have divided this kingdom. But, when the prince laid down his life for the princess, he redeemed the first king's offense, and now the kingdom will be renewed."

Erik and Rosa gazed in wonder at each other, and Erik humbly realized that they had played a part in much larger story than he would ever understand.

The Green Lady spoke again. "We of the Faerie Company would remain with you for the evening and then crown you king and queen of Lothene on the morrow."

"My lady, do as you will. You honor me and the kingdom."

Erik and Rosa then led the faerie company within the castle, and all the noblemen and women, all the castle servants and guards, all the people from the city and the country, looked after them in awe, for living myth and legend stood in their midst.

The kingdom held its breath at the mystery of it.

AS the company left the courtyard, it was as if a cloud of reverent silence had been lifted, and Dunstan looked about him. "Where is Emma?" he asked sharply.

Kenelm held up the circle of jangling keys he had lifted from Edgard. "I believe she was imprisoned when the princess first escaped."

Dunstan snatched the keys and ran speedily down to the dungeons and found the princess' handmaid. He saw that she had been crying, and, when he opened the door, Emma exclaimed, "Oh, Dunstan! Have you found the prince? Everything is terrible! The princess is imprisoned and will be sentenced to death."

He took her outstretched hand and said, "You don't have to cry anymore, Emma, for everything is marvelously changed. The king and queen are dead, the prince and princess have been saved, and a faerie company stepping out from one of the old stories is staying at the castle. Erik and Rosa will be crowned King and Queen of Lothene on the morrow."

Emma face was full of disbelief, but then she gave a cry and bent over to look at one of his wounds. "You've been hurt! How did this happen? You must let me bind this for you."

"In a moment, my ministering angel," said Dunstan, taking both her hands and drawing her close to him.

"Danger seems to find me more often than not. How about you marry me, so that you can make sure that I survive all my wounds?"

Emma did not answer him in words, but she said "yes" all the same.

THE Silver Lady waited in her rose garden and looked up at the moon. Its gentle light illuminated the flowers and cast her fair hair in a silver sheen. The faerie lady turned when she heard footsteps, and her eyes lighted upon the Golden King as he stepped into the moon's light. Both the king and the faery gazed at the other for a long while, and finally the faerie lady said, "Your golden hair has grown white, my lord."

"It grew white with sorrow watching the suffering of mortal kind."

"You have seen much in your wanderings."

The king approached her and took her hands gently into his. "I have wandered much and seen much with a weary heart, for all was broken and forgotten, and I was far from home."

Then the Silver Lady spoke. "But now all is healed, and Erik and Rosa's love will renew the broken kingdom. The seeds of their love will supplant the seeds of jealousy planted long ago, for love is without measure, and jealousy will eventually expend itself. How long it takes for mortals to learn what is truly beautiful and lasting in the world."

"It takes a lifetime, and, when it is discovered, our lives are over, and the young pay no heed to words of warning learned from bitter suffering and tears."

"Time's wheel has come around full circle, and no revolution is ever the same. Yet there is always hope. Though the faerie and mortal realms will never again be one, here we see a new beginning. The mortal realm will continue to wrestle and strive for its full growth in governing its dominion, but Faerie will always whisper in the mystery of things for those who have hearts that listen. Both Rosa and Erik have such hearts, and they will govern the kingdom well."

Auryn smiled at his faerie lady, and his dark eyes took on the light of faerie kind. "And at the completion of the wheel's circle, my time in the mortal realm has ended. May I return home with you, my lady?"

"Indeed, my lord, for the faerie realm is also no longer my home unless you are in it. I took on mortal guise, so that I could in some way partake in your suffering."

The Golden King kissed the Silver Lady and said, "But now the time for tears is over, now is the time for joy."

The two stepped out of the rose garden and into Faerie.

THE next morning Erik and Rosa were crowned King and Queen of Lothene in the great hall of Midloth castle. The Green Lady placed golden crowns upon their heads, and the faerie lords and ladies bestowed new gifts on them and their children.

Erik looked at the gathering before him and saw Dunstan and the dark-haired Emma both smiling at Rosa, their faces alight with their own happiness. He saw the Grey Hawk and his men, for the Lord Gavin had heard that Rosa was in danger and had mustered his forces in her defense. He had arrived a day too late to save her, but just in time for the coronation. Beside the western lord stood Kenelm, wearing the insignia of the king's chief steward, second only to Erik in all the realm.

Then King Erik looked at his new queen and saw in her a beauty and a strength that emanated from within and he knew that it was through their gifts and shared love that the kingdom would be renewed. The king kissed his queen before the entire court, and the great walls of the castle echoed in thunderous cheers and applause.

King Erik and Queen Rosamund ruled the kingdom of Lothene through the new golden age, and their children grew up and reigned as kings and queens after them, and an age of peace descended upon Lothene that lasted for a hundred years.

CPSIA information can be obtained
at www.ICGtesting.com
Printed in the USA
BVOW11s1302230917
495663BV00001B/6/P